The group cast a moving frieze of shadows. Those who had been runaway slaves, and then miserable exiles squabbling among themselves in a caricature of their former servitude, were an army now.

A small army, Alldera reminded herself. Small, and hard-worn by the desert crossing. *Look at us*, she thought. *Not at our shadows, but at ourselves: dirty and scabby and thin, on ribby, dull-coated horses.* People's elbows and knees had broken through their clothing. The provision sacks hung slack and leather water bottles jounced emptily.

They would soon find out whether they were heroes claiming their destiny, or a packed of doomed idiots who should have stayed home in the Women's camps and died out peacefully, in comfort.

Whatever the answer, it will be on my head; and after all these years and tears and flailing about, so be it. Alldera chirruped and flicked the rein ends over her mare's shoulders. She was happy.

THE
FURIES

SUZY McKEE CHARNAS

A TOM DOHERTY ASSOCIATES BOOK
NEW YORK

This is a work of fiction. All the characters and events portrayed in this book are fictitious, and any resemblance to real people or events is purely coincidental.

THE FURIES

Cover art by Rick Berry

A Tor Book
Published by Tom Doherty Associates, Inc.
175 Fifth Avenue
New York, N.Y. 10010

Tor Books on the World-Wide Web:
http://www.tor.com

Tor® is a registered trademark of Tom Doherty Associates, Inc.

ISBN: 0-812-54819-1
Library of Congress Card Catalog Number: 94-2349

First edition: June 1994
First mass market edition: December 1995

Printed in the United States of America

0 9 8 7 6 5 4 3 2 1

This book is dedicated to readers who have asked me for it; and to those who did not know they were waiting for it until it appeared; and to those who, harshly constrained by illiteracy, mutilation, starvation, slavery, and every other kind of abuse and exploitation, do not even know that such books are written. I hope that, imperfect as it is, *The Furies* spurs others to write better books into a need so great that no number of books of any quality can ever fill it: not until the conditions giving rise to such writing have been utterly eliminated everywhere and forever.

Acknowledgments

Grateful thanks to those who have kindly taken the time to read this work for me and make suggestions: Mary Morrell of Full Circle Books, Vonda McIntyre, and of course my editor at Tor, Debbie Notkin.

CONTENTS

CONTENTS

BOOK FOUR

BOOK FIVE

EPILOG

Author's Note

The story of Alldera as a slave in the Holdfast and of her time among the Riding Women and the Free Fems in the Grasslands is told in *Walk to the End of the World* and *Motherlines,* which are available in one volume from The Women's Press, 34 Great Sutton St., London EC1V 0DX.

For readers unfamiliar with the earlier books, a shortened version of the tale is retold in this book by Daya the Storyteller, on pages 12–23.

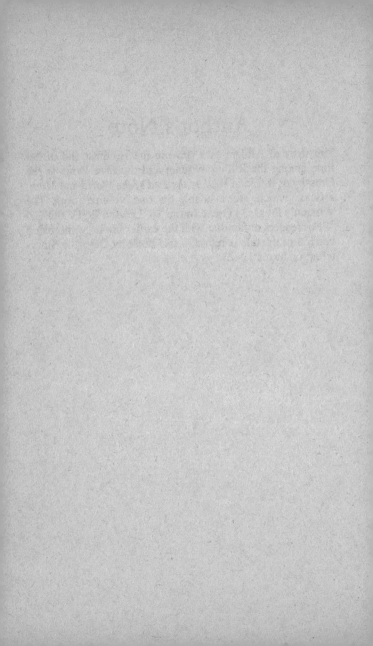

When I think of all the wrongs that have been heaped upon womankind, I am ashamed that I am not forever in a condition of chronic wrath, stark mad, skin and bone, my eyes a fountain of tears, my lips overflowing with curses, and my hand against every man and brother!

—Elizabeth Cady Stanton

I

A Maiden Raid

Four Women on foot and lightly laden hid in a dusty dip where sharu came at another season to roll. The Women watched Red Sand Camp, whispering scurrilous comments to each other about the activities of the inhabitants.

Sheel could hardly believe their good fortune. In addition to the well-known raiding and hunting mounts they had come for, a certain Hayscall Woman from Waterwall Camp was visiting. She had brought with her a famous racehorse with which the Hayscalls and their relatives had been making themselves rich in winnings this past year.

Sorrel, with the eagerness of youth, wanted to go in and get the Hayscall Racer immediately. Her friend Gallados Berrig egged her on.

Sheel said, "No, not till dusk."

"But why wait?" Sorrel said. "They may spot us before then! It's such a long time, Mother Sheel!"

The fourth raider, a heavy-faced Chowmer with a dark down of hair on her upper lip, said, "Not so loud."

"Dusk," Sheel said firmly. "So that the Red Sand Women have a chance to mistake us—if we carry ourselves properly—for Torrinors, Chowmers, and Berrigs of their own camp going about their own affairs."

Sorrel said, "Then *I* can't go into their camp? Have I come on my maiden raid only to hold horses while other people take the risks?"

Sheel had not considered this. Sorrel was, after all, unique, the first child of what the Women hoped would be a new Motherline of descendant daughters. There were no Women of the historic Motherlines for her to be mistaken for.

Tyn Chowmer said doubtfully, "You look a little like a Faller, in bad light."

"I could, I know just how those red-haired Fallers ride and everything about them!" Sorrel said in a rush.

"Oh, let the child go and lift what she can," Tyn said to Sheel. "What's a maiden raid without risk to the maiden? You and your daughter here can do the lifting and holding. This Berrig and I will keep the Red Sand Women entertained."

The two older Women swiftly squelched Gallados Berrig's predictable protests. They turned the talk, as the hot sun sank, to the subject of the Hayscall Racer—its parentage, progeny, winnings in past races, how long it might go on winning future ones, its various owners—only leaving off when a band of Red Sand riders passed dangerously close to their sharu-wallow hide. But no alarm was raised.

The light grew more oblique, the shadows denser. "Time to go," Tyn Chowmer whispered.

They all rose and slipped away through the tall grass, returning to the gully where they had left their own horses ground-tied. While Sorrel kept the spare animals soothed and still, the Chowmer and the Berrig would ride together toward Red Sand on a long curve as if traveling from the south (if they appeared on foot everyone in the camp would ride out to succor the poor strangers who had lost their horses in some no doubt interesting disaster).

Sheel, going in first and on foot while Red Sand Women were distracted by these approaching riders, padded alone toward the camp using every dip, ridge, and tall-grass tuft as cover. Close by Red Sand's squats she lay down and caught her breath, blotting the sweat from her face with her sleeve. It was years since her own maiden raid. She could hear Red Sand Women talking. She could hear time blowing through the air on the wind. Time was much in her mind these days; it had recently dealt her, and Holdfaster Tent, hard blows in its passing.

Abruptly she rose and entered Red Sand Camp as if she had every right to be there, striding boldly through the patches of shadow and the flat, bright washes of late light.

A Woman hailed her by the name of a Torrinor of Red Sand and shouted to her in passing about a necklace of horse teeth that would be ready very soon, payment of some debt. Sheel waved acknowledgment without breaking her stride.

If they caught you and you admitted to coming to steal horses, they could fine your family's herd. If you were stubborn in denial, they might try to beat an admission out of you. A Woman could be crippled during such questioning. With the Hayscall Racer at stake, Red Sand Women would not be gentle with would-be raiders.

The sense of danger spiced her blood.

She heard laughter and comments from people grouped on the farther edge of the camp, and turned that way. Three Women stood admiring a horse tethered beside a large, busy tent. Sheel stepped into shadow and watched.

They felt over the legs and chest of the horse and fed it dried ground-egg strips and grain from their hands. The horse was a ragged-coated beast with a hammer head: the Hayscall Racer, without a doubt. Its early successes had beggared many gamblers. No one had believed that such a scrubby-looking gelding could run so fast.

Sheel reluctantly moved away as the Red Sand Women

drifted toward suppertea at their tents. This was Sorrel's maiden raid, not hers.

For herself she chose two spot-rumped horses tied behind the Chief Tent. As soon as the predictable hullabaloo was raised over the approaching strangers, Sheel moved up between the tent and the horses and bent as if to look at the forefoot of one of them. She cut its tether. The smaller horse, its foal no doubt, nuzzled and nipped at her hair.

In one fluid movement she hiked herself up against the older horse's flank, her heel hooked over its spine and one hand wound in its mane. The foal would follow its dam.

She got the mare moving in a desultory way toward the perimeter of the camp, ambling among the tents like some sleepy stray. Always she kept the mare's body between herself and the heart of the camp.

It was growing dark. The sounds of conversation, shouts, and laughter fell behind. Once well past the perimeter, Sheel pulled herself properly astride and moved the mare on, but not so quickly as to leave the foal calling noisily in her wake. Dusk thickened between herself and the outermost tents.

At the gully, Sorrel leaped up to greet her. "Where's the Racer? What are these horses?"

"They belong to the Carrals of Red Sand Camp," Sheel said, dismounting. "It's Wellfinder and her foal, Dainty. The main prize I've left for you." She told Sorrel where to look for the Hayscall Racer. "Go, it's your turn."

Sorrel sprang away, darted back again. She leaned close to Sheel and whispered, "I can feel your heartmother Jesselee looking down on us. She may be dead in the world of Women and horses, but she's watching me on my maiden raid."

She hugged Sheel hard and was gone.

Sheel waited with the horses, calming them with pats and murmurings, but her thoughts wandered. Her own aged heartmother Jesselee had only recently died of the lung fever that killed people sometimes near a change of seasons. Jesselee had always said that Sorrel's maiden raid would prove that the child was more Riding Woman than Free Fem, no matter that her bloodmother was a runaway slave from over the mountains. What a pity Jesselee had not lived to see her faith vindicated.

A Red Sand rider, a Golashamet by her terrible posture in the saddle, trotted past. The rider never turned her way. Sheel took it as an omen.

The Berrig and Tyn Chowmer returned, signaling with soft calls, the first three notes of each one's self-song. Young Gallados, nearly bursting with excitement, led a mare she had snagged somehow from the camp's grazing herd.

Then Sorrel appeared, a dim figure against the somber sky.

"Which horse?" the Berrig hissed.

"Don't you recognize the Hayscall Racer?" Sorrel made her mount rear.

Tyn Chowmer let out a muffled whoop and punched Sheel's leg. At the same moment, shouts erupted from Red Sand Camp.

"Gently," Sheel whispered. "Let them wonder awhile which way we've gone."

The four of them moved off at a rapid walk, ignoring the mounting uproar behind them. Sorrel, riding beside Sheel, constantly turned to look over her shoulder.

"Can't we gallop yet? Shouldn't we go? They're after us, Sheel!" The Racer, fretted by Sorrel's nervous hands and legs, threw foam from its mouth onto Sheel's leg.

"Ease up," Sheel said, "or you'll wear him out."

Just then they heard a high, yipping cry of triumph: they were seen or someone had cut their trail.

"Go!" Sheel said.

The spare horses fled ahead of them in a swift stream. The Carral foal, Dainty, was soon left behind, yelling for its mother. Only Sorrel looked back; despite the struggles of Wellfinder to rejoin her abandoned foal, there was no point in trying to take the little one along. It could not possibly keep up.

They raced over rock, over great sweeps of thick grass that would hold no tracks, over blowing sand. They stopped only to give their own last ration of water to the horses, and so avoided wells where their enemies, with fresher remounts along, might have sped ahead to lie in wait for them.

But when they got home to Stone Dancing Camp, tired, hungry, dirty, and triumphant, the news of the lifting of the Hayscall Racer was lost like a drop of rain in a river. The Chief Tent was jammed with Women deep in an uproar of argument and peroration.

The Free Fems who followed Alldera Holdfaster had taken all their own horses and left the camp.

After years of talk and planning and warlike practice, they had done it at last: taken weapons, horses, supplies, and their inexplicable longing for the land of their bondage, and they had ridden east for the mountains and the Holdfast beyond.

In Holdfaster Tent Sorrel's other sharemothers were gathered. Not many were left, with Barvaran dead several years ago and Alldera newly departed. Shayeen was there, and Nenisi Conor sat hugging her long thin legs to her chest and blinking at the fire.

"We should have suspected," Shayeen said, looking up as Sheel entered. "They've been working their horses for weeks, hardening them up for something like this."

"For a late-season raid, people thought," Tyn Chowmer said, broadly hinting, "like the one we've just made with Sorrel."

But nothing could deflect attention to such a minor affair from the major event of the fems' departure. Like everyone else, they sat up late, arguing about the fems. Gallados Berrig, looking tearful and very young, left as quickly as she could. Sorrel herself tethered her prize horse close by the rear of the tent and came back in to lie listening on her bedding, her expression unreadable.

Nenisi took the milk bag from its cradle. "They've been at it two days in the Chief Tent. My ears are sore from listening. My throat would be sore from talking, if I knew what to say. But I don't, so I left.''

"Why say anything?" the Chowmer said. "It's simple. The fems' old leader, Green-eyes from the Tea Camp, finally turned them all loose. They felt free to follow Alldera, that's all.''

Nenisi shook her head and stirred milk into the teapot. "No, no. Watching our youngsters prepare for this year's Gather upset these fems. They can't conceive to a stud horse as we can, and if they don't get pregnant soon, they never will. They're like a weird, varied Motherline on the brink of dying out. No wonder they're willing to risk a return to their horrible homeland!"

The Chowmer snorted. "So much fuss, you'd think no one had ever ridden to the mountains before. I hope there'll be other things to talk about soon.''

Shayeen took over stirring the teapot, firelight gleaming on her copper-red knuckles. "You're dreaming, Tyn. This isn't just anybody, it's Free Fems. Whatever the reason, they'll cross back into their homeland. The men who were their masters will learn about us, and then what?''

Nenisi rubbed her lean hand across her forehead. She looked more elegant than ever these days, with silver netted through her springy black hair. Imagine that fool Alldera, leaving such a person to go back to the men's country, that land of shame! The Free Fems might ride and shoot and even raid for horses as if they were Women of the camps; when you came down to it a person raised in slavery was not the same as a person who had grown up free.

"We've had years to consider this possibility," Nenisi said sadly. "Years.''

Tyn Chowmer nodded. "So you have often said, Nenisi Conor, and everyone knows that the Conors are always right.''

Shayeen said, "Did you hear what the courier from Steep Cloud Camp said? They want the Gather called early, to talk about sending a force after the fems.''

"Good," Sheel said. "Someone has to stop them." She had no appetite for her tea. She smarted for the neglect of Sorrel's achievement, and she missed the wise counsel of her own heartmother, Jesselee, with an aching bitterness.

"You mean hunt them down like enemies?" Nenisi said, obviously dismayed. She had always been too close to Alldera Holdfaster: lover, friend, defender.

"People in Steep Cloud want to," Shayeen said. She cut her eyes toward Sheel. "And maybe some others. I know some people who may just ride off eastward on their own, if something doesn't happen pretty fast."

"What happens fast in the Grasslands?" Nenisi countered, glancing at Sheel too. "Only flash floods and grass fires, which tells you the good of haste."

Sheel wondered if Alldera had told Nenisi she was going, perhaps even invited her along. Surely not. There would have been too much chance of Nenisi speaking up beforehand, if she'd thought it was right to do so. But Nenisi must have guessed; which would make the fems' departure no easier for her to bear.

Damn the Free Fems, Sheel thought furiously. They should be rejoicing with the Women of Holdfaster Tent over Sorrel's accomplishment. Nenisi should be laughing, giving away her best arrows and trinkets to friends and lovers come to celebrate with her, all the while modestly decrying the cleverness and good luck of her successful sharechild.

But everything was spoiled.

Sorrel got up suddenly and walked out of the tent.

Shayeen pointed after her with a jerk of the chin and said lowly, "Sorrel herself will go, if no one prevents her."

"She can't," Nenisi said firmly. "With her maiden raid behind her, she must begin finding sharemothers to tent with. She should have her first daughter soon, for everyone to see."

"I'll talk to her," Sheel said, rising.

I'll go put a stop to this, she thought as she strode through the camp, *if I have to ride all the way to the Holdfast to do it.*

These Free Fems have slipped their tether and gone to put us all in danger.

But in her heart she felt approval too. She had not thought they would ever really have the nerve to return to the land of their bondage.

Daya Tells a Tale

Alldera sat leaning against her saddle, as bloody-handed as any of them from butchering two more horses. There was a limit to what could be done washing with sand, even if you could find clean sand to scrub with in this filthy desert.

I never thought to see this place again, she mused, only half listening to the murmur of voices as scorched strips of fresh, sinewy meat were handed out. The desert seemed less harsh than she had remembered it—but then, crossing it the other way nearly fifteen years ago, she had been alone, pregnant, and starving. And perhaps even this wasteland of the Ancients had the power to renew itself, however slowly, over time.

I was young then, she thought, looking down at the raised veins on the backs of her hands. *We're few of us young now.*

They were, however, tough; tough enough, tougher even than the horses. The journey over the desert and the mountains was harder on the herd than on the Free Fems themselves. People cut up the slaughtered animals and bundled the meat in strips to hang from their saddles to air-dry.

Those who had already eaten bent over the work of packing up hides, sinews, and bones. Nothing could be wasted. They might find only barren lands all the way east to the sea.

When Alldera thought of the Holdfast, she pictured high-walled halls and strings of river barges, busy factory floors and figures moving in rain-moist fields. She saw all the settings the Free Fems had talked of for years, planning to conquer the land they had worked as slaves.

But no one had come west over this desert since Alldera herself. They might find that the Holdfast was nothing but a scorched wasteland, devastated by war.

If they got that far. The Riding Women would surely pursue them. Everyone looked back from time to time. Sometimes she thought she saw hope in those glances. Sometimes she felt hope herself.

If they stop us, she thought, *if the Women of the camps catch up and turn us back, then we'll never see the Holdfast as it is now, or test ourselves against what's to be found there. And it wouldn't be our fault.*

They were camped on a dusty flat near a black spoil bank that loomed huge against the evening sky. The stream below stank. Most of the horses had refused to touch it and had been given small portions of the fems' own water ration mixed with dry milk instead. People spoke in hushed voices, huddling anxiously together in the hot dusk.

Alldera woke late at night, hearing a horse whicker outside. She went out, wrapped in a blanket and carrying a lance in each hand as she padded among the sleeping forms. The horse herd was drifting restively in search of something to eat. She saw no sign of the sentries.

Circling anxiously in search of them, she heard whispers and murmurs from a sandy wash. She guessed from the tone of the indistinct voices and a rush of stifled cries what that must be about. As she hesitated, she heard the soft susurration of bodies shifting and rubbing against each other. The voices sank to the guttural level where words and moans were indistinguishable from each other.

If this was one or both of the people who were supposed to be guarding the horses, she wanted to know about it. Careful to make no sound, she put her lances down and hunkered onto her hams, peering into the wash.

Two figures grappled there in languorous underwater motion. The knee of the one above was bent and braced beside the other's hip for leverage as she flexed against her, and one hand of the topmost was lost in the dark press of their bellies and thighs. Clothing lay twisted on the sand beneath them.

The fingers of the one below flexed on the back of the other's neck, pressing her head closer, as if their faces could merge one into the other through the sheer force of desire.

Alldera, pulse rushing in her ears and mouth dry, was nerving herself up to interrupt when she heard whistles and calls nearby, and a scatter of hoofbeats. The riders of the watch were off on the left, driving back strays to the herd.

The two people below froze, one muttering breathlessly in alarm. The topmost of the figures raised up a little and looked around. Alldera ducked back out of sight immediately, thankful that she had not made her presence known.

She knew one of the lovers by the giggle that accompanied her whispered comment. It was Tua, the youngest of their number, whose impulsive emotions and tireless interest in snuggling, jokes, and sex should have caused problems among the Free Fems. Yet because of her sweet and cheerful nature, she managed to indulge her whims freely without setting off destructive jealousies. Yearnings and resentments, yes, but no fights.

Alldera retreated, wistfully wondering how it would be to find Tua waiting, soft-faced and wet-mouthed, in her own bedding. Daya had told her that the youngster was far too much in awe of Alldera to approach her.

Alldera felt herself to be simply too old, too plain, and too influential among the fems to fairly make an approach of her

own. If she were free to, which she was not; Daya was a possessive partner.

She hesitated at her own tent, unsure whether Daya was
there, in her lumpy-looking blankets. She ached for the pet
fem's warmth and responsiveness, and her own share of the
slippery pleasures she had glimpsed in the wash.

But if Daya was not sleeping there in her place, where was
she? Better, perhaps, not to ask. She went back to her own
bedding without disturbing Daya's.

When she woke in the morning, she found the pet fem
waiting by the cook pot with a dozen other early risers. They
sat hunched with blankets over their shoulders, heads together, talking in low voices of the dreams of disaster that
people had every night in the desert.

They fell into an uneasy silence when Alldera came over.
She squatted down with them, holding her palms out for the
warmth of the fire, and said lightly, "Dreams are just
dreams, they make no sense. Let's have a real story, Daya;
one for the start of a good day."

So Daya told a story, as the others gradually assembled
with their cups for a meal of hot tea and porridge.

"The men of Ancient days," the pet fem said, "wor-
shiped the sun, and they put the sun's heat in their tools and
in their carriages and in their great cities. They put it in their
hearts, where it burned in the form of limitless greed."

She writhed her scarred cheeks and showed her teeth in a
hungry grimace. The Free Fems nodded and murmured as if
they remembered Ancient times themselves. What they actually remembered was the many times Daya had told the
tale of the Wasting.

She had never told it here in the barrens, with the Holdfast
so near. Tall Kobba said that in another day's ride up onto
the spine of the mountains ahead they would see their homeland again.

All this is my doing, Alldera thought, glancing around at
them for the hundredth time. There was Lexa, once leader of
a watch that had beaten Alldera for her headstrong ways.

Next to her squatted Emla the masseur, sinewy and sly, on whose false accusation Alldera had suffered that beating. And Fedeka, the one-armed healer, who had given Alldera refuge. As always she traveled on her own strong legs, keeping up without apparent effort and still finding new plants along the way, to pluck and pack into the pouch at her belt for later examination.

All the Free Fems looked about themselves as wonderingly as if freed from some years-long, paralyzing spell, and never more so than when sitting together to hear a story from Daya. Old Tea Camp grudges had no place here, now that they were committed in reality to what had been only a childish game of "what if" under Elnoa's rule.

How strange and unaccountable people were. Well, probably Daya's life was a mystery to Daya too; and how much mystery must be contained in the round, shiny head of Bald Roona, their eldest since the death last year of Fossa?

Alldera smiled to herself, incredulous: *I never thought I'd miss Fossa.*

"So when Moonwoman saw the men burning up the world," Daya went on, "she was angry. The world as it was then, all green and bright with clear waters and warm, rich soils, was her jewel and her joy. So she raised the winds against men, and the tides, and the earth's own roaring and shaking voice.

"The men were, as usual, fighting each other over everything valuable. Now they saw all those coveted things blown to ash and ruin. There was a howling of accusation everywhere, and war upon war upon war over the scraps.

"Now, Moonwoman works by a time that is not our time and with a grasp so large that our little lives cannot be held singly by her. She could not reach down and pick up our ancestor-mothers one by one with her great hands and set them aside in safety. And she would not stop the destruction until the greedy men were humbled.

"Yet here we are! Because with their world dying around them, the men who were the leaders ran away to the underground city they had built as a refuge from the far-flying weapons of enemy-men. They took with them some young females, and made on them generations of sons to follow them and daughters to serve those sons.

"But being sheltered, the men learned nothing from their own errors. Moonwoman allowed this. Maybe she was angry with the females of those times for allowing the men to run things to ruin instead of doing what was needed to stop the Wasting.

"As even Tua, who is young and foolish, knows—" People grinned and nodded at Tua, who blushed. Daya liked to tease her. "—as the moon turns in the sky, time turns; and nothing lasts forever. And when the world had cleansed itself, the men's descendant-sons left the Refuge and ventured into the open again. And they could not face what their fathers' fathers had caused to happen there. So they blamed it all on those who couldn't speak for themselves: all the beasts, and all the people whose skins were not white, and all the people who were poor, who had been left outside to die of starvation, disease, and deadly sun-blast.

"But most of all the descendant-sons blamed the ancestor-mothers and their female descendants. So those they had always called 'our women' the men now frankly enslaved by force, and ruled them as chattels called only 'fems.' The men made them hew from the ragged wildland by the sea a cleared place for people to live in, the country called 'the Holdfast.' Fems built it and worked it for food and fuel.

"Now these new men, masters of fems, ruled in the old ways with greed and violence, squabbling over the little wealth they could still wring from the Wasted world. They fought each other, company against company, sires against sons, and trampled the fems underfoot as casually as they would piss against a wall. They turned to each other for comfort, being too high above their degraded fems to ever share love with them. They shared sex for the making of progeny, but they didn't share love.

"By their Law of Generations they kept themselves in

willed ignorance of which boy came from which sire, so the
boy would never know which old man to attack in the inevitable rebellion of sons against their fathers. And they took a
drug they call 'manna' to dream with, dreams designed to
tell them how wonderful their ways were so that they would
not see their own smallness and their meanness and their
doom.

"Now, Moonwoman lives by a time that is not our time,
and she was content to have it so."

They groaned. Daya smiled her scarred-cheek smile.
"But not forever. She thought and thought through her many
turnings about how to make the world better again, using the
men's own ways against them so that this time they might
learn. And when the time ripened to her will, Moonwoman
spoke in the sleeping-dreams of Raff Maggomas the Engineer.

"She told him how to recover secrets of his forefathers
and how to steal strength from the sun; and she told him how
to seed and identify and train up a known son of his own
body to carry on his work after he himself was dead.

"It was all a false dream, but how could he know? Moonwoman's true mind was closed to him and all his kind.

"So Maggomas' son was born, pale and cold because he
was Moonwoman's instrument; and the tale of his femmish
dam, burned for a witch, I will tell another time. Maggomas
named him Eykar Bek and left him to grow with other boys
until the time for his inheritance should come.

"But there was another boy, Servan D Layo, Bek's lover
and his enemy, and he was a hot, cruel, golden lad as greedy
and merciless as the sun itself, and as beautiful.

"For Moonwoman loves a good story."

Around Alldera fems laughed and nodded, and passed the
teakettle around. Close by, one tongueless fem served another. Their fingers interlinked around their tea bowl to signify that server and served were lovers.

Daya poured for herself, and her gleaming eyes met Alldera's as she raised the cup. How she loved telling the tale,

and how young it made her look, and almost beautiful! Alldera smiled at her. They were lovers again, now that black
Nenisi of the Riding Women was left behind. Alldera knew
as well as anyone how quickly Daya tired of her partners.
But the pet fem liked to be close to power too; and Alldera
was power.

But where had Daya slept last night?

"Servan D Layo used the men's drug as he pleased, outside the old men's rules. For this he was outcast as a Dark-
Dreamer. Maggomas' son, Eykar Bek, guilty with him of
this crime, was sent to be Endtendant of Endpath, the place
where sick men went to die in a drugged and painless sleep.

"Now, there was one other, whose birth and nature no one
had noticed because they were insignificant in the world of
men. She was a fem-cub called Alldera, taken early from her
dam's side and sent to Bayo to be raised as a slave, as male
cubs were put in the Boyhouse to learn submission to their
elders and hatred of fems. In Bayo's kit pits and then the
femholds of her first masters Alldera became a speaker, a
trained runner, a bearer of men's messages among themselves. But in her heart there burned from the beginning the
white fire of Moonwoman's design."

People turned toward Alldera, ducking their heads to her
in deference, murmuring. Fedeka the dye-maker made the
circular sign with her fist that she had devised to signify the
blessing of Moonwoman. This sort of thing made Alldera
uncomfortable, but she had learned that there was no effec-
tive remedy.

"Now, in her own time Moonwoman sent the tides of
change surging through the lives of these three. Here is how
it began: feeling himself growing old and a great revolt by
the Junior men building, this man Maggomas sent for his
son, Eykar Bek. With Moonwoman's help, the Endtendant
and his sun-gold friend D Layo came through many dangers
to the town of Bayo, which was the fems' home as much as
anything in the Holdfast could be called the fems'."

A tongueless fem emitted a high, gargling sound of derision.

"At Bayo Alldera joined them on their journey westward to the black town of 'Troi. Why? you ask. Now, Moonwoman does not move the ocean by stirring it with her hand. She sends her thoughts which move the wind, and the wind blows the waters, and the tides obey. So into the minds of the Matris, the elder-fems who ruled Bayo under the masters there, Moonwoman put a plan.

"Legend told of escaped fems living in the Wild beyond the borders of the Holdfast who planned to return, conquer, and set free their bound kindred. Alldera was to go and seek the aid of these fugitives against the repression that must soon come. The poor food harvest that year must lead, as all bad fortune always did, to blame and punishment for the fems.

"So Alldera traveled west with these two men who thought she was merely a slave sent along to serve them. She passed through perils, and tended Eykar Bek when he was injured, and was mated by both young men whether she would or no in the manner of the masters of the Holdfast with their fems."

Hands shyly touched Alldera, comforting pats to her back and her arms. Warmed by the surge of their feeling, Alldera turned and embraced the person behind her. It was Kenoma, homely and gruff. She had never been a friend in the Tea Camp days but she now stayed close, like a personal bodyguard.

"But the mind of the man Eykar Bek, which Moonwoman had already prepared, was opened to what Alldera told him on that journey west. Brave and steady in Moonwoman's service, she said true things about men and fems, and her words sank like sharp-pointed arrows into his soul.

"So they met Maggomas in his black town of 'Troi, and he told them of his great plan: in future the fems would be not only the slaves of men but their livestock too. Their flesh would become the staple food of their masters. So he boasted—having first fed his guests some of this new food, and they all unaware!

"In reply, Moonwoman lashed out through the right hand of the man's own son, Eykar Bek. And that blow was strong enough to kill Maggomas the Engineer, in the midst of an attack on 'Troi by an army of young men from the City.''

A cheer rose from the seated audience, as always at this point in the tale. Tua threw off her sleepy look and yelled rapturously at the sky. Let her caress whom she chose, for she was the blithe, high heart of them all. Maybe each of them loved herself more because Tua could love any one of them she wished, and not be blamed for it.

"Moonwoman watched over Alldera in the midst of chaos, for Eykar Bek turned to Alldera with the Lady's own silver light in his pale eyes and he set her free to escape into the Wild, where she had all along wished to go.

"She fled west from the slaughter, carrying inside her a cub sired on her by one of her two young masters. Alone, hungry, trusting in Moonwoman's guidance, she crossed the empty silences of the Wild and entered this desert.''

Daya spread her hands wide, indicating their own bleak surroundings. Each one of them had spent some time lost in this land-between during her own escape from the Holdfast to the Grasslands of the Riding Women's camps.

There were longer versions of the tale (Alldera had heard Daya spin it out over a week of mealtimes), but long or short, it always gripped them. Daya's timing was magical, and the play of her voice was an art in itself.

"And in that desert, Alldera found that the legend of the Free Fems was not legend but truth. Beyond the mountains she found the land of a free people calling themselves 'Riding Women.' She gave the Riding Women her daughter, a child of rape born in freedom, and lived among them as bloodmother of that child. Her sharemothers in that child were Women of the Grassland tribes: Nenisi Conor, black as storm and speaker of righteousness in the Chief Tents of her people, who loved Alldera the runner; and Sheel Torrinor, proud warrior of an unforgiving line, who despised the messenger as a coward and a slave.

"Now, other escaped Holdfast slaves lived on the plains, 'Free Fems' inhabiting the luxurious wagons of the Tea Camp under the rule of one of their own, Elnoa the Green-eyed. And they lived quarrelsome, futile, petty lives." Daya paused meaningfully. When no one commented, she went on calmly: "But Alldera grew restless among the Riding Women with their strange ways. Strangest of all, they mated with their horses to obtain daughters!

"Lonely among them, Alldera slipped away to live instead with her own. In the Tea Camp she found a friend and lover—" Daya bowed sweetly to their applause "—but treachery drove her out, wounded and dismayed, for Alldera demanded that the Free Fems ride home and conquer their masters, but Elnoa's followers only played at planning their return. So she traveled, healing, with Fedeka the dyer. At last Moonwoman drew Alldera away alone, on foot, to learn her destiny.

"The messenger returned with horses she had found and tamed for herself: one gold like the sun, one black like the night, one white as our Mother Moon." Alldera bit back an objection: let the tale flow unchecked in this telling of all tellings, in this place, at this time. "These horses carried her into the midst of a raiding party of Women and thus—with her companion, Daya, the pet fem—back into the tents of the tribes. Her horses carried her to chiefship of the Free Fems, who came to join her and to learn at last to be not slaves or even escaped slaves but warriors, as you all know."

"Warriors and lovers!" Kenoma shouted, and people whistled and clapped their hands.

"And in Moonwoman's own time, back these warriors rode, armed and mounted and sure of their own strength and their own anger. They rode homeward to take the Holdfast for themselves, from the Wild to the bright shores of the eastern sea, under Moonwoman's shining, smiling face."

They followed the line of her pointing finger, toward the late-setting moon.

Lifted on the pulse of their exhilaration, Alldera rose and stood with her heart beating hard and her eyes moist. Amid the roar of their approval she raised her cup and toasted the tale and the teller with a hot gulp of milky tea.

Alldera's Army

Was it only imagination, or was that the tang of the sea in the air? Around Alldera the others were a silent, straggling group, looking down on the Holdfast from a windy pass.

They had halted above a canyon that cut down through the tree-studded slopes east of the mountains. The whole plateau below was forested as far as could be seen on either hand, except for a single spread of clear, green tableland just below them. It was divided by a bright strand of water flowing eastward toward the coast.

How beautiful, Alldera thought, with a bursting of emotion under her heart. She had not remembered the Holdfast as quite so narrow, with margins so poignantly ragged. It seemed cozily small after the endless reaches of the Grasslands, jewel-like with the ripe coloring of late summer. How could such a compact tract of country ever have contained as much death and terror and desperate loving as the Free Fems carried in their combined memories?

Tua stood in her stirrups and burst into a song that Alldera had not heard sung for years: "Land of my suffering, land of harsh joys!" Young as she was, Tua had the least clear memories of Holdfast life. But she had a romantic soul, and the throb of her voice made Alldera tremble.

Look at our faces, Alldera thought, *now that we have this homecoming we fought over for so long.* There were closed and bitter looks, cold stares of resolve, puzzled blinking eyes; and here a startled softness, there a dazed smile.

Tua stopped singing. Kenoma cleared her throat expectantly. Alldera realized that they waited for some sign from her. Whatever she had planned for this moment she could not now remember. Something else came in its place.

Leaning steeply from her saddle, she snatched up a sun-warm stone from the ground. She hurled the stone out into the air and a wild yell burst from her throat: "I, Alldera, I am here!"

Apart from a nervous start from Kenoma's horse alongside her, the only reply was a faint echo. She felt foolish and wished she had let the moment slip by unmarked.

Then Daya shouted, "I, Daya, I too am here!" Other voices surged, overlapping, outward into empty space, and died away into a taut silence.

"Let's go down," Kobba exclaimed. "Let's go down!"

They hazed the horse herd along a defile cut by a small stream. Alldera watched Daya's slim back, swaying with the jolts of her mount's footfalls. What elaborate ceremony would the storyteller make of this moment in her stories?

Daya glanced back at her and smiled her scarred-cheek smile. She began singing in sweet, lingering tones.

"It was done, the hard crossing,
The quarrels and hunger, the weary-foot ponies,
Behind them the water that shone with bright poisons,
The dead, dirty earth of the Old People's deserts.
Before them the homeland, fruit of their labors,
Within them their eagerness, burning with questions,
Above them the home-sky the color of oceans.

What will they find here, and who will come greet
them?
Their muscles are hardened, their weapons are
sharpened,
Their hearts are resolved.''

Alldera improvised a verse, untuneful but clear:

"Their butts are all blistered,
Their footsoles are stirrup-numbed,
Their mouths taste like tree bark.''

People laughed. Thus the Free Fems entered their homeland singing and laughing. Up ahead, Emla, with a girlish
blush in her thin olive cheeks, reached to catch at the ragged
fringes of Lexa's sleeve. She rode twining love knots into
them. Lexa's stern, imposing face softened with fondness.

Reality clubbed Alldera's senses: the different rankness
of the dust, the deeper coloration of the soil beneath the
horses' hooves, the dampness in the air. She felt her hold on
her life in the Grasslands waver, and she had a flash of panic.
What if all that evaporated? What if this reality—so shock-
ingly intense now—obliterated that life entirely?

What nonsense, she thought, inhaling the good smell of
horses and leather. Where did Fireheart come from, then?
While the mare's back swelled and dropped again beneath
her rider, there could be no doubt of the reality of the Grasslands and its population of horse-herding nomads.

All miles away now, perhaps never to be seen again. So be
it. *We are not Riding Women, and their country was never
ours. This is our country,* she thought, watching her shadow
pass over the stony upland soil. *I have been made to eat this
earth with my man-bruised mouth. This earth, not the prairie
sod of the Grasslands.*

Surprisingly, this flash of ugly memory brought not anguish but exultation. She sensed a similar surge of feeling in
the others around her.

*I ate this earth under a man's cruel weight, but I survived;
I return a free person, in spite of all they could do.*

Kenoma's shadow, rippling over the uneven ground, was
no slave's shadow hurrying along on a master's business. It
was a rider's shadow, with tailored leather clothing and the
weapons of a warrior. Over the shadow's shoulder rose
the curves of two unstrung bows. Back from the shadow of
the horse's rump projected the straight dark bars of a clutch
of javelins.

The group cast a moving frieze of such shadows. Those
who had been runaway slaves, and then miserable exiles
squabbling among themselves in a caricature of their former
servitude, were an army now.

A small army, Alldera reminded herself. Small and hard-
worn by the desert crossing. *Look at us,* she thought. *Not at
our shadows, but at ourselves: dirty and scabby and thin, on
ribby, dull-coated horses.* People's elbows and knees had
broken through their clothing. The provision sacks hung
slack and leather water bottles jounced emptily.

They would soon find out whether they were heroes
claiming their destiny or a pack of doomed idiots who
should have stayed home in the Women's camps and died
out peacefully, in comfort.

*Whatever the answer, it will be on my head; and after all
these years and tears and flailing about, so be it.* Alldera
chirruped and flicked the rein ends over her mare's shoulders. She was happy.

After that first surge of energy their progress slowed. The
rush to get across the mountains without interference from
the Riding Women was over. The fems needed to rest their
mounts and the riders too. Old Roona nearly fell from her
saddle when they stopped at last.

Dark was settling down the sky by then. For their first
camp in the Holdfast, Alldera wanted to choose a place of
significance that would speak to them all, but if they passed
such a place she did not see it and no one called it to her

attention. They camped at a dip in the wall of a steep canyon, still high above the river below.

Alldera recognized the bright smell of rain on the air, a different, sweeter smell than that after Grassland rain. It woke memories of dawn risings with the ache of yesterday's labor still throbbing in her limbs. What a joy it was to breathe that scent with no weariness but that which she herself had chosen.

People shared meager rations, sitting in small groups and feeding morsels into each other's mouths with their fingers—they who had once squabbled, starving and desperate, over the scraps from their masters' tables.

That night Alldera woke moaning, in a sweat of dread.

"What, what, it's all right, I'm here." Daya's arms gathered her in. "Hush, people will hear you and be frightened."

Alldera grew aware of the sounds of other people sleeping in the tent. She shook off the grip of her dream—a blond man sharpening his knife, a black-haired man staring into the distance in which Alldera herself stood concealed. She got up and drew Daya after her into the warm night outside. Stars drifted between pale swathes of cloud.

Out of earshot of the others, Alldera sat down on a boulder beside the trickling stream. Daya stood behind her. Daya's hands drew Alldera's damp hair free of her neck and cheeks.

"I'm sorry I woke you," Alldera said.

"I was already up. I couldn't sleep." Now that they drew close to the Holdfast, Daya often woke in the night herself, whimpering or crying aloud. She said she dreamed of a man stabbing a food skewer through her cheeks over her master's dinner table, years and years ago.

"Were you dreaming that Sheel Torrinor caught up with us and turned us back?" she asked.

Alldera shook her head. Real dreads surfaced, sharp and painful. "What if we fail?"

"We won't."

Alldera bent to dip her hands in the cold water. "What if there's nothing to eat here, and no graze for the horses?"

''Then we'll eat them,'' Daya said sharply. She loved the horses and hated butchering them. ''And if there's anything to harvest in the Holdfast, we'll harvest it for ourselves now. We've talked about all this, over and over.''

Alldera splashed water from the stream onto her face and neck. The icy shock made her gasp. *''If.* We could all die here, and never get word back of what had happened to us. My daughter Sorrel would spend her life as a freak in the Grasslands, and we would vanish into the legends of the Riding Women. In a few generations they'd have it all wrong besides.''

Daya chuckled. ''You always get gloomy after bad dreams. But I saw your face yesterday when you said, 'I am here.' Your gladness, our gladness, was truer than these night terrors. And now it's too late for the Riding Women to stop us.''

''I wasn't dreaming of being chased by Sheel,'' Alldera said, ''although I can recall her face more clearly than that of my own bloodchild.''

Daya sighed. ''Move over, I want to sit down.''

''There's not enough room, pick your own rock. Why hasn't a clear memory of my own child's face come here with me?''

''Sorrel is no child anymore.'' Daya stepped across the narrow stream and perched on a stone on the other side. She scooped up water in her hands and drank, making delicate slurping sounds and smacking her lips with satisfaction.

''Good water. Grassland water never tasted right to me. Look: you have been as fine a bloodmother to Sorrel as any fem from the Holdfast could be. To the Women she's a daughter, but to us of the Holdfast she's a rape-cub, just as all our kits were in the old days.''

Shuddering with memory (the weight of the DarkDreamer D Layo pressing her down, the swift and terrified assault by Eykar Bek), Alldera breathed a steadying breath of the water-sweet air. Some way off, a horse whuffled and stamped.

"You're not making me feel any better, talking about Sorrel."

"I didn't bring her name up, you did."

Alldera wasn't sure whether she had in fact been the first to mention Sorrel. Daya was perfectly capable of lying about this as about most things.

"Don't pick a fight with me, Daya. It's the pit of night, and I wonder what we're all doing here. We're too old. I'm thirty-four at least, and I'm one of the younger ones."

"But we're strong," Daya said. "And some of us are even still pretty, don't you think?"

Alldera remembered with a pang the first time she had seen Daya, firelit and sleepy-eyed in Elnoa's luxurious wagon in the Tea Camp. She had recoiled then from the pet fem's ruined beauty. " 'Pretty' isn't going to help much if we start having to nap every afternoon and forgetting our own names."

"I was always afraid I would live to be old." Daya began flipping small stones into the water with juicy, plunking sounds. "Old and ugly and hated, like old Fossa, or some doddering Matri. Outside of them, how can we know what 'old' is like?"

"We've picked a dangerous time to find out."

Plunk, plunk: "Elnoa would say that we would be better off aging grouchily but peacefully in the Grasslands."

Alldera moved her shoulders uncomfortably. "No one had to follow me. I'm here for my own posterity—for Sorrel."

"Whose face you can't remember," Daya gibed, falsely gentle.

"Well, all right—I'm here for myself as much as for her. This is something I can do, before I sink into my dotage or get carried off by a fever, like Fossa. I want my homeland back, in case my daughter ever wants to see it. In case she ever needs a place to come to that isn't the Grasslands."

Daya reached over to touch her arm with cool, wet fingertips. "You always said you would come back here, even in the Tea Camp where no one wanted to hear it. You said it until we beat you for it. We all remember, now that we're back in the country of our pain.''

''Why didn't Kobba lead you all home, years ago? Did you hear her snoring back there? She has few doubts.''

Daya stood up and stretched. ''Kobba isn't entirely sane. Not many of us would follow her far.''

Alldera snorted. ''Everyone would, if you told such outrageous lies about her as you make up about me.''

''What lies? You are the fem of legend who went into the Wild and now rides home with warriors to save her own kind.''

''Legend!'' Alldera scoffed. ''There was no legend. There was a useful falsehood made up by the Matris to keep rebellious young fems quiet, so they would wait for this mythical rescue instead of fighting and dying for themselves.''

''You're angry,'' Daya said sadly. ''Is it at me? I saw how you looked when I told about how you brought horses back to Fedeka's camp. You didn't like it.''

Impulsively, Alldera reached toward her. ''I did. I did like it. But I get itchy when I hear how I rode up driving a black horse and a golden horse but riding a horse as white as the full moon. It was only a brown horse and a gray and a dun—''

''I don't remember it that way—''

''Wait, listen to me.'' Alldera paused. If she said this wrong, the volatile pet fem might truly leave her. These days, she did not think she could bear to be left. ''I'm not an imaginative person. People sometimes mistake me for one because I look ahead, I plan. But you know me, Daya, better than anyone. You know how I get an idea into my head and go after it, that's all. I'm a runner, a messenger, and my mind is—steady, at its best.

''So when I hear you—embroider things about me, on the one hand I cringe at the—the exaggerations, do you see? Because for me accuracy in a message is basic.

"But at the same time—at the same time I love all the color and ornament and—and the patterns you see in my life. I love it, and I want to thank you for it. I could never dream up such satisfying richness for myself. If I criticize, it's because in your telling I start sounding like a stranger to myself, a myth instead of a person."

Daya murmured, "I dress you in myth with the hands of love."

Alldera was suddenly aware of the scent of Daya herself, all mixed with the clean tang of the water. She leaned forward to catch the pet fem's tapered fingers, with which her own had been interlaced around a love drink often since leaving the Grasslands.

And yet the heat of their lovemaking had cooled lately. She was almost afraid to ask: "Come back to bed, Daya."

"It's a warm night," Daya said, delicately drawing open the knotted leather lace that held her shirt closed. "And this bank of the stream is grassy and soft. Even the Lady in the Moon won't see us through those clouds."

Alldera found she had been holding her breath, and she let it out in a low laugh. "Moonwoman rejoices in our joys, isn't that what Fedeka says?"

She stepped over the rill and sank herself into Daya's sinewy embrace. Tracing the miniature labyrinth of the pet fem's ear with trembling lips, she imagined the ghost of Servan D Layo watching, helpless and aggrieved.

Corpse Hill

One plan was to establish a base near the western border of the Holdfast, from there send a small party of fast-moving scouts downriver to the City, and improvise according to what was found there. Or they could gallop straight past 'Troi and the City and then turn to sweep back westward from the coast.

Alldera was for a cautious approach, going settlement by settlement along the river. She argued it all over again with Kobba as they descended toward the smudge that marked the remains of the town of 'Troi, which looked unreal at this distance, like a fault of vision.

Kobba had slept badly too. Today the lines stamped between her brows and bracketing her mouth seemed harsher. There were liverish rings under her deep-set eyes. She had a long-jawed face, her high, wide brow fringed with straight, straw-colored hair. One cheek was scarred from an old blow.

She wanted to ride full tilt to the City. She was sure that men would still be living there at the Holdfast's center if anywhere, with the summer's harvests stored away.

As for Bayo, she maintained that it would surely have been gutted long ago by fem-hungry men. Heading straight there might mean trading an empty ruin for the precious element of surprise. Others had argued that if young fems survived, they might still be found at Bayo. Femmish cubs had always grown up there until being sent to auction in the City.

Alldera felt that the worst possibility would be for men at Bayo or elsewhere to be alerted to the Free Fems' arrival by premature contact with far-ranging scouts. If there were still fems at Bayo, men could then use them as hostages. She mulled over this unthinkable eventuality and the possible responses to it.

There were a hundred considerations of how to hide the little army's presence longest. Alldera worried about keeping communications quick and accurate between fast-moving scouting parties and the main camp, which was slowed by the horse herd, the laden pack animals, and the older Free Fems.

Then there were questions of food supplies, good drinking water, and a dozen other matters. Everyone had something different to say about everything, but left it to her to take a stand and force a decision one way or another.

It was in some ways a pleasure to have a good, firm argument with Kobba. The tall fem pressed a plan to lead a small group forward herself. "If there are men here," she said, staring out over the bright plain below, "I want to make sure we find them before they find us."

Alldera knew that no refusal would restrain Kobba for long. Any of them might choose to fly off on her own now that they were home. But she was determined to hold them together as long as she could.

"I'd rather take a leaf from Elnoa's book," she said. "The one that advises patience and observation, rather than hasty action."

Kobba grunted, turning down the corners of her narrow lips. "I remember when you would have wiped your behind with such a page."

Alldera grinned. "My perspective has changed."

Kobba and Elnoa the Green-eyed had been close back in the Tea Camp. Alldera wondered if Kobba dreamed still of Elnoa, or of her former masters, as Alldera dreamed of Eykar Bek and Servan D Layo. Kobba must surely wonder whether Elnoa was alive or dead.

According to the last Free Fems to abandon the Tea Camp for the Riding Women's tents, Elnoa the Green-eyed had arisen one morning and ordered them to leave her. Huge and soft and tyrannical, she must have seen that there was no future for her in the nomads' camps. Elnoa could never have made the crossing, either. Still, the loss of her must hurt Kobba.

The little army, heading east two full years later, had found the Tea Camp deserted and no sign of their old leader or her books or belongings.

Suddenly Tua stood up in her stirrups with a cry, urgently pointing. All heads turned, and reins tightened.

On top of a bald hillock they were about to pass, someone stood watching them.

The first to move was Kenoma. Yelling something incomprehensible, she galloped her horse up the hill. The others stared after her as she closed on the unmoving figure that stood dark and menacing against the morning sky.

"Circle!" Alldera shouted.

They had practiced this move many times, and at once formed a defensive ring at the hill's foot. Alldera, surrounded by fems with weapons glinting in their hands, maneuvered her horse with a hard hand, determined to keep a clear line of sight to Kenoma. Her breath caught at a shallow level in her chest where it could do her no good.

Then people began to exclaim in disgust, pressing the loose lengths of their headcloths to their faces. On the hilltop Kenoma burst into loud laughter.

Alldera caught the scent too, and ducked her own head, coughing.

"Whoever's up there must have been dead a good while!" Tua craned her neck to see better.

Waving her back, Alldera urged her own horse up after Kenoma's. Excitement burned in her veins. She hoped that Kenoma's laughter meant that it was not a dead fem up there but a man.

At the summit, Fireheart shied sideways, snorting. Alldera steadied the mare and made herself not only look but study what was there to be seen.

The contorted corpse was clumsily fixed to a tree with woven fiber cords. Exposed for days to the weather, it was shrunken to ropy meat and dull, exposed bone. Its outspread arms were pinioned, and its head was held upright by a twist of its long hair knotted to a branch above. One foot was pegged to the tree trunk by a wooden stake driven through below the instep. The other leg dangled above the ground like a haunch of horsemeat hung over a fire to smoke. The whole distorted figure was too tall for a child, too narrow in the hips to be a fem.

Reining up close beside Alldera, Lexa said, "A man, surely, but where's his bag-and-hanger?"

Wordless, Alldera indicated the shrivel of blackened flesh at the corpse's groin. At once the body jinked like a speared sharu, as if her pointing finger had emitted lightning. Someone had shot an arrow into the lifeless chest.

Another fem drove her mount close and, leaning from her saddle with knife in hand, began hacking at the body. Someone else rushed forward with a keening cry and Alldera saw the glinting, sharpened edge of an unsheathed hatchet. Even haughty Lexa pulled a knife from her boot and spurred forward.

Alldera held Fireheart back as one after another the Free Fems rode forward to curse the corpse and strike it. There was no stopping them, she could see that. What a story the Riding Women would make of this if they were here!

Shaken, Alldera left the others and rode down the far side of the hill. Behind her rang the shouts and laughter of the

fems' sport. Ahead lay inviting silence. But she had only
gone a little way when her mount snorted, planted its front
hooves, and stood with its ears pricked sharply forward.

The roots of her hair stirred. She felt the stare of living
eyes.

She patted the mare's shoulder and swept the horizon with
an anxious gaze. If she had led them into a trap—if all was to
be lost here, before they had even begun—

With a jolt she realized that a person sat calmly on the
ground not fifteen feet away, in the midst of the wide, grassy
swale behind the death-crowned hill. This one moved no
more than the hill corpse had.

Its source found, her unease gave way to irresistible curiosity. Heedless of the danger, she rode closer, squinting:
what was it, another body, fixed to sit upright on the ground?
What other crazed and revolting things did Holdfast people
do with the dead these days (what Holdfast people—men or
fems)?

The person raised its hands and covered its eyes, then
stared at her again, giving an absurd impression of coyness.
The face was youthful beneath its grimy tan. The shoulders
were wide and bony.

Someone galloped up and past, startling Fireheart into a
bound that almost unseated Alldera. It was Tua, drawing her
bow as she screamed, "Stand up, you!"

The person jumped to its feet, fluttering its empty hands at
shoulder height. "Welcome, Christs!" it cried in a clear,
light voice. "I have waited long by this offering! My name, I
am glad to tell you even though you most certainly know it
already, is Setteo. I welcome you."

The harsh manspeech grated in Alldera's ears so that she
could barely make out what was said; and what did it mean?
Then memory sparked: some men had held to an Ancient
belief in an avatar called "Christ," who ages before had
been punished with death for disobedience to God his Father.

How absurd, to be hailed in the name of that old supersti-

tion! She laughed. Of all the things she had expected to find
in the Holdfast, an honest surprise was not one of them.

Tua shrieked something, a curse or command. The stranger fell forward like a lance toppling, ending supported on his
two hands with his nose to the ground. Tua's wildly loosed
arrow wobbled away over his shoulder and landed harmlessly in the grass. He stayed motionless. Tua grabbed for
another arrow.

Alldera kneed Fireheart closer, and—by design—into the
young fem's line of fire. She looked down at the creature
that named itself Setteo and that was undoubtedly a male.

He wore a thick woven belt holding up a kind of ragged
skirt. His hair was dirty, brown, and shaggy, and old scars
had faded into the skin of his back. All this paled before the
astounding fact that the creature was doing the impossible,
the thing that all slave fems had been called upon to do
before all men at any and all times.

"Let be, Tua," she called back over her shoulder. The
youngster put up her bow and stared with huge eyes. "He's
touching ground to us."

At her words Setteo sprang up again, looking ridiculously
pleased with himself. His chest was bony, his nipples small
and flat like a little girl's.

"I knew you would come! I waited long after the man in
the tree got dry and broken, and look how many great
Christs have come to me!"

Tua yelled, "Shut your mouth, muck!"

Down he went again, and Tua came on at a flat gallop,
another arrow nocked to her bow. Alldera nearly collided
with her, turning Fireheart to stop her charge.

As they grappled, Daya raced past them, slid her mount to
a halt, and whipped one rein around the stranger's neck.

"I claim capture!" she cried. Her face shone fiercely as
she completed the formula used by Riding Women in taking
a prisoner on a raid. "He is mine by the rein!"

And so Daya led him, walking by her horse's shoulder
and smiling all the way, back up the hill. Tua, wild with ex-

citement, galloped on ahead to alert the others. Alldera rode behind Daya, feverishly trying to think out what the finding of Setteo might mean.

On the hilltop the riders, still hot from their action against the now hacked and broken dead man, stared and exclaimed at the sight of Setteo. Several fems grabbed for the lances slung from their saddles. Alldera steeled herself to intervene, but how? She was nervous of her own people in this savage mood.

Setteo saved himself.

He slipped Daya's rein with a deft movement, darted forward, and, diving into the air, landed upside down, standing on his hands, comically inverted. He walked on his hands before them, his legs waggling in the air and his ragged clothing flopping down around his torso.

Someone laughed. Weapons were lowered, faces slackened with surprise.

Fedeka the dye-maker walked over to him. Her several white bracelets clicked down her muscular arm as she thrust her hand between Setteo's legs. He squawked and collapsed in a heap on the ground.

"I thought so," Fedeka commented, wiping her palm on her shirt with a rattling of moon jewelry. "He's gelded. He's some man's bondboy, fake fem and no man."

Shouts and groans of derision greeted this discovery. Daya's face flushed red. Her captive was one of those boys whom powerful Senior men used to have mutilated to make soft but acceptable mates, effeminate but not actually female.

Alldera gave them all a moment to gape and point and laugh. Her flash of panic was past. She said briskly, "So, now we have someone to answer questions, but there's no need to ask them in this foul-smelling place. Am I the only one who's getting sick from this corpse stench?"

Riding on, Daya now ignored the cutboy who trotted unbidden in her wake. Alldera reached out and gave the pet fem's slender hand an approving squeeze. "You'll have to tell a story about yourself now, taking our first prisoner!"

Daya pulled away. "People will make fun of me for seizing damaged goods." She looked at Alldera from under lowered eyelids. "Why do you still ride with me, when I've made such a fool of myself?"

"Because I love you, idiot." Alldera caught her hand again and kissed the inside of the pet fem's wrist. She turned in her saddle to look back at Setteo and the phalanx of riders following and discussing him in lively conversation. "And don't worry, Setteo will have his uses, cutboy or no."

They made a cold camp a few miles beyond Corpse Hill. Setteo sat on the ground with his outstretched hands lashed to the ends of a yoke fashioned of branches. People asked him over and over, Are there fems at Bayo? Are there men in the City, or in Lammintown?

He said, "Oh, yes, Christs," each time, no matter what the question. When pressed for numbers, he said he could not possibly count, for folk shifted around all the time, coming and going in the wink of an eye; and some were brighter or dimmer than others, some vocal and some without voice; and did they also want him to count the bears?

"He sounds like Grays Omelly," Kenoma said, scratching angrily at a rash on her forearm. Grays Omelly was a Riding Woman who had been Daya's lover back in the Grasslands. Like all Women of the Omelly Motherline, Grays Omelly was mad.

The twentieth time Setteo mentioned bears (whatever they were), Daya lost her temper and smacked him, which made people gasp, and then laugh nervously at their own startlement.

Alldera said mildly, "It might be better not to addle his brains any more than they're already addled."

Setteo said, "Thank you, Christ." Then he added plaintively that if they wanted only the living accounted for, they should say so; but that he doubted he could give accurate figures since he often had difficulty distinguishing the living from the dead.

"Kill him," Kobba said, slicing the air with the edge of her palm. "He's cut, he's crazy, and he'll only slow us down."

Alldera bit back an angry answer. She had not spent all those hours listening to debates in the Chief Tents of the Riding Women's camps for nothing.

Fedeka interposed in a thoughtful voice, "He says he sees ghosts, Kobba. We may need someone who can see ghosts before we finish here."

"He's male." Kobba spat on the ground. "Or was. What can he see that's true or useful to us?"

Alldera said, "We might wait and find out."

Fedeka slid her bracelets up and down her arm. "The mad belong to Moonwoman; she protects them. And as you say yourself, this one isn't even entirely male anymore."

Everyone began to argue at once.

Setteo spoke in a soft, anxious voice. "Why are they angry? I gave a sacrifice to bring you, Christ. Wasn't it good?"

Daya looked down her fine-boned nose at him. "Nothing a piece of muck like you does is good, but if you learn to keep your dirty mouth shut we might let you live awhile."

Setteo bent forward from the waist in a bow so deep that his face touched the earth in front of his folded legs, and his bound, outstretched hands were pressed likewise to the ground. His physical suppleness was perhaps partially due to his cut status, for up close Alldera could see that he was not as young as she had thought at first.

She found the sight of him prostrated like this profoundly disturbing. He looked so like some specially trained house fem, contorted on command for the entertainment of an audience of casually cruel masters.

She stood up. "Why would he tell us the truth, even if he knows it? There's still light enough to reach 'Troi today if we move along now. We'll get answers for ourselves."

With gratifyingly little further discussion, they resumed their progress. They were in high spirits, eager and full of jokes and laughter. The yoked prisoner trotted again at the shoulder of Daya's horse. When he saw Alldera looking at him, he smiled shyly and quickly looked away again.

Now she felt depressed by a sense of having been cheated. They had found one dead man and one mad one. She would give a great deal to have found one living fem.

A Terrace in 'Troi

They sat along the border of a patch of pavement, talking. At Alldera's prompting, they had made a map that all could read.

She had started it off with a length of rope that represented the river, running from the mountains (a heap of rubble) to the eastern coast (another line of rubble opposite the first across the breadth of the paving). Fingers of shadow reached eastward from the markers in between.

People crouched to point or stood up and walked around the map as they argued. Alldera thought of how the Riding Women "gave the plains" to a daughter fresh from the childpack. They sketched a map on the sandy floor of the sweat tent and walked her over it, telling her all the stories they could remember about each place represented by a symbol drawn in the sand.

She remembered her own child, Sorrel, struggling and scowling mutinously among her sharemothers—all left behind now. And that gave her a strange, exposed feeling.

The markers here were, westernmost, a black stone for

'Troi; moving eastward down the "river," crossed sticks for Oldtown; farther down, nearly dead center on the map where the river branched, a knotted rag for the City. At the river's northern outlet, a shard of frosted green glass marked Lammintown. Bayo, on the delta of the southern branch, was represented by a twist of leather strung with five metal bells each no larger than the ball of Alldera's thumb.

Daya's bells, an old love gift, seemed completely right for marking the Holdfast home of all fems.

A breeze had risen as the sun sank. Alldera turned up her shirt collar. At her back she felt the presence of 'Troi, its jagged, blackened ruins like the remains of a rotted tooth. Over the voices of the Free Fems echoed other voices that existed only in her mind's memory.

Men's shouts and screams, the bellow of explosive weapons, the crash of falling masonry, the hollow rush of fire— that was what she had fled from, running westward as if speeding off the edge of the world. It had been only a little later than this same season too, in early autumn.

Past and gone; these warrior fems were her people now, live people, in a dead place. Her nostalgia, if that was what it was, attached to her vanished youth, not to the ugly, strenuous, dangerous events of those past times.

The fems had spent the afternoon crossing and crisscrossing 'Troi ruins on horseback and on foot, making sure no one was there. One had brought back a torn fabric sleeve patch, the gold-wheel sign of Trukker Company.

Alldera herself had spent the time making the map and thinking about it. Everyone seemed relieved that she did not insist on going herself into the ruins, where anything might lurk. She was touched by their concern.

With the onset of evening suppertea was prepared: dried meat, fat, and blood stewed up together. Carrying their food bowls, the fems talked over their options around the map. Now and then someone would duck into Alldera's tent to look at Setteo, who slept (or pretended to sleep) securely tethered there. Under Kobba's sharp eyes, one camp watch relieved another, and a new crew went out to guard the horse herd. They walked past leading their mounts, talking of cut-boys they had known in the old days.

Alldera put aside her bowl untouched. The pull she had resisted all day was too strong: she must see 'Troi for herself. She rose silently and padded away, following a channel of flowing artificial stone into the dark, fragmented maze of ruins.

The moon cast pale light and deep shadows. She could not help stopping with a jerk of fear every time her booted foot turned a fragment of stone or ground the grit of broken glass that lay everywhere. But nothing else moved around her.

I should have come riding here in daylight, she thought, *like the others.* Yet there was satisfaction in walking into 'Troi alone and unguarded; she had last left it running, prey to any who might see her. At any moment she might surprise her own younger self, dressed in men's clothes and wearing a hip pack stuffed with scrounged provisions, slipping away westward to freedom and undreamed-of adventures.

Now 'Troi was shattered stone. Rusty machine hulks leaned forlornly among the ruins or lay crushed and twisted in the streets. If there had been useful objects left lying around—metal blades, tools—they had long since vanished.

Scavenged? Setteo had survived, and he was crazy. Others must have made it too. Even fems. Some would have come here to scratch through the rubble for what they could find.

The blond man in her dreams who sometimes sat and sharpened his knife had been a survivor if ever there was one. She remembered him running, eager and intent, down-hill toward this place when it was nothing but smoking wreckage in dawn light. She could not imagine him older than he had been on that day. Youth had seemed the Dark-Dreamer's right, the core of his cruel and cheerful identity.

Suddenly her attention was caught by something jarringly familiar. Two massive, broken walls still formed the corner of a once-tall tower beside the river. High above, a section of flooring thrust out from the join of the walls.

A soft sound echoed back the way she had come: a footfall, a whispered curse? Her heart slammed with terror. What if she was surprised here by men (D Layo, of course, summoned magically by her thoughts) and killed; or, worse, taken prisoner?

She scrambled up the rubble toward the looming corner. Stones rolled under her hands and feet. She looked down and saw the gleam of the river on her left, and the bent metal cage of an old walkway sticking up out of the water end-on. She saw where her panic had brought her.

This was Raff Maggomas' tower. Her muscles twitched with terror of the height, the uncertain footing, and the creaking of the breeze-swept ruins all around her. That jagged plane sticking out from a split in the wall was a shard, milky with dust, of the great map incised on a sheet of "plastic" that had divided his room into living and working areas. The floor groaned ominously under her feet as she teetered an unthinkable distance from the ground.

She stepped through a partial doorway and onto the slab of paving that leaned out into the night. From this terrace Maggomas the Engineer, his men, and his son and his son's friend (and their unregarded serving-fem) had observed the attack on 'Troi by City Juniors from downriver.

The pavement underfoot vibrated to the power of the river rushing by the base of the tower. The whole ruin seemed to sway as if preparing to throw her off with a shake of its shattered shoulder.

Come all this way, to fall? She squeezed her eyes shut and spread her fingers on the pitted surface of the nearer wall.

"It's dangerous up here!" said someone behind her, and she gasped.

It was Fedeka, half-crouched and clinging to the frame of bent metal and slanted stone that had been the doorway onto the terrace. Weak with relief, Alldera sat down with her back against the wall and stretched out her rubbery legs.

"More dangerous for you than for me, Fedeka," she said vengefully. "It's a scary climb even with two hands. Why did you follow me?"

"I saw you leave," the dyer said. "I think you need to talk to someone besides Daya or Kobba. And I was tired of everyone oohing and aahing over the cutboy."

"Is he still calling everybody 'Christ'?"

"Less now," Fedeka said. "You know that old story? God's own son in revolt like any rebellious child and running about preaching femmish softness, until his outraged sire had him nailed to a tree to die. Setteo says he followed a man out of Oldtown, waited until the fool died of hunger or cold, and then pinned his body up in that tree to bring back 'Christ.' And then we came along!"

"Such an ugly tale," Alldera said. "It's better forgotten."

"But everyone needs gods," the dyer said. "And there is a kind of virtue in what Setteo did. I spent some time with him today. He says he was trying to bring about the salvation of the Holdfast—the 'Second Coming,' he calls it."

Alldera smiled in the dark at the idea of Fedeka talking theology with Setteo. She was sorry to have spoken unkindly before, but the moment for apology had passed.

"I think I'm afraid of heights," Fedeka muttered. "What is this place? Ah. This is where Raff Maggomas died, and his plans with him. I've heard it told so often."

"Yes," Alldera said. "Afterward, in that room, where you stand now, I was handed my freedom by a man I had called 'Master.' " She looked down at the moonlit river. "What a child I was! I listen to Daya's stories about me with disbelief now, sometimes."

"Your disbelief in general is a problem," Fedeka said. "I wish you would come to our ceremonies, Alldera. People notice that you don't attend."

Alldera shook her head. "I have to think about who our strongest riders are, our best archers, who is more skillful with hatchet or lance, how to arrange everyone best for an attack, or for defense—for a retreat, even. Kobba and I discuss these things often. We don't find Moonwoman much help.''

Fedeka nodded. ''People respect your planning because it's taken us this far. But there are other concerns. You came to my camp once to heal and remake your life, and so it happened. If you won't trust Moonwoman, will you trust me?''

''Fedeka, I do trust you. That's what I'm saying. You attend to religion if you think people need it. You have a feel for it, I don't.''

''I'm not talking about that,'' Fedeka said. She made her way nearer, a dark figure, long-waisted and slightly bowed in the legs. ''I'm talking about you, and what happens in your own mind. You come up here, solitary, thinking of what? Of those men, I think: your masters that were. That's not good to think about, alone like this, and with the moon hidden by clouds.''

Alldera looked outward to where the parapet had been. She imagined she saw someone standing there, whip-thin, bitter-faced, a man whose scent she could almost remember and whose pale, observant eyes she could never forget. Sorrel's sire, maybe. But what in the world could that mean, to the man, to Sorrel, or to Alldera herself?

''It's all so long ago,'' she said.

With a faint groan and an audible cracking of joints, Fedeka sank on her heels beside Alldera. She nudged down onto her wrist the half dozen bracelets that she had jammed together near her elbow so they would not make noise and alert Alldera that she was being followed.

''That's why,'' she said patiently, ''the support of Moonwoman is so important to us all, the strong as well as the weak: to keep our memories and our purposes clear and true even after such a long, long time.''

They were as private here as they would ever be, and Alldera felt that she owed it to Fedeka to try to explain. ''The worship of the moon is a slave religion, Fedeka, invented by the Matris to keep fems docile in their bondage.''

She felt the older fem turn toward her in the dark. "Are you thinking that in that old life I'd be a Matri by now, an overseer of other slaves? Well, maybe. But I learned something, wandering the Grasslands alone for years and thinking about things under the moon. Nothing that gives strength is evil or useless. Moonwoman gave us strength to endure slavery. She'll give us strength to win freedom. You must see the truth of this, Alldera. You can't take back the Holdfast alone."

"I'm not alone. I have the Free Fems with me. I have you with me, Fedeka; don't I?"

"The others turned on you once," Fedeka said thoughtfully, "years ago, in the Tea Camp."

"They thought I was challenging Elnoa's rule. Which I was, of course. But Elnoa's spell is broken. People feel themselves aging. They want to come home, take what revenge they can, bring freedom to the friends and lovers and daughters they left behind, if any still live, and to any children there may be. So they follow me where they want me to lead them, as if we had never quarreled. Where is Moonwoman in any of that?"

Fedeka scratched her calf with the rasping sole of her other foot. "Things change. People can be scared into acting against their own best interests and their natural affections. Be careful, Alldera."

Alldera sat very still, chilled. "Are you threatening me, Fedeka? Is that what you climbed up here to do?"

"No." The dye-maker's big hand smoothed Alldera's hair so delicately that it might have been the tug of the breeze. At once, as if in embarrassment, the touch was withdrawn. "Can't an old friend give you a commonsense warning without being suspected? You worry me, Alldera. You worry me."

"Well, don't worry so much," Alldera said. "I pay attention to the lessons of my own life. I don't need reminding."

This was coming out all wrong. Fedeka had probably saved her life, back in the Grasslands. *Maybe that's why I hate this Moonwoman nonsense,* she thought; *because Fedeka assigns to a white stone in the night sky all the thanks I owe to her, herself.*

"Did Daya send you after me?" she said.

"Do you think I'm a slave?" Fedeka said testily. "I go where I choose, not where I'm sent. I couldn't help thinking, in this terrible place—what if the Endtendant or the Dark-Dreamer is still alive, lurking in these ruins?"

Alldera shivered at this echo of her own fears. "They won't be alive after so long."

"You're alive," Fedeka said. "What if you find one of them here tonight, or somewhere else tomorrow?"

Alldera bit her lip. "That's everyone's question, isn't it? If so-and-so survived, master or fem, what then?"

"If it's any master of mine, I know what I'll do," Fedeka said positively. "But you don't know what you'll do, because you don't listen for the whisper of the Lady in your heart. You came up here tonight to try to imagine what you would do, because you don't know."

"Oh, horseshit," Alldera said, gathering herself to rise. The crooked pavement thrummed unpleasantly beneath her. She had a sudden nervousness of standing up and seeing again just how high off the ground she was. What if she couldn't bring herself to climb back down?

"Weren't you thinking about those men when I joined you?" Fedeka insisted.

"You helped me once, Fedeka, but you're not a mother of mine and neither is your phantom Lady in the Moon. Leave me alone!"

Without another word, the dyer withdrew. Alldera listened to her awkward descent and the clatter of dislodged debris falling on the broken pavement below. Only when all the sound had died away did Alldera herself climb down, annoyed at her own childish defensiveness, but angry with Fedeka too.

On the way she put her hand on something rounded and hard half-buried in rubbish. It was one of the glass globes with which the Engineer Maggomas had once lit the rooms of 'Troi, using power extracted from the river. The globe was partly shattered and wind-scoured to a cloudy gleam, a small, fragile moon of the men's own making.

She crushed it with her heel before continuing down.

Moonwoman's Portion

Alldera gently sponged Kenoma's face and neck, whispering words of comfort and encouragement. Kenoma, moaning and hugging her belly, tried to smile, baring her teeth that were squarish like a horse's teeth.

"I'll do that," Emla said. "She's strong, she'll be all right, I think. Fedeka says so."

"Fedeka should know," Alldera sighed, patting Kenoma's shoulder and rising to stretch her own back. "Though you're becoming an expert in these things yourself, Emla."

Lately Emla had been studying healing herbs with Fedeka. Now that four people were down with belly cramps and fever, she was the dyer's assistant in healing. Her sallow face with its long, straight nose and dark, clever eyes wore a concentrated expression of concern instead of her more customary look of calculation. She wore a Lady-token, a smooth pale stone drilled through and hung on a leather thong.

She was changed from the person who had been Daya's

ruthless rival for Elnoa's most personal favors. They never alluded to that time now, but Alldera thought of it sometimes.

"It's the older sick ones that I worry about most," Alldera said. She worried too that illness kept them all stuck in this camp beside dead black 'Troi, where for all they knew the source of the sickness itself lay hidden. But she did not voice this concern, which would only alarm people more.

Emla felt Kenoma's forehead with the back of her wrist. "They get so thirsty, with this fever! How much longer till the water party gets back?"

"Soon." The Mercy Wells, the one stop allowed the old labor gangs bringing metal from the mines to 'Troi, were only a day's walk away along the base of the foothills.

"In Moonwoman's own time, I suppose." Emla raised Kenoma's head and tilted a small clay vial to her cracked lips. "She must be holding us here for her own reasons."

Such pious cant! Alldera still smarted from Fedeka's intrusion last night. She watched Emla's deft fingers pack up Fedeka's medicines. Where *was* the water party? Maybe she should have gone with them herself—but she could not do everything and be everywhere.

Voices rose suddenly, excited calls. The ground drummed faintly with the rush of horse hooves. Alldera ducked outside.

A rider came tearing through the camp to draw up in a rearing halt a scant yard before her. It was Daya, flushed and breathless.

"We found men," she gasped. "We got to the wells so quickly—Kobba said that if there were men still living, they would be working the old metal mines, farther up the road. We went to see if we could find traces of them." A circle of listeners pressed close around her, transfixed by her vivid excitement. "We almost rode into a whole crew of them. We fought them. We won."

Smears of blood streaked Daya's sleeve and the flank of her gray mare. The horse shivered its sweat-darkened skin.

There had been eight in the scouting party, Kobba leading. Kobba had once worked in the mines. She knew every inch of the mine road north from 'Troi and of the mine pits themselves.

Now, Alldera thought, *don't stand still like a dazed fool: take hold.* She stepped forward and smoothed the mare's wet shoulder with a long, calming stroke.

"Are all of you all right? Did anyone get hurt?"

"None of *us,*" Daya said with a spasmodic grin. "None of *us* got hurt."

So that was not femmish blood.

"Where are the others?"

"Coming," Daya said, looking back up the river. "Men are smaller than I remembered. Isn't that funny?"

Now Alldera could see the knot of fems riding quickly down the river road, their mounts' hooves churning dust. The pack string bobbled along after them. She saw no one walking. Men—captive men—would surely be on foot.

"Where are these men you found?"

Daya's scarred cheeks twitched with that wild smile that was like a tic. "We killed them. We killed six men."

"Killed them? You found men living, and you killed them?" Alldera's hands shook with an upwelling of incredulous rage. She forced herself to speak in level tones. "Give me your horse, Daya. Go to your prisoner. He's not to see this."

White-faced, Daya swung out of the saddle. Alldera mounted the lathered horse. Other people at once scattered to find mounts where they could. She felt them pressing at her back as she rode out of the camp. But no one passed her or even came up abreast.

They were afraid of her anger. Good. This was not to have happened. She had thought that at Corpse Hill the first murderous, thoughtless impulse had been spent. Whatever she did now must be swift, vehement, public, and sure. She was grimly certain that there would not be another chance.

The party of scouts approached, whooping triumphantly.

Heart pounding, she pressed forward. They reined their horses aside, calling to her, exultant. Fat water bags swung, dewed with moisture, from their saddlebows. She pushed through to the spare horses at the rear.

These animals carried other burdens: dead men, stinking of raw and fearful deaths. Their slack flesh jerked and sagged with the steps of the horses that bore them. Lexa rode alongside one of them, her handsome face ruddy with excitement. She brandished a trophy that had already spattered her clothing with brown stains.

On a cold, furious impulse Alldera turned in her saddle and snatched the heavy thing from Lexa's hand. Greasy hair cut into her clenched fingers. She spun her mount and thrust the bloodless head aloft at the full stretch of her arm. Her horse shied, snorting, but she wrenched it in a tight little circle, showing the dead and sagging face to the startled riders, scouts, and onlookers from the camp, who fell back in confusion. Only tall Kobba met her glare from a masklike face.

Alldera flung her words at them all. "Is this what we've come for?"

"Yes!" someone cried, and others roared approval.

"No!" Alldera screamed, so hard that she thought her throat would split. "Think before you speak! Can this make reparation for our suffering? Can this give us a lifetime of payment for the debts owed to us? *Can this sire a child?* Answer me!"

They grew quiet, staring at her and at the bloodstained trophy, or looking frowningly at each other. Memory of a thousand Tea Camp conferences and strategy sessions in the Women's tents, countless conversations about when we go home, when we take back the Holdfast for ourselves, fueled her rage.

Lexa brushed back her silvering hair, leaving blood smears on her own cheeks. "But, Alldera—"

"This dead scrap can do nothing—nothing that we need or want. It can only rot and stink. Here, Lexa, you took this prize—see what good you can get from it!"

With a grunt of effort, she slung the head away as hard as she could. Lexa's horse reared, almost throwing its rider. The head struck earth, rolled, and stopped, its face mercifully hidden.

Alldera turned back toward the camp, kicking the tired gray into a trot. Excited talk and laughter bubbled up behind her again as the scouting party was surrounded by the other riders come out from the camp to meet them. Her pulse still pounded, but the rush of fury was gone. She could have wept with frustration.

Emla ran to meet her, offering to cool out the gray for her. Excitement touched the masseur's sallow cheeks with color. Her eyes were bright with greedy curiosity. Alldera handed her the reins without a word.

Daya was in the tent, shaving slivers from a tea brick.

Alldera snapped, "I hope you washed the blood off yourself before you started that."

"I am bleeding," Daya said, not looking up from what she was doing. She had pulled on a clean shirt. "I didn't know you could tell. It comes on me unexpectedly sometimes now, a sign of maturity from Moonwoman, according to Fedeka."

"That's not what I meant and you know it. I'm talking about men's blood."

"My hands are clean," Daya said softly. "I've given Kenoma water to drink, and Setteo is tethered where I left him."

Alldera sat down by the fire cage. "What happened?"

Daya put more tea shavings into the kettle. "These men were carrying supplies and stacks of metal in two carts. A wheel had broken, dumping one of the carts down a gully. They were trying to shift all the loads to the other wagon. We heard them, we smelled them." Her pupils looked enormous as she focused, inwardly, on that scene.

"One of them saw us and tried to shout a warning." She grinned, an involuntary rictus. "Someone shot him in the belly—I have to find out who it was before it gets all confused in people's memories. We rode down on them. They ran, or tried to hide behind the carts, under them—everyone was screaming, us, them. When it was over, they were all dead.''

"That's all?"

"I need time to make a good story of it," Daya flashed. "You should have been there."

"If I'd been there, it wouldn't have happened," Alldera said. "Did you try, at least, to stop it?"

"I'm only a pet fem turned storyteller. No one *obeys* me. Kobba was in charge."

"Who else should have been?" came a new voice. Kobba stepped into the tent, bending to avoid the sagging ceiling. "You gave people something to talk about, Alldera, but you might have waited for a better time to crack the whip of command."

"If I'd had a whip in my hand, I'd have done more than crack it!"

Disturbed by their voices, Kenoma raised her head and peered blearily at them. She groaned and rolled deeper into her blankets. Kobba stepped around her and sat down near the fire cage. She took a cup in her big-boned hand and turned to Daya for a serving of tea. But her eyes were fixed on Alldera.

"I don't understand why you're angry. If there are six men, there must be others. These were no use for breeding anyway."

"Do you *know* that?"

"Most of them were older, and we've always said that all Senior men should die in any case." Kobba leaned back against a pile of saddlebags and sipped her drink.

"We did agree on that," Daya said. "They'd be too steeped in the old ways to be taught new ones."

"No one can be taught anything if he's dead." Alldera took the kettle from Daya's hand and poured for herself. "I can't believe you allowed this to happen, Kobba."

"I made it happen," Kobba said. "You should be glad.

Instead you abuse people, and now they're afraid to talk to you. Your feelings are too strong. I told them I would come speak with you.'' She leaned forward intently. ''You know this had to happen.''

''It's exactly what everyone knows must *not* happen. We agreed to take captives whenever we could.''

''Some prices can only be paid in one coin.'' Kobba slowly swirled the tea in her cup. ''And the debts owed here are bigger than the world. But it should be easier to take men alive now that we've done this.''

Alldera said, ''Where are the other scouts? We shouldn't be speaking privately. Everyone should hear.''

''They're busy unloading what we took from those men, and the water we brought. We did fetch what you sent us for.''

''Oh, Kobba, of course you did. But then to go on to the mines like that—''

Kobba said quietly, ''It was so close on horseback, instead of how we had to do it in the old days, on foot and burdened.''

Alldera refused to be distracted. ''You could have missed one of these men, and had him run off to warn the others you're so sure exist. Can we not trust each other out of sight for fear of somebody's impulse undoing everything in an instant? This is not what we came here to do!''

Kobba set her cup aside and hugged her long legs to her chest. ''It's what I came to do. I'm too old to bear cubs. Many of us are. You yourself might not be able to carry another cub to term. People are dreaming, when they sit around the suppertea fire talking about naming their new children after friends and lovers and heroes.''

Daya murmured, ''There are other purposes than mating to put a man to, for people who remember.''

Alldera glared at her. ''What, mindless killing? That's not worth the journey.''

Kobba said, ''I think it is. The fems who rode with me today think it is. Don't cut our pride away from us, Alldera.

We've killed some of the masters who used to brutalize us. We needed to do this. We all need to do it, each of us; even you.'' She pointed her finger at Alldera like an accuser.

"Each Free Fem needs to know she can face a man in battle instead of groveling or running away. And each of us needs to know that the Free Fem riding beside her has done that and can do it again, so we can trust each other in a fight.''

With a hollow feeling at her center *(Must I do such a thing? Could I do such a thing?)* Alldera said, "You think chasing a man down on horseback is 'facing the enemy'? I saw the wounds in the backs of these corpses. Look, if what you say is true, Kobba—if everyone agrees with you in this—you should lead. Go ahead, you take over. I won't object. Daya has the maps, she'll show you.''

"Alldera, don't!'' Daya exclaimed.

Kobba shrugged. "Everyone knows that Moonwoman has chosen you as our chief.''

"Oh, great Witches of the Past,'' Alldera groaned, slapping the nearest tent pole so that the leather roof above them trembled. "Don't refuse on account of Fedeka's superstition! What is it, are you punishing me? Paying me back for being right years ago, when I tried to drive you all home while we were all still young and strong?''

Kobba stared at the fire, fingering the rough skin of the scar under her eye. In the quiet they all heard footsteps and voices approaching the tent.

A crowd of fems came leading a horse among them, a horse lumpily laden. Alldera could see an arm hanging down, gashed and unnaturally bent: the arm of one of the dead men. Fedeka halted the led horse and spoke to Alldera in a clarion voice.

"I have here an offering to Moonwoman, something from our first true blooding in our own land. Moonwoman walks full in the sky this evening. She's not to be neglected, just because our enemies were killed in daylight.''

Alldera saw her in the mind's eye as the dye-gatherer in a

solitary camp, the self-reliant collector of plants that the Free
Fems used for colors and potions. This corpse-taker with her
one arm ringed in white bracelets symbolizing her deity was
a new Fedeka. Currents of zeal and otherworldly desire
swirled around her, attracting others and obscuring her former gruff and simple clarity.

Alldera tried not to sound challenging. "Are you sure the
spirit of the moon wants anything from this dead man?"

Old Roona, wraithlike at Fedeka's side, said, "It does no
harm to try to please the Lady."

"It does no good to mutilate dead bodies," Alldera replied with asperity, "even those of enemies. Would you do
that in the camps of the Riding Women?"

"We are not in the Grasslands now," Fedeka said. "And
Moonwoman watches here differently than she did there."

With that the little procession moved on, heading out from
the camp toward wherever Fedeka had chosen for her lunar
rites.

Kobba said, "You would do better to use Fedeka and her
cult, not criticize them."

"I'm surprised to hear that from you, Kobba. Are you
wearing white tokens now too?"

Kobba's teeth gleamed in a quick, hungry grin. "I'm
waiting for tokens of a different kind. Do you mean to say
you yourself don't carry a pebble for the Lady?"

"No Woman in the Moon is going to make our victory for
us."

"In that case," Kobba said, getting up, "we'll manage
without her."

"Where are you going?" Daya called after the tall fem.

"To Fedeka's ceremony."

Daya looked at the floor. "I'm going too."

"Who will look after the sick while you're all praying to
your imaginary god?" Alldera picked at a splinter the tent
pole had left in her palm.

"They won't begrudge us a little time with Moonwoman," Daya said heatedly. "We won today. We deserve

to celebrate.'' The way she said ''we'' patently included the scouting party but excluded Alldera herself, along with everyone else who had not ridden to the mines.

Alldera was suddenly sick of looking at the pet fem's scarred, defiant face. ''Well, go ahead. Enjoy yourself.''

''Is there water?'' Kenoma whispered, and Alldera got her a drink.

She busied herself among the sick fems, giving them the herbal tea Emla had steeped for them that afternoon and helping them settle for what sleep they could get. These chores soothed her and helped her mull over again the deployment of the little army for an attack on Oldtown.

But her thoughts began to run in circles, freighted with obsessive worry. After moonrise, she drew on her cape and prowled through the camp on foot, making sure sentries had been posted. Kobba might have forgotten that detail, in her enthusiasm for Fedeka's Lady in the Moon.

She was jittery, starting at every sound. Men had died at the hands of fems today, a thing scarcely believable except when she looked again at the remaining bodies, examining the faces—all unfamiliar—by torchlight. In other times, such an occurrence would have touched off savage retaliation. Echoes of old rampages by angry masters, witnessed or heard about, nagged at her and would not let her rest.

In the end she walked out to watch Fedeka's ceremony, from a little distance. Unnoticed herself, she saw Daya, with the others, taste the hot marrow from human bone and dance in a dance of hatchets and knives that left the corpse a gutted ruin.

But I, Alldera thought, *the one who led them here—I haven't ever raised my hand as high as that against any man.*

Stone Encampments

S haru drink my blood,'' Sheel swore, ducking to avoid a
straggling branch. "What a country! You can't see
anything with all this spiny growth everywhere!''

She was in a foul mood. They had not caught up with the
fugitives in time. If they ever did, there was no plain good
thing to do about it, not now with the Free Fems back again
in their own land.

I should have ridden ahead alone as I meant to, she
thought. Eight riders were too slow, and too few to make any
more difference than one would make. *I would have caught
up with them by now. I would have shot Alldera Holdfaster
from her saddle, if that was what it took, and gone into exile
for killing my own sharechild's bloodmother.*

*Nothing but wrong choices, wrong decisions, from begin-
ning to end,* she thought glumly. *My decisions. So here we
are, too late, chasing them in this green country swept by
wet winds.*

And where the hell were they anyway? She drew rein and
crooked one leg around her pommel, squinting ahead past

what appeared, at long last, to be the edge of this tangle of borderland brush. The others drifted to a stop around her.

Before them lay a long, smooth slope of grass, islanded with young trees and dappled with the shadows of passing clouds. Sheel had never been nervous of being in the open before, and her feelings—that they were abandoning the shelter of the forested mountains for dangerous exposure on the plain—irritated her. What was forest but a trap for riders where enemies could hide in the trees, jump down on you, pull you from your saddle, and cut your throat?

They were all edgy, although they had found nothing alive since leaving the Grasslands. The fems had left plenty of sign—they certainly weren't counting on being undetectable to pursuers from the west—but that was all.

Sheel's mount shifted its weight and reached for more of the thick, lush grass that grew here. She was tired to death of hearing the others exclaim about the stuff and speculate admiringly on its merits. It seemed there was no Dusty Season on this side of the mountains, but early rains well before the fall equinox. Grassland people would still be sticking close to their camps' wells. Here there was the river to drink from, now that the springs in the hills were left behind.

But what did people eat here? Their own supplies were running low. A strange, damp country to starve in.

Tyn Chowmer spat past her horse's shoulder and dabbed at her lips with her headcloth. "Well, they've made it home. Maybe we should leave it alone?"

Picking off stray men along the border was one thing, but venturing into the Holdfast itself was another. All their training was against it, everything they'd all been taught about protecting the security of the camps. They had a right to prickling scalps and darting, nervous glances.

The Salmowon in the group, a pale Woman with sunburn blisters on the high bridge of her nose, shook her head. "We need some word of the fems to bring back, so that Women will know what they can expect from this mad venture."

Suasayan Tulun raised her hand to shade her almond-shaped eyes. "From what we've seen, there is nothing to expect. Soon the Free Fems will see that this place is worthless and come back to live among our tents again."

"Not everybody thinks they belong in our tents anymore," the Salmowon sniffed. "Now that they've run off and taken all Women's ease of mind with them."

"What kind of Woman lets her peace rest in the hands of people who were slaves?" the Tulun said scornfully.

Sheel snapped her fingers. "No quarreling! This is enemy country as it is."

"If there are any enemies left," Tyn said with a distasteful pursing of her mouth. "Besides that sack of hacked manbones hitched to a tree back there."

Sheel held out her hand. "Who's got the map?"

"It's not much of a map," Ayana Maclaster said dubiously, handing over the roll of thin-scraped leather. "A fem made it as a love gift to a Mellers Woman. She was more interested in pretty squiggles and little pictures than in accuracy, I think."

Sheel unrolled the soiled page and flattened it on her thigh. Now that the Free Fems had fulfilled their promise and their threat of so many years, it seemed a criminal madness that no one had ever thought to make them draw maps of the Holdfast for the Women: many maps, good maps.

She rolled the map again and turned to tuck it into the bedding lashed behind the cantle of her saddle. "The fems have followed the river so far, and we've followed the fems. Let's continue, until there's something else to do."

After some discussion they rode on, hazing the spare horses in their midst. Out in the open they grew more confident and cheerful, even though the sky was an alien sky and the grass was different grass than they knew.

The fems' trail zigzagged downhill toward a great swathe of scorched and fragmented walls, its two parts linked by broken bridges over the river. If that was what remained of 'Troi, it was where Alldera had originally escaped the Holdfast, according to femmish tales. How did these ruins look to Alldera's eyes now?

"People made this?" the Salmowon said incredulously.

Sheel nodded. "If you consider men people, yes, people made it. Then they unmade it again."

Tyn Chowmer snorted. "From what I've heard, men planned it and men destroyed it but the labor of fems built it."

The Salmowon blinked her pink-rimmed eyes. "But what was it for? Why would anyone make such a place?"

"Something about working metal, I think," Sheel said. "If you do it on a large scale, instead of piece by piece and for one Woman at a time, you end up housing your giant anvils and crucibles and so on in a permanent camp like this."

The Tulun said sagely, "They made it to show how rich they were. The Free Fems say that 'Troi walls were once clad in flattened metal sheets, as we dress our bodies in leather."

At this, both the dark young Rois cousins nudged each other and emitted soft sounds of amazement and disbelief.

No one seemed anxious to go any nearer. The wind blew among the clutches of weed and brush that overgrew the place. Grass rippled along the foundations and up over the piled rubble. The only sound was the river's murmur.

"All this water and no one to drink it," Margora Garriday observed. "No herds to graze these sweeps of grass. If you told me, I wouldn't believe it: these Holdfaster people had so much wealth, and what did they do? Huddled together in stone buildings, rubbing shoulders with each other until they went crazy and killed each other!"

The Free Fems' trail led to a camping place just above the ruins. The Women paused there to drink and refill their water bags. Sheel hoped no spirits drifted in the river, invisible watchers with hungry eyes. Her skin crawled at the thought.

Holdfast men had fought each other here and must have

died in great numbers, by Alldera's account. There were no sharu on this side of the mountains to consume the flesh of the dead and free the angry, injured souls. The wind must do it, a slow, ugly process, surely. The spirits might never get free, or forget where to go when they finally did; if there was someplace for them to go.

She kept glancing uneasily back the way they had come: what might be following them?

"Gayala Rois, Ray Rois," she said, "will you keep watch on our back trail?" The cousins nodded and turned back.

When Sheel knelt to fill a waterskin, she found the smooth back of a human skull gleaming up at her out of the mud. Standing again hastily, she saw that there were bones everywhere, scattered on the ground, sunk into the soil and overgrown with grasses and weeds.

They found no signs of recent life around the ruins— except the Free Fems' own tracks—but 'Troi was eloquent in its own silent, windswept way.

"Let's go in and look around," said Tyn Chowmer. "We can't stop the Free Fems now, so why rush?"

"We didn't come all this way just to go home without seeing what's here to see, did we?" Ayana Maclaster added. Wearing her rain cape over her shirt, she looked dumpy and soft, but she could put a lance through a sharu's eye at twenty paces. And she was a sweet, imaginative lover when she was in the mood to be, as Sheel had discovered in the past.

"We three, then," Sheel said. "Some people have to stay with the horses."

So she rode down into 'Troi with Tyn Chowmer and Ayana Maclaster, both of whom she trusted in a fight.

'Troi was a terrible place. She was afraid the leaning slabs of wall might collapse on her. The footing was a rough, hummocky quilt of rubble and ash that made her worry about laming her horse. Or herself, for that matter, if she must dismount and walk.

Sunlight glowed on scatters and heaps of bones that wind

or water had moved among the ruins or that lay where they had fallen, still delineating human forms. Tyn picked up a tangle of thin black rope which disintegrated in her hands to expose the scorched metallic core inside. She threw the gleaming thing away.

Sheel was deeply relieved to leave it all behind. From a distance, 'Troi looked like some blighted pasture from which the soil had been blown by a monstrous wind, so that only these stony, smoke-streaked shards of wall could grow there now.

They lost the trail over a flinty stretch of land below the ruins. Everyone agreed that the Free Fems had probably continued eastward along the river's course.

Sheel rode listening to the creak of saddle leather and the thud of the horses' hooves on the alien ground, and thinking, *This place is empty the way no place is empty at home. This is a hungry emptiness. It has swallowed the Free Fems and now it is swallowing us.*

They would ride and ride but never find any living thing. One day they would ride into the sea, which she imagined as a rushing river with only one bank, and they would never be heard of again.

Haunted by these thoughts, she reproached herself as she rode. She should have come alone, causing no risk to Women of other Motherlines than her own. But how could she have said no to her old raid-mate Tyn Chowmer of the heavy, homely face, or the plump Maclaster, not only an old lover but someone to whom she had twice been related by the rein and once as a sharemother? Anyway it was too late to change things now.

Down the river on the north side they followed what had once been a broad trail lined with worn, flat stones. This would be a "road," she supposed; a silly thing, unless you only went from this place to that place and back again. It was as if the Holdfast people had been so afraid of getting lost in their little patch of country that they had had to mark its trails permanently with rocks.

Grass had broken the paving up and covered much of it. The Women rode alongside the road, not on it. When they picked up the Free Fems' trail again it led them to the trampled traces of another campsite.

They were discussing camping close by themselves—the land made a shallow dip with a rim from which good watch could be kept—when Ayana Maclaster came galloping back from scouting the area. Her round face looked green.

"Come look," she said.

Leaving the others with the spare horses, Sheel and the Garriday followed her to the far side of the ridge. A large stretch of grass had been flattened and a fire had burned in the center. Fragments of bone lay scattered in the ashes: bones stripped of flesh, charred, crushed, and emptied of marrow. They were not the bones of horses.

The three Women silently quartered the open space on horseback, examining the ground from the saddle. Not one of them wanted to set her foot on that stained and beaten earth.

"Milk and welcome, what is *that*?" Sheel said through clenched teeth.

In a shallow trench lay the mutilated body of a man, his gaping torso stuffed with scorch-marked rocks. Ayana Maclaster leaned beside her horse's shoulder, gagging. Maclasters were squeamish people, though steady in a fight.

"The tracking is terrible in this country," Sheel said, turning away. Men had been enemies all her life, but her own stomach heaved. "We missed the place where the Free Fems met men."

"You can't miss how it ended, though," the Garriday said, wrinkling her freckled face up into a mask of disgust. "Phew."

They rode back to where the others waited. The dark Rois cousins were too young to have patrolled the Grassland border. Through debts and favors called, Sheel had been maneuvered into bringing them along. She was more sorry than ever for it now.

"Go look, over there," she said. "The next man you see might be alive, and if he sees you first you won't see him at all."

They looked at each other and rode off to do as she said.

"We should all go see," the Tulun said uneasily.

"Well, go then," Ayana Maclaster snapped. "See if you like it any better than we did."

They moved farther from the river and made their own camp, and they sat at their small tea fire, thinking more than they talked. The Tulun kept shaking her head so that her sleek black hair swung.

Sheel said darkly, "We'll see worse sights, I imagine, in this country. Better get used to it, Suasayan."

"I was just thinking," the Tulun said, "about how they used to mate with these men. That's why they've come back, isn't it? To mate while they still have some chance of having children. Is this what they do after mating?"

"You could hardly tell what it was," said Tyn Chowmer. "Men aren't so bad when you see them living. Funny-looking, mostly, but pretty too, some of them. I remember, one that we chased down on my first mountain patrol had a strong neck and shoulders, like a good horse. My patrol-mates had four arrows in him in a flash. They die just like anybody else. That one back there never felt most of what they did to him."

Ayana Maclaster took a stick in her dimpled fingers and poked at the dirt, making curved marks. "All those circles cut in the ground, and then part-circles—it looked like some of their Moonwoman magic. As if a Woman in the Moon would have any use for bits of dead men, or people who cooked and ate them!"

The black-eyed Tulun stared, frowning, at the moving stick. "Not even sharu tear and raven as they did here."

Tyn Chowmer glanced at Sheel and kindly saved her the trouble of trying to defend her femmish relations. "Every one of the Free Fems came to us from slavery under male masters. There must be debts owed, many, many old debts."

She paused and then added in a lower tone, "It must be much harder even than we thought, this 'slavery' thing."

"I think I'll go back home, I've seen enough," the Garriday said. She stood up and spat emphatically on the ground. "Will anyone come with me?"

No one answered. She walked away.

Sheel thought the Garriday would not ride home alone so it wasn't worth an argument. Better to let it just happen that she stayed with them instead of doing what she had said she would do. The Garridays often spoke rashly and later changed their minds.

Suasayan Tulun said, "I'm glad you told those Roises to go look, Sheel Torrinor. When I jump out of my sleep screaming tonight, I don't want to have to try to explain my nightmares to someone who didn't see what I saw."

The Garriday came back. "Is it going to rain tonight? It smells like rain, but who knows what that means here?"

Tyn Chowmer wagged her big head and sighed. "What a place. It has no seasons, it just rains whenever it feels like it. What a place you've led us to, Sheel Torrinor!" She stretched her arms over her head. "I'll be happier when we're just telling about all this by our own fires at home someday."

The Tulun took the first watch and the others lay down to sleep. Sheel scooped ashes on the fire, thinking, *I always wished them ill, the men of this country. Now it has come, but it's nothing to do with us. We should not be here.*

She had never been homesick on patrol in the borderlands, but she was homesick now.

II

Scouts and Spies

Oldtown was barely a remnant of the great, humming center of hemp-processing that Alldera remembered. The overpowering stink from the retting ponds seemed thin on the breeze now. The scouts lay on the backslope of the river levee where they could see without being seen.

In the midst of wreckage that marked the longer, wider shape of the original town, an earthwork of heaped-up brick had been thrown together, topped by a palisade of stakes. Above this composite wall a few rooftops could be seen. The bridge across the river had been replaced with a sagging patchwork of logs and boards. The land surrounding Oldtown was laid out in orderly-looking fields, some standing full for harvest, the rest already cleared of crops.

"Setteo meant real people in Oldtown, at least," Daya said. "Somebody made all this."

"I was a slave in Oldtown," Roona whispered, "when they scalped me for my hair. Master Veejam had it done, to add to his wig for a party.'' She stared, nervously licking her lips. ''What do we do now?''

Alldera hushed them both. The place seemed inhabited, no telling by how many. The Free Fems' only sure advantage was surprise. She must make a plan out of that.

As the scouts watched, gates in the palisade swung open and a file of figures emerged. These workers spread out in a thin line among the green rows, cutting and stacking the mature hemp plants.

The sight of these people struck Alldera like a physical blow. She smothered an exclamation with her knuckles, realizing with horror and guilt that she had not really expected to find any fems alive.

At the gates and watching from a high platform inside the stockade were other people, of unmistakable form and carriage: the laborers' masters; men.

''They know we've come, they're waiting for us!'' Roona said, gathering her quivering old limbs for flight.

''They don't know,'' Alldera said. ''Be quiet and listen to me: they watch their slaves as always, but they don't suspect we're here. Otherwise they would never have let those fems outside the gates.''

''I count sixteen,'' Daya said breathlessly. ''Sixteen fems, sixteen slaves. Sixteen slaves,'' she repeated in a voice that cracked. ''Slaves.''

Alldera counted for herself: sixteen fems and perhaps half a dozen men at the walls and gates, but no Rovers in sight. A patrol of Rovers would have been instantly recognizable, thick with muscle, shaven-headed, mad and menacing.

Her memory served her the painful picture of a single fleeing figure converged upon by running Rovers. Thankfully, from her workstation little had been visible but dust rising from a struggle soon ended. That had been a hotter day than this, with great cloud pillars standing in the sky.

This was a grayish morning fresh with breezes that might bring more rain. The packed dirt of the levee behind which they hid was moist to the touch.

Her mind kept shying away, reviewing their preparedness for elements that might have been forgotten. She could concentrate on everything but the action that must come, while her eyes devoured the proof that fems still lived in the Holdfast.

Most of the slaves wore broad-brimmed grass hats, a rare luxury in the old days. All had their smocks belted at the waist. No master would have allowed such a fashion then. Contraband might be hidden or carried secretly inside a belt or in the folds of bloused clothing.

So some things must have changed here, but not this: fems worked while men watched. The stooped figures were slaves on the brink of their freedom, all unaware. They were the key.

They had only to know it.

A plan unfolded silent as a cloud spreading in the sky. Charged with its energy, Alldera signaled Daya to come with her back to the bridge stem, leaving Roona to watch with her faded but sharp eyes.

"Watch the men too," Alldera admonished her softly. "Don't just look at the fems!"

Hidden by the brush that grew thick between the riverbank and the levee, Alldera and Daya made their way back to where the others waited. Alldera told her plan.

One Free Fem would slip down to the fields and contact the bond fems at work. With their aid, she would return to Oldtown tonight as one of them. Masters seldom noticed the looks of individual fems, and all femmish work parties were adept at hiding gaps in their ranks, or unofficial additions to them, at need. Once inside the Oldtown fem quarters, the Free Fem could prepare her slave kindred for the attack.

"They all looked young," Daya pointed out. "It will have to be someone young who goes to them."

Over cold food and drink scarcely touched by anyone they settled it quickly. The draw of long and short grass blades among the six youngest fell on Tua, to the evident dismay of everyone.

"Oh, good," she said. "I missed the trip to the mines."

Pale but composed, she took everyone's hand in turn, or kissed them. She took off her pants and her boots and ripped out the sleeves of her long leather shirt. She tied the shirt at the waist, smock-fashion, with a cord of plaited straw. Then she slipped away, just another bare-legged labor fem to any eye not looking for something else.

They watched her suddenly appear at the end of a row of plants near the other workers. When no alarm was raised, the watchers quietly withdrew downriver to their hidden camp. Time was what Tua needed now.

The night passed slowly. People wandered up and down the riverbank, whispering anxiously together, staring intently toward the dark bulk of Oldtown, touching each other reassuringly in the dark; touching Alldera's hand with quick, shy touches and slipping away again.

Fedeka said, "The legend is about to come true for those bond fems—the return of the Messenger, with help from the Wild! It is Moonwoman's gift to us all."

"Well, give me a hug, then," Alldera said, "because I'm terrified. I'll tell that to no one but you, because I know you won't pass it on except maybe to Moonwoman."

"Oh, she already knows." Fedeka's single powerful arm closed her in briefly, her several bracelets digging into Alldera's flesh, and then propelled her away again. "She chose you for this years ago."

Alldera slept deeply and had no dreams that she remembered. When she woke—or was she dreaming now?—Daya was sitting nearby, her shoulders bowed, rocking and muttering in an agonized undertone, "Will the sun never come up? When will it rise, when will the sun rise?"

Then she was shaking Alldera awake, all but gibbering with excitement. It was daylight, and a stranger came walking shyly toward the camp, escorted by Kenoma and two labor fems.

For a moment Alldera thought she knew the visitor. But no grown fem of the Holdfast that she had left would still be

young as this one was. Alldera felt the solid weight of her
own maturity, and she could not help but notice the gray in
the hair of the watching Free Fems. They wanted to reach
out and touch the newcomer. Alldera could see their longing
and feel it in her own body. She restrained them with a
frown. Touch without permission was a prerogative of masters.

The stranger wore her dark hair in a braided coil. Her thin
figure was draped in a smock pinned at both shoulders and
belted with a colored rope. On her feet were sandals of
woven grass, the sides smeared with river mud.

"Look," Emla muttered, nudging Alldera with her bony
elbow. "See that earring she wears? How did she earn that, I
wonder?"

Metal was precious in the Holdfast. What sort of fem
wore a metal ornament?

"A pet?" Alldera murmured. This newcomer was slight
of build.

Daya said dryly, "Not pretty enough." Absently fingering the knot of scar on her own cheek, she studied the stranger intently.

The stranger halted, her eyes very wide. She had a triangular face, the forehead rounded, the chin pointed. Her nose
pointed slightly downward to a small, precisely curved and
shaped mouth. Her hair rose in a thick brush of dark brown.
Her ears, thus exposed, by their inward slant at the lobes and
slightly peaked tops added to the impression of a delicate,
artificial tapered quality, elegant and pleasing.

And she was white as salt and plainly terrified.

Emla said, "She's going to run." Her fingers tightened on
the coil of rope she held.

"Wait," Alldera said. "Don't do anything, it's all right."
She spoke to the newcomer, pitching her voice to carry
pleasantly: "You are welcome."

The stranger stared from face to face. She said in a tremulous voice, "Which one is Alldera the runner, Alldera Messenger? Is she really here?"

Alldera felt a lurching of the earth under her feet, a wrenching of time. Her voice almost left her. She cleared her throat. "I am Alldera," she said.

The stranger-fem rushed forward, fell to her knees, and burst into tears. She gasped and gulped, her upturned face astonished and shiny with tears.

A murmur went up from the group and several moved toward the new fem. She shrank from them. "Please," she whispered. She patted at her face with her skirt hem and looked up at Alldera again, brilliant-eyed. "We have songs about you. But they say you are very tall."

"I'm as tall as I can manage," Alldera said. Kenoma guffawed and covered her mouth in embarrassment.

The bond fem's face flushed. With a palpable shock Alldera realized that this person was only a few years older than Sorrel, her own daughter.

"I mean, I thought, they say—" the newcomer stammered painfully. "The songs say—"

"Get up," Alldera said. She hadn't meant to sound angry. "We don't abase ourselves to each other in this camp."

Hesitantly the bond fem got to her feet, looking over the Free Fems with a flinching glance. "You're so few. And where are—the—the—beasts that serve you?"

"They are nearby," Alldera said cautiously.

The stranger gave a little gasp of fear. "This fem would like to see one."

Alldera smiled. "What's your name?"

"Beyarra is the name of this fem, so please you."

The old usage "this fem" avoided the assertiveness of "I," "me," "mine," which the masters had always forbidden their fems. It fell on Alldera's ears like the flick of a whip. For a moment she hated this slave.

She forced herself to relax. "Let us look at you, and you look at us. It's years since we've seen a Holdfast fem, and I imagine you long ago gave up hope of ever seeing us."

Beyarra smiled tremulously and stood with downcast eyes under their scrutiny. She was a dainty young person, scented with some sweet fragrance. Her clothing was mended but clean.

She accepted a cup of cold tea and managed not to spit out the first sip. The Free Fems watched her avidly, nudging each other and reminding each other that tea was a Grassland drink.

"Sit down," Alldera said. "Let's talk. You know our plan?"

Beyarra nodded. "So please you, the fems of Oldtown will come out tomorrow as if to work, but run instead toward the river where you lie hidden. Those of us inside the walls will try to hold the gates open for you." Another little gasp, of excitement and fear.

"Good. How many of you are there all together in Oldtown, and how many men?"

Beyarra counted on her fingers: "Twenty-two masters. Twenty of us, but not all come out to work in the fields."

"How many will stay inside the walls tomorrow?" Alldera asked. "Will they join us?"

"They say they are resolved," Beyarra said solemnly. "Though not all can fight. Gredda is sick after a miscarriage." She paused at their startled looks. In the old days a fem who miscarried would simply have been burned for witching her cub dead. "Since she did at least conceive a cub, the masters are careful with her health now in hopes of another conception when she recovers. She is old for bearing, as old as—as—" She faltered, lowering her gaze.

"As old as we are." Roona grinned, showing her few remaining teeth.

"And Tezza," Beyarra added hastily, "my friend; she won't be sent out to the fields. She is the favorite of Master Jodd since last winter. He still keeps her late in his bed sometimes. And of course Matri Mayala will stay in to oversee the cooking."

Several people repeated the word "Matri." A fem who could not speak spat on the ground.

Daya asked silkily, "Did many Matris survive the wreck of the old ways?"

Beyarra ducked her head as if avoiding a blow. "Why, many Matris died," she said softly, "at first. But most of us are young and headstrong, and masters like order. The older fems who survived those first days were the steady ones. And so . . . the masters themselves now call our overseers Matris, which this fem believes was a secret name before."

Daya said, "But this puts Tua in much greater danger, going into a femhold run by a Matri!"

Alldera held up her hands for quiet. "Tua is clever and strong. The risks she runs can't be altered now. We must trust her to protect herself."

She hoped they couldn't see how anxious she was. *They will never forgive me if it goes badly for Tua,* she thought.

The rest of what Beyarra had to tell soon ranged beyond the immediate facts of Oldtown life. She said that the fems who had survived the Fall were treated better, after a frightful interval of slaughter and abuse, because they were fewer and so more valuable.

The Rovers, the armed force of the ruling Senior men, had been prime targets of the rebellious Juniors. So far as Beyarra had heard, not one Rover had survived and no new Rover teams had been trained up since to police the fems for their masters. Fems who ran away from harsh treatment these days could always find a new master offering milder conditions of work.

Yet men still kept fems as chattels, worked them, and tried to breed cubs on them, this last with limited success. Some fems who had survived the Fall were now too old to bear. Some younger ones had not menstruated for long months because of starvation during the worst of the fighting, and were still slow to conceive.

The different bands of men tried to keep up appearances of health, strength, and vigor before each other to discourage attacks and to attract defectors from other bands. Lies were told and rumors were rife. Newborns that lived were sometimes fought over, traded, and stolen in raids, like valuable horses among the Riding Women.

Men and fems still lived in the City. The current Oldtown cohort was in fact based there, but had come upriver with their fems for the growing season and harvest. Men lived in Lammintown also, Beyarra said.

Men were armed with knives, of course, and some had learned to use bows and arrows as well as slings. From her description, they were not proficient with the bow to anything like the range of Grassland archers. She had heard of the guns of 'Troi, used in battle during the Fall, but so far as she knew the weapons themselves and those who knew how to use them had perished.

Beyarra thought there were upward of one hundred eighty men in the entire Holdfast, perhaps as many as two hundred; and seventy-five or eighty bond fems, many of them under twenty years old. Of cubs, she thought perhaps a dozen, no more.

Kobba had been right about one thing: there were men to spare.

Beyarra said, "For a long time men fought over food, over us, over each other—who was to blame, who had injured whom. They fight less now, but sometimes despair takes them and they kill themselves, or us."

Beyarra didn't know about Bayo and said no one did, though many stories were told of fighting there. Balked in this inquiry so close to their hearts, the Free Fems turned to asking after friends they had long ago left behind.

Beyarra shrank from these inquiries. "Many died. They say that some young fems of those times, who had pledged themselves to resist, died defending themselves and others." She made that little gasp of shock, as if the idea of fighting the masters was still almost unthinkable.

"The masters retaliated at random," she went on, her voice sinking so that Alldera had to strain to hear her, "as the Matris always said they would. I am too young to remember, but I have heard—ask who still lives. That this fem can say.''

Alldera found she couldn't remember names of fems she had known in those days. She sat as mute as the tongueless, more so—they used hand speech to convey their inquiries.

Beyarra closed her eyes and reeled off the names of the living that she could remember. No one cried out in the joy of recognition, perhaps because so many friends sat stone-faced, hearing no names that they knew. Lexa put her arms around Emla and stroked her hair where the white streak ran through it. Everywhere people held hands as they listened. Here and there a face shone bright with tears of rejoicing or perhaps surrender of long-held hopes.

Then people wanted to tell Beyarra all about the Grass-lands, but she hunched her shoulders and covered her head. Alldera said the young bond fem should be allowed to rest. Besides, it was time to relieve those on watch and guarding the horses. The audience reluctantly dispersed.

Beyarra sat by Alldera's bedding and cautiously drew from a quiver a single arrow, which she examined with won-dering eyes. Alldera watched her run her fingers up the slen-der shaft between the sharp stone point and the fletching of parchment vanes.

Beyarra saw her watching and froze, clutching the arrow. ''May this fem touch it? Is it a weapon to be used against the masters?''

Alldera said that it was, and showed her a bow as well.

Beyarra said, ''If instructed, this fem can learn to make arrows.''

''Learn to shoot,'' said Daya, who did not herself use a bow. ''People make their own arrows. It's archers we need.''

Beyarra shook her head.

Alldera said gently, ''Even pet fems will have to strike at their masters, Beyarra.''

The bond fem blinked and looked away. ''This fem has had many masters, so please you, Alldera Messenger. Every man in the Holdfast is her master; she would not know where to aim. She is master of nothing, not hatchets or bows or the demon-beasts they say you ride. But this fem thinks—I think,'' and again came the little gasp of shock at what she was daring to say out loud, ''I think I could learn to make arrows.''

A Well in Oldtown

Alldera smoothed her pony's mane, whispering soothing words. Any loud sound might carry to the men at the open gates of Oldtown.

The three sentries looked small from here, but muscular and tough. Alldera was alternately terrified and burning to close with them. No doubt the others felt the same—all the Free Fems who waited with her, lying along the slope of the levee with their horses, which they had brought and made to lie down when the light, predawn rain had stopped.

Beyarra had told the names of the men in Oldtown. None were familiar to Alldera. She stared at the sentries, trying to evaluate them in terms of the fighting to come. They were hung about with straps and pouches, but she saw no bows, lances, or spears. One lookout had a bit of bright cloth bound around his temples, confining his long, fluttering hair.

Another kept turning aside to cough, hiding his mouth with his hand. This reminded Alldera uncannily of old Jesselee Morrowtrow back in the Grasslands, during her brief last illness. She thrust the memory away, but it returned every time the man coughed. The explosions of sound from him seemed minute at this distance.

She imagined how the men would react if they knew they were watched by fems; or worse, that under the root of the old bridge one of their own, Setteo, was the invaders' prisoner.

It seemed hours since she had settled here. Could she have been shaking and sweating so long? Down the line, she heard someone trying to be very quiet about throwing up. In the foreground the stooped figures of the bond fems moved steadily, sawing at the hemps with sickles. Alldera could see the sweat rings under the arms of their smocks.

Close, they were very close—

One of them straightened her back and called after the two nearest the levee. Innocence or treachery?

"Now!" Alldera screamed. Behind her came the sound of Kenoma's bow and the flight of a hollow arrow cut to whistle as it flew. Along the levee horses lurched to their feet and people scrambled frantically into their saddles in a tide of unleashed motion.

Alldera swung astride and lashed her horse forward.

"Wait, Alldera!" Daya cried, snatching at her arm.

Swearing, Alldera rode up over the levee. Others pounded behind her. Kobba pulled ahead, lips curled in a snarl.

Alldera glimpsed a bond fem cowering openmouthed as they raced past. A howl of triumph and terror burst from Alldera's throat. Her yell was taken up around her, a yipping cry streaming back like a flag.

The sentries sprang into action. Two of them rushed to close the gates. The one with the colored headband snatched a long thong from around his waist, loaded a stone, and began whipping the weighted sling around his head.

The stone whizzed harmlessly overhead. Used to aiming at slower enemies advancing on foot, he was off his aim.

"Wait, wait," Daya screamed, surging up and grabbing at Alldera's rein. "You can't go in first! Dangerous!"

The words were lost as Alldera fought to free her mount.

Daya was light; it took only one strong heave to tumble her from her saddle. Galloping on, Alldera glanced back and saw her climb up behind another rider who had paused beside her.

Many others raced well ahead now. Bowstrings hummed in the air, sending a cloud of arrows at the few men visible on the palisade. One leaf of the gate was now shut, but the other was jammed, aslant. The men straining at it ran inside as the foremost riders closed on them. One paused to lash out at the lead riders and then darted inside after the others.

Kobba's spotted horse went down, and Kobba hit the ground running, yellow hair flying, lance in hand.

Alldera spurred her horse through the gate and was enveloped in a whirl of dust and noise. Someone ran ahead of her, not Kobba—the slingsman. She drew a lance and kicked her mare in pursuit down an open corridor between long wooden sheds. She heard the whip of arrows and thick sounds of impact everywhere. Her skin flinched continually, but it seemed like someone else's skin.

The mare shuddered and swerved, and Alldera caught a glimpse of a heavy-browed face glaring up at her. The slingsman had hit her mount with a stone. He sprinted on again.

She kneed the horse and spoke in its ear, begging for speed. The mare trotted on, snorting and favoring its right foreleg.

Another rider pushed past on the left—Kobba, mounted now on a bay horse. Others shoved by and blocked Alldera's path—Kenoma, her square teeth bared in a grimace, and Emla with an anxious grin on her thin, sallow face. Beyond them, Alldera saw Kobba harry the slingsman into a corner where two walls met.

With a wide-bladed knife he slashed wildly at Kobba. Sweat flew from his hair and beard.

"That one's mine!" Alldera yelled, trying to get past the riders ahead of her. "Damn you, let me pass!"

"Fedeka said to guard you!" Kenoma shouted. She had

picked up a bright red garment somewhere in the fighting
and wore it knotted around her shoulders, a blaze of color.

Kobba's arm swept forward. The point of her lance took
the man through the thick part of his thigh. He shrieked and
grabbed at the shaft with both hands. Kobba leaned from her
saddle and wrenched at the bobbing butt of the lance. Alldera heard the blade grate on bone. The man collapsed forward in a spout of blood. Emla and Kenoma stared, riveted
at the sight of that blood.

Alldera backed her horse and drove it down a twisting
side passage that she remembered from years ago. It led to a
loading yard near the hemp-oil sheds. She emerged into the
yard in time to see a Free Fem borne down from her saddle
by two men who had jumped from the roof of a shed. An
arrow from somewhere slapped into one of them and he
dropped.

Teeth clenched on a scream of anger—how dare they
touch one of her people, how *dare*—Alldera rode up and
slammed the other man on the back with her coiled rope. He
fell without a sound. The fem he had unhorsed—it was
Roona, moving swiftly despite her age—grabbed his hair
and slugged his head against one of the shed timbers. He
said "Guh" and lay still at her feet.

"Are you all right?" Alldera's arm tingled with shock.
Her thoughts were numbed, except for anxiety that someone
else would try to keep her from the fighting. "Roona?"

"I'm not hurt." Roona sliced a thick leather lace from her
saddle strings, straddled the unconscious man, and lashed
his wrists together behind his back. "Your horse is lame.
Take mine, if you can catch him."

"I can't leave you afoot in this," Alldera began, but
Roona overrode her.

"It's an honor. I hate riding anyway."

Alldera grinned. "If Kenoma finds you, or Fedeka, don't
tell them you've seen me."

She jumped down and slapped her own mare's rump, hoping the injured animal would find its way back to the main

herd. Catching up Roona's chestnut gelding, she turned toward a major concentration of noise.

The layout of Oldtown had changed in the rebuilding. She spent a frustrating time galloping up and down between rows of sheds, unnerved by the screams and bellows from hidden sources. Fire cracked nearby. Heat shimmered in the air.

Up ahead the roof over the old beating-out floor burned under curtains of smoke. She saw a figure—man or fem?—leap screaming from a high storage platform, hair and clothing in flames, and vanish behind some stacked hemp bales. A horse dashed by, riderless and panicked by the fire. Two figures came running from the smoke, wailing—bond fems, Beyarra's people, by their dress.

Alldera urged the chestnut toward them, trying to think where she could send them for safety. *They are what we came for,* she thought, *never mind the men.*

Seeing her bearing down on them, they screamed in terror. One would have run back into the fire if the other hadn't stopped her. They retreated through a dark doorway.

"Don't be afraid!" Alldera shouted. The chestnut shied from the fire. The bond fems did not come out.

Someone waved at Alldera from a gap between two sheds, crying, "This way, this way!"

It was Lexa, on foot. Her eyes glaring wildly in her soot-streaked face, she beckoned Alldera to follow. In the roar and rout of the fire Alldera could not understand what she shouted, but her urgency was clear.

Ignore the flurry of fighting over by the retting ponds; leave for someone else the man reeling in a daze like a drunkard's from one wall of a narrow alley to the other, holding both hands to his eyes; follow Lexa, who pushed on past everything, her pale hair gleaming.

Alldera still clutched the coil of rope in her hand: *I have struck my first blow against them. I have knocked a man to the ground with my own hand.* She ached to turn back and beat him to death where he lay—the master, pulled down at last. The thought was so exciting she thought it might stop her heart.

At the far end of an open court, between walls all but one of which sagged into the fires within, stood another Free Fem and a bare-legged bond fem in a smock. Both were peering into a well that Alldera remembered drawing water from with a rough, creaky rope that hurt your hands. The well cover had been flung aside with its dark, nether face turned to the smoky sky.

Several yards away a man lay hugging himself, puking.

Alldera drew rein, squinting through the smoke. She was seized by the conviction that if she only turned her head at the right moment, if she just looked with the right slant, she would see people she had known, labor fems staggering by under bales of hemp, Rovers staring and quivering like nervous horses, an overseer idly drawing pictures in the dirt with the butt end of his whip—the past.

But there was only Lexa, running to join the other two. Alldera rode closer to the well. "Where are your horses?"

The other Free Fem, Fedeka it was with a big bruise swelling around a cut on her forehead, yelled back, "Quick, your rope—give me the free end."

"What for, what are you doing?" Alldera demanded. They stared at each other. Lexa opened her mouth to say something but instead turned away.

The bond fem touched Alldera's knee: the touch of a pet fem, the ghost of a touch. "Messenger."

Alldera looked down at her, suddenly chilled with foreboding. "What?" she shouted. "What do you want?"

The bond fem, a long and rough-built person much painted under the dust and sweat on her face, gave a propitiatory smile and murmured inaudibly.

"What does she say?" Dread tightened Alldera's throat.

Fedeka bent her head, dabbing at her eyes with her single sleeve. She began to explain that something was in the well that they must haul back out. They needed a horse and a rope. Fedeka's tone was odd, barking. She said a name too, but Alldera didn't hear it over the sound of the fire.

She tossed them the free end of her rope, turned the chestnut, and trotted it away a little. Fedeka bawled at her to stop, wait until they had fastened the rope. What was the matter with her, why was she screaming like that?

Looking back, Alldera watched Lexa climb into the well with the rope's end tied around her waist: a very strange and unlikely thing for that proud person to be doing.

Time passed in tiny increments. Alldera noted the ache and smart of various cuts and bruises she did not remember acquiring; and noticed a swelling (she had no idea how it had got there) forming on her right forearm; and wondered where Kenoma and Emla were, and where Daya was. She ran over and over in her mind the last sight she had had of the pet fem, riding behind someone else.

The wounded man continued to gaze dully at the earth under his face and to spew small quantities of frothy spit. Not far off, someone was screaming repeatedly, and from another direction came the grunting squeals of an injured horse.

At last Fedeka shouted at her to go. Alldera clamped her knee over the knot in the end of the rope and urged the chestnut forward. The rope creaked. They shouted at her to stop, to go slowly, there, there, pull, no, gently, the rope will break, here she comes, easy, easy, here she is.

The rope went slack. No one spoke. They huddled close around the well's mouth. Strange, stricken looks flashed furtively in her direction.

This will be bad, she thought. *There must be bad parts, and they start here.* She dismounted and walked toward the well. The chestnut horse stepped nervously behind her, pulling back on the reins every time a gout of fire flared inside one of the buildings around the court. Fedeka took the chestnut's reins from Alldera's hand.

The gray stone mouth of the well was choked with something wet and bulging, from which little runnels of water trickled busily down the outer wall to the ground. Not something. Someone, once. It was a corpse, the rope trussed around its torso and the skin scraped from its shoulders and upper arms by the walls of the well. The water-darkened garment dragged down from its shoulders and breast was not the belted smock worn by bond fems, but a sodden leather shirt.

When Lexa lifted the lolling head, Alldera saw the dark ligature mark around the throat and the deep bruise where the knot had been twisted. No other marks were visible, no signs of abuse or torture. Just death. The dead fem had been very young.

Lexa cradled the dead face and cried tears onto it, which she surely would not do for an unknown bond fem. This was the corpse of Tua, strangled and stuffed down the well; Tua of the sun-warm smile, once a slave and then a Free Fem, come here to conquer her homeland.

She who had fired their first shot against a living enemy— in the mind's eye her arrow wobbled its erratic course again over the shoulder of Setteo the cutboy. She who had begged again and again for stories of the old life, their weight and lacerating meaning registering visibly in her solemn eyes.

Alldera thought, *If I look long at this, I will lose all my strength and become useless, a danger to others.*

She lashed the chestnut horse out of the wellyard at a gallop. She could not bear to be there when Daya came, or Kobba. Or anyone.

New Rules

Beyarra, standing among the mounted strangers, shifted from one foot to the other and peered out at her people from hiding. The bond fems of Oldtown huddled near the sagging wall of the stockade, keeping well clear of the invaders, at whom they scarcely dared look.

Now and then one would dash a short distance from the others and scream curses at the men. Shania, hysterical and shaking, had done this several times already. Now there was an outburst from Tamansa, who only moments ago had stumbled out through the gates hugging a bundle of her fire-scorched belongings.

The masters bunched together at the broken gates looked battered and smoke-streaked, like everyone else. Thin fingers of fire licked through the wall behind them, nearly invisible in the shimmering air. Cinders looped drunkenly on the updrafts.

Beyarra chewed her fingernails and whimpered to herself. The last time she had seen such flames a Lammintown fem pen had been burning. Three fems had been driven inside by the masters to die. Beyarra had been a child then, but the memory was keen.

The masters had put that fire out with seawater when the flames had threatened to spread to an adjoining roof. But Oldtown was made of wood, not Lammintown stone, and no one was going to the river to bring water now. It might all burn, and perhaps these captive masters with it before all was over. Not fems but masters: the idea was dizzying.

A rider emerged through a gap farther down the wall, driving a staggering man before her with the butt end of a lance until he fell among the others. Looking at these demon-riders from the Wild was enough to chill Beyarra's blood, with their strange expressions, so grim and yet exultant! How could the men even look at them and not fall down wailing in fear?

Beyarra knew each man by name, of course, and which ones were missing; and the scent of Jodd Galgar, who had fucked her just two nights ago along with her friend Tezza, and who now sat on the ground clutching his wounded knee. He was handsome, and clean, and not as rough as some. Should she speak up for him? Tezza, who had been his favorite, said nothing.

Beyarra did not think she could speak at all, for anyone. The men looked beaten, but she was still afraid of them. What if they suddenly pounced on the strangers, and what if the horses ran away and the men overpowered— overpowered—fear made her feel sick.

Where was Matri Mayala? Where was Janiega, kind and sweet-tasting, who shared food even when there wasn't enough? Beyarra moaned to herself, wanting to run to the others and ask, but afraid to.

"It's burning," she said timidly, glancing up at the gray-haired rider nearest her—Lexa, her name was. Look at the knife sheathed at her back, her regal profile, the animal she rode! If a person like that didn't want Oldtown to burn, surely she could stop it. "It could all burn down."

Lexa laughed bitterly and ended coughing. "Let it. What

does an army of riders want with walls and rooftops anyway?''

"There is food stored there," Beyarra dared to point out.
"Our harvest." These Free Fems were all lean people, she
had noticed. Her meals with them so far had been meager.

"We have our own food," Lexa said curtly. "And fewer
of us to eat it than there were two hours ago."

Beyarra had seen two Free Fems carried out of the gate.
Oldtown had not been taken without cost.

Beyond the rebuilt part of the town three riders galloped
back and forth, standing forward in their stirrups as their
mounts jinked this way and that. Figures on foot fled desperately among the ruins of the older settlement: men. Masters,
this morning. Masters, now, of nothing.

Her pulse pounded at the sight of this strange hunt: what a
thrilling, shuddering wonder! She did not know how to feel
about it. Her body buzzed with unfocused excitement and
she could not stand still.

One of the men by the gate strode forward, crossing his
arms on his broad chest. There was blood on his jaw and in
his pale yellow hair, and soot smeared his skin.

Beyarra cowered back. Gunder was a hard man; he never
forgave anything in fems or men. But he ignored the bond
fems, and what he said to the Free Fems made no sense.

"What are you, scrappers gone astray in the Wild all these
years?" he demanded hoarsely. "Is that where you found
those beasts you ride? Christ-God-Son, we don't raid each
other anymore here!"

No one answered, though the Free Fems leaned to look
along their own rank expectantly. One rider advanced toward Gunder and the men behind him. It was Alldera, on a
big, light brown horse. She didn't say a word, she only
looked, her face with its wide cheekbones set like a gleaming mask. The corners of her broad, full-lipped mouth were
turned harshly down.

Close behind her Beyarra saw several of the others shifting and murmuring, plainly uneasy to see their leader ap-

proach alone so near to the enemy. But the big one called
Kobba, on a droop-headed horse with an oozing shoulder
wound, gestured with her lance. The others settled back,
leaving Alldera alone between the Free Fems and the men.

Gunder squinted at her from under lowered brows.
"Look," he said in that same bluff manner, "we're always
looking for able fellows to join us. You never know when
the Ferrymen might come roaring down on us from Lammintown. A truce means nothing to those wild lads. Now, us,
here, we're the City's Oldtown crew, twenty-two strong
men—well, we were twenty-two. Those fems belong to us.
We live in the City most of the year, with other good men.
It's a fine life."

Alldera pulled off her headcloth and shook free her hair.
She said in a raw, strident voice, "We are not men but Free
Fems, come home to take what's ours. We have beaten you,
and we will break you, and we will own you."

A shout like a storm wind went up from the riders.
Beyarra covered her ears, then snatched her hands down
again. This storm was not raised against her.

"Fems?" Gunder's jaw dropped and his big, hurtful
hands dangled at his sides. Strong Gunder, always ready to
slap you bloody for the smallest error; a hard driver in the
breeding room who left you sore for days. He looked so astounded that Beyarra giggled behind her hand.

Rab, who had a weakness for beer that often got him into
trouble, turned ashen and began to sway from side to side,
eyes closed. Beyarra felt a pang of pity for him.

"Free—?" Gunder started, on a rising, menacing note. A
wave of color mounted in his neck and cheeks. "Free *fems*?
There's no such thing!" he roared.

None of the riders flinched. The bond fems clutched at
each other and tried to keep out of Gunder's line of sight.
Beyarra felt her own knees weaken with fear.

"Here we are," Alldera replied stonily. "And there you
are. There's such a thing now."

Gunder glared over his shoulder at the others. "It's not

scrappers or devils, men! These are renegade fems, that's all! Are we cubs here, still wet with our dams' filth, to let fems take us? I don't care what kind of monsters they've got on their side, it's us that'll take them!''

"Try," Alldera said, reining back her horse, which had begun to fret and tug at the bit. "Come and try. I'm waiting." Again that terrible sound went up from the ranks of the Free Fems, a growl and a cry and wild laughter all at once, a sound that made Beyarra's guts loosen.

"Shut your mouths!" Gunder set his fists on his hips. "Fem bitches! You, the talker—get down here on your own feet and fight me, and we'll see who's free!" He flashed the other men a ferocious grin. "I can smell this mouthy one from here. I'll have to scrub myself clean in the river when I'm done with her!''

But beneath his bluster, Beyarra realized with a thrilling shock that he was afraid.

Alldera walked her horse forward.

Gunder hawked and spat hard on the ground. Alldera's horse danced sideways, rolling its eyes. The man guffawed and drew back his fist.

Oh, Moonwoman, a man's fist, a big man's thick, hard-knuckled fist cocked in anger—any fem born and bred in the Holdfast might cry and cringe from that fist, unable to face it, let alone oppose it. Any fem, even Alldera the Runner. That knowledge was in the face of every fem watching.

Behind Beyarra someone swore in a low, anguished voice. It sounded like the scarred pet, Daya. Beyarra did not turn to look. Her gaze was fastened, like everyone's, on Alldera Messenger. Her blood thundered in her skull.

Alldera dashed sweat from her forehead with the back of her wrist, dug in her heels, and charged. As the brown horse pounded down upon him, Gunder shouted and lashed out with his fist. She took the blow on her thigh and returned a sharp kick to his chest that sent him staggering backward. He fell a scant yard from the burning stockade.

Beyarra's voice leaped in her throat, a cheer, a sob, wordless and delirious.

The other men retreated, jostling each other. Alone, Gunder got up slowly. His cheek twitched. He backed away along the earthen wall, below the palisade that seeped smoke and flame between its palings.

Alldera sat rock-still. Then, with awful, silent deliberation she took her coiled rope in both hands and shook out a long loop. No one moved to stop Gunder's retreat down the open space between Oldtown wall and the ranks of riders. He was a large, heavy man. He did not move very fast.

Alldera whirled the loop in the air and flung it. The rope sailed after Gunder as if controlled by some magical intelligence of its own. It licked around his chest with a loud smacking sound. He snatched at it with both hands, trying to throw it off over his head.

Alldera wedged the knotted end of the rope under her leg, wheeled her mount, and made it spring into a run. Gunder flew off his feet with such an expression that Beyarra crowed with involuntary laughter. He hit the ground and was towed rapidly along, rolling and bounding at the end of the rope, still struggling to free himself.

A hungry howl broke from the mounted watchers, overwhelming the terrified cries of the bond fems. All heads turned together each time Alldera's horse wheeled and dragged its burden back again.

Beyarra sobbed, her streaming eyes stretched wide to miss no instant, no detail. Unknowingly, she pounded her fists on her thighs. It was like a fit, a dream, a bursting dam flooding her body with ecstatic energy.

When the dragged man was only a lump of loose, bloody meat on the rope's end, and the neck and shoulders of Alldera's horse were lathered white, the Messenger turned in her saddle and slashed the rope in two. Then she trotted the brown horse on, coiling up the portion of the rope she retained and watching her own hands doing this, as if the ruin left behind her were not even worth her glance.

A sudden rush and thunder of timbers crashed into the fire behind the stockade. Everyone jumped. The horses banged into each other, squealing and tossing their heads.

Ardur, unwounded but filthy, screamed a curse and ran to Gunder. Without hesitation, warning, or change of expression, Alldera snatched a lance from her saddle slings and hurled it. The blade tore through Ardur's back and spiked him to the ground, bent bowlike in his death spasm over the body of Gunder.

Alldera rode closer, braced her foot against him, and jerked her lance free. Then she turned away from the men, the dying ones and the living ones, and rode straight toward Beyarra.

Beyarra thought her heart would burst. She blinked up at the Free Fem leader and reached out to touch her. Alldera glanced briefly down, empty-eyed, and then spoke over her head to Lexa.

"I rebuked you the other day for killing men. I apologize."

Lexa said, "Tua was worth a hundred of them."

Alldera turned again toward the other men, who scrambled back from her mere glance. Her voice rang like hammers on iron, stroke after precise stroke: "Listen, you pieces of dirt. We are Free Fems. We do not answer to your bidding, we do not bend to your violence or run from your anger, and we do not fight you fair. Think hard before you speak or act. The man who tries to be a leader here, or who does anything he isn't told to do by one of us—that man is a dead man, like those dead men there. You will have no leaders, because we won't allow you to have them. You will have masters. We are your masters, the only kind of masters the Holdfast will ever see again."

"Is that what you came for?" called a new voice, quavering but edged with scorn. "To be our masters in the men's place?"

Beyarra started wildly, in a sweat of guilt. She knew that voice. On the one corner of the palisade that was not yet aflame stood a slight, white-headed person with the sprung-hipped stance of one who had borne many cubs.

"Matri Mayala?" Alldera called up to her. "Your femhold is down here. Why are you up there?"

The Matri answered over the dull roar of the flames, "Fems of this hold still live because I have protected them. If I had known I was doing it only to turn them over to you, Alldera Runaway, I might have acted differently."

Someone shouted abuse and Beyarra heard scuffling somewhere among the riders. A bond fem cried, "Matri, come down! We will speak for you!"

Alldera said, "A Free Fem came to you out of the Wild, Matri Mayala, to say that we were here to fight for you. You had her killed. We found her body stuffed down a well. One of your femhold showed us where to look."

The Matri answered, "Who could be sure that this stranger-fem spoke the truth? She might have been a spy set among us by our masters to winnow out malcontents for a trade to some other hold, or worse. And now that I see you and your handiwork, I see too that my caution was justified. Holdfast fems will die because of you."

This brought roars of protest, one shriek rising furiously above them all—Daya's voice. "You had Tua killed to protect your place and your masters, bitch!"

"No, the masters killed her," the Matri countered. A mistake; she was more frightened than she showed, to say that now. Beyarra felt a stab of contempt for her.

"Liar!" Daya yelled. "Men would have killed you with her, and they would have tortured you both first. You are alive, and Tua was unmarked except for the bruise from your strangling cord! You killed her! When have the Matris ever hesitated to destroy a brave young fem with their own hands, for the 'safety' of all?"

The Matri regarded them silently, ignoring the fire's heat wavering up behind her. Finally she said, "You have been away a long time and forgotten a great deal."

Beyarra's heart said, *Maybe they can teach us to forget as well.*

"Matri Mayala, will you come down?" Alldera demanded.

The old fem looked behind herself and turned back to them all again.

"No, Alldera Wildrunner. You have brought your message—here it is, all around us. I have no answer for savages from the devil-haunted wastes."

Alldera pointed her bloody lance at the bond fems, who stood together staring upward. "Some of these say they are willing to speak for you. Take your chances with the rest of your hold, or stay where you are and burn."

Burn, then, Beyarra thought, staring with the rest. No one, she knew, could speak any word magic enough to save the Matri's life. *Keep your dignity, at least.*

"Let her burn!" called someone, and others took up the cry. It became a raw-throated chant, accompanied by the stamping of the bond fems' feet. "Let her burn, let her burn, let her burn!"

Alldera lowered her lance. As if it were a signal, new riders came, pouring over the levee. They drew rein in a rough arc around the Free Fems and their captives.

The one in the lead called out in a strange accent that Beyarra could barely understand, "So, is this large fire what you call the liberation of the Holdfast?"

And then the whole front portion of the stockade wall collapsed, taking the old Matri down with it into the heart of the burning town. Beyarra dropped to her knees and covered her stinging eyes with her hands.

Old Grudges

Sheel saw that in this tent full of fems, there was no doubt who led. Every face was turned toward Alldera as, brilliant-faced with the flush of victory, she rose to speak.

"I want to say—I want to say, we've won—" A wild cheer rose from the group. Sheel saw fems with their heads thrown back and their eyes closed in tearful ecstasy as they screamed. Alldera stood quietly, head lowered almost as if shamed by the sound, until it died down sufficiently for her to be heard.

"We've won, but it's more than that. I mean, we fought, for the first time today, we all fought a battle, as an army, against those who used to be our masters—in a place that the men have always called their own. We fought, and we beat them! *We* beat *them*!"

Her voice caught, and she stopped again, her expression open and amazed. Into this pause the pet fem Daya rushed, raising one clenched fist overhead in a violent, circling motion as she cried, "The men's rule is over! Our sky-mother rejoices—"

"I'm not finished," Alldera said, and people laughed. Daya flushed deeply and shrank into herself. Alldera seemed not to notice, perhaps because her eyes were blurred with tears.

"Just give me, let me have a moment. In spite of all that, in spite of everything, I want to say—the men's rule is not over, not yet." She lifted her chin and her voice grew stronger. "What we did today—we've announced in blood—their rule is bounded not by the western mountains anymore but by us. And from here we will roll the men's power back and back before us until we drown it in the sea!"

All around Sheel, fems pounded their hands together or stamped on the ground. The tent shuddered with sound.

"I dreamed for years," Alldera went on when they had settled again, "we all dreamed, and that was all we did. Well, if we had tried to come home when I wanted us to, who knows what would have happened? Only women of the Conor Motherline are always right, and I'm not one of those!" She looked, briefly and with high humor, at Sheel.

"Anyway, it was worth waiting to see—I am so proud—" Again her voice left her momentarily. Eyes wide and fixed on her, they nudged each other for quiet.

"I am prouder than I know how to say," Alldera said at last, "to be with you, to be one of you today. That is my message, that I bring back to my homeland." Startlingly, she burst into a song, one of those ugly Holdfast tunes that always made Sheel want to cover her ears.

"Where is the power we could not wield?
Look, look around you, say where you see it!
Where is the freedom we could not earn?
Look, look around you, say where it is!"

They listened, silent. Alldera's bright glance moved from one grimy, glowing, worshipful face to the next. "And it adds to my joy, if anything could, that we've taken our first great victory under the eyes of our teachers, the Riding Women of the Grasslands.''

She pointed, her glowing eyes fixed on Sheel's, and added with the lightest edge of irony, ''Kindred, we knew you would come.''

''We are sorry to be so slow,'' Sheel said dryly. Her heart was beating hard, for their excitement had affected her. She needed time to collect herself. ''We've brought tea to share.''

In a general loosing of tension, tea was brewed to drink. People passed around slivers of dry tea to be chewed by Free Fems who still preferred it in that form.

Downwind of the campsite the remains of the place called Oldtown still smoldered and stank. The Free Fems, many with bruises and rough bandages, occasionally glanced out at the smoking wreckage with grim expressions. The femmish slaves they had rescued sat huddled together near the center of the tent. Dazed and frightened, they only dared look at the Free Fems and the Women with quick, flinching glances.

Sheel, on edge to begin with, started at every smoky breeze. She remembered prairie fires windblown across thousands of acres, consuming everything. But that was at home, and this was a new place, where former slaves had killed or captured today more Holdfast men than Sheel had seen in her lifetime. She tried not to show how much their victory had impressed her.

At length Alldera said, ''Tell us your news,'' very politely, as if she and her people had nothing to tell themselves.

One by one the Riding Women rose and spoke of their home tents, their families, their horses. Many of the Free Fems had lovers, friends, and rivals among those named. All that must seem very far away to them now, and diminished.

Sheel stood in turn and told about Sorrel's maiden raid, but what could that mean to these people now, with their ancient enemies' blood on their hands? They were polite, no more. ''Now,'' Sheel ended, ''she prepares for her part at the next Gather, at which the presence of her bloodmother and others of her parents will be greatly missed.''

"I am sorry about that," Alldera said, her face cramped by a painful, anxious expression, "but glad that you can go back for the Gather, Sheel, with good news from us. I don't know when I will return to the Grasslands myself."

Tyn Chowmer nudged Sheel's leg ungently with her elbow. Sheel pushed her back, annoyed. She knew without prompting that now was the time to threaten, if threats were to be made. But threats on what basis, and to what purpose?

She had seen the captured men and the dead ones too. These fems were still fresh from combat, high-hearted with confidence in their own strength. They were as dangerous as Women of the Omelly line, who were always capable of violence and never easy to herd to where you wanted them to go.

Anyway, the damage was done. Free Fems had fought men, killed men, and taken male prisoners. The world was altered.

I'm not fit for this, she thought resentfully. *We Torrinors are stubborn, we balk at the new. The others should prevent me*—but the pursuit had been her idea. And who would wish to be in her place, speaking things that had never been spoken before, in circumstances no other Women had ever seen?

She said, "We followed you to prevent your homecoming, so that you would not reveal to any people of this place the existence of our land across the mountains. Well, we failed."

Somebody laughed, a loud, nervous laugh, and was hushed. Tyn grunted and cast up her gaze in wordless exasperation.

"We were too slow, held back by the way that people of the Grasslands make decisions," Sheel went on. "And by our own caution, as we traveled in strange territory."

Every eye was on her. These bruised, streaked, hard faces were warriors' faces. She could not speak falsely or badly to such people, for her own honor's sake and the honor of her entire line. Everything was changed, and kept changing now as she was speaking.

"We Women have spoken together briefly, and we want you to turn back." Silence and blank, disbelieving stares. "You have a victory to sing about. People of your own kind are free today because of you. Be content with what you've done in this place, turn back, and let time show the result of your raid here before you push on."

Someone expostulated in outrage and was hushed. They all looked from Sheel and the other Riding Women to Alldera and back again. Alldera leaned forward, elbow on knee and chin on fist, studying Sheel's face.

"I agree that there are arguments for doing what you say," she said reasonably. "We ourselves have been over and over them a hundred times before we ever came here. Everyone knows that you are a seasoned raider and warrior with your own kills of men to your credit. But we have no more interest in these arguments, even from you."

"As leader of these people," Sheel said warmly, "it's your place to consider anything that might make your strike into this country more successful."

The runner said, "It's too late, Sheel. We've tasted the blood of those who were our tyrants, and freed others of our own kind, and we know the job has only started. We won't go back, and we outnumber you almost five to one. You can't stop us or turn us, and you know it."

Sheel held the Free Fem's gaze for long moments. The matter stood as she had feared it would. Now, with failure breathing in her face, she felt unexpectedly light with release.

"I know it," she answered at last, "and I don't like to waste people's time, either. Well, my friends must decide for themselves and their lines what they will do. As for me, I'll accompany you awhile, my arrows and my lances with yours."

Tyn Chowmer shook her head in disbelief. The Free Fems yelled and whooped triumphantly.

"I think," Alldera called over the renewed din, "your offer is welcome." She raised her arms and spread them for quiet. "We have stories to tell, boasts to make—" More cheers. "But not yet. Not with the taste of our own losses fresh in our mouths."

The shouting and excited talk was instantly quenched. Alldera sat down again in silence, her expression closing into flinty impassiveness. Now Sheel noted the absence of at least two fems she had known at Stone Dancing Camp. Some people would be watching the horse herds or guarding the captives. But the looks on the fems' faces around her told her that there were grimmer reasons.

Alldera looked around with a stare that excluded Sheel and the Women. "We have some questions for the newly freed fems that were bond fems this morning in Oldtown. Beyarra says, and others confirm it, that one of you was lover and Second to Matri Mayala. And I say, speaking for the many who have spoken to me about it, that we hold that dead Matri and her Second responsible for the death"—her voice broke and she paused to clear her throat—"the death of our friend Tua, murdered in Oldtown before we attacked. Stand and defend yourself, Gredda."

Sheel swore silently. She remembered Tua as a pretty youngster with an expressive voice that could sing pleasingly even the harsh songs of the Holdfast.

With some scuffling and shoving, one of these newly freed people was bundled forward alone. A lean, rawboned person with large head, hands, and joints, Gredda tried to stand but her legs failed her. She sank into a graceless squat, her face stark with fear. Disconcertingly, she looked like a Woman of the Jowoness Motherline back home.

"I had nothing to do with killing the stranger," Gredda said with energy. "I showed you where to find her!"

Alldera nodded. "Yes, but why did you show us, and how did you know her body was in the well?"

The Free Fems roared. Engulfed in that raw emotion, Sheel had never felt so far from home, or so glad of the presence of other Women with her.

"Let's leave," Ayana Maclaster whispered in her ear under cover of the noise. "This is ugly and I don't like it."

"Go if you like," Sheel replied. "I want to know what I'm talking about when I tell people at home what happened here."

Gredda cried, "I don't need to defend myself. You defend *your*selves! You come here and break and burn everything we have, you decide our lives for us according to what you want, and you claim our masters as your property! What happens to them should be our business, not yours. Well, I think you want to make us your property too."

"What are you saying?" asked an old Free Fem with no hair on her head; Ruwanna was her name, or some such. Sheel was surprised to see that she had survived the desert crossing. "You are free today because of us!"

"We were free enough without you," Gredda said. "We were working toward our own betterment, we didn't need you. But how would you know that? No one asks, no one cares. You present us your plans and expect us to touch ground to you. I see pride in your faces, nothing but pride."

Alldera said, "We have earned that pride."

More cheering.

Gredda seemed to take courage from the hopelessness of her position. She shook her finger at Alldera.

"Oh, yes," she declared, "so much pride that we are nothing to you, we aren't fit company for you! What makes you think *you* know how life should be lived in the Holdfast? You are strangers here. You ran away; we stayed to try to make that life. Go away, go back where you came from! No one asked you to come turn everything upside down and shed blood as if it were the times of the Fall come again—which you ran from, leaving us to endure it."

The one called Kenoma, wearing a bright red garment

slung around her shoulders, stood and called, "You make me angry, bitch! Look here!"

She pulled up her tunic to show a great weal of scar along her ribs. "The hemp machines of Oldtown did this to me, years ago. A lot of my blood ran out through this wound before I healed. Are you going to stand on soil that drank my own body's blood and call me 'stranger'? Are you going to tell me I have no rights here?" She sat down again and folded her arms.

Tall Kobba clapped her hands down on her knees in nightmarish joviality. "You were nearly a Matri yourself, weren't you, Greedy Gredda? Look at you, going well shod, keeping well fed, holding yourself higher than the rest." Her feigned jollity vanished. "You and Mayala have been the men's whip hand over these others for years. Maybe you have some debts owing to the fems of Oldtown, and you're afraid they may come around now to collect?"

Gredda said stoutly, "If any of them has complaints against me, let her say so."

Sheel saw some vindictive looks flashed in Gredda's direction, but none of the bond fems spoke up.

Daya stood. She had hacked her hair off, in mourning for Tua, no doubt; several others had also done this. "I have a complaint: Tua's death."

Gredda said sullenly, "We did what we thought was best. Everyone agreed."

One of the freed slaves, with large, long-lashed eyes and an odd, upward-flowing style to her hair that gave her head an intriguing wedge shape, cautiously put up her hand. "Not everyone was asked for an opinion, Gredda. But," she added, to the others, "Gredda's way of thinking is not unreasonable for fems who stayed here in the Holdfast."

Another of the elder bond fems, a bony person with a crooked arm, said suddenly, "It's true. We who survived the Fall made new ways to live, but it wasn't easy. Your friend Tua's message scared people. No one is so brave or so foolish as to imagine she can survive chaos twice."

"I know you now, Kastia!" bald old Ruwanna exclaimed. "You were a coward when you served the Seniors of the Blues, and you are a coward now. Is that all you think of, survival?"

"What do you think of?" the fem with the crippled arm retorted, but she shrank down again and said no more.

The big-eyed newly freed fem nervously fingered a metal ring in her earlobe. "What was done to the scout Tua was done by fems still bond. You Free Fems have not been slaves for many years now. But we have."

Alldera said sharply, "And how is that an excuse, Beyarra?"

The big-eyed bond fem colored. "It is only offered as an explanation, not an excuse."

Kenoma got up again. "I am tired of these bond fems' reproaches. How was it braver to settle for slavery and help the masters patch up a new life just like the old one? How is that better than escaping so you can come home to set your own kind free, ungrateful though they are for it?"

Beyarra tried again, unsuccessfully, to be heard. Alldera called peremptorily for quiet. "Beyarra is the first bond fem to join us and help us by her own choice. Let's hear what she has to say."

So, a recruit, Sheel thought, this timid creature with the peculiar haircut. But she was too uneasy to be amused. The Free Fems were no longer only dedicated students of the Women's skills. They seemed to have absorbed power and weight from the earth of their homeland and to have become more alien than ever.

They were kindred to these slaves. Suppose they were all to join together and turn on the Women among them? Would there be any sign of their intention that a Woman might recognize in time to defend herself? She was appalled to find that she was a little afraid of them.

Gredda tried again. "Beyarra is alive to join you because of Matri Mayala and me; she and her friend Tezza who sits with her, and all the rest too, because we kept discipline and used our good sense—''

She was drowned in a roar of denial. When that died down to a few cutting remarks, she threw back her head and cried, ''Mayala was right! We should have run from you, or fought you, even—outlaw fems, renegades! Oh, you don't like that, do you? Will you murder me, then, in front of these monster-people that you've brought into the Holdfast? Have you come to give 'freedom' only to fems who kiss your feet and call *you* master?''

Fedeka the dyer pointed accusingly, bangles gleaming on her arm. ''Freedom isn't our gift, it's Moonwoman's gift. You could at least be grateful to her.''

Gredda rounded on her, crying, ''Oh, you people with Moonwoman's name always in your mouth—your Lady of the Night did nothing for us who live here! We had to do all for ourselves, with no more help from Moonwoman than from Free Fems. There was never any help, never, only our own strength, and the Matris nurtured and protected that strength. If you offer praises for the survival of Holdfast fems, offer them to people like Matri Mayala and me, not to some dream of a moon-witch with great and wonderful powers! I am real, and I did what I could. Now pass your judgment on me if you dare!''

Sheel thought Alldera seemed moved by Gredda's words; but Daya said savagely, ''Tua's death is your judgment!''

Alldera looked stricken. Had she just realized that Daya and young Tua had been sleeping together ever since the pretty young fem had come to Stone Dancing Camp? Tua had effortlessly taken the place of mad Grays Omelly in the pet fem's regard, even as Daya had moved back into All-dera's bed.

Sheel felt a pang of sympathy. To her mind, one of the maddest things about the Free Fems was their peculiar notion that any two people should be permanently sealed together by any act of sex between them. Naturally they were not able to live up to this foolish standard, any more than any group of human beings would be able to.

Alldera had never been perceptive about such matters. Given the inevitable jealousies and grudges among her followers, this was a serious lack.

Composed again, Alldera said, "Does Daya speak for us all?"

There was an uneasy moment of silence. Then Fedeka stood and said gravely, "Moonwoman will accept this fem's life at our hands and send it back cleansed when the time for new life comes."

Which sounded like nonsense to Sheel, but they all yelled in support of it.

Then steel-haired Lexa suddenly stood up and vehemently announced that she was taking a new form of her name, originally given to her by the Matris of Bayo, to mark the occasion of the fems' freedom from their own collaborators as well as from their former masters. From now on she would be *El*lexa, sharing the initial sound with her friend and lover Emla.

"Oh, no," one of the Roises murmured to her cousin in Sheel's hearing. "I have trouble remembering which is which as it is. Now they're going to start changing their names?"

People laid hold of Gredda to drag her out of the tent. She shrieked despairingly, "Is this your liberation? Kastia, Beyarra, they're going to murder me!"

The little recruit turned away, hiding her eyes with her hand.

At Sheel's side, Tyn Chowmer said lowly, "They kill their kindred like this, with a little yelling back and forth and no deliberation, no law?"

Sheel said, "Sssh, keep still. It's their business."

But she too was shaken.

White Bears

There were many Bears about tonight, more than Setteo had ever seen. They prowled in the dark, low-slung heads swinging, small black eyes gleaming now at the prisoner men, now at the Blessed, and sometimes at the horses, which at dusk were only a dim mass drifting slowly along the ground some distance away.

He loved the horses. When the fire and the screaming and the rushing back and forth had started, Setteo had slipped away, yoke and all, among them. He had worked off his gag and spent the hours of the battle pulling grass with his teeth the way they showed him, which had brought great peace to his mind.

After all, nothing he could have done would have changed matters substantially. The Bears would not be thwarted. Their time had come with the coming of the Blessed, as foretold in the holy books.

Setteo had worked out some answers: the horses were the Bears' children. The Angels were supernatural warriors sent to help the Blessed (called by the men "fems") to rule over the Holdfast at long last. He suspected that the Angels were great dead heroes of the past, remade by the Bears to be guides for the Blessed in modern times.

The clearest truth was that the reign of men was over.

What he was most curious to see was whether the Blessed, with help from the Cold Country of the Bears, would try to make something other than men of the captives. That, of course, was the underlying fear of the men themselves: that maleness, derived as it was from femaleness through physical birth, could only be maintained by total domination. Otherwise femaleness would invade, conquer, and transform everything in its path, as indeed the Blessed were well on their way to doing.

Setteo, having been himself made something other than male by men trying to master this transformative process with typical masculine crudeness, was keenly aware of such concerns. Surely there would be transformation—the Second Coming was irresistible—but he did not think that the men could be made into females, or that the Blessed wished to achieve that radical a change.

With his scrotum emptied and withered Setteo was not, strictly speaking, a male, as the one-armed Blessed had pointed out. On the other hand, no one could truly mistake him for one of the Blessed, either. Other states, between the extremes, must exist. He was curious to discover, as the Blessed wrought their will in the Warm World, what those states might be.

A pity he could not discuss this with anyone. He had long ago learned that there were matters best kept to himself, most particularly when people were under pressure and therefore more than usually cranky.

As now, for instance. Men sat together, their rough wooden yokes tilted in the effort not to strike each other with the ends where their hands were pinioned. They tried to hide their chanting from the guards by keeping their voices low and their bodies massed together, as if to contain and protect the words they remembered of the old Chant Protective.

Other yoked men lay crookedly on the ground, asleep or unconscious or moaning in pain. Jodd Galgar sat massaging his swollen knee and cursing steadily under his breath. He had sometimes been kind to Setteo and listened to reports of his ventures into the country of the Bears. Now Jodd had no interest in anything but his own injury.

Two others nearer to Setteo uttered smothered, effortful grunts: one tried to hold his yoke steady while the other gnawed at the leather thongs that bound his friend's wrist.

How foolish! Nothing could succeed against the Blessed. These were the times of the Second Coming. At the return of Christ, all the dead of the world were supposed to return too, and here they were, the Blessed themselves, angry and invincible.

He watched the other men wistfully from a little distance, soothed by the good sharp stink of their sweat and the comforting rumble of male voices. He longed for contact, for a touch, a hug, someone's breath on his cheek.

But they were too frightened to be kind to him. If he spoke up, said anything to draw their attention to himself, the men would probably beat him. Even bound and defeated, they would find some way to reject his unwelcome message. The blindness of others amazed him.

More terrors were coming, he knew. One of the Bears would undoubtedly reveal itself in time to be the Seventh Seal, herald of the end of the world. He knew from his reading that once Bears had eaten seals; and you are what you eat, as the Ancients wisely said.

When the damp wind shifted, you could still smell dead flesh mixed with smoke and scorch. The Blessed and sometimes even the strange, hard-looking Angels would walk by and go scrutinize the dead men where they lay in a pathetic row on the grass.

Then there were those who paused to study the live captives too. He was always glad when the gaze of these visitors passed over him. The ones who looked at the dead walked with their heads bowed in somber thought, but these, who kept drifting back to the living men, had a hungry aura that frightened him very much. They made him think of Bears in a bad mood.

Setteo could not remember when he had first seen the Bears, pacing about on their own business with their great padded feet like drumheads. He thought now that he had always heard their steps echoing deep in the sky, like thunder. He looked out of the corners of his eyes, and there they were, moving with their slink-shouldered gait: great silver beasts with black tongues sliding out along their black lips.

Oh, they were tasting blood in the air, all right. And Setteo, yoked as he was so that his shoulders were raw and his wrists ached, could not make the warding gestures that had kept him safe through all his wanderings in the Bears' territory (the world of the Dead of the World, though it was not polite to say so to their faces).

When he wasn't secured by spells the Bears themselves had taught him, they might easily forget who he was and tear the soul out of his body with their yellow teeth. It was not his time yet, he was sure, but anyone can make a mistake.

Especially in times like these; though truth to tell, he had never seen times like these: he, who thought he had seen everything!

Some of the Blessed Ones approached from the wide tent where they had been meeting since noon. They walked with purposeful steps, and the echoing crashes of the Bears' feet made a continuous roaring accompaniment, like music for a dance.

Setteo began to sweat. Clumsily, he tried to get up. One of the sentries thwacked him across the back with her lance.

"Stay down, muck!"

Another one said, "It's only Daya's creature."

The first went to meet the newcomers. Setteo saw rage smoking in the air around them and wanted badly to be somewhere else; but he was clearly chosen to stay and endure the power of the Blessed, under the eyes of the watchful Bears. They tested and tested, the Bears did.

One of the visitors was his own Blessed, the knot-cheeked one called Daya. She ignored him; he was glad. She had only touched him once, that slap to make him stop speaking with disrespectful openness of the Bears. He was terrified of her.

They conferred, and then one of those secret Blessed who had formerly served meekly in Oldtown stepped forward and said something in a squeaky voice (the thunder grew louder just then). Shania, she was called, Setteo knew her from the City: dark, with a sulky mouth and big, brown, wounded eyes.

Shania began to weep in angry, barking sobs. It was comforting that the Blessed could shed tears.

The sentries walked in among the men swinging their lance butts, driving the prisoners apart from each other. Shania followed, glancing furtively at each man by the light of a little fire basket that Daya-Blessed carried. Shania shook her head, no, at each one.

Then the light fell on the face of a man called Jaygo, who wore a colored headband. Shania nodded once and looked away, twisting her hands together in agitation. "I don't think I can," she whispered.

"Why not?" said Daya-Blessed. "He had your lover burned for witchery. If we Free Fems can take revenge against our enemies, so can you. Do you want one rule for Free Fems and another for bond, just as Gredda and Mayala said?"

Shania didn't answer. One of the sentries said anxiously, "Did Alldera say this unslave could kill this man? Did you hear her say it herself?"

"I know Alldera's heart," Daya said. "I speak for her, and I say these bond fems won't really be unslaved until they have spilled men's blood with their own hands."

Jaygo opened his mouth to protest, or to beg. Then, perhaps remembering Gunder's fate, he hung his head and was silent, even as they prodded him to his feet and walked him away toward the smoking remains of the town. The sound of the Bears' footsteps was loudest in that direction; Jaygo would not be coming back.

Another man bellowed suddenly, "What are they doing to Jaygo? Run, Jaygo, run!"

Young Givard actually staggered to his feet and tried to bolt, yoke and all. The sentries descended on him with a flurry of blows. That was how it would be: the anger of the Blessed would fall upon the just and the unjust alike.

Discreetly, Setteo inched farther from the others, keeping as close to the ground as his yoke would permit. Sometimes if he moved like the snake of Ancient times, the Blessed disdained to notice and let him pass where he wished. He made for the horses again, where he hoped he might shelter from danger.

After an unclear interval (he was not very good at Warm World time) he became aware that someone walked beside him as he squirmed along. Setteo gulped up air, stopped moving, and tried not to cry. The Bears hated crying. It was such paltry mourning. They grieved constantly but silently for the loss of everything that had lived in the Warm World before the Wasting, from Leviathan to the small creatures of the air.

A cold metal edge touched the back of his neck where the wooden yoke did not cover. He was some distance now from the others. No Bears thundered close, waiting to gobble up his unhoused soul. Setteo had some hope of living. He lay very still.

"Where are you going, Setteo?" Daya-Blessed said softly.

"Only a little way, Blessed," he whispered.

"How am I 'blessed'?" she said; testing, always testing. "And how do you know that I am?"

Setteo turned his face clear of the grass. "I know only what I've read for myself, and what the Bears have revealed to me. I know that I am ready for new times."

"What kind of new times?" Her interest was caught, but

not too much, he hoped. You had to be so careful of the powerful as they toyed, in their strength, with lesser beings.

"Why, the times of love, Blessed," he said. "It will be a great change. The ruler of the Holdfast was always not love but fear."

"How do you know, idiot?" she said.

Oh, careful, careful! "Men ruled by love would never have done to me what was done."

She sneered. "Men are capable of any horror, Setteo, in the name of any 'rule.' "

"They do horrors when they let their fear drive them," Setteo replied, breathless with terror. If he didn't correct her according to what he had read in the Christ-books, he failed her test. On the other hand, she might destroy him for having the temerity to correct her. Squeezing his eyes shut, he added, "In the times you bring, Blessed, even men will act from love, and everything will be different."

She lifted the lobe of his ear with her knife tip. He sobbed and almost jerked his head away.

"Do you know what happened today in Oldtown?"

"F-fire," he stammered. His neck and shoulders had begun to burn with tension. "The Bears licked up the souls of dead men."

"Some of us died too, did you know that?" she said. The knife point described a small circle on his cheek. "One was killed by those she had come to save. She was my friend. I loved her. But she's dead, so how are things different? And where is the rule of love?"

"Will you put marks on my face like your own, Blessed of the Bears?" he said faintly, wishing desperately that he were braver. It would be very hard not to scream if she cut his face. "I would be honored."

"That's not what I want to do, Setteo," she said. She was weeping now, which terrified him. He whimpered. So newly arrived in the Warm World from the country of the Bears, even a Blessed One might have only a vague awareness of the effects of physical mayhem on mere living flesh. "Tua will never get to pay back the masters for her pain and her exile. She will never have a free child to raise in her own free land. She's dead, and you're alive.''

Setteo closed his eyes and saw enormous jaws opening on great yellow teeth, and a long black tongue convulsing in a hungry gulp. It was her tears that landed hotly on his back, but he envisioned saliva dripping from the ravenous maw of a Bear.

''Run, Setteo,'' she whispered. ''Run from me.''

He got up and ran clumsily toward the herd of horses. But they were Bearers of the Blessed and would not shelter him from her. So he stopped running and stood, panting and swaying and trying hard to be ready to die and have his soul devoured.

She stepped close behind him. He gasped for breath, staring straight ahead. The horses were telling him things with the flicking of their rears and the tossing of their heads, things that might save him, after all. They told him that this Blessed One loved them deeply.

He said, ''Please, Blessed, I want to die among the horses, if I have to die now.''

''The horses?'' she said sharply. ''Why?''

''Because they are beautiful and wise, like the Bears.''

''Be quiet!'' He felt her warm breath on the back of his neck. Next it would be the knife, he was sure. Well, it wouldn't be as bad as the other time, because nothing could ever, ever be as bad as that had been. ''You have no right to admire the horses, you have no right to speak of the horses, you have no right to look at the horses.''

He saw the horses nodding. Yes, they were saying, the great jaws are about to close upon you as they have closed on others today. Only one thing can save you.

He read the one thing in their slowly milling forms, and accordingly he said, ''The one you want to feed me to, Blessed, can never be filled. Never, never, never.''

Silence. Then she moved in front of him and looked into

his face, holding up the clay lamp she carried which had only glowing embers in it now.

"Are you really crazy, boy?"

He tried to smile. "Everybody says so."

She turned him so that she could reach the twisted ropes that bound his right hand in one end of the yoke.

"In the Grasslands it's a disgrace to hurt crazy people," she muttered. Something in what she said was false, but he had no way of knowing what. "Women try never to do it."

"Oh." Did she mean by "Grasslands" the country of the Bears? "Woman" was a word for Angel. She was telling him lies, but also very great secrets which he didn't understand, and which he had a strong feeling he would be better off not knowing anyway.

Her knife flashed and the yoke's weight was knocked from his shoulders. He danced, keeping his feet clear of the pieces as they thumped to the ground. He hissed with the sting of the raw place on his shoulders.

"Go stay with your Bears; stay away for a while," she commanded.

"Shall I see you again, Blessed?" he said timidly.

"Go!" She turned and walked quickly toward the horses. He saw her catch one by the hair of its neck and draw its head down into the crook of her arm. She whispered into the animal's ear.

Setteo set off eastward along the river and trotted along toward the City. Whenever he saw Bears, which he did frequently, they were traveling in that direction too, licking their shiny black lips.

A Naming of Names

The wounded mare kept shifting its weight to ease its leg. Sheel talked steadily to the animal, keeping her curses and her anger to herself: these damned Free Fems shouldn't keep horses if they couldn't attend to them better than this! Who ever heard of not bothering, after any sort of clash, to check your mount for injuries?

Sheel sipped sleeping mixture into her mouth and pulled the mare's head down with both hands. She blew the liquid into its nostrils in a burst of spray, pulling back at once to avoid the horse's violently upflung muzzle. A second blast made it settle, standing with a glazed look on its long face for several moments before it staggered and knelt. Sheel stepped to one side and tugged on its withers. Groaning like an old Woman, the mare keeled slowly over onto its side, turning the wounded shoulder to the gray dawn sky.

Relieved to have the first stage done with, Sheel took her bottle of clean water and rinsed her mouth out. The spike-leaf she had chewed earlier braced her against drugged drowsiness now. She unplugged the larger medicine bottle slung from her waist.

Overnight she had brewed up a potion from some freshly gathered plants that looked, smelled, and tasted very much like what in the Grasslands was called "fever-eater." These Holdfast plants, gathered from the rubble under the broken Oldtown bridge, had yielded a good bowlful of medicine. She had dispensed small amounts to injured fems, but plenty remained.

It took a Woman to think of the horses.

She was glad to have a job to do. She was much disturbed by a conversation overheard this morning in which Suasayan Tulun had remarked in a speculative way on the fate of the captive men at the fems' hands. And the younger Rois had replied that she would love to get hold of one of the comelier ones among the prisoners and see what it was like, lying with a man as the fems proposed to do.

Much ribald chatter had followed, and Sheel was shocked to hear several others expressing a similar, unseemly curiosity. They had spoken satirically, but Sheel thought she detected an underlying tone of serious interest. Was it the air in this place, or what?

She lay across the injured mare's body and began mopping at the glistening wound and thinking dark thoughts about the undisciplined imagination of youth.

Someone spoke softly. She looked up and saw two of these fems everyone was calling "newly freed." They stood side by side clutching each other's hands like bashful girls, each keeping the other from running away.

One was trim and lithe with a great tumble of dark ringlets around her face—a striking face, with enormous, challenging eyes, turned-up nose, and a long upper lip. She wore a smoke-stained garment belted at her narrow waist.

The other, younger but no child, was short and broad in the hips. She had coiled and knotted her washed-out yellow hair above one ear.

"What do you want?" Sheel said, sitting back to wring out the medicine rag.

The blonde one said boldly, "People say you are some kind of men, you strangers."

Sheel stood up, untied the drawstring of her pants, and dropped them. The two fems buzzed and fluttered while she did up her trousers again. The spotted horse blearily lifted its head a little off the ground.

"Hey," she said, annoyed with them for having roused the animal with their chatter, "if you want to talk to me, come and make yourself useful. You can sit on this horse's head and keep her down while I'm doctoring her."

The dark-haired one backed farther away, but the other pulled free and edged closer, staring at the horse with wide eyes.

"Sit?" she said. "Just sit on it? It won't bite me?"

Sheel showed her how to drape herself over the horse's neck and cheek. "A horse always lies down or gets up front end first. If they can't get their heads up off the ground, they can't figure out how to stand. They're not smart, you know, only large and strong."

Like some fems, she thought, but kept that to herself. She sat down again cross-legged in the dewy grass. Bracing herself against the curve of the spotted mare's back, she threaded a long needle with a length of fine-drawn gut.

"So," she said, "your friends think only men could tame creatures from the Wild, is that it?"

"Some think so." The newly freed fem patted the horse's neck gingerly. "How hot its skin is!"

"They have warm bodies. I don't think she's feverish, no thanks to her rider. Some people shouldn't have horses."

"This one is Kobba's," the blonde girl said. "I saw her yesterday, in the fighting." Her eyes glittered with remembered excitement.

Sheel grunted. "Kobba's too tall and heavy to ride this mare. Or most horses, for that matter. Some people are built to go on foot."

"Is it true that the Free Fems will give all the masters to you horse people?" the fem said.

"We don't need men," Sheel snapped, thinking of the remarks she had heard among her own people about these cursed prisoner-men. "We kill them when we can."

"Oh, but—then how—?"

"We mate with our horses," Sheel said. "Not this one, don't worry—she's a female. Among us, the stud horse's fluid starts our babies—which are all human, mind, not part horse or any such foolishness. So, that's over with; will you run away shrieking, or stay and help? This won't take more than a few stitches, but she might thrash around."

The Newly Freed paled beneath the faded tattooing that patterned her cheeks and forehead, but she stayed where she was. "Won't you just sew fever into the wound? Our Matri used to say—"

"Your Matri wouldn't know anything about it. Though it's true that given another few hours, I wouldn't take a needle to this. Anyway, I've sluiced the wound with a fever-killing tea. There, she's feeling the needle. Hang on where you are, that's the safest thing you can do anyway."

The spotted horse made an unhappy sound and heaved its weight upward from the shoulder, but between them it was no trouble to hold her down. Sheel worked quickly, drawing the edges of the wound together and repressing the swollen tissue beneath Xs of coarse stitching.

"My name is Juya," the Newly Freed said, her gaze following the swift movements of the needle. "My friend there is Tamansa-Nan. She used to be just 'Tamansa,' but now she wants to be called by more than her slave name. So she added 'Nan' to make her free name."

"What does 'Nan' signify?" Sheel said, glancing over at Juya's companion. She had sat down some distance away, nervously twiddling a lock of her curly black hair.

"It doesn't mean anything. I mean, it signifies that she's more than a slave now, but she took 'Nan' because she likes the sounds together: Tamansa-Nan. It's pretty."

"It sounds childish to me," Sheel said.

Juya was still for a moment. Then she said, "We have never been 'children,' only cubs. Perhaps we need some childishness."

"I'm Sheel Torrinor," Sheel said, "of Stone Dancing Camp." The little slave had embarrassed her.

Juya said shyly, "Everyone knows your name. And I knew you couldn't be men because some of you Wild people have black skin, like the unmen of the old chants. Only the unmen were supposed to be all dead."

"Your masters thought so."

Juya giggled. "Oh, yes. They were very surprised by the Free Fems' attack, but horrified when *you* showed up!" Her eyes widened. "No one's ever seen any animals or any black people here."

"Dark skin is nothing special where I come from." Sheel bent over to pull the knot tight between her fingers and her teeth. Then she cut the thread and sat back, wiping her hands on the rag. "I asked you before, Juya of the Newly Freed: what do you want?"

"Nothing," the fem said quickly. She worked her fingers cautiously into the horse's tangled mane. "I am only talking to you, and helping. You asked me to help."

It certainly didn't take them long to move from slavish subservience to bald impudence. "You want something, or you would be sitting over there with your friend Tamasaya."

"Tamansa-Nan," Juya corrected with a nervous laugh.

Sheel packed her supplies back into the medicine kit. "Move away now," she said. "I don't want you in the way when this horse gets up. You can ask me for something. You helped, you've earned a favor."

Juya squatted on her heels, trying to neaten her hair knot, which had colored threads bound into it. "I want a new name," she said so lowly that Sheel almost missed it.

"Move back, I said." Sheel got up and walked a little way off. She stopped and turned to make sure the horse could stand. Juya followed her, all meekness now.

This name-changing was spreading rapidly among the Newly Freed. No Free Fem living in the Grasslands had ever added a "freename," and Sheel doubted any of them ever would. Of course the fems were such a jumble of people, with no clear lines of relation or descent among them, that you never could know what to expect from them.

These freenames would at least set off the Newly Freed from the fems who had returned from the Grasslands. Of the latter, so far only that pompous Lexa had been moved to make a name-change of her own devising. Sheel suspected that if any other Free Fems made such a change, "Ellexa" would switch back again, out of pride in her uniqueness.

"What's wrong with the name you've got?" she said. " 'Juya' sounds fine to me, for a fem's name."

The spotted horse lunged to its feet and stood, breathing heavily.

"They say that in your country everybody looks alike." Juya blushed deeply. "I mean, lots of people look like you, the way the two black ones with you look one exactly like the other."

"They are cousins, of the Rois Motherline," Sheel said, baffled. "How else should they look?"

"I think I look a little bit like you," Juya said, eyes downcast. "I don't ask a name from your own family, I'm not asking that. But I would like you to be the one to give me a new name. I want a name from a place where no one has ever been a slave."

Sheel was flattered. Juya could have gone to Alldera Messenger, Alldera Conqueror, for a name, or to another among the Free Fems as several of the Newly Freed had already done. It was incredible, the way these Holdfast people invented new ways as they went along. They were like contrary winds blowing in every direction.

"Your friends, the other ex-slaves, what will they think about your getting a name from me?" she said cautiously. She did not want to be maneuvered into doing something politically stupid.

There, the spotted horse took a shuddering step and did not fall down.

Juya muttered resentfully, "What does it matter what they think? They are not my masters! I want a name to pass on."

The gesture she made, a proud and possessive stroking of her as-yet-flat belly, was unmistakable in meaning. Sheel's pulse leaped. She took Juya's arm and turned her away from the watchful eyes of Tamansa-Nan.

"You're pregnant?" she said intently.

Juya smiled. "No one knows, I haven't said anything. Mine will be the first cub to be born after the Free Fems came."

"Child, not cub. You're pregnant with a child, you'll be its bloodmother." Sheel's mind raced. "Listen, little Juya, I will do what you ask, and more than you ask, if you invite me to be a sharemother of this child when it's born."

Juya's blank look reminded her that these people seldom shared; not the rearing of children, not anything much.

She shifted to another approach. "Two of my companions are talking about going back to the Grasslands. Go with them and stay there until your child is born. Then the child will be a daughter of both lands—" Inspiration came. "Like Alldera's own daughter."

"Alldera's daughter," Juya repeated, awestruck. "She is one of you, they say. A 'Mare.' " She hugged her arms across her belly and backed a step away from Sheel.

Careful, now. "No one knows yet whether Sorrel Hold-faster can truly be one of us and breed as we do. But come what may, she is still Alldera's bloodchild who has never been a slave and has free people for her relations. No one can change that. It can be the same with this child of yours. Isn't it worth a name, to share your child with a Riding Woman of the free Grasslands?"

"But how can I go there?" Juya said, looking anxiously over her shoulder at her watching friend, who had not moved. "Crossing dangerous country to live among people with—with strange ways—and leaving everyone else here to fight! They will call me a coward, a poor slave with no courage—''

Sheel interrupted impatiently, "Once they find out you're pregnant, do you think your own people will let you fight? And if they did, would you really risk your baby's life in a battle against men? What if you were captured by the enemy? Then your child would be born a slave.''

Juya shifted from foot to foot and stared at the ground. "I will do it,'' she whispered at last. "Give me a name.''

"Joyahanna,'' Sheel said, naming a Woman who had died thrown from her horse right after coming out of the child-pack; a Golashamet, not a Torrinor, but what would that matter?

"No,'' Juya cried. "Not a name that ends in 'a'; all our slave names end in 'a.' Another name, a name like yours.''

She frowned with a fierceness that startled the Woman. A true Torrinor might look at you so, if she were insulted and would not suffer it. Could this creature with inked designs under her pale skin possibly be in some way related—? No, not with that broad-hipped build. Still—

"All right, here's a better name, an old name of my line: Veree. It comes with a self-song that is never sung. Veree Torrinor fought for her honor against a woman of her own Motherline, and for that she was exiled and went away to die. Her case is still argued; not everyone agrees that she was wrong. It was honor against Motherline, and people's opinions sway this way and that way on such matters. In her own Motherline, she is accounted a hero. Will you accept her name?''

Juya looked searchingly into her eyes. "Is it really a good name? I want my cub—my child to carry it proudly.''

Sheel touched her shoulder lightly, turning her toward the horse herd. "Walk along with me. I'll sing you Veree Torrinor's self-song. It's the story of her life. After you've heard, then decide. But if you accept, you must tell nobody about this child of yours. Just go when I tell you it's time, with my people as your escort. Will you do that?''

Juya glanced back once at her watchful friend. She said, "Yes, Sheel Torrinor."

So Sheel began to sing, softly, that old self-song of pride and tragedy. Her heart exulted.

Margora Garriday still wanted to go home. She had argued much of the night for a dash back over the desert to tell the Riding Women what was happening here in the Holdfast. And Ayana Maclaster was beginning to speak of being homesick herself. Sheel had argued, citing the risks of such a crossing, and the turmoil that their news (which would moreover be long out of date by the time the Women heard it) would create.

The Garriday had given in again and agreed to stay. Before long, though, she would go, and the Maclaster might go with her. All the Women were nervous, being in alien territory without the comfort of consultation with others. Sheel was nervous herself.

Singing the self-song of the dead outlaw for Juya, now Juya-Veree, she kept thinking of how her own self-song would grow. It would come to recount how Sheel Torrinor had wrestled a triumph for her line from this careening, baffling venture into the perilous land of men and fems.

Kobba's Daughter

Alldera drew the rawhide rope through her hands, inspecting the frays and nicks in the leather. Her mind was filled with erratic impressions of violence: Tua's wet hair clinging to her swollen cheeks, flames leaping from behind the Oldtown palisade, scorched and bleeding bodies pulled from the wreckage and laid out on trampled grass.

She was haunted by Gredda's homely face, first glimpsed beside the Oldtown well and then distorted by terror and rage during her doomed defense. She saw again Matri Mayala vanishing in the inferno of Oldtown; and the slashed corpse of a captive called Jaygo whose body had been found at dawn in the squats outside the camp; and Tua again, and again.

She glanced around at the fems gathered on the riverbank to bathe, wash their clothes, and check over their gear. People were splashing and shouting in the shallows where the river had carved itself a side channel through a gap in the levee.

If I died now I would die happy, she thought. *No, better than that: vindicated.* Under the cheerful racket around her she kept hearing in her thoughts the breathless grunts driven from blond Gunder, jouncing at the end of her rope.

I did that, she thought, *in front of everyone. And my lance went through his friend like a hot knife through fat.* She had killed those men as a deliberate, public act of policy, and with her heart locked tight in rage over the death of Tua. Looking back, she was proud, but horrified too, at the speed and sureness with which she had acted.

Now she was blooded, tested as Kobba had said all must be tested. She hated it when Kobba was right about such things.

She wished the rope could be washed clean on the broken poured-stone slabs people were using as scrubbing surfaces.

Down along the riverbank a tall skinny unslave with joints that seemed limitless in their range kept jumping up to strut and posture as she talked. She was mimicking someone—probably a gawky young master, by the look of the performance—to such effect that the others kept erupting into shrieks of laughter. One threw her wet garment over her head and rolled backward, holding her belly and gasping while the others now laughed at her.

Alldera remembered something she had seen the day she had first arrived at the City from Bayo to be sold. Three Juniors of the Quarterbacks had noticed a fem, one of a loading crew, splashing up a handful of river water onto her sweating face. The men had made her swim back and forth across the river, timing her with rhythmic shouts, until she had come staggering onto the bank and fallen, unable to move.

The sport had been entertaining, the betting high. The men had gone on their way with no further attention to the exhausted fem. Soon after, she had rejoined the work gang to drag weakly at the sacks and boxes they were loading onto a flatbed wagon.

Alldera remembered the black stubble of the swimmer's hair—she must have been recently shaved by the fur-weavers—and the bright drops of river water rolling down her skin. She had thought at the time, with the disdain of youth, that she herself could have swum faster and farther.

The swimmer would be a crone now. All fems aged quickly, labor fems quickest of all. She had probably died long since, on some less fortunate day.

When we get to the City, I'll go down to the docks and make some kind of marker in her memory, she thought.

Kenoma, seated nearby, sang under her breath as she cut down the red shirt from Oldtown to fit herself. Like all the belly-cramp victims, she had recovered, but she still had bluish shadows under her eyes. Today she smiled, sitting at her tailoring with her legs stretched out and her strong feet paddling contentedly in the water to the tune of a new verse of her self-song. The words were largely boasts of her own bravery during the taking of Oldtown.

Emla whispered something to Ellexa, into whose fresh-washed hair she was braiding loops of dyed leather. Ellexa snickered.

Kenoma broke off her song, frowning and abashed. "Well, I suppose everyone was brave yesterday, compared to the enemy. How they ran from us, sweating and screaming! Why were we ever afraid of them?"

"Hmm, I wonder?" Daya said, patting at her short hair to fluff and dry it. She did not sit naked on the bank as other Free Fems did, the pale, water-beaded skin of their torsos startling against their sun-browned limbs and faces. She had wrapped herself in a long robe. She was sensitive about the scars of an old sharu-attack. "It must have been a silly mistake, all our generations of fear."

Alldera nodded vigorously. "The rest of the men won't be so easy to confuse once they know that it's just us, fems, armed and organized and riding on animals—"

Kenoma laughed. "Only their nightmares turned real, you mean! I'm telling you, they'll all be terrified. Look at that Jaygo who tried to run away last night. The Holdfast is ours. We can send scouts down to Bayo, or whatever we want."

"It's not ours yet," Alldera answered, "and it may never be, if we let one victory make us lazy and overconfident."

This brought murmurs of concurrence from others sitting nearby. Two tongueless ones slapped their callused hands on the water for attention. They stood hip-deep in the purling water, arms loose around each other's waist, and gazed earnestly at Alldera with speaking eyes.

"They want to go on now," Ellexa said for them, "galloping all out for Bayo. They left cubs there—babies, I mean—when they fled the Holdfast, and they think maybe there are traces, records, something. We should go. I don't speak only for myself, Alldera."

"Neither do I, I hope," Alldera said. She cut out another ruined section of her rope. "We need to rest the horses and ourselves and think about the lessons of this fight. Then, when we move on, we can do it quickly and decisively."

"The lesson is that we can win," Ellexa said, the challenge of the words blunted by the way she looked over her shoulder at Alldera with a softened, almost girlish expression. This was an effect of the curtainlike fringe of ornaments Emla had already fastened into her hair. "We can win, Alldera, without the help of the Mares."

"Let's see first what kind of stores we can salvage from Oldtown. And we must learn what we can about what's ahead by talking to the Newly Freed, one by one and carefully."

"But that will take time," Ellexa protested. "If word of our coming gets to Bayo ahead of us, all the fems there could be killed to keep us from freeing them!"

"There may not have been any fems in Bayo for years. We need to gather news of the place first."

The bloodstained bits of her rope were gone. Someone must have taken them, but what for? To be kept as relics of what Alldera had done at Oldtown, probably. An ugly idea.

"We always said we would go to Bayo," Kenoma put in, holding up the red shirt for a measuring look. "Bayo was home for all of us as cubs. Ellexa's right; there may be secret records hidden there, about our foredams. About us."

This was Daya's doing, with her stories of hidden bands of rebels escaped from Bayo! Didn't the pet fem ever think before saying such things?

Two of the Newly Freed yelled and laughed, struggling to duck each other in the deeper part of the water. Both wore their smocks—to wash them, the Newly Freed all said when they did this. The nakedness of fems to their masters' eyes had always been fraught with danger in the Holdfast.

A pity. Many of the Newly Freed were young, and their physical beauty and exuberance fed Alldera's heart. Her eyes lingered on the sun-gilded down on the round, full arm of Beyarra-Bey, who squatted by the water absorbed in washing a delicate bone comb she had found. Its teeth were clogged with what Alldera hoped was only dirt.

Ellexa wouldn't let things alone. "We could at least send a messenger, in case there are still fems in Bayo. We could send someone to warn them."

"Send who?" Alldera countered sharply, thinking of Tua. "We can't spare anybody. And if we could, who would you send out alone between here and Bayo, to run the risk of capture by men along the way?"

One of the Newly Freed—Alldera didn't know all their names yet—noisily dropped the garment she was rinsing in the water and stood up with her arms crossed on her breast like a shield. Her wild glance darted from face to face.

"My name is Shania," she said rapidly, "and I have something to say. You must all run away. Other masters will come and kill you, all of you, and us too, for what you did in Oldtown." She stopped, breathing distressfully.

"There are no 'masters,' " Kobba said quietly. She lay sunning her scarred, muscular length on the grass. "Only men, who will all end up as our slaves."

Shania hid her face in her water-darkened skirts and cried in an anguished, muffled voice, "Run and hide, ride back over the mountains and be safe! There have always been masters. Look how big and cruel they are, and we—we are smaller, weaker. They have always been, they will always be the fist that beats us! How can you think you can change this? The masters will punish you and your creatures terribly if they catch you!''

People sat stunned under this tearful onslaught, paralyzed by conflicting impulses (bash her, hug her, shout her down—*make her stop*). Only Kenoma uttered an angry laugh that brought a flush to the cheeks of other Newly Freed fems.

They are so young, Alldera thought; look at Beyarra's inseparable friend, Tezza. She had a soft, plump, mobile face which just now expressed utmost anxiety. *Are they going to be any help to us? What if underneath their bravado they're all like Shania?*

Kobba made a disgusted sound. Rolling over, she rifled the heap of her discarded clothes and drew something from a pocket. She got up, waded out into the water, and thrust her hand in the weeping fem's face, showing something that lay in her palm.

"These are ears from a man's head," she said conversationally. "I cut them off yesterday. I killed him afterward, and I took other things of his too. Next time, you fight at my side, Shania, with a knife of your own."

Shania wailed and sank to her knees in the water, holding Kobba's hands and kissing them. Kobba bent to hug the Newly Freed's shaking shoulders and to straighten the tangled mass of her long, damp hair.

"This girl is young enough to be my daughter," she announced. "I claim her as kindred. When I was a slave, I bore at least one cub that lived. I say this is she, her name is Shania. No, Shanu*ay,* that will be her freename. When you deal with her, remember: her name is Shanuay and her mother is Kobba of the mines."

The two of them together were like a monument, a moving statue set in the river, tender and eternal. Alldera's eyes stung.

Old Roona, all sags and wrinkles and clearly not caring

who saw, stepped carefully over the wet clothes spread out to dry and sat down, effortfully, beside Alldera. "Good, very good, but we can't splash in the river forever. Alldera is right; winning brings its own worries, if you think ahead."

The two young Newly Freed sporting in the river stopped to clap mightily, mocking the old fem with a daring they surely would never have shown to their Matri Mayala.

Roona ignored them. "What about these men? The captives, I mean. When we do move on, to Bayo or the City or wherever, we should move fast. But can we? It's bad enough you've got an old stumbler like me dragging you back. Now there's these men to take with us. And the Newly Freed may all be eager and able to ride off like Free Fems first thing tomorrow morning, but I don't think anyone here wants to see the captive men put on horseback just so they can keep up."

Daya muttered fiercely, "Never!"

"We'll see them dead first!" someone else shouted.

"No, fuck them first," Ellexa said, "and then see them dead."

The laughter that greeted this was unnaturally hard and loud. Under the cover of it Beyarra-Bey said timidly, "When are we going to—to begin using the men? I would like to make a cub at my will instead of theirs, a free cub with warriors for her relatives."

In Kenoma's face Alldera saw the disdain of one who thought that was about all the Newly Freed (like Shania, or rather Shanuay) were good for. Fortunately, Kenoma said nothing.

This business of mating with the men had been little more than an occasion for jokes and threats back in the Grasslands. It was going to have to be handled seriously, somehow, now that the little army had its first success.

Luckily, the time to make decisions about this could be postponed; Alldera had trouble thinking about it, and managed not to, much. She thought it was much the same with the other Free Fems, not one of whom had raised the issue since the captives were taken. It was easier, and far more exhilarating, to concentrate on the possibilities of bringing liberation to more femmish slaves, now that everyone knew that there were slaves to free and that it could actually be done.

People were looking at her, waiting for her answer. Briskly she said, "First things first: Roona's right, we'll be held to the prisoners' pace on our way to Lammintown. Since some of them are hurt, that won't be fast."

"I try to earn my keep," the old fem said with a quelling glance at the young Newly Freed who had mocked her. They laughed and pulled each other under the water.

The others took up Roona's questions. No one wanted to compromise the tremendous assets of mobility and speed that the horses gave the little army. But Oldtown was too far west to serve as a base where the prisoners could be penned and guarded, and Alldera was adamant against splitting the femmish force. Maybe the centrally located City would serve as a holding place for the captives, once it was reached and taken.

Alldera sat back and let them talk it through, seeing where they must come out. There were few realistic alternatives. By late suppertea back at the tents, word was spreading: they would all move on to the City as soon as possible, driving the captives along on foot at the best speed they could make. Men who couldn't keep up would be killed where they fell.

"We don't want weaklings to breed from anyway," Kobba pointed out; a mild comment, for her.

"I don't want to breed from them at all," Emla said, her lean face growing drawn and shadowed. "I won't have one of them touch me ever again."

There were thoughtful looks as others around that particular fire considered their own histories of rape by Holdfast men: old histories or, in the case of the Newly Freed, fresh ones. Alldera saw Ellexa quietly take Emla's hand and hold it to her lips. Ellexa's eyes, just visible past the fall of her silver hair, were closed above tear-slicked cheeks.

No one said, "But breeding is what we came for." Now that they had begun to take male prisoners, there were teeth in that purpose, and the teeth were sharp.

That night they disposed of the dead. Surviving men might call their own dead "martyrs" and make sacred places of their graves if these were known. These bodies were dragged out into the deepest, fastest part of the river in the dark of night and let go to be carried away. The corpses of fems were buried as secretly, without markers, so that no men might find them and know how many the fight for Old-town had cost, or try to desecrate the graves.

Alldera, restless and grieving, stayed with Daya, who walked over and over the returfed burial site trying to memorize the place. The pet fem had argued for memorials to be raised later so that people could come honor their fallen friends and lovers, and make offerings to Moonwoman on their behalf.

Alldera said, "Come with me, back to the tent, and tell me how you're going to make a story out of the taking of Old-town. We depend on you to remember that, not where certain bones lie in a country paved with bones."

She took Daya's arm and walked her back toward the camp. The pet fem's sinewy frame trembled continually.

"I think of Tua also," Alldera said. "I'm very sorry, Daya. I can't tell you how sorry. You'd been sleeping with her again?" Daya's silence confirmed this. Alldera thought of the two lovers in the dry wash that night in the desert. "I thought you broke with her long ago. Has everyone known but me?"

Daya still didn't answer. *Some comfort I offer,* Alldera thought; *it comes out as reproach. Why am I so clumsy at these things?* "I'm sorry. It doesn't matter. Listen, I heard old Roona asking one of these Oldtown fems if she had any curdcake, because she hadn't had any in years and missed the flavor."

"Did she have any?" Daya said hollowly. "The bond fem."

At least she answered.

"If she did, she kept it for herself. The point is, you would think to hear Roona that curdcake was something to miss, not the horrible food that was left to slaves to eat. We need to keep hearing your tales of the truths of the old life, to help us remember straight. To keep from making it—I don't know—romantic."

"Anybody can tell those tales," Daya said. "Setteo could tell them."

"Setteo!" Alldera said. "Don't joke. I've been meaning to talk to you about him. Make sure he stays away from the other men. Mad or not, he might tell them things that they could use against us."

"He won't tell them anything," Daya said. "He's gone."

"Gone?" Alldera gaped at her. "Where?"

"Somewhere," Daya said with a vague gesture. "I sent him away. Don't look at me like that. It doesn't matter where he goes or who he talks to about his stupid 'bears.' "

Alldera seized her by both arms and shook her. "Are you as crazy as he is? He'll go straight to the City and warn them!"

Daya jerked free. "You said we won't always have surprise on our side. Were you going to try the same trick again, sending someone to talk to the Citymen's bond fems and get herself killed?"

"Daya, it was the best, the best plan I could think of," Alldera said, scarcely able to find words in her shock and alarm. "We had to do something. If someone had come up with a better idea—"

"No, no," Daya said, "they stood back and waited for you to do their planning for them, and you did, of course. Tua is dead from your planning! Make a better plan, Alldera! You and Kobba and the Riding Women, all you great warriors—make a better plan next time!"

The Library

The men of the City's midnight watch marched Setteo through black, echoing halls and broken streets. He had often walked these rough ways alone for hours, hoping to solve the maze of ruins. They hustled him along with no awareness of the vast puzzle through which they moved.

He had used to think that if he once found the way he could show it to the Bears, and they would reward him lavishly. How vain and foolish such hopes seemed now! He sniffled forlornly as, chivvying him along in their midst, they started across the square on which the Boyhouse fronted.

Setteo had lived there dim eons ago, when the halls had been alive with bustling, hungry boys. Only the Librarian lived there now. Yellow lamplight shone between the slats holding together the great round Library window on the second floor: up there was his den.

Setteo pretended to be as scared of the Librarian as everyone else was. Actually the man had always treated him well.

He let Setteo look at the books, if he kept very quiet and
restrained himself from asking too many questions and naming the word-marks out loud.

The man Setteo thought of as the Erl King was waiting at
the entry doors, accompanied by two others. He always had
guards with him. The head watchman started to explain, but
the Erl King cut him off.

"I'll hear it inside as we go, and it better be good."

Someone struck a light, and they filed in under the sagging lintel with its props of fire-blackened timber. Setteo
knew the route, but he let them find their own way over the
piled rubble and fractured stairs. At last they halted before
one leaf of a great door that hung slanted from a single
hinge. Much of the doorway was blocked with a rough wall
of salvaged masonry.

At the far end of the room within, the Librarian looked up
from his work table, his face lit by the glow of three clay
lamps. Around him the worst of the wreckage had been
cleared and shelving rebuilt. Books marched in rows along
the walls and were stacked in neat pillars on the floor, emitting the scent of pressed time and thought.

Without haste or comment the Librarian set aside his
tools, a soft rag and a small bowl of water. He had been
gently sponging clean a loose page on the work surface in
front of him. At his elbow was a pile of similar papers,
wavy-edged and discolored from age and exposure.

The City men lingered near the entry, clearing their
throats and uttering gruff, uncomfortable apologies for disturbing him.

"Sir," the Erl King said, diffidently approaching him.
"You know this cutling here. He's telling us a crazy tale.
We thought maybe you could get some sense out of him."

The Librarian had other names besides that and "sir," but
they were seldom used. His good eye fixed on Setteo, alert
as a held breath. "Come here, Setteo. Come and sit down."

Setteo obeyed. The man made order around himself in a
disordered world. Order meant less pain and fear, which was

not *always* appropriate—there were places in all mazes that required pain and fear. But for the moment the Librarian's calm created a welcome air of security. Possibly he had some secret knowledge of the Bears, but mostly Setteo thought not.

"I meant to come and tell everyone," Setteo said, perching on a tall stool by the desk. "But I was hungry. I stopped to pick some wood-faces down under the piers—"

Nazon Morz, the watch captain, broke in. "He was caught stealing mushrooms that are supposed to be food for all of us."

"Don't call them that," Setteo muttered. " 'Mushrooms' are poisonous."

"Then," Morz went on ominously, "he started raving about fems, and other sorts of creatures, coming out of the Wild. He says they attacked Oldtown and took it." Morz laughed, but his big red face did not crinkle with humor.

The Librarian kept very still. Banked excitement crackled off him like fire on burning wood. "Setteo? What fems?"

"They're *like* fems," Setteo said cautiously. He had already been roughed up by the watch for speaking of Angels and the Blessed. His left arm throbbed and his nose seeped blood. "The ones we call fems, I mean. But these ride on the backs of horses—"

"Horses!" the Librarian exclaimed.

"And they're very strong, these people. If men challenge them, they beat them down. I think they're the Blessed Ones of the Second Coming. I could be wrong," he added, too late.

One of the men grabbed him by the ear. Setteo screamed. The Librarian said, "Stop it, Givard, what's the matter with you?"

What was wrong with Givard was that he was very young and unsure of himself. When nervous he turned brutal. He let Setteo go. "What if the younglings heard him, or one of our fems caught wind of this crap he's spouting?"

"If you can't let Setteo speak freely," the Librarian said,

looking down again at the papers on the table, "don't bother me with this. Go and work it out for yourselves."

"Our fems are all locked up for the night," the Erl King said. "Don't worry about it, Giv. Nobody here will be stupid enough to repeat anything the cutboy says outside of this room, either. We'd really like your advice, sir."

Why weren't they as nervous of Setteo as they were of the Librarian? Setteo alone went journeying in the country of the Bears, but it won him no honor. It was a sad puzzle.

The Librarian turned to him again. "What happened, Setteo?"

He told the story over again, of the Second Coming which had brought the Blessed Ones riding out of the Wild to crush everything that resisted them; how they shot arrows great distances from their short, curved bows; and how the Angels had joined them at the taking of Oldtown.

"She dragged Gunder on a rope," he said in agitation, "and the earth skinned him and filled up his mouth. They want no talking, they say. But when my Blessed One first brought me to them they wanted me to talk, and talk—does everyone understand me suddenly, to want so much talking from me?"

Someone muttered, "Not hardly," and laughed unkindly, but no one hit Setteo. The Librarian's power protected him.

"Describe these people to me."

Setteo wasn't sure whether he was intended to describe the wavering lights, burning hot orange and brown that he saw in the Blessed when they were angry—"Hungry Lights," he called them to himself—or how the people appeared outwardly.

"My Blessed has wavy hair," he began tentatively, "and scarred cheeks. Some of the Angels are black as charcoal, or yellowish, or very brown. The Blessed themselves are all light-skinned, like us."

Givard snorted. "Is he trying to tell us that the Dirties are back? Everybody knows all the Nigs and Mexis and those died Outside, in the Wasting."

With a cold look at the young man, the Librarian continued his questions, his customary remoteness replaced by eager interest. "Are there more of them than there are of us here in the City?"

"If the Angels are some other form of the Blessed," Setteo ventured slowly, in an agony of indecision at this new thought, "or if maybe even the horses might become Angels at the will of the Bears, who could count them? The horses pour over the land like a river in flood."

"The cunthead doesn't know what he's talking about," Morz said disgustedly. "What's 'horse' anyway?"

The Librarian held up his hand for silence, and got it. "What are the . . . Blessed Ones . . . doing here? Do they say why they've come?"

Setteo shivered. "The Blessed are very hungry, having been away so long in spirit places where there's no real food. I think they want to eat the Warm World as they go, though it makes them sad. They walked all night in 'Troi, murmuring and crying."

" 'Troi," the Librarian repeated, blinking. "They knew it, then, if they had memories of the place to cry about." He frowned. "I've heard what I need to hear. Thank you, Setteo."

Setteo relaxed gratefully on the battered stool, hugging one thigh to his chest and resting his chin on his undamaged arm. He wished he could sleep.

"It's crazy," the Erl King said, "what he says!"

"But what if it's true?" Givard said, his opinion veering again. "Didn't the old chants warn about a fem revolt, and femmish alliances with unmen and ghosts? Well, then the Fall happened, and now there's this, whatever it is—good men dead or captured—and what are we going to do about it?"

"It's just renegade fems," Morz said. "What's all the fuss? We'll go grab them, and their damned beasts too."

"Think," the Librarian said. He was always saying that to people: think. People hated when he said that, but they didn't actually hit him for it. "One way or another, they did take Oldtown. That means they must be a formidable force."

"Then they're not fems," Givard said, pacing and turning so that his flared vest swung out behind him. "Fems don't fight. These must be demons from the Wild."

"If it was demons, they'd be here already on a magic word," said Bavell, a quiet youth with a broken nose.

The Erl King nodded. "They're no demons, then."

Givard interrupted fiercely. "They're witches, and they've brought beasts to fight us. But we can beat them. The men of Ancient times went up against witches and won, didn't they?"

Morz rubbed his hard palms together. "We should head upriver tonight and take them before they realize we know about them. We'll send a messenger to Lammintown, to the Ferrymen, for help. We can pin these renegade fems in the jaws of a trap."

The Erl King forgot his manners and spat on the floor. "The Ferrymen are thieves. We don't need them."

An old argument ensued. Setteo got off the stool and sat on the floor so he could lean his aching shoulder against the cold wall. He dozed.

Eventually the Erl King asked the Librarian what they had come to ask. "What do you think, sir? What would you do?"

The Librarian looked down at the pages on his worktable. When he lowered his pale gaze, they forgot a little their fear of him and heard his words.

Setteo listened too, ignoring the sense and concentrating on forcing the sounds outward through his own skull into the air beyond the building, so that the Bears would be able to hear. He could do that because it was in this room of books that he had first seen the Bears, smiling at him from the scratched and faded pages.

"Whoever these people are," the Librarian said, "I think you should prepare to treat with them."

"Treat?" the Erl King said after a long pause. "You mean, talk with them? With *fems*?"

"You asked my opinion. My opinion is that escaped fems have come back from the Wild with allies we never dreamed existed. Together, they may have much to teach, as well as being more than a match for us."

The Erl King cried, "Blood and bone, sir, don't talk like that!"

The Librarian leaned toward him over the table. "This is the first infusion of life into the Holdfast in years. Whoever these incomers are, they may be the only hope we have for a future. Be grateful, be flexible, and be glad."

Strange; there were tears glittering in his eyes, his cold eyes that never wept that Setteo had seen.

Morz rushed the Librarian, roaring curses. The Erl King grappled with the infuriated watchman while the Librarian bent over his papers, protecting them. Morz threw off the Erl King and turned away.

The Erl King kept his eyes on Morz, although his words were for the Librarian. "We'll leave you to your work, sir. Thank you for your thoughts."

He shooed the others out ahead of him. Their voices, rising in anger again, faded as the men retreated down the shattered corridor.

The Librarian came around the end of the table with his crooked, limping gait. "Nose stopped bleeding? Show me. What did you do to make them bring you to me? Tell them you were frightened to death of me above all things?"

"It was their idea. Bavell didn't like Morz deciding anything. He and Givard ganged up on Morz and insisted on coming to you."

"And you said, 'Oh, please, anything but that,' " the Librarian said. "Why can't you focus that well-hidden cleverness of yours on something useful?"

This was an old complaint. Setteo said nothing.

The Librarian rubbed his eyes. "Well, come help me find

some food to pack. We have a journey to make, just you and I.''

''Don't want to go back there,'' Setteo whispered miserably.

''Erl will never deal with your 'Blessed Ones,' so we must do it, if it can be done.'' He looked around the book-filled chamber. ''Before they get to the City. Take me where they are. It'll be slow going, but with your shoulder to lean on I may reach them in time.''

Setteo wailed softly, knowing it would do no good. Nothing would. The Librarian was the one who must approach the Blessed, of course—who else? So Setteo must go with him. This was the price of being close to greatness.

''And on the way,'' the Librarian added, ''you can give me detailed descriptions of as many of these strangers as you can remember clearly.''

Setteo felt the axis of events (which reached all the way through the Warm World and into the world of the Bears as well) tilt as it had tilted when the Blessed had come—suddenly, drastically, and irrevocably.

Favoring his mauled arm, he climbed wearily to his feet. The Bears could at least have forewarned him. You would think they could do that much.

Men Fall Like Rain

B undled up against the predawn chill, Alldera rode a
slow, wide circle around the prisoners from Oldtown. An escape of these men was the common
nightmare, stronger here, so close to the City where they
might join other men. She stood her watch with tingling
nerves, her gaze constantly sweeping, probing, darting over
them, determined to miss no movement, no stir, no warning
sign of trouble.

How difficult it still was to believe: masters turned slave,
men gone from puffed-up lords of all they surveyed to these
clumps of sleepers, lying in leaden exhaustion on the bare
earth.

As we once had to lie, she reminded herself.

But how was it going to be possible to take these creatures
as mates? She had seen other fems, Free and Newly Freed,
come wandering out here to stare at the men, to ride or walk
around the group of them, staring and staring.

Behind their eyes they must be wondering, as Alldera
wondered, what it would be like to couple with a man now,

with the world all changed. Could a person make something of it other than an ugly necessity to be endured? Or even a triumph, as Fedeka said it could be if the event was dedicated to Moonwoman and the memory of all the dead fems gone before?

She couldn't imagine this, but it had to be imagined. Something had to be imagined besides what everyone remembered: brutality, pain, danger, and degradation; or how would they ever be able to bring themselves to create the future they had come home for?

One of the men moaned in his sleep. She remembered the moan of the first man to have fucked her as he strained upward from their joining, trying to fly away from his terrifying duty in the breeding rooms. She remembered the hot grip of his hands on her biceps, pinning her down.

Better to stop remembering. It must be different. They would make it different.

Someone rode up beside her. "God, they do stink, don't they?"

It was Daya, with whom Alldera had spent little private time lately.

"At least there are fewer of these now," Daya added. As expected, the man-pack had dwindled on the forced march from Oldtown. The surviving dozen were dazed and dumb. "Fewer and quieter. I do love to see men quiet."

"Well, it is a new thing in the Holdfast," Alldera said, more lightly than she felt.

Three men had died on the way from Oldtown, dispatched where they fell of weakness, wounds, and exhaustion. Coached by Kobba, Shanuay had killed one of them, jabbing him with a lance. The remembered image weighed on Alldera's mind. There was a time when she would have talked her feelings over with Daya.

I've missed you, she thought. *Can't you feel me missing you?*

Daya said, "It's a good rule for them, your rule of silence."

"I'm not so sure. Were men's rules ever able to stop us from talking among ourselves?"

"We'll do better. An ex-slave is a wise master."

Alldera rubbed at the place on her leg where Gunder had punched her. She was an ex-slave, all right. "I used to hear that boastful tone in the voices of our masters. Look at them now."

In a small voice Daya said, "Are we going to argue?"

Before Alldera could answer, Fedeka walked up to them carrying two javelins together in her one big hand. Someone had given her an elaborate necklace of carved bone pieces which clicked as she walked; you always knew where she was.

"Relief watch on the way," she said. "Right behind me. Why don't you two go rest? The City isn't far now, and we want to come to it fresh."

"So you're speaking to me again, Fedeka?" the pet fem said sardonically. "Has Moonwoman excused my letting Setteo go, then?"

"No, but I have." Fedeka planted the butts of the lances on the turf and leaned on the shafts. "I just had to think about it awhile. And what I think is, our own cleverness can carry us only so far. If the Citymen have been warned, Moonwoman will send us a different way to beat them."

Alldera said, "Even without more sacrifices, Fedeka?" There had been, thankfully, no moon ceremonies on the march from Oldtown.

Fedeka's shrug was just visible, the rattle of her necklace loud. "There have already been more sacrifices," she said placidly. "Just because I didn't take the men who fell by the wayside and offer them myself at night, that doesn't mean they escaped Her. When a man dies at any fem's hand, Moonwoman rejoices; even at the hand of someone who was the man's slave just days ago."

Daya drawled, "The Newly Freed call themselves 'un-slaves' now." She had taken to gibing at people in a way that made them wary of her.

Fine rain began to fall. Holdfast rain had a sweetness Alldera did not remember tasting in the cloudbursts of the Grasslands.

Fedeka set down the lances and rewrapped her headcloth, one-handed, with practiced ease. "It doesn't matter what they're called."

"It does to them," Alldera said.

"What matters to them," Fedeka said, "is these men, I think; even more than to us, maybe. Of course there are grudges and old scores people want to settle. But these Newly Freed are eager to start making free children, Alldera."

"Or eager to lie down with men again," Daya remarked. "I've seen some looks . . . Beyarra's friend Tezza likes men."

"Likes them?" Fedeka said. You could hear her frown in her voice.

"She's attracted," Daya said, drawing the word out derisively.

"Some of our own may be also," Alldera said. "I knew someone once who—she liked the way they smelled, and their hard muscles. She always said that fucking with them could be pleasurable, if only they weren't so frightened that they had to make it terrible."

After a moment Daya said, "Do you believe that?"

"I don't know," Alldera admitted.

"Thank the Lady, I'm past all that, speaking personally," Fedeka said. "Maybe we could drug them, milk them, and use syringes on ourselves."

Daya said sharply, "Who suggested that?"

"Oh, it's come up a few times, because of how people used to try to start children with my concoctions in the Tea Camp." Fedeka snorted with self-mockery. "Goodness, I was arrogant, to think I could come up with such a magic formula!"

"And who's going to do this 'milking'?" Daya said. "Or are we counting on the men to cooperate themselves?"

"Maybe," Fedeka said. "Fems cooperated with their masters, didn't they? In all kinds of ways."

Alldera cast about in her mind for some change of subject; the whole discussion made her acutely uneasy, and she could practically feel Daya's own anxiety burning close by. Daya had been a pet, and Alldera knew from nights with her—although they had never spoken openly of this—that being penetrated had come to gratify her in some inexplicable way.

"As long as we don't, any of us, forget who our enemies are," Alldera said. "No fem is ever another fem's enemy as totally and viciously as any man is."

"So Moonwoman teaches," Fedeka said.

Daya said nothing.

"So where's this relief watch?" Alldera said, peering around into the lightening gloom.

Someone ran up and fell flat on the ground in front of them. Alldera's horse shied and nearly threw her. Fedeka grabbed up both lances in her fist, brandishing them, dark streaks against the paling sky.

Daya said, "It's only Setteo, back again."

Alldera's skin prickled with alarm. "Fedeka, go alert the others. This could be a diversion to distract us. Daya and I will deal with the cutboy."

Fedeka set off at a shuffling run, whistling a signal to the other watch riders on the far side of the man-pack.

Setteo lay with his hands clasped over his head as if to protect it. Belated anger flared, that the cutboy had come so close to them without an alarm being raised.

"Put a rope on your creature."

Daya said, "He's tame. Get up, Setteo."

He jumped to his feet and said in a rapid, nervous voice, "Daya-Blessed, I have brought someone who needs to speak without dying for it."

Someone. Alldera was struck still with icy foreknowledge. Her bones turned to water and she sagged in her saddle.

"Some Dirtmuck man?" Daya spat. "Where is he?"

"I will take you?" Setteo inquired anxiously.

Daya touched Alldera's arm. "Wait here, I'll go. We don't know, it could be anything."

Alldera sat speechless, transfixed by certainty. Daya rode off after Setteo. Alldera at last found breath and impulse, and gave her own horse its head to follow them. Her mind was mercifully blank.

"Show me," Daya ordered Setteo, up ahead, so intent that she seemed to have forgotten Alldera entirely. "But keep close. This is the point of my lance in your back, do you feel it? One mistake and I'll stick you through your stringy little heart."

"Yes, Blessed," the cutboy's voice drifted back.

Alldera thought of galloping away somewhere. Her horse carried her on after Daya. Setteo led them in a wide curve away from the bare hillside where the prisoners slept, all the way around the horse herd and beyond. The rain trailed off as the sky grew light ahead. They were moving eastward, some distance from and parallel to the river. No one else was in sight now.

"Hurry up," Daya shouted at her guide. Alldera thought, *She'll kill Setteo right in front of me, and we'll never get to meet—that other.*

"There!" Setteo cried.

Ahead and to the left on a rise, Alldera saw the dark form of someone standing alone in the dew-gemmed grass.

Daya halted her horse and hefted the lance in her hand. "Setteo, get out of my way."

Alldera's mount stood with its ears pricked forward. She sat staring from its back, unable to move or speak. Daya rode past Setteo and without dismounting circled the stranger, menacing him with quick stabs of her lance point that stopped just short of touching him.

"Man-muck," she yelled in a high voice, "show me your hands!"

She's afraid, Alldera thought with distant surprise. *Daya is terrified, for all her brave talk.*

Hands were raised, fingers spread against the sky. Alldera could see the crookedness of the man's stance, the favoring of one leg. Her own hands trembled on her cold, wet reins.

Daya was silent now; she must guess. She had told the story often enough. She had described this man, repeated words he had spoken, told what he had done, wondered aloud whether he was Sorrel's father.

Alldera suddenly felt intolerably exposed: did he see her, or was his attention fixed on Daya and her weapons? Alldera slid down off her horse and leaned against its warm, damp shoulder.

Daya cleared her throat. "Eykar Bek."

"Yes," the man said.

His voice? Suddenly Alldera wasn't sure.

Daya said, "Where have you come from?"

"From the City."

If only the sun were not rising behind him. Alldera burned to see him clearly, to know for sure. Someone coughed: Setteo, who stood nearby. She had forgotten him completely. She forgot him again at once.

She shielded her vision with her raised hand. Now she could begin to make out the hard planes of the man's face. How could she have thought—? His features were creased and lined, one cheek sunken, a scar puckered at an angle down the forehead. His shoulders were stooped.

This was some battered stranger, not the elegant and steely person she remembered.

He spoke again, perceptibly softening the sounds of man-speech in some mad attempt at courtesy. "I must speak with Alldera."

Daya's lance shivered against the sky. She cried hoarsely, "Your kind doesn't use our names, Muck!"

The man stepped backward and fell, in comical silence, on the ground. Alldera's throat unlocked.

"Leave him, Daya! He's mine."

Daya glared over her shoulder, then reined her horse back

toward Alldera with a hard and angry hand. "Are you sure it's him?"

Uncertainty vanished. "Of course I'm sure!"

Daya offered her lance. "Then you do it. Only a spy would come alone like this. If he is alone! A dozen men could be hidden out there waiting for his signal to attack."

At their backs, the camp was stirring. Free Fems whistled as they moved the horse herd. Alldera became aware of the hum of conversation as people gathered at the fires for a meal before traveling. She did not trust this man—of course not, why should she? But against all that forceful life in the camp, what could a crippled ghost do?

She said, "I think he's come to talk to me, just as he says." She took a deep breath and addressed him for the first time in her life by his given name, as a master would naturally address a slave. "Stand up, Eykar."

After a suspended instant in which he seemed too startled to reply, he answered huskily, "I'm not sure I can. I have an old injury."

A pulpy burn, raw and hideous, pulsating under her hands; she saw it again, she smelled the tingling stink of the wound. She remembered the feel of his skin and the bright, alert, invisible flame of his trembling attention—to his hurt leg, to his situation, to her. That flame had burned away her caution and her necessary detachment, as her words had burned away his.

All that might have happened just this morning, it seemed.

She let her horse trail after her with its reins hanging and walked toward him through the wet grass. Without thought, as naturally as she might pick up a stone from the ground, she bent to take his hands and pull him to his feet.

His fingers, wiry and cold, closed unhesitatingly on hers. Oh, yes, that was the grip, this was the weight and the balance of him. She could almost believe that they were back there in the past again, both tense and wary, both young.

Hissing through his teeth, he lurched upright and steadied himself against her grip.

"How well you look," he said. The sun had risen.
"Strong."

"I can't believe," she said, and stopped, shocked and
frightened by the happy roughness of her own voice. There
should be no joy. But, against reason and sense, there was.

They looked into each other's faces, both breathing softly,
expectantly. *I am who I was,* Alldera thought. *I survived, you
survived. We did not die.* She saw him thinking the same, she
saw incredulous, exultant laughter brimming in him too.

"What are you doing?" Daya screamed.

What are we doing? Alldera's mind echoed. She felt the
suspended moment, with its riot of impermissible feeling, jar
and slip. She tried to hold it, but it was gone.

He drew his hands away and backed a step, his weight on
his good leg (into her memory flashed a luridly lit scene, a
smoking brazier flung aside and spilling coals, a deep
scream of pain). He was crippled, as she had left him. And
lean, still. He had always been lean.

She swallowed. "What are you doing here?"

With a gasp of breathless laughter he said, "Risking my
neck. Is your friend going to kill me?"

He turned a little toward Daya. Alldera was struck with a
sickening amazement that she had recognized him at all. His
hair, once black, was now shot with gray. One eye was still
the pale ice that she remembered, but the other looked
blurred. She knew the look of cataracts: the man who had
never turned his gaze away from anything was half-blind.

She felt again the lurch of the camper under them as they
were borne inland by the carry-crew. He had had a fierce
young face then, eyes keen as stars, and a voice wintry
enough to wither oak. A long time ago. They had lived, for
that short, chaotic period, as closely as any pair of femmish
cubs in the terrible kit pits of Bayo. Such proximities could
not be canceled.

She did what she had learned to do in the Grasslands: she
put wonder and anger and sorrow aside and took charge.

"Others will come soon," she said rapidly. "Walk with me. Speak while you can."

"Setteo says you're the leader here, and I see it must be true. Even these animals serve you." He was staring past her at her horse, which nodded along at her shoulder. Suddenly he rubbed at his eyes and muttered something in broken tones. Was he touched in his brains, perhaps like Setteo, all the gleaming strength leached out of him? Or worse yet, had there been no such strength, was it only an illusion of memory?

He said painfully, "Captain Kelmz would have given both arms to see that horse." It was for a friend dead nearly two decades that he wept.

Excited voices sounded distantly. Riders were milling along the edges of the camp.

"What are you doing here?" she said, walking slowly beside him.

"The Citymen know you're coming. It's not Setteo's fault; they more or less beat it out of him."

"So you've come to ask a pardon for Setteo?"

"More. The City is ruined—"

"Keep your voice down."

Daya rode slowly abreast of them less than a lance-cast away, all malevolent attention. Alldera was afraid of what the pet fem might perceive between them; still between them, after all the bitter things that had happened (and the good), and after all this time.

"I've been salvaging what I can," he said more softly, "records, books, pictures, anything usable I could find in the Boyhouse Library. I live there now."

"Live there?" she exclaimed. "But you used to hate the place!"

"I came to beg you," he said, lowering his voice still more to speak these words unimaginable from any man, "to help me keep these poor scraps I've saved from being destroyed."

Involuntary laughter burst from her, an incredulous guffaw. "You want me to protect the place where you were tortured and humiliated as a boy?"

"That was the doing of men, not books," he said stiffly.

"Books," she marveled. "I thought you would ask for the lives of men."

"Oh," he said, "men fall like rain and vanish into the ground as if they had never been. But knowledge endures if we let it. It waits to be harvested, like nourishing grain."

She thought again of the men who had died on the march down from Oldtown, one silent, one crying, one wheezing the words of an old chant. And fems fallen too, fighting against men. *Dead bodies lie between us already, his dead and my dead, with more to come;* and here came her own people, with a drumming of hoofbeats and cries of alarm. *He and I will never speak like this again.*

Good, she thought, with immense, painful relief; *good. So it should be.*

"Your father read books," she said coldly, "and he planned to raise fems for meat. My people would pile up your books and happily burn them, and you with them."

"Burn me, then," he said. "But not the books!"

The riders thundered close, calling, afraid for her.

"Listen, Eykar, if you want to stay alive: you don't address me directly. You don't speak unless you're spoken to first by one of us. You do not carry petitions or offer bargains or try to use your connection with me ever again. Now kneel down and kiss ground to me so they can see it."

His head jerked back as if she had slapped him, and she thought with rage, *He won't, and I'll have to kill him, the fool.* But he obeyed, just as riders jolted to a halt all around them.

Saddles creaked, lances were unslung. No one spoke. They waited for her. These were her people. Her past with Eykar Bek was long since over, and everything was changed. That was the point of having come home.

"This man," Alldera said with a calm descended from somewhere outside herself, "I know from old times. He came to surrender to me, as you see."

"Look at him, he's a wreck," Daya said. She raked Eykar with a blistering stare. "He'll only slow us down."

Ellexa added, "Why not give him to Moonwoman?"

Alldera said evenly, "He has submitted himself to me, not to you, and I say no."

Ellexa's horse thrust against the bit, shaking its head irritably. She pulled its head up hard. "Well, if you want him as your Setteo," she said dryly.

Alldera said, "We said we would hold our prisoners in common. Put him with the others."

"He won't be able to keep up," Daya objected. "I should have killed him as soon as I saw him. Someone should kill him now."

Heart beating hard, Alldera turned and caught up the reins of her own horse. "Put him with the others and have him not come to me again. I don't want to see him. Setteo can help him. One lame man and one mad man will likely add up to one whole man."

"And if not?" Daya demanded.

"Then not." There was no point trying to conceal who this man was; Daya might not say, but others must already have guessed. Alldera raised her voice so that everyone would hear. "There are no indispensable men in the Holdfast of the Free Fems, not even the former Endtendant of Endpath and my old master, Eykar Bek."

She rode on toward the camp without one look backward, and all the way she felt filled with the rich, racing energy of release. She had met him, dealt with him, and paid an old debt: a gift of life for a gift of life.

They were quits.

But another part of her mind said quietly, *That man fucked me, and it was nothing but a passing moment of ordinary brutality, one among many in that lifetime. Could we do it again, if I wanted to make another child? Of course. Why not? It would be nothing again.*

But what if we did it and it was not nothing?

"Quits," she said aloud.

III

III

History

B eyarra stood in awe of Alldera, but she loved the sinewy column of Daya's neck and found the pet fem's scarred, smoldering beauty irresistible. And besides, Tezza said that she had heard that Alldera and Daya had been lovers themselves, on and off, for years; which made being close to Daya something like moving nearer to Alldera herself, to whose bed a young but newly freed fem could scarcely aspire except in dreams. Passion only lasts so long between any two people, and though they might remain close in some ways, sex together was bound to diminish. Probably Alldera was grateful that someone was helping to distract Daya from any pain and regret she must be feeling at their growing estrangement, which was plain for all to see.

And anyway, Alldera would forgive in an instant, if she knew how much Beyarra was in love. She was in love as she had not been in love in—oh, in more than a year now. She kept stealing glances at her beloved, so thrillingly near.

Beyarra hated outdoor labor, the lowest of slave work. Her sense that Daya had no use for it either (unless it involved horses) had first brought her close to the story-maker. Out of this had come something unbelievable and wonderful, but it was still just beginning. She was terrified of ruining everything with stupid mistakes.

On this wet morning, the worst of the rain had stopped. The wind still blew occasional gusts of rain against the tent and chilly drafts knifed through.

Beyarra sat where daylight gleamed past a raised wing of the tent. While sorting arrows retrieved after the fight for the City, she hesitantly retold the story of the battle.

"No," Daya cut in. "No, no, no. Didn't your masters teach you to listen? Get it right or don't tell it at all."

"I'm sorry," Beyarra said humbly. "Please, you tell it to me again. I'll try harder to remember everything."

Daya rested her chin on her folded arms, staring out resentfully at the gray sky. "I don't remember so much rain in autumn. We would be better off inside the City, but the place is barely livable anymore."

"There was a lot of fighting after the Fall," Beyarra offered timidly. "And we were not so many as in the old days, to keep up with repairing things."

"But you *lived* there. Civilized people fix up their homes." Daya fixed Beyarra with an accusing stare. "In the Grasslands we've talked for years about how we came from a place where people lived better than they can in a nomad camp. Now here we are squatting in tents outside the wreck of the City. Sheel and her friends are laughing at us!"

Beyarra ran an arrow shaft between her fingers. "There are some sound buildings. But people talk of ghosts—"

"Ghosts!" Daya said. "Ghosts! It's the decay everywhere that encourages such ridiculous talk. The City used to be such a glittering place. Now I have to make a story worth telling about the conquest of a batch of filthy, patched-together hovels." Beyarra accepted her lover's scorn in adoring silence. This did not protect her. "And it doesn't help when I find my chosen pupil so stupid."

"I am trying," Beyarra whispered. "I am, Daya."

She was amazed that Daya would even consider teaching a mere unslave the stories of the Free Fems and their conquest of the Holdfast. But Daya herself had suggested it. "In case I get killed," she'd said. "Someone should remember."

"Concentrate," she said now. "Pretend your master will whip you if you don't learn. I'll start again. There's no point trying to fix that shaft, can't you see it's ruined? No, save the vanes; good fletching leather doesn't fall from the sky!

"So: the Army of the Free camped across the river from the City, which the Newly Freed from Oldtown had described in every useful detail: where the men now lived, where they locked up their bond fems, which parts of the City were still fortified, and where food and drinking water were kept.

"Now, Alldera, who had questioned the Oldtown unslaves one by one, explained her plan to everybody, going around from tent to tent with Sheel Torrinor and the fems chosen as war leaders after the fighting at Oldtown, which were Kobba and Ellexa.

"So the men of the City woke that first morning of the siege of the City and saw fifty tents set out across the river, with fems and horses in constant motion among them. Erl Scrapper's men wanted to rush out and fight there and then. One man whirled his sling and flung three stones. They fell short, into the river between. And Kenoma of the Red Shirt, not a Riding Woman but a Free Fem, shot an arrow upward and killed him. That made the others scramble back and think again!

"Now, the men had bows too, but these were bare wooden staves, not backed with strong horse sinews as our bows are. Their arrows too fell short, except for one that nicked the ear of Ellexa's gray gelding. So Erl Scrapper, the master of the City, brought all his men to him to make a plan.

"They made the walls ring with their boasting, but if you want to know how pale they were with shock, and how shaken with confusion, and how dry-mouthed with foreboding, ask the Newly Freed who were still bond then in the City and who served them their food and drink while they talked inside the safety of the walls!

"We showed them the freedom of life without walls. That first afternoon we went down to the riverbank and bathed, and drew water for ourselves, and watered our horses. We sat together for our tea and meat on the old stone-paved docks alongside the shore, out of their bowshot of course.

"We, who had so often gone hungry in our bondage, fed each other hot morsels from the stew kettles. We, who had labored for our masters unwashed and unrested until we stank, washed and combed and dressed each other's hair, tying into the tresses of our chosen companions—we, who had never been able to choose—the bright ribbons of friendship and the red threads of love. We, who formerly went nowhere except on our masters' business, ran footraces and gambled and shouted and laughed together.

"And they watched us, from their walls.

"That night the men chanted for hours to the beat of drums and gongs. We heard them cheering when clouds drifted over the face of the moon. But we were not afraid.

"And on the second day we held a pillo-game, Riding Women against Free Fems on strong, fast horses. Ellexa of the Silver Hair pulled the pillo and won the game for the Free Fems, while the Citymen watched from their parapet.

"That day at noon Erl Scrapper's men took a bond fem of the City and threw her down to her death in the sight of all of us. This was Brita, once owned by the Tekkan Company where she cooked for the Senior men's banquets. Remember her name; she died in the taking of the City.

"Everyone came to Alldera and said, 'We must attack, we must avenge Brita's death and free the rest!'

"But Alldera said, 'No. For us to win, the men must come out into the open, and they are not ready to do that yet.'

"And the Newly Freed of Oldtown said, 'Bond fems are penned up in the City, friends and lovers of ours. What if the men kill one every day? You say you came to free us, not to get us murdered by our masters!'

"But Alldera said, 'You yourselves tell us that there are more men here than we are, fems and Riding Women together. Our strength is in our horses and our bows. Horses are no good in the City with its paving and narrow passages, and our use of bows and lances would be hampered. Inside the walls, the strengths of the men are greatest and ours are least.

" 'We can't bring back Brita, whom the Citymen killed to provoke us into attacking like the foolish and impulsive slaves they think we are. But we have a plan, and we will win.'

"And so the dead fem was buried by her friends. Her name will not be forgotten: Brita, of the Tekkan Company that was.

"Now, that night all the bond fems in the City were locked up in the old brewery buildings while the men argued. Meanwhile three of Erl's sentries sneaked away to a small boat hidden under the ruined bridge. The boat belonged to Erl Scrapper himself, for his own private comings and goings. These men meant to take this boat and escape to Lammintown.

"But the Newly Freed of Oldtown knew about that boat, as they knew everything there was to know about the City. Holes had already been cut in that boat under cover of dark by Jida and Ganedda, who crossed the river on horseback to do it. They can now boast of it in their self-songs, so you won't ever forget their names.

"So the boat was sunk when these coward men reached it, and the men were stoned from their own walls because other sentries thought they were enemies attacking from across the river. One of the deserters was killed, and two slunk back to face their leader's anger; and their names are of no importance.

"On the next morning we brought our Oldtown captives to the riverbank. Those men we had so far kept upriver a little way. They had been set to cutting and smoothing the walls and floors of the old clay pits there, in which they were penned each night.

" 'You are making this clay house for your brothers,' we said to them. None answered because of the lesson Alldera had taught them all with rope and lance outside Oldtown.

"Now, on this morning these men, yoked and bound together, were driven naked to the riverbank opposite the City to wash the clay and filth from themselves as best they could. We cut the hair of their heads and shaved their faces as Alldera decreed, so that we could recognize one from another; for we know how useful anonymity can be to slaves.

"On the wall appeared every man of the City, and there was not a sound from them, not a cry or a curse, as they gazed out on the sight of men like themselves helpless in our hands. Then the prisoners were driven back to their slimy pit, to work under the eyes of guards who kept their bows bent and their arrows ready to hand.

"But one who had tried to escape and one with a festering wound were kept back and offered to Moonwoman by Fedeka. Alldera said that we would soon take many more prisoners, and Moonwoman's aid should be sought by every means—"

"Alldera didn't say that," Beyarra said, startled into interrupting. She bit her lip.

"No?" Daya paused dangerously. "You remember more clearly than I do?"

"This fem—I heard people arguing. Alldera didn't want to offer Jodd Galgar and Beery Rab to Moonwoman."

"And what was the result of the argument?"

"Those masters—those men were given over to Fedeka—" Beyarra stumbled. She had not wanted to see poor Rab killed. He had looked so wretched and desperate, helping blank-faced Jodd Galgar stumble along on his swollen and discolored leg.

"So," Daya said inexorably, "the decision was to give them over to Moonwoman through Fedeka's hand, isn't that so? And Alldera, as our leader, knows and does the will of us all, as she did here, ultimately. Any discussion of the matter was unimportant.''

She paused. Beyarra waited, her gaze lowered.

Daya continued: ''So on the riverbank, out of range of the Citymen's slings and bows but clear to their sight, Fedeka offered these two with her half-moon blade, while we all asked for Moonwoman's protection. And nobody spoke for these sacrificed men, because of the memory of Brita, who died thrown from the walls of the City.''

No, Beyarra had not spoken for poor Rab, and she did not speak for him now but kept a melancholy silence.

''Late that night, four bond fems got out of the breweries, eager to warn us that the men meant to attack us before dawn. If you want to know how they escaped, wait for their self-songs. They crossed the river clinging to bits of the wrecked boat and were carried far downstream. But by the guidance of Moonwoman they found our camp anyway.''

Daya either didn't know the names of those bond fems or did not think they were worth including. Beyarra knew that the leader had been Paysha, Erl Scrapper's bedmate for the past eight months. Paysha was a high-strung, wiry person who had risked her life repeatedly by reporting to other bond fems whatever useful bits of information she had managed to pick up while in her master's company.

I will find out the names of the others, Beyarra thought solemnly. *I will include them all, when I tell the tale.*

''But how surprised these bond fems were,'' Daya went on with relish, ''to find that there was hardly anyone there! They were frightened to see so many empty tents and dummy tents, and were afraid that they had been tricked by demons from the Wild, or that the Army of the Free had been driven away or destroyed by the men's chanting.

''But Alldera came to them and said, 'Don't be afraid.' She sent them to the care of the Riding Women at the clay pits who had charge of the prisoner-men there, saying, 'You cannot ride horseback to either attack or escape, so you must stay with people who can look after you.' And so they went."

Daya paused, running her spread fingers through her hair so that her damp, springy curls were freed from her neck and forehead. "Do you have something to add here?"

Beyarra thought of the screaming protest the City bond fems had raised against being put in the care of the Riding Women, whom they had believed to be demons. But she shook her head, and Daya gave a satisfied sniff and continued.

"So then in the pit of night the men came, crossing the river with ropes fastened to old lashing rings sunk in the docks. They slipped among the tents of our camp, and at a signal—an iron gong set crashing with noise that was supposed to terrify the Free—they attacked the empty tents.

"Our taunting voices were heard from the levee, and blunt-headed arrows fell among the men as gestures of contempt—although one put out the eye of one man, and he has died since.

"Some men turned back at once and tried to swim home to the protection of the City walls. But some charged the levee, cursing and stabbing at riders as they came galloping down upon the men and lashing at them with whips and lances. One managed to pull down Jebekka off her horse and hack her to death before he was killed himself. That story will go into the self-song of Kobba, who took a cut on her face while trying to save Jebekka. And one horse, a yellow mare called Sunny, broke her leg in a fall.

"So the men were herded this way and that by riders they could barely see, until suddenly on the parapet of the City across the river a great flame leaped up. This was a signal fire made by fems: the City was taken. The men, guessing its meaning, lost heart and scattered, to be captured and put in the clay pits with the rest.

"The main body of the Army of the Free, increased by the numbers of bond fems they had found in the City and released, came back across the river to the camp at sunrise.

They brought out too all the men they had found within the walls, living and dead. Some men killed themselves rather than be taken alive. Erl Scrapper fell to the hatchet of Ellexa of the Silver Hair; remember her name. And if you want to know more of that fight, listen to her self-song.

"Now I will tell you Alldera's plan that won the City for us, because she is too modest to put it in her own self-song. Under cover of night she had secretly sent half the Army of the Free to cross the river lower down where it is broad and shallow. They hid themselves below the southern walls, where the causeways linking the City and Bayo once stood. Erl Scrapper had set a small watch here, but those men could not see down beneath the remains of the old causeways.

"So Ila, a bond fem freed at Oldtown, advanced alone and called to the men of this watch, begging them to let her back into the City. She had valuable information, she said, that she had spied out among the invaders for the sake of her masters. The men on watch lowered a rope for her. As they held their torches high to watch her struggle up toward them, they were killed by arrows aimed from the darkness below.

"Ila climbed the pillars and secured the rope. Then others joined her and moved down the streets of the City, not on horseback but on their own feet, that knew every corner and every cranny of the place. They swept through in silence and stealth, searching for men posted to defend the rear of the City, and for bond fems to set free; and their tales of victory you will hear in their self-songs before long.

"So at last they made their signal from the parapet, and that is how the City was taken, on a night of cloud and wind. At dawn the sky cleared and a horned moon was seen.

"There. Do you think you've got it this time? I hope so. It's not hard. I haven't even put in all the names yet."

Beyarra said, "Tell me where your own name goes in the story. I won't forget that."

Daya rose abruptly. "I don't boast like a Riding Woman."

Hadn't she said before that she had been first, after Ila, up the causeway ruins? Perhaps it was part of the storyteller's true art to hold herself out of the tale and leave the glory to others.

Moved by this notion (for she had thought Daya anything but modest by nature), Beyarra shyly took the pet fem's hand and raised it to her lips. She closed her eyes and inhaled the scent of the sweet oils with which Daya anointed herself each day.

Daya pulled away. "I'm not your master, to have my hand kissed."

"I only want to thank you for the story."

"You can thank me by memorizing it properly, which would make you of some use to us at least."

Beyarra got up and left the tent to walk to and fro in the mizzling rain, repeating what she could remember of the story over and over while her eyes streamed tears. How terrible, how beautiful, how painful it was to love a free person!

Petitioners

S oon," Alldera said. "I just haven't got it all organized
yet." Sheel cupped the chin of the gray horse they
were examining. The soft, puckered, bristled skin
quivered in her palm. "If I were your enemy I would attack
now, while you loaf around celebrating your victory."

"Things take time, Sheel. You know that."

They stood at the line of tethered horses. Two of the
Newly Freed were watching from a short distance away.
Beyarra (Beyarra-Bey, after a freename ceremony under last
night's moon) had probably volunteered to get more used to
the horses, of which she was obviously still very frightened.

She squatted some yards from the picket line, list in hand
and marking stick tucked behind her ear, her neat, triangular
face looking strained and attentive. Her friend Tezza-Bey
(they had taken the same freename for the sake of their
friendship) stood beside her, hands on knees, whispering
questions and studying the list. The earmarks of each pick-
eted horse had been inscribed by Sheel herself on a bleached
fiber page from one of the City record rooms.

"This gray is broken-winded," Sheel said. "Hear how she's breathing? And she was barren the last two years besides. Move on or stay here, she'll serve you best as meat and hide."

"Agreed." Alldera made a broad throat-cutting gesture. Beyarra-Bey marked the list.

Sheel stretched, pressing her back with both hands. "I remember lifting this horse from Waterwall Camp years ago, when she and I were both younger. Don't worry, I'm not going to tell you the story of that raid. It means nothing here. Pity she fell into the hands of people who don't know how to take care of their mounts, eh, Briar?"

She slapped the horse regretfully on its matted shoulder.

"Not all Free Fems are hard on the horses," Alldera said. "Look at Daya, for instance."

"She's a natural rider," Sheel agreed. "But some people aren't cut out to ride at all. Beyarra-Bey will never be easy on a horse, in any sense."

"She won't need to be," Alldera said, "once we've settled here. We're not nomads by nature, Sheel. We all walked before we ever saw horses."

Sheel studied the two Newly Freed from the corner of her eye. "Still. Any woman can do whatever needs doing in the Grasslands. Each Motherline has its strengths and weaknesses, but there are no Women who fear horses, or can't ride or shoot an arrow. Unless they are too old or too crippled, of course."

"You should keep your voice down," Alldera admonished tartly, "when you're talking nonsense. There must be Women who are afraid of horses, but they can't admit it because then nobody would respect them." She ran her hand over the back of the next horse, a bay gelding. "Saddle sores, getting bad. Rain seems to make it worse, doesn't it? He needs to be rested."

"I've got some lotion that might help," Sheel said. "I'm talking about the basic skills of life. Tessaya, there, the soft-faced one, falls into hysterical laughter at weapons practice whenever someone strikes at her. As if laughter will defend her! These people will always be dependent on others to protect them. They're pathetic.''

Alldera made an impatient sound. "Listen, Sheel: I was never pretty enough to be a pet, strong enough for hard labor, or specially talented as a cook or a weaver. I did have a solid butt and quick, strong legs, so I was trained to run. I did what I could do, and that kept me alive. I ran for my life. Now I'm home as a conqueror—so far anyway. But I still can't do everything.''

"*You* don't have to. If they hadn't made up this Lady of the Moon, you'd be their god. Look," Sheel added, pointing with her chin. "Here come some more of these worthless but respectable people, looking for you, no doubt. Why they can't work anything out for themselves is beyond me.''

A small group approached on foot. Daya led them, resplendent in a tunic made of banners; signal flags, Alldera had said they were, that the Citymen had used to send each other messages from hall to hall when they couldn't be bothered to use a runner like herself. The Newly Freed had begun enlisting Daya to speak for them, and she now dressed the part of an important personage.

Alldera, like most of the Free Fems, wore simple leather pants and tunic, scarred soft boots tied under the knee, and her headcloth draped around her neck and shoulders, as the Free Fems had taken to wearing it here. You would not know, to look at her, that she could call these other people, in their smocks and wide hats, ''hers.''

The little party came raggedly to a halt at Daya's back. They stood uncertainly eyeing the horses and Sheel as if from behind a defensive wall.

"What is it?" the runner said. "You all know anyone can come to my tent at suppertea to talk.''

"Some friends speak more freely in the open, without so many others to shout them down," Daya said in the unctuous tone she adopted in such circumstances.

Sheel noted Beyarra-Bey watching the pet fem anxiously;

she was spoken of now as Daya's bedmate. Matters had been strained between Daya and Alldera since the death of Tua, and maybe before that even. A pity; Daya had a destructive streak that needed soothing. An unslave's uncritical worship might not suffice, after the love of Alldera Conqueror herself.

Sheel was glad not to have made any approaches of her own to this intriguingly attractive little person Beyarra: life was complicated enough.

Besides, this very thin, watchful City fem called Paysha was interesting too, and had distinguished herself in the battle. Let the Rois cousins snigger together about what mating with a man might be like, and the Tulun and the Salmowon bed down, passion-stricken, in each other's arms; Sheel had her own ideas of where to look for the surprises and delights of love here in a foreign land.

Perhaps Paysha would tell her what it had been like, meekly sleeping with the head City man, Errol, and meanwhile spying for her own people. The details promised to be fascinating.

Sheel slitted her eyes and made a subtle motion of acknowledgment with her head, and Paysha smiled faintly and glanced away. *Oh, yes, there would be pleasures there,* Sheel thought. *Don't rush; act as if there is plenty of time, and there will be plenty of time.*

Alldera gave up. "Walk along with us, then. We have work to do here today."

As Alldera and Sheel moved on to the next horse, a ribby black, Daya beckoned to the little group of petitioners—for that was inevitably what they would turn out to be—with the whip that she wore looped from her wrist. It was not a rider's twist of rawhide but a slave-driver's wand of tough, thin wood with a splayed end.

Daya had taken the whip from one of the Newly Freed she had found using it on a horse. Sheel had thought since of stealing the evil thing and burning it, and thought of it again every time she saw it.

The black horse was hale and strong. Beyarra-Bey stopped whispering with her friend and hastily made another mark. The delegation stood there, mutely intrusive. Sheel saw Paysha looking at her from under lowered lids, and let herself be observed studying the slim fem's body, caressing the angular grace of her with her gaze.

One of the Newly Freed stepped forward, flanked by two of the tongueless ones. She was a coarse-built person of some years, with a squarish face falling away to dewlaps. One arm had been broken once and had mended awry. She made a sketchy bow.

"You are choosing horses for travel on to Lammintown, Alldera Holdfaster?"

"Yes, Kastia-Kai," Alldera said. "Not all of them are fit."

"Well," Kastia-Kai said, looking anxiously over at Daya, who remained impassive, "some of us are perhaps also not fit. Some of us prefer the protection of the City walls to that of mounted warriors, no matter how brave the riders may be."

On the words "mounted warriors," all eyes turned to Sheel, who busied herself running her hands over the legs of the black horse. Perhaps these were the fems who had argued late into the night after last night's moon ceremonies, disturbing other people's sleep.

That smooth Emla had persuaded Ayalees Salmowon and Tyn Chowmer to attend Fedeka's latest moon-doings, and the Salmowon had reported passionate speeches and exhortations. Most of the Free Fems were ready to move on at once, but there was a core of opposition that included both Free and Newly Freed.

Come to think of it, hadn't this Kastia-Kai spoken up for Gredda after the burning of Oldtown? Now she sported what was obviously (once you looked carefully) a thick braid of horsehair woven into her own scanty locks. Correcting for this change, Sheel knew her heavy face.

"We need to secure the coastal towns before the winter

storms begin in earnest," Alldera said rather stiffly. She was much easier with the Free Fems than with some of these diffident but stubborn unslaves. "Our slower travelers will go protected by an escort of armed riders, like moving walls. Daya, I've explained this; couldn't you have answered these people's questions?"

Did Alldera see the tightening of the pet fem's mouth, the dart of anger in her glance? Sheel saw. She saw Daya drawing closer to Fedeka's zealots, as if folding the currents of the dyer's spiritual authority around herself in place of the shining armor of Alldera's love.

Daya said, "I am only a storyteller, Alldera. They want to speak to you."

Alldera sighed. "Speak, then." She still had not learned to disguise her feelings very well.

"These are new ways for us," said Kastia-Kai sententiously. "We have no experience at what you call a 'camp,' always moving or preparing to move."

The dumb ones made hooting noises into their cupped hands, a sign of assent.

Kastia-Kai continued, "Some of us are older and might fall behind even the pace of 'slower travelers.' "

Kenoma, who had ridden up leading two geldings she was now knotting onto the picket line, said scornfully over her shoulder, "Then stay behind, we don't need you. Hide behind the City walls that protected Erl Scrapper's men so well."

She shifted a wad of tea to her other cheek and spat on the ground. Kenoma Red-Shirt even sucked seeds and stones because she was always hungry, a bout of belly-sickness having left her with a raging appetite. Sheel liked her better here than she had in the Grasslands.

Another of the group on foot, pale Tamansa-Nan with the curly dark mane, friend of Juya-Veree, said in a sweet, husky voice, "May I speak?" She counted on her fingers. "Here we have full storerooms for the winter. We know how to harvest food from the old laver ponds. The lands around the City are good for growing manna plants and grain, but someone must be here to break the ground and do the planting early next spring. There is grass here for your animals. Why not stay?''

Beyarra-Bey spoke up. ''But we'll be back by spring, with more captive masters to put to this work of planting.'' Everyone looked at her. She blushed.

Sheel guessed that the little unslave didn't like Tamansa-Nan. The Newly Freed had lived together for years under the Citymen. They must have many secret grudges and alliances stored up.

''Go on,'' Alldera said, bending to pick up the forefoot of one of the horses Kenoma had brought. ''I'm listening.''

No one spoke for a moment. Sheel knew that bland stillness of Daya's. She had come here leading the opposition, and she wouldn't budge or let her troops turn back until plenty of trouble had been made.

''I don't want to leave,'' Tamansa-Nan said, fiddling nervously with her dark curls, which she had cut off at earlobe level as an offering to Moonwoman. Her large, liquid eyes seemed fixed on some inward vision of disaster past which she spoke with effort. ''Slow camp or fast camp, I don't want to go anywhere.''

Paysha nodded and seconded this in a light, reedy voice: ''The City is my place too, that I helped fight for. I belong here more than I ever did before.''

Tamansa added hesitantly, ''Maybe it means nothing to you Free Fems any more, since the City is so changed from what Free Fems remember. But I want to mend what I can, and walk the streets and alleys as a free person before I am killed in some other battle somewhere else.''

''You run no risk,'' retorted Kenoma with a scornful toss of her thick gray hair. ''You'll be plodding along in the slow camp, behind the real warriors, where you belong. I certainly don't want you or any unslave at my back when we meet the Lammintown men.''

Uproar: the tethered horses started back from the Fems'

shouts, snorting and rearing along the picket line. Sheel grabbed the head of a piebald mare that broke its tie with one terrified lunge. Cursing, she dug her heels into the sod and hung on.

She caught glimpses of Alldera clinging to the bridle of another rearing horse, dancing about to avoid its flailing forefeet. Over the snorts and stampings of the horses Sheel heard people yelling and the sounds of grunts and blows.

She wrestled the piebald to a panting, stiff-legged stand just in time to see one of the tongueless unslaves kick Kenoma like an angry horse herself.

Other people were racing over from near the main horse herd.

Daya, mounted on Kenoma's horse, drove into the struggling mob and lashed downward with her whip. One of those on foot shrieked and stumbled out of the press, shielding her head with her arms.

Everyone froze. They stood panting, staring at the spectacle of a mounted Free Fem with an overseer's whip in her hand looming over an unslave—Tezza-Bey—who cowered, wailing, before her. Beyarra-Bey darted between them, white-faced with shock.

Sheel assured herself that Paysha was all right—yes, there she was, holding Kastia-Kai by her good arm and speaking urgently. Well, now there would be something for Sheel to chat about with Paysha.

Kenoma, bleeding from a split lip, stalked back and forth along the picket line and yelled, "Cowards! All you know how to do is insult everyone, whine, and bother people at their work! You were too cowardly to run away to freedom, and now you're too cowardly to fight for yourselves!"

She was not the only one to scorn the courage of the Newly Freed. Sheel had heard tales of bond fems who had barricaded themselves in the City brewery with two of their masters and held the Free Fems off for an hour. Complaints were made about certain Newly Freed from Oldtown who had been found not fighting, as they had been sent to do, but looting the old Boardmen's Hall of men's belongings. Incidents like these did not show up in Daya's stories, but rumors were rife.

Alldera had laid down rules since about equal shares in the spoils, and hearings for charges of treachery. But anger that still simmered had just boiled over. What was dangerous about fems was not so much their cowardice as their cowardice combined with their repressed rage.

Kastia-Kai pushed Paysha away from her, screeching at Kenoma, "Who's done all the work and taken the beatings these past years? Cowards are people who run away, not people who stay the course!"

"Be quiet, both of you!" Alldera commanded. "We are all the same people, and we were all slaves. Anyone who tries to set us against each other is a fool and a traitor. We've all done the work and we've all fought, in our own ways."

"So why do fems fight fems?" asked Kobba, just arrived from the horse herds. Her long, stern face was newly marred by a scabbed-over cut she had taken in the fight for the City. "This makes no sense, but there is a reason for it."

Sheel rubbed her palms together to ease the sting of a rope burn. She watched with interest as Alldera set her face and body sturdily against the coming challenge, for which she sensibly made space by saying nothing. Kobba clearly had not finished.

"Everyone knows," Kobba went on, seemingly off on a tangent, "that the Newly Freed Leeja-Beda was fined for killing a captive Muck two days ago."

She should have been rewarded, Sheel thought. The killing was not what she would have expected from gawky Leeja-Beda, a plain person with a penchant for jokes and mimicry. But news of another man dead and harmless was always welcome.

"I fined Leeja-Beda," Alldera declared. "I stand by that judgment, Kobba. The man did nothing to provoke her. Ellexa says she won't be Chief Whip if fems can murder any man of any work gang at a whim."

"Leeja-Beda struck for Brita, that the Citymen threw from the walls," Kastia-Kai said, adjusting her false braid, which had slipped down over one eye in the scuffle. "They were lovers."

A hit; Alldera's eyelids fluttered painfully, but she recovered herself at once.

"Many men died in the taking of the City," she reminded them, "including Erl the Scrapper, who ordered Brita's death. Isn't that payment? The man Leeja-Beda stabbed was captured by us in Oldtown, days before Brita died."

While she was speaking Daya dismounted, furtively tucking the whip inside her shirt. No one but Sheel was looking. The others hung on the discourse of Kobba, who squinted into the distance at some list of debit and credit that only she could see.

"All of the men are guilty," she said. "All of them owe every one of us. Killing them at random is better than many other things—singling one of them out for special attention, for example."

Alldera threw Sheel a frustrated look. Well, if she was vulnerable on this score it was her own doing. Everybody knew about her meeting with Eykar Bek. That man of all men Alldera should have put down at once with her own hands.

Daya straightened the collar of her shirt of flags and said diffidently, "This is the message repeated over and over in Fedeka's dreams from Moonwoman: our anger is our gift to the men who were our masters, and we need to give it to them, not to each other!"

So they came back again—as they almost always did, no matter where they began—to the subject of the captive men. Sheel found this profoundly disturbing. What a pity that Kobba, Fedeka, and Daya did not simply join forces, finish the prisoners off, and argue Alldera and the rest around afterward.

True, this would leave the fems with no hope of creating future generations, slave or free. But what difference could that make to people who had never raised their children in a human fashion anyway, and who had no society even now, only an army?

Alldera said, "The men are already dying in the clay pits of wounds and fever."

Paysha said sharply, "If they don't like it, they should try the kit pits." Others laughed and nodded approvingly.

Alldera went on, "If they're to survive at all, we may have to take more care of them, not less."

"How many Mucks were counted last time?" Daya said. "Over two hundred all told? And a scant hundred and twenty of us. In the old days some fems escaped. If we did it, men can do it, and tell tales of escape to hearten each other. Better to kill them now than regret it later."

Kastia-Kai thoughtfully rubbed her twisted arm. "I know one of them in particular, and he knows me. I would like him to feel the edge of my knife, not die of fever or the viciousness of another of his kind, or even the whim of another fem, Free or Newly Freed. Maybe we need to settle scores more than we need all these men."

"Kastia-Kai," Alldera said, turning an intent look on the older fem, "you know the history songs we used to sing as slaves. Do you remember how the songs end? Do you remember the warnings against becoming what we hate most? We fought against letting men distort our souls when we were bond. Should we let them turn us into murderers now? Do you want to spit in the faces of our foredams, who endured every filthy thing and still held on to their human decency?"

Daya said, "Moonwoman preserved us then and she will preserve us now."

Sheel stood with her arm over the neck of a roan mare, listening in silence. How had Daya gone from Alldera's friend and lover to her opponent? Among the Riding Women, people came together for love and parted in sadness when their passion was spent, but they did not turn against each other because of it.

She thought she saw a kind of stifled agony in Daya's expression when she looked at Alldera these days. Of course Daya had been a pet fem, a plaything of men. Her behavior was sometimes exaggerated and odd (just look at that outlandish shirt she was wearing!). Still, could this be simple jealousy?

Sheel could not tell. But she thought that if the Free Fems would follow Kobba or Fedeka as High Chief instead of Alldera, Daya would quickly change her allegiance.

Not much chance of that, though. Alldera was not someone to be set aside lightly. Look at her now, assailed but standing fast. Too bad Sorrel couldn't see this. It would make her proud.

Kobba pressed on remorselessly. "I say Leeja-Beda did us a favor in cutting the Mucks back by one, just as my daughter Shanuay helped out when she gave a man called Jaygo what she owed him, after we took Oldtown. Oh, yes," she added, smiling faintly at Alldera's evident surprise, "ask Daya about the 'mystery' of that Muck's death, him that was found in the squats where he belonged. Daya knows. She was there."

Tezza-Bey, rubbing at the red mark of Daya's whip on her neck, burst out, "Oh, she's always *there,* but she never does anything. Unslaves like Shanuay and Leeja-Beda slaughter their enemies, but Daya the Free Fem hasn't struck a master yet. Everyone knows she took a crazy cutboy captive, but for the rest she only uses that whip she carries on other fems, as if she were a master herself!"

Daya looked up, stark, the color drawn from her face in an instant.

Kobba frowned. "True, I have never actually seen you strike one of them, Daya. Not even that day at the mines when six Mucks died at our hands. Not your hand, now that I think back on it."

Sheel saw the pulse beating desperately at the pet fem's temple. She felt a stab of mixed pity and disgust, and a righteous warmth at the confirmation of her own judgment of Daya's character.

Alldera did not see, or, seeing, chose—with a reckless loyalty that took Sheel's breath away—to speak vehemently in defense of Daya, whose bitterness Sheel could all but smell.

"I don't have to ask Daya anything. She was a slave of men, as each of us was. She was punished for not serving them perfectly, as you can see by the scars on her face. And yet she took prisoner the first man we encountered here alive—"

"Because she couldn't bring herself to kill even a cutboy outright," Tezza-Bey muttered under her breath, with an angry look at her friend Beyarra, who would not meet her gaze.

Alldera said, "I myself didn't let a man's blood until after Oldtown was taken, as you all saw. And what if Daya *never* kills a man? Have you all forgotten her courage during the sharu-swarming at Stone Dancing Camp? I saw her gathering arrows for other people, at terrible risk from wounded sharu savage with pain. She has scars from that day. Must she show them to convince you?"

Kobba shook her head. "Men are not sharu, and sharu aren't slave-masters."

"Our masters," Alldera said roughly, "said we must all be crawling, craven slaves or die. Are we now going to say that each of us must cut a man to pieces to be respected? Is that the only way a fem can prove that she is no slave but a free person?"

She stepped forward and put her hands firmly on Daya's shoulders. "I say Daya is our singer, our poet, the keeper of our story for the future generations we mean to establish in this country. I say the work of the singer is as valuable as the war deeds of Kobba, Ellexa, Ila-Illea, Paysha—or myself. If we compel each other in anything as our masters compelled us in everything, Matri Mayala will be proven right: our victories will be an ugly joke at our own expense."

Kobba turned without a word and walked away, her big hands curled into hammerlike fists at her sides. The others looked uneasily after her.

Alldera lifted her chin, her nostrils flared like those of a spirited horse, and said firmly, "We were talking about leaving the City. When we have taken our entire homeland back, I hope some of you still want to come back here and make this place thrive again. Until then, I ask you to trust enough in your kindred returned from exile to travel on to the coast with us."

Kastia-Kai lowered her head submissively.

Kenoma caught up the reins of her mount. "I have more horses to bring." Glowering and fingering her split lip, she mounted and rode off.

The tension eased. The others began to walk toward the camp talking quietly among themselves. Paysha looked back once at Sheel, but did not linger. Only Beyarra-Bey and Tezza stayed, avoiding each other's eyes; and Daya the pet fem.

"Don't touch me!" Daya cried. She twisted violently free of Alldera's hands. "You think I don't know you despise me? It's true, I shake when I see a man, I tremble. You wouldn't know about that because you're a hero, nothing scares you! Well, I'm only human, and I'm afraid!"

She ran for the camp, her brightly colored shirt billowing.

Sheel shook her head. "Too bad. She won't forgive you."

"Forgive me!" Alldera cried. "For what?"

"For her cowardice, of course."

"You have always underestimated her!" Alldera's eyes glistened with unshed tears.

Christs

Setteo was too excited to sleep. His consciousness spread outward, feeding back to him through his ears, his skin, senses that had no names, the reverberations of voices, of movements, of the strike of footsteps and of the hooves of horses on the earth. In the bumps and shallows of the clay wall at his back he read future upheaval.

Men were awake late tonight in the prisoner pits. Givard had been beaten by the Blessed for trying to hide a metal fragment he had found while working. They had not killed him outright because he was young, and marked for breeding. But on his account no one had been fed tonight. Lezandar and two others had beaten him some more for that, until the Librarian had shamed them into stopping.

How impatient people were, how foolish in their sudden rages! This was an old story to Setteo.

"It's not fair," Givard mourned. "Why did they treat me like that? I was never a fem-basher like the old masters. I've been a friend to fems."

Someone else snarled, "You don't know what you're

talking about, boy! They're devils, Witch-kin, coming here with black beasts and black riders too. They don't need a reason to strike down a true, strong man, let alone a damn-stinking boy like you.''

"Shut up!" hissed another voice. "If they hear you—"

"I'm not afraid of them. Wait till the Lammintown men come and get us out of here. You'll see something then."

"Who's going to fetch them?" the other said scathingly. "You? You know a way out of here?"

"There's free men still unaccounted for," came a bolder response. "Even the Witches know that."

"Won't do us any good if we're killed for talking."

Givard moaned, "We were getting along fine here. It's not fair. Why can't they let us alone?"

Setteo moved nearer to Givard and, setting his mouth very close to his ear, tried to explain. "It's about the skins of the fathers, which are visited on the sons. It takes years of growing for a young fellow to shed the resemblance to his father, and you know how those fathers behaved before the Fall. The Blessed Ones punish harshly, but this is the Last Judgment."

"Hush, Setteo," came the Librarian's voice. "Let people sleep, if they can."

He was sitting alone, with space around him as always. The prisoner-men taken in Oldtown had been baffled by his arrival among them, but no one expected him to account for himself. Even in these circumstances they regarded him with awe. This seemed perfectly natural to Setteo. If anyone could ameliorate the anger of the Blessed and temper their destructiveness, it would be the Librarian.

If he had vision—and how much could he have, with one milky eye?

Setteo had vision; too much of it. He wanted to give some to the Librarian, who might actually be able to receive it as most men could not. Bad feelings came to Setteo tonight, through his skin and his blood. He didn't want to be alone with these feelings. He moved over to sit next to the Librarian.

"They are doing something," he whispered anxiously. "I can hear it: busyness in the darkness, hurtfulness is happening. You can turn it, maybe. You can divert the flow."

Without raising his head that he had pillowed on his crossed arms the Librarian said, "Let me think, Setteo. Be quiet and let me think."

His thinking was visible in the form of a pale wash of steady, intense light surrounding him and setting him off in the murk of the pits. This visible thinking was full of flares of tension, leaping flashes of hope, and dark ripples of despair. Entranced, Setteo watched the Librarian think.

He had seen Alldera-Blessed, Beloved of the Bears, touch this man. She had reached through the wall of icy air between the two of them and taken his hands. In that moment a charge of enormous power from the Cold Country had rushed from her into the Librarian.

He was banked fire still, but there was fuel for a great blaze there. You could be burned up in the conflagrations such people made of their lives if you happened to be standing too close. But if you had studied in the land of the Bears for years, you might survive.

"The night is buckling in on itself," Setteo said. "Something is twisting it, something is—"

The Librarian caught his arm in a painful grip. "Be quiet!"

Setteo shivered in the darkness. "Too late," he whispered. "It's begun, don't you smell it? A great fire in the river—" The grip on his arm spasmed tighter, then released.

"Fire?" the Librarian said fearfully. Setteo knew he was alarmed not for himself but for the books in the Boyhouse Library, so many of them already charred and battered.

"Not fire that burns paper," Setteo hastened to reassure him. "More like—the air is shaking with pain, and pain is a form of heat. Don't you feel it?"

The Librarian sighed. "Things are bad enough, we can't

afford panic. So keep it to yourself, will you? Whatever it is, keep it to yourself.''

Setteo hunched away from him, hurt. The Librarian was proud in his masked power, but even he would come to realize that he couldn't achieve great things alone. He would need his vision-seeker, his shaman. Setteo had once thought to become a chantsman, to preserve and teach the old ways. Hardly anyone bothered remembering the old chants now.

He drifted, almost without knowing it, into a corner of the Cold Country where a voice was singing a new chant, one that might have power for these new times. Before he could draw near enough to make out the words, someone shook him back into the Warm World.

The eyes of other men, awake and silently watching, gleamed. Light shone from the lamp fixed to the outer rail of the lifting platform, which had been lowered from the edge of the pit.

''Setteo.'' The Librarian's voice was tremulous. ''I need your help. They want me, up above.''

The lift slowly rose on creaking ropes. The Librarian held tightly to Setteo's shoulder. He had banked his thought-fires to a faint glow, and his breathing was quick and shallow. Setteo too was afraid when he saw the guards who waited at the rim of the pit. They radiated something too dark to be seen, but bitter and stinging when inhaled: the fury of the Blessed.

Out in the surrounding landscape the Bears still lurked, their thick paws shivering the earth underfoot. The darkly blazing air drew them. Setteo feared that his own pathways to the Bears' country would be burned up tonight, and would have to be remade later at enormous risk.

He staggered a little as he stepped off the platform onto solid ground. No one touched him or the man with him, but there closed around the two of them a silent escort of six of the Blessed. As the sun edged above the horizon, they were marched southward toward the bluffs overlooking the river.

The Librarian had the sense to keep his mouth shut. He

must know the danger of unwittingly ingesting the raging currents in the cold dawn air. Setteo set his own lips tightly and matched his stride as best he could to the Librarian's halting one. Hurried wordlessly along between the clay pits and the dark tents of the Blessed, he was terrified. But it was always by moving into the heart of what he feared that a seeker learned things worth knowing.

They trudged up onto the bluffs above the old loading docks, from which they could look across the river at the lightless hulk of the City. Others were waiting for them on these modest heights: a small group of the Blessed, most with blankets drawn around their shoulders against the spiky breeze that had risen with the sun.

From beyond them and below, where the river ran, waves of thick, sickening heat rolled upward, making Setteo's teeth chatter and his skin slicken with sweat. Here lay what the Bears had come for. They padded like shadows along the edge of the bluffs, beyond the Blessed gathered there. Setteo could only look that way between quivering, half-closed eyelids.

The Chief Blessed came forward. Her face was set like stone. She said, "Come to the edge and look."

The Librarian faltered. Setteo helped him forward, wondering if he could remember in time how to escape the body and fly. This was not something he had ever done before witnesses (except the Bears of course). Could the Blessed pursue his spirit body into the sky if they so wished?

At the bluff's lip he looked down, shut his eyes, made himself look again.

Though he did not think it appropriate to say so, Setteo had seen what was to be seen before, in the Library, in pictures: the three raised figures, the barren sky, the atmosphere of suffering, injustice, and disaster. In this current manifestation of that timeless paradigm he recognized a response to the sign he himself had made, when he had raised his single Christ as a signal for these Blessed to come.

Here now were three Christs, in answer.

Under cover of the windy night, three wooden poles had been set up in the mud beside the half-sunken slabs and timbers of the old docks. It had been done with deadly care—each mouth was thickly gagged, the arms of each body had been bound tightly to the sides—so as not to rouse the camp before the sign was assembled and its meaning made complete.

With flinching inward vision he imagined the whole process: the sharpened poles laid out on the ground, the busy, whispering, straining men (they had been men, of that he was sadly certain), the gagged and terrified victims. Onto one end of each stake a struggling human body had been thrust, legs forced apart to admit the rough-hewn point.

Then the heavy-laden spits had been reared upright, raising their writhing, muffled loads high into the whipping winds. Once secured in place, the makeshift lances had slowly and inexorably impaled the three dying bodies.

The dead hung still now. Their bare feet were shredded and black with blood from scrabbling uselessly for purchase. Fluids still dripped, making small, evenly spaced, distinct sounds of impact on the ground below. Beneath this horror, a number of the Blessed worked frenetically but in near silence to bring the stakes and their burdens carefully down.

The Librarian, clinging to Setteo, turned aside and retched as if he would bring up the world.

Setteo stood quietly, speaking in his mind to the tumultuous air. First, he apologized for his own foolishness: he had thought the night's turbulence had to be the doing of the Blessed or the Angels, but it had been men's work. Then he prayed to the Bears to take away from the newly dead souls the memory of their frightful passing.

Even in this light he could identify the distorted faces: three of the secret Blessed, bond fems in the City until a scant week ago. That very thin one, stick limbs bundled like firewood, was Paysha, bedmate of the Erl King himself, occasional advisor in matters of crops and harvests and a hero of the Blessed's conquest of the City. Another had been sold away in a lean year and come trotting back along the bank of the river, preferring her accustomed masters to the rougher men who had taken her in trade. The pretty necklace of bright plastic pieces she had been given to reward her loyalty was gone now.

The third Setteo had fondled and played with sometimes in the days of his desperate interest in such things, before he had been taken up by the Bears to levels beyond mere curiosity about physical matters. He remembered with melancholy the warmth of her mouth on his maimed body.

Blesseds whispering in breaking voices lowered this last one's body, still pierced by the killing shaft, to the stained and trampled mud. Her hair fluttered under the confines of the rag bound between her gaping jaws. Setteo could not remember her name, though he knew it well.

"Look carefully," Alldera-Blessed said in a heavy voice. She wore only a loose vest over pants tied at the waist, and her arms were rigidly crossed, hands cupping opposing elbows. Her hair hung loose and wild around her face. "You're here to look and listen. I will only tell this once. Some Citymen hid during the fighting. Later they came sneaking to three Newly Freed fems, begging for protection. Drunk on victory and freedom, these fems were tricked, captured, and treated as you see.

"The men then tried to escape to Lammintown riding horses stolen from our herds. They should have run away on their own feet, that they know how to use, but being masters of everything, they thought they could master our animals at a whim. We have caught them and killed them tonight.

"But they left us this—sign, which we have no trouble understanding. Do you see? Do *you* understand?"

They were all staring, waiting, except for those gathered around the second lowered stake and its burden. Now only one pole leaned, creaking, over the water on which the new sun glinted like gold.

The Librarian uttered a single dry sob. "I see, but I do not understand."

"You will understand this," the Chief Blessed said. The parallel lines between her brows were as deep as a brand. "We will take reprisals. Not against all of you, because we don't let passion drive us against our own best interests. Not against enough of you for justice—there is no way to do that. But against as many as we choose, without excuse or explanation. If you are asked, say so."

With a cry a Blessed threw herself down, tearing the gag from the face of one of the corpses. The others stood back helplessly as she closed the slack jaw with tender hands and kissed the blackened lips.

"Kill them," said a voice of fathomless bitterness. It was the tall, broad-shouldered Blessed with the strength of the Bears themselves visible in her frame. If you had doubts of the origin and sponsorship of the Blessed, you had only to look at Kobba. She had even the mark of their claws on her cheek, fresh and livid. "Here, in the sight of these poor corpses, kill these two Mucks to begin with."

Alldera answered steadily, "I sent for this man, whom other men know as a truth-teller, so he can bear witness to them. How else can the prisoners know the reasons for their punishment? Do you want to bring them all here to look, Kobba, to gloat? Eykar will explain to them when they ask why."

"There's been enough explaining," Kobba roared. "There's always been too much talking, and not enough bleeding, not enough screaming, not enough pain—from them. The pain and the bleeding and the screaming have always been ours. But not anymore."

Alldera squared her shoulders before this storm, her face shadowed and grim. "We are going to the same place by different trails, Kobba. You asked me to make a judgment about this. I have made it."

There was silence. Then Emla-Blessed said through stiff lips, "I want to hear Alldera's judgment, word by word."

Alldera nodded once. Her eyes dwelt not on Setteo—he was glad of this—but on the Librarian, who blinked dazedly as she announced her judgment. "Every man will be brought up from the clay pits, to be yoked and tied and driven to the old Boardmen's Hall. There every fem will choose one man and do to him what she will, in memory of her own sufferings and those of all her mothers and her mothers' mothers and now the sufferings of these three Newly Freed and newly dead. Surviving men will be returned to their prison, and not be punished for this atrocity again."

Kobba-Blessed looked at the faces around her from eyes like stars of anger sunk in their deep sockets. "As you say, Alldera Conqueror." Her voice rose again, Bear-like in its ferocity. "But everyone should know that this is the last time that I, Kobba, make way of any kind for any of these *things*."

She suddenly stepped forward, seized the Librarian's chin with her long fingers, and spat in his face. He seemed to hang, shivering, from the vise of her fingers. She withdrew her hand with a jerky gesture, as if his skin burned her, and throwing back her head she sang in such a harsh and tearing voice that the words were distorted past Setteo's understanding. He would have covered his ears except that the Librarian was clutching his arm like a strengthless old man.

Well, no wonder: he had just felt the jaws of the Bears close on him, and yet survived. If he had dared, Setteo would have pointed out that by naming them witnesses, Alldera-Blessed had guaranteed that they two at least, the Librarian and Setteo himself, would survive the slaughter to come.

Clay Pits

The sodden cloth dropped behind two more men who had squeezed into the shallow cave after Eykar, out of the rain. These days men followed him and sat near, watching and listening. Friends of the dying came begging his attendance on their friends' behalf. As Endtendant he had dispensed a swift poison mixed with manna-drink to make sweet, and final, dreams. Of the kind of death that struck in the clay pits these days, he knew no more than anyone. But he came when they asked for him, and stayed as long as he was wanted.

Such grotesque differences between his fate and Alldera's—he dreamed about it sometimes, and daydreamed too, and came to himself dazed and helplessly angry.

If only he had said something different to her at their meeting. Out of that moment when she had helped him to his feet anything might have come, if he had been quick enough, brave enough to have spoken differently, acted differently, than he had. Or if only he had made some inspired gesture on the terrible day of the impalements, something to win absolution; then things might be different now. He often fell into useless, painful circles of thought around these events and their consequences.

Also around his need to think about her, to catch glimpses of her, to argue inwardly over how powerfully the sight of her affected him. Her survival, her return, was like a miraculous gift—a gift with a sharp and poisoned edge that he could not deal with but could not let go of, either.

That night years ago in 'Troi when he had helped her escape, he had—unknowingly?—freed a demon, a demigod of malign endurance and purpose. How could he have recognized such a future being in the alert young fem who had dared everything to tell him her most wrenching truths? For which he had punished her at the time, appropriately and despicably. So if now he was her slave, and with all his kind a slave of all her kind, how on earth was he to feel about that, and about her?

Attending on the dying was a refuge from useless brooding.

This time it was Nazon Morz, down with pit-fever. A man needed no injury to die, not since the increasing rains had turned biting cold. Not since water had begun seeping in from a nearby pit in which the fems had the men throw their own dead.

Using rags and the panels of an old screen of reeds, Morz' friends had made a seat for Eykar. He maneuvered himself down beside the sick man.

"Well, Morz; they've asked me to come."

"It's that bad?" Morz whispered. Sweat gleamed on his face and neck. "Should have let some damned Witch-bitch kill me clean the night we lost the City."

Eykar took Morz' hand and began to speak of the smooth black walls of Endpath and the orderly processions of men entering the great central chamber for their last Dream. The air at Endpath had sparkled with the taste of the sea. This low-ceilinged chamber hacked into clay stank of Morz' sheddings of fluid and salts from his collapsing system.

Eykar breathed this air and talked of Endpath. Memories of that life were the only comfort he had to offer.

"It was really like that?" said Lezandar, Morz' friend.

"As I remember it, yes." Eykar's father had said of Endpath that it was a lethal device designed by the Seniors to control the energies of Junior men and limit the Holdfast population. At times since, Eykar too had spoken such heresies—raving in manna-induced frenzy to anyone who had paid to listen. But men here who remembered those occasions said nothing of them in his hearing. They had too much need of the soothing memories of Endpath that he raised for them.

"Will he die tonight?" Wiry and vigorous, Lezandar had one wounded hand tied up in a scrap of filthy rag. Checking automatically, Eykar was relieved to see no tell-tale dark streaks on the skin of his forearm.

"He'll die soon, at any rate," he said quietly.

One of the others said, "We'll all die, that's their plan. They don't need us. They can mate with their demons."

"Horses," Eykar said, "not demons."

At least today no one argued. He had heard it all, over and over, in the days since the capture of the City: the Free Fems were Witches, they would destroy everything and then fly away on their four-legged demons that could sprout wings at full moon. They weren't fems at all but spirits from the Wild mimicking the appearance of fems. They were a test sent by a secret empire of invincible men living in the heart of the northern forests.

"Our own fems, that we've fed and protected, want us dead," Lezandar grated. "Look how they tore into us on Murder Day. They won't rest till we're all dead."

"If they wanted that," Eykar said, "they'd have massacred us by now. They've had plenty of provocation." The dying man mustered a smile at this allusion to the three impaled fems. "As for Murder Day, I've seen men do as bad and worse to captives after a fight, and so has every man who lived through the Fall of the old Holdfast. I expected much worse from the fems. You might consider what a nuisance it must be for them, keeping guard on us and seeing that we get a little to eat and drink.''

Young Bavell, who wore a permanent look of devastation since Erl's death in the battle for the City, awkwardly ventured an opinion: "They're scared of us because there's still more of us than them. They want the fever to thin us out.''

Eykar snorted. "What makes us sick can make them sick; and if nothing's done soon, it *will* make them sick. You can be sure they haven't planned on that.''

"They don't plan," Lezandar said. "Fems can't reason. It's all impulse with them.''

This willful blindness was maddening. "They took Oldtown and the City on impulse? When will you realize that you're not dealing with the fems you're used to? We have to face what these people really are—''

"Witches!" Young Givard was still inclined to these outbursts, when safely out of the enemy's presence. "Witches from the Wild, that's what they are. They've poisoned the minds of our own fems that have served us happily all these years. We need new chants to hold them all off until the Lammintown Ferriers come help us fight them. Then we'll show the bitches, we'll teach them! Next time it won't be just a sharp stick up their cunts. First we'll fuck them bloody, and we'll tear their skins off in strips and stuff their mouths with their own roasted meat.''

Eykar let the tirade wash over him without protest. Silence often meant surrender and quiet death, but Eykar found bluster harder to bear. He heard so much of it.

Morz began whispering wildly and turning his head from side to side. Eykar shifted his own aching leg again and bent nearer to listen.

"I saw them from the walls, just like Setteo said: femmish archers, riding beasts! How could we match them, when bows had been banned in the Holdfast for generations by the Seniors? The old men have won after all, years after their own deaths. Will you chant it, Endtendant?''

No amount of blood, terror, and death could wipe out what Eykar had been and done. He was never allowed to keep for long the illusion that he was simply a salvager of tattered books, a harmless and hopeful gleaner of knowledge in a darkening age.

Or he had been, when there were still books.

"Nobody would believe it if they didn't see with their own eyes," the dying man said, pressing Eykar's hand. "If it's not put in a chant, how will anyone know what happened to us?"

The clay-smeared cloth billowed suddenly. The men tensed, the whites of their eyes gleaming. This room could become their tomb if femmish guards found it. But there was no other privacy, no other shelter from the rain.

No one came in.

Morz' ragged nails dug into Eykar's skin. "We didn't have a chance. Tawmon was a great slingsman, but they killed him."

"Tawmon was stupid." Lezandar reached past Eykar to pat the sick man's forehead with a wadded rag. "He thought he could bring one of them down even at that distance. Whing, whing," he said, imitating the whirling of a sling strap. "Next thing, there's an arrow through his neck."

Morz groaned. "Slave-bitches shaking out their fresh-washed hair. I had a sweet one once, did I ever tell you? Not like these, she'd never have——" His voice faded, then came back strong again. "I'll never forget. You could almost smell them, and you could hear them across the river, talking, laughing."

"And men's screams," Givard whispered. "The Old-town crew."

They were quiet. Only Morz' struggles for breath sounded in the rank little chamber, and the tiny lamp flame sputtered. Outside, the rain's voice swelled for a moment and more water slid in under the curtain.

Bavell's friend Arjvall scratched raspingly at his scalp; femmish knives trimmed men's heads roughly, close, and often. "We had bad luck. If you'd been in the City, sir, you'd have foreseen it. You'd have reminded Erl, 'Keep a strong watch on the south side too.' But you'd gone."

Eykar sat silent, letting the reproach sting until its toxin was spent. Yes, he'd been gone, shambled off to plead with the enemy to spare the damned books. God, his leg was killing him.

"He's dead, sir," Lezandar said flatly. "You can let go of his hand, he's finished now, and thanks."

Bavell began to cough and kept coughing. *Him too,* Eykar thought; *first the coughing, then the fever.*

He drew his fingers from Morz' cooling grasp. "Don't bury him in here to rot beside the living."

Lezandar said fiercely, *"They're* not going to know that another man has died."

Arjvall said, "They count us every day."

"Shit they do," Givard shrilled. "Fems can't count, everybody knows that. They only pretend."

"I'm not giving Morz to those Witches," Lezandar said stubbornly. "They can spell a dead man hard and ride him to steal his seed, if they get him fresh. He stays here."

Eykar had to stand upright or scream.

"Where are you going, sir?" Bavell caught at Eykar's shirt. "If they see you come out of here—"

"They won't notice. I must straighten my leg."

Bavell clung mutely to the rotting cloth.

"Let go, boy," Lezandar snapped. "What do you think you're doing?"

"It's all right," Eykar said, twitching his garment free.

"Where was all this in your visions, your prophecies?" Lezandar cried suddenly, brandishing his swollen fist. "Why didn't you tell us, why weren't we warned?"

Eykar hunched his shoulders, a reflex from his days as an unwitting prophet. "I did see it. I can't help it if my *keeper* didn't tell you things he knew you didn't want to hear."

"You *saw?*" Lexandar repeated. "All this?"

Eykar's momentary flash of certainty faded. "I think so.

But would you have believed in an army of fems if I'd spoken of it? Would any of you have stood watch in the west, to guard the remains of the Holdfast from mere manna-visions?''

Lezandar turned away to shake out a rag and spread it over Morz' face. Bavell bent to his coughing. Eykar drew the dripping curtain aside and, after a glance upward for the sight of a sentry's form silhouetted against the gray sky, limped out into the rain.

It fell more lightly now than earlier in the day, but it was cold. He regretted the odorous warmth of the jammed little cave. Out here other prisoners huddled, men of mud and scabs and streaming water; coughing men, shivering men. Some of them looked dully over at Eykar, but no one approached.

He leaned against the slippery clay wall and flexed his bad leg. It hurt. He thought of the touch of Alldera's deft hands, tending that old wound in those old days. He saw her sitting her horse on the afternoon of Murder Day, watching in stony silence as her followers selected victims for their rage. The torsion between these two visions made him blink and shake his head.

If Lezandar ever learned that Eykar had helped Alldera escape years ago, all pains and questions would be over. But though Eykar's life as Endtendant and after was commonly known among the men, the inner truth of his journey west to meet his father was never spoken. It was about Eykar and a fem, after all; nothing important.

A plashing sound caught his attention. Setteo crouched nearby, paddling in the mud with a stick.

''Lovely, whether for ducks or not,'' he said brightly. He had picked up many obscure words and sayings while sheltering in the Library with Eykar, in relative safety from the rough humor and darker moods of Erl's men.

''How are you, Setteo?'' Eykar said. ''No coughing yet? No fever?''

Setteo moved nearer to him. ''I have been on a journey.''

"Really? Where did you go?" Eykar had grown used to carrying on meaningless but somehow comforting conversations with the cutboy.

"I went with the Bears to the Cold Country. We passed the burning water and the frozen water and the water that runs uphill. They gave me signs to show the guardians—" Setteo fell into the singsong delivery that always accompanied his more bizarre ramblings.

Eykar concentrated on massaging his aching thigh. How much longer, he wondered, could he last here with the fevers and the sudden, bitter fights that erupted among the confined men? And when he was gone, what would happen to Setteo?

"—this token for you." Setteo slipped something small into Eykar's free hand. It was a glazed clay game counter in the form of a house, one of Setteo's little hoard of meaningless treasures that he insisted came from his "Bears."

"What's this for, Setteo?"

"To pass you safely among the Blessed Ones," Setteo said. "When you go to speak to *her.*"

"Her? Who?" Eykar's pulse raced.

Rocking, Setteo crooned, "The runner of wilderness, the bringer of anger, Chief of the Blessed, Beloved of the Bears. You know her; and she knows you."

Eykar stared into the boy's filthy face, blinking hard in an involuntary effort to clear the occluded vision of his right eye. So Setteo did remember something about the meeting with Alldera. If he spoke of it to other men—but no one would understand him, or believe him if they did, would they?

"And you know," Eykar said grimly, "a great deal more than you should."

"I learn a lot," Setteo said placidly, "traveling in the Cold Country. Maybe you can come with me sometime."

Arjvall ducked out of the clay room, hunched in the rain like an old man. He moved close to Eykar, head lowered. "Sir—about Bavell, my friend. We—we're really close, a long time now." He chewed his lower lip. "We never had anything against fems, Bavell or me. We only talked rough so we wouldn't look soft, like Givard just now, he's still doing it; specially after what happened to Doverdo.''

"Doverdo?" Eykar said, fixing the name to the pointy-nosed young man to whom it belonged. "What are you talking about?"

"Oh, you mean they haven't—nobody's told you—"

"Told me what?" Arjvall's face showed that the boy regretted having spoken at all. "Where is Doverdo?"

Arjvall blinked anxiously at him for a moment, then said reluctantly, "Over here," and led Eykar to another curtained alcove across the slippery clay court. Inside, alone and still, the corpse of Doverdo lay on a black patch of muddy earth. He was on his back, naked and contorted, and his dead skin gleamed whiter than bone.

"There was no one to call me?" Eykar said.

"Lezandar said not to." Arjvall wiped his nose on his wrist.

Eykar squatted painfully beside the corpse. "Hold the corner of the curtain up so I can see—but Doverdo was all right yesterday! He was one of the strong ones."

In the pallid daylight he could discern a wad of rags jammed between the teeth of the dead man. He was looking at murder, not fever.

"Who did this? Was it Lezandar? Arjvall, who did this?"

"Some people," the lad said uneasily, sinking down beside him and gazing curiously into the dead man's face.

"For pity's sake, *why*?"

"Consorting," Arjvall whispered, "with the enemy. Telling our secrets."

Eykar said, "What secrets?"

Arjvall glanced furtively over his shoulder. "Well, nobody knows what he told them; that's what's so dangerous! Maybe the names of men who talk against the Witches and plan rebellion!"

"Ah," said Eykar. "All of us, you mean."

"And besides," Arjvall added, moving nearer and all but

whispering, "they say he had that stuff in payment, see, for sleeping with her—with Shania, you know her. Erl used to make her do that stupid dance somebody taught her, he thought it was funny."

"What stuff?"

"Food," Arjvall said. "He was hiding strips of dried ground-egg and some mushrooms. Well, where could he have gotten hold of anything like that? One of *them* must have given it to him. What would the bitches do that for, except in exchange for him trying to make a cub for them?"

Eykar's voice came out clotted with anger, a stranger's voice: "Someone saw this transaction?"

"Well, no, sir, but Shania's been seen watching him." He smiled a sickly, leering smile. "Doverdo always said all you had to do was sort of touch them right and cozy up a little, and they'd cave in, couldn't help themselves. Anyway, how else did he get hold of extra food?"

"Good question," Eykar said caustically. "Here's another: where did these unlikely lovers find the privacy to act on their impulse, and when? Or is it all rumor and a chance to hit out at somebody, with the food going to the accuser? Oh, hell, it's too late now. And I was sleeping!"

"Everyone has to rest," the boy said. "Anyway, he deserved to die alone."

"Because he slept with a fem."

"And for informing." Arjvall frowned. "Lezandar says you can't deal with them at all without being, you know, *tainted.* Look how Doverdo kept that food for himself. He didn't even offer some to Chigg Vargin, and they've been lovers since the Fall."

Eykar could not bring himself to ask whether it was Vargin who had accused Doverdo in the first place.

"Didn't anyone think about how the fems will view the fact that we've murdered—"

"It was an execution, sir," the boy protested.

"—murdered one of our own? A young man, capable of exactly what he was accused of doing?"

"Lezandar says *they* won't bother to look him over carefully. Who'd know he didn't die of fever?"

"Lezandar says!" Eykar ran his hand beneath Doverdo's neck and showed Arjvall his smeared palm. "Who bleeds to death from fever?"

"Nobody will know, not without a careful search," Arjvall insisted doggedly. Some fellows held him down and gagged him, and Lezandar cut him in certain places with really small cuts. He used a sharpened tooth from an old skull, pointed real fine. They're going to take away the gag and dump him out in the rain tonight. By the time the Witches see him, the blood will be all washed off. Nobody will know but us."

Unless someone tells. Arjvall did not say this, clearly did not even think it in connection with Eykar, fortunately. "Anyway, like you say, it's all over. It's nothing for you to trouble yourself over, sir."

"You think not, do you?" Eykar said savagely. "It's not enough that our conquerors destroy us at will, but we must murder each other over scraps of food and supposed treacheries?"

"They say that he confessed," Arjvall said with a hurt look. "What's it matter anyway? He's dead."

Eykar closed his eyes and pictured Lezandar's big-knuckled hands, so tender with Morz' corpse, inflicting secret, deadly wounds on Doverdo while others held the "traitor" down.

"There's the living to think of, people that can still be helped. Like Bavell. We were going to explore the Wild together someday," Arjvall went on, his voice already grieving, "me and Bavell. He'll die down here if you don't do something."

"What makes you think I can do anything that you or anyone else can't do?" Eykar snarled. "Go ask Lezandar to help you."

"You were Endtendant of Endpath." Arjvall looked away from him, at the rain falling outside Doverdo's death chamber. A muscle under his eye twitched. "You're the Man Who Killed His Father, the Oracle. You have to do something."

He began to cry.

Eykar clenched his fist around the token Setteo had given him. "I know I do. I know."

A Mating

The ceramic pipes leading from the boiler to the bathing tubs had been shattered by a great fall of fire-scorched stone, but Beyarra was glad to carry water bucket by steaming bucket. She wanted work to keep her hands busy, while her thoughts whirled with anxiety and eagerness.

What they were doing was wrong, of course. Everyone said wait. Alldera herself had said it. But young and vital men who should be good for siring cubs were sick and dying daily of the clay-pit fever. How long would *they* wait?

Today events had fallen into place so easily. The hand of Moonwoman could be seen in any harmonious pattern, that was what Fedeka always said. And Moonwoman would never encourage any truly wrong action.

Everyone was busy tearing great holes in the City walls so that the place could never again be fortified by enemies. Horses, men, and fems worked at four different points to pull stone down from stone. Now and again the paved floor of the old Games Hall basement would shudder underfoot as another section of wall crashed somewhere on the outskirts of the City. Even down here in the bathing rooms she got an occasional whiff of the dust the destruction raised.

In all that activity, who would miss Beyarra, a weak, useless Newly Freed, or her friend Tezza, another? Undependable, sulky, childish people who slipped away to gossip or explore the empty rooms of Lammintown without a thought for those who did real work; she knew what Free Fems said about the Newly Freed behind their backs. They said also that because Beyarra was the first bond fem to have joined the Free, she and her friend could get away with anything.

Maybe not this, though, when it became known. But the opportunity could not be passed up. Who would notice that one sickly man had been taken from the pits, to be secretly mated under the careful watch not only of sympathetic Free Fems but of three Riding Women?

Tezza pretended to be scalded by water splashed from Beyarra's bucket and jumped about yelping, but there was a nervous edge to her clowning.

"I don't know why we can't just dunk him in cold," she said, testing the tub water with her hand. "Isn't this hot enough?"

"He already has the cough. We don't want to kill him."

"Speak for yourself," Tezza said, rolling her small, sparkling eyes ferociously. "Anyway, lying down with me might stop his heart with pure terror."

Beyarra wiped her palms on her smock hem. When she thought about what they were doing, she was frightened for Tezza. She was frightened for herself. "It's only Bavell," she said quickly. "He was never bad with any of us in bed. And now—"

Tezza giggled. "Now he'll be so petrified, he probably won't be able to stand to it." She leaned over and stared at herself in the surface of the washwater. Her voice softened. "I've slept with him before, but he won't remember. I'm not pretty enough for them to notice; not like you, Be."

Beyarra patted her friend's plump arm. They had been

lovers as adolescents, but were since then best friends without the yearnings of sex. She wanted this mating to go well. "The manna will make it safe and easy."

Tezza glanced askance at her, biting her lip. "Why don't you take my place? You go first. I like that boy Givard better anyway—"

"Givard? That loudmouthed—"

"But he's nice-looking, you have to admit. And he smells good, well, when he's clean. I can wait; you take Bavell."

Beyarra emptied another steaming bucketful of water into the tub. "I can't. It's too soon for me, after—Paysha, and the others, and everything."

They were both silent, thinking about the impaled ones.

"You'll have to sometime, though," Tezza said in a subdued tone. "We have to start doing something between men and fems that isn't about killing and pain. Even Alldera says so; you told me that yourself."

"Yes. But I can't yet."

"Who's always saying we have to be strong and tough and everything, so the Free Fems will respect us?"

Beyarra said sheepishly, "Well, me, I guess. But that doesn't mean all the time, about everything. Nobody's strong all the time."

"Is that what Daya says?" Tezza said, putting on an exaggerated, languorous expression with fluttery eyelids. She didn't trust the pet fem and disapproved of Beyarra's affair with her. "Well, maybe I'm not so strong today. Maybe I want to put it off to another time."

"You can't! Too many people are involved. You can't just change your mind about something as serious as making a cub!"

"A 'child,' " Tezza said. "That's what the Mares say. Where are they anyway? Let's get this over with. What if someone sees our smoke and comes sniffing around? We should have him wash in cold water."

"Kenoma will warn us if anybody comes," Beyarra said. On cue, a faint, explosive sound echoed down to them from above, making them both giggle. Tezza mimed a huge sneeze that sent her doubled over and skidding backward across the room. Kenoma, left off the work roster because the dust of demolition made her sneeze until she wept, was standing lookout on an upper terrace of the building.

"Remember when Bavell ate blow-weed last summer and almost died sneezing?" Tezza said. "Who slipped the stuff into his food anyway? I don't remember."

"Charjodda, I think," Beyarra said, nervously folding and smoothing a large piece of faded toweling. "Because he took away that belt buckle she found in the north field that day."

Charjodda had died of cubbing fever months before the Free Fems had come. Tezza shivered, and Beyarra impulsively flung down the towel and hugged her.

The floor shook suddenly. As the vibrations died away they heard the lighter thud of footsteps near at hand. They both turned toward the ramp that led down from the floor above.

People were coming, their voices sounding over other diffuse and muffled sounds. Was there a man's voice among them? Beyarra nearly knocked the folded towel into the bath. This was going to be harder than she had thought.

The man, a skinny phantom dressed in fluttering brownish rags and bound with heavy rope, was hustled in with his feet barely touching the ground by the two Rois cousins. He writhed and made desperate, strangled sounds into his gag. They plunked him down on a bench across from the row of sunken tubs. He sagged back against the pitted wall and closed his eyes, breathing heavily through his nose.

Kenoma followed them in, with Tyn Chowmer. She had gone to the Mares for medicine against her sneezing fits. None of their remedies worked for her, but from her talks with them had come the idea of inviting some of the curious foreigners to the covert mating.

Kenoma dabbed at her reddened nose with a wipe rag. "Let's get his clothes off," she said.

Beyarra watched the young man as he was shaken with a series of choked coughs. Well as she knew him, she did not want to touch him. "Why not take the ropes off him and have him undress himself?"

Kenoma scowled and started to object, but Tyn Chowmer walked over to the prisoner and, pressing his shoulders forward and down with her elbow, began working at the knots that bound his hands behind his back. One of the Roises, Gayala by the blue beads around her neck, helped. The other strolled to the doorway and leaned there, cleaning her nails with her knife point.

Bavell did not struggle. His head, downy with new stubble after the close-shaving of Reprisal Day, bobbed dispiritedly as they tugged him this way and that, cursing the stubborn knots. If it had been, say, Lezandar there, Beyarra could have enjoyed seeing him brought so low. No, she would have been too frightened. Lezandar was a hard man, cruel and selfish, whom she could not imagine ever being truly subdued.

Bavell, who was moody but could be cajoled out of it, seemed merely pathetic. Even Tezza relaxed. She pranced around the tub, whistling a men's love song.

Tyn Chowmer and the Rois lifted Bavell to his feet and glanced questioningly at Kenoma. Kenoma sniffed angrily and said, "Take your clothes off, Muck."

Still gagged, Bavell whimpered and looked at her with stricken eyes.

"You heard her," Tezza said loudly. She stamped her foot on the tiled floor. "Do what she says!"

He did not look as if he recognized her—he was too terrified, perhaps—but he obeyed. He shed his rags into a little heap on the floor and stood shaking, his hands clamped in front of his genitals. His toes curled on the tiles. Beyarra had never noticed before how hairy he was all over, like a horse.

Ray Rois, at the door, kept looking him over from head to foot and shaking her head incredulously. Tezza now stood

quiet with a distant look on her face, her arms crossed over
her chest. She rubbed at her upper arms as if she were cold.

"You have to clean up," Beyarra said to Bavell. "Come
here and get into the water." She almost added, "We'll help
you." Here he was, and here they were, and why make it
nastier than it need be? He couldn't help what he was, could
he?

Gayala Rois had to catch his arm to keep him from falling,
and she kept her dark fingers clamped around his biceps as
he crossed the floor on stumbling feet. She wrinkled her
nose.

"I've tended sick horses that smelled better," she remarked. She stood staring in open curiosity as the young
man was hustled into the tub.

"Wash," Kenoma barked, slapping a pad of new-made
soap into his palm.

Beyarra pried the fingers of his other hand free from the
edge of the tub and curled them closed again on a washrag.
His skin was clammy. She was sorry for him and so handled
him gently. He lifted his head and stared blindly up at her,
his face grotesquely distorted by the gag, kept in place to
prevent biting or screaming. He seemed to be having trouble
breathing through the flattened passages of his nose, which
had been broken two years before in a fight.

She thought of Paysha, impaled, her gaping jaw dis-
located by the force with which her torturers had gagged her,
and her concern evaporated.

It was hard to stand here and think about Tezza's soft
body that Beyarra herself had hugged in friendship and plea-
sured in love, soon to be impaled on this hairy fellow's sex.
She wished she had never agreed to be part of this mating.

"I'll go up and get things ready," she said.

Tezza followed her partway up the ramp. "He's a coward," she said disgustedly.

"He's afraid we're going to cut his cock off," Beyarra
muttered. "After what happened on Reprisal Day—" She
shuddered violently and had to stop and lean against the pas-

sage wall. "We shaved off their hair and beards first that day. Maybe he thinks the bathing is like that; it comes before punishment."

"Oh, he doesn't have that much imagination," Tezza said. "And you have too much. What are you shaking for? I'm the one who's going to open my legs."

"Maybe you should be the one to drink the mannabeer, then, instead of him," Beyarra said, and Tezza giggled and said maybe that wasn't a bad idea; it would certainly be a change from the old ways.

The great Hall of Games was empty and silent, its roof partially collapsed onto the warped wooden flooring. They made a couch of old exercise mats in one of the small side rooms once used for storing equipment. The little chamber had a long ventilation slit in one wall. Nothing was left from the old days but some moldy netting which they fed into the fire.

They crouched by the flames. Tezza, her short legs folded under her, emptied a small pouch of grayish powder onto a flat tile. She stirred the substance back and forth with the edge of her knife.

"About half the dose they used to take, you think?" she said. "I don't want him thrashing around in some dream of battle from the Hero cycles. I could end up with a black eye I would have to explain to everybody with a ton of lies."

"You think the men remember any of those dream stories?" Beyarra said. "I don't think the younger ones do."

"Oh, it's the young ones who really tried to hang on to that old men's religion," Tezza said.

"How do you know?"

"The same way you should," Tezza chided. "Didn't you ever listen to what your masters said?" Her face grew serious. "They have to listen to us now."

She sighed and reached under her smock to rub slowly, almost absentmindedly at her nipples. Beyarra had a brief flash of the tingling lust that had once drawn the two of them together.

"The thing is," Tezza murmured, "it's not just—oh, greediness, or revenge or anything. Kastia says, if we wait for those Free Fems to say yes to matings, everybody will be all withered and dry, men and fems alike."

"I think you're very brave," Beyarra said.

"Well, if anybody does find out, you can get Alldera to make things easy on me. You would, wouldn't you?"

"I'd try. But we're not going to get caught, not until you show pregnant anyway. And you will, too. You had a cub once already, didn't you? After the Fall, I mean, when you were still in Lammintown."

Tezza blinked. "Yes. It was taken by Rozag."

"You said it hurt, a lot, birthing it. That's what I mean about being brave."

"Mmmm," Tezza said, rocking slowly on her heels. "Well, you sort of forget that part after. I keep thinking about—if he'd lived, my cub would be a proud young master, I mean ex-master now. So I guess he'd be with the prisoners in the pits. I don't know how I would feel about that.

"How will it be, when a fem knows which youngster is hers? Maybe it was better the old way. Just that part of it, I mean." She carefully put half the manna powder back into the pouch with her knife tip. "After all, think of the Man Who Killed His Father. Maybe it's better not to know." She glanced at Beyarra. "Does Alldera think of mating again with him, do you think?"

"Oh, I'm sure she doesn't!"

"Here they come," Tezza whispered, turning her head so that the firelight glittered on the ceramic cuff she wore on her ear. "See if you can get Kenoma to go back on watch, just in case. Somebody should stand guard, and I don't want her around anyway. She really hates them; she'll be thinking horrible thoughts the whole time."

The others came bustling in through the doorway, Bavell secured among them. The corners of his mouth looked raw around the gag. His back and chest were pink with scrubbing. His hair curled moistly on his chest and arms and legs, and clung in small, neat curls at the base of his belly around his fear-shriveled genitals.

Beyarra felt an unexpected tenderness toward him—he looked so skinny, so hunched, so hopeless—tempered by exasperation. Couldn't he see by now that they meant him no harm?

His escort pushed him to his hands and knees on the heap of bedding by the wall. Gayala Rois crouched beside him and let the point of her knife rest on his panting flank in warning. She murmured something in his ear and with her free hand lightly stroked his bare back from head to spine's end. He shuddered and made a whining sound through his nose.

"What are you doing?" Kenoma said sharply to the black Woman.

"We try to gentle the stud colt first," the Rois said, "for the safety of the girl he's to mate with."

Beyarra took the beer pot out of the ashes at the edge of the fire and tipped in the manna dose. Not having a proper whisk, she had brought a stick with its end chewed flat to mix with. She had seen men making mannabeer for themselves often enough to know how, but she was nervous. The stick, awkward in her fingers, slapped the mixture dangerously close to the rim of the cup. At this rate she might lose the whole dose in the ashes, and then what would they do?

"What are you burning in here?" Tyn Chowmer said, making a face. "It stinks!"

"Old rope," Tezza said. She laughed and began to undress. "I don't know if I can stand all this romance."

"Blindfold him first," Kenoma said, stepping between her and Bavell. "He doesn't get to look at you. We look at him as much as we like, but he doesn't get to look at you."

"Oh, let him look," Tezza said, stroking her own heavy breasts with comical affection. "He never looked at me before, just climbed on, slappety-slap, and climbed off again. It's supposed to be different now, isn't it?"

Beyarra leaned close to her and whispered shyly, "Let's

go in the next room, and I'll lie down with you and warm you a little.''

Kenoma said, ''No. I've brought some slippery stuff to use. This isn't love, it's only sex. She should do it cold, and think about people like Brita and Paysha while she does it too.''

''Hush, Kenoma,'' Tezza said, color staining her cheeks. ''You'll wilt Bavell for good, talking like that.''

Beyarra whimpered. She had not seen Brita flung from the City walls, but she had heard about it often. Maybe Bavell had helped to do it.

''Someone should be on watch,'' Tezza said. ''I don't want just anybody marching in here and finding me spiking with a man.''

''We're staying,'' the Rois by the door said.

Kenoma grunted. ''You just want to satisfy your curiosity.''

''Yes,'' the Rois answered readily, amusement softening her dark, angular face. ''I don't think it's going to be much, to tell you the truth. But when Sheel Torrinor finds out about this, she's going to be angry. Ever since that Paysha-fem was murdered, Sheel's been seething. If I have to fight with her about going against her wishes, it's going to be over more than just watching a man take a bath.''

Beyarra remembered how Sheel Torrinor had been held back by the other Women from riding in among the men and chopping them all down on Reprisal Day; because of Paysha, rumor had it. Correctly, it now seemed. Paysha, who had always had such terrible breath and that irritating voice? People were so strange! Had the Riding Woman actually bedded Paysha? she wondered. Ask Tezza later, she was a magnet for sexual gossip. Soon she would be the subject of the hottest gossip of all, if they weren't all very careful.

The beer pot sat round and warm in Beyarra's hands. The fumes of the mannabeer were already making her feel woozy and filling her mind with hazy images of people twined in each other's arms. She asked Kenoma to check the strength of the dose.

"I can't smell a thing, but the color looks right," Kenoma said. "What a joke! First we thin them out on Reprisal Day, then we give them their precious drug and sex too! Those of us who can bring ourselves to do it, that is." She grimaced. "I never could stand them, not their look nor their touch nor anything about them. 'Men to men and fems to fems,' that always made sense to me. I'll go back to keeping watch. I've seen men fuck before."

But she lingered, staring at Bavell. Gayala Rois, crooning and coaxing, had one hand between his legs and was working there. The top of his head was pressed against the wall as if that were all that held him up on all fours. His skin was shiny with sweat.

"Besides, if I saw him enjoying it," Kenoma added grimly, "I might just brain him with a brick before I thought about it. Maybe we shouldn't have come home until we had all stopped bleeding, and let the future take care of itself."

She blew her nose hootingly twice, wiped at her eyes, and left without a backward glance.

"Well, it's not much but it's up," the Rois said, still reaching under Bavell as if she were milking one of her mares.

"If he doesn't need it to get stiff, we can drink the beer ourselves," Tyn Chowmer said slyly. "After, I mean. To celebrate."

But as soon as they laid hands on him to turn him on his back he lost his erection and collapsed into a gibbering panic. So they pinched his nose shut and poured the brew down him. The knot in his throat jumped as he swallowed. Released from their hands again, he slumped on his side, panting and hiccuping.

"Oh, Moonmother," Tezza said suddenly, hugging her knees tight to her chest. "What if I get a male cub off him?"

Beyarra said quickly, "We need them too, everybody says so, Tezz."

"Sure," Tezza said with an anxious cackle of laughter. "Give me what's left of that drink."

"Wait, I'll find you a fresh cup," Beyarra said, but her friend grabbed the beer pot from her.

"I'm not squeamish," she said, and swigged down the rest of the contents, then tossed the cup against the wall with a muted crash. She licked her lips, belched mightily, and reached for a shallow, widemouthed jar that Kenoma had set near the fire.

Tezza scooped out a handful of milky grease. Bavell, staring with his neck craned, squirmed and moaned. Gayala Rois took a fresh grip on his wrists, looking intently into his face. The other Rois and Tyn Chowmer held his ankles.

Beyarra knelt close by, painfully aware of the heat in her groin. Not because of Bavell; because of Tezza, who, firelight gilding her skin, rubbed the lubricant between her own legs.

"Hold him tight," Tezza said, and crouching beside Bavell, she closed her oily hand on his shrinking penis. With a few swift, firm strokes she brought him quiveringly erect. She leaned close over him, her face gleaming.

"Be quick, boy," she said in a hoarse imitation of man's speech. "Answer the demands of your Senior!"

Bavell groaned and tossed, lashing his head backward and fluttering his eyelids. Beyarra thought they should have used thicker bedding. He might knock himself unconscious before he could perform. She bit her palm, stifling a nervous laugh.

Tezza threw one leg over Bavell's twitching body and lowered herself onto his nodding spike of flesh. He arched under her and made weak upward lunges with his hips. She set her hands on the floor on either side of him and rode slowly up and down on his red and swollen cock.

It seemed to Beyarra to take a very long time. Bavell writhed and whispered and hunched his body under his rider, whose face was now hidden by her swinging hair. Kenoma was right: sex between males and females was absurd and

disgusting. Beyarra looked away. But she could not shut out
the moist sounds of their contact and the strenuous rhythm of
their breaths.

The two Rois Women held Bavell firmly down, watching
closely. Tyn Chowmer, the only one whose face Beyarra
could see clearly, looked rather bored.

"What's wrong with him?" the Chowmer said at last,
shifting her grip on Bavell's ankle. "He's so slow!"

"It's the drug, I think," Beyarra ventured. "The men
sometimes used it to—to prolong things."

Tezza threw back her damp-streaked hair. "Soon," she
gasped. Her gaze was heavy-lidded and unfocused, and
Beyarra realized with a shock that her friend was coming to
climax: her nipples were engorged, and she was grinding
forward on the upstrokes to obtain pressure from Bavell's
body where she could feel it the most.

Sometimes in the past Tezza had spoken admirably of the
better-looking, younger masters. Sometimes she had come
back weeping and pale from the breeding rooms, but now it
came to Beyarra that maybe she had cried for being cheated
of the pleasure that she now took from Bavell.

Tezza stiffened, trying to conceal her own climax when it
came, but Beyarra knew the signs—the pursed lips and the
chin straining upward, the whole body trying to take off into
the air from the explosion of sensation below.

If the Riding Women noticed, they made no remark.

Tezza redoubled her efforts, and almost instantly Bavell
bucked and shouted, straining at the hands that held him, and
then collapsed, coughing and groaning and rolling his head
weakly from side to side.

Tezza sat where she was for a moment, chest pumping.
Then she pulled off and rolled away, and lay with her back to
the others. Beyarra wanted to go to her, but did not know
what to say. Her throat ached with tension.

It was Tyn Chowmer who pulled up one of the blankets
from the bedding and wrapped it around Tezza.

Beyarra sat by herself, gulping back tears. Why cry?

Tezza had learned to suck sweetness from the bitterest pit of bondage. Wasn't that a victory, like the victory of being able to lie down in lust and joy with other fems in spite of the brutalities with which the masters had infused the whole idea of sex?

"Just to see what it feels like," someone was saying.

Gayala Rois stood astride the loose-limbed body of Bavell, pulling at the tie of her leather trousers.

"You can't," Beyarra cried, jumping up and shaking her hands at the Riding Women, no no. They stared at her. "I mean," she stammered, "it's not—they're only good for one go at a time; isn't it like that with your horses?"

She was sick at the idea of these foreign people riding the lean boy themselves to satisfy their curiosity, or perhaps— even worse, somehow—their casual lust. They had no right. *They hadn't earned it.* Frightened but stubborn, she held Gayala Rois' gaze with her own.

The Rois shrugged and stepped away. "I thought maybe a young male was up for more than that."

Beyarra smiled apologetically. "Well, he's got that cough, and then with the drug and everything—"

For all she knew, Bavell, sunk blissfully in manna-dreams of whatever kind of lovemaking he favored, might well enjoy the Wild Woman's attentions even right after Tezza's. But the Women were not to know that, and Beyarra was not about to tell them.

"We'll take him back, then," the Rois said, "before he's missed. Come on, Tyn, what are you doing? There's nothing left in that beer pot."

When they had gone, Beyarra said, "Tezza, are you all right? Let me help you wash the smell of him off you."

Tezza nodded. "Then I'll help you clear up," she said matter-of-factly. But she sat in the tub of hot water and let her hands float, doing nothing as Beyarra gently soaped her down.

"He enjoyed it, didn't he?" Tezza said. "I'll never understand why we can't get what we need from them without giving them pleasure. I have to have a talk with Fedeka about Moonwoman's design of life.''

''She says it's all mechanics.''

''Oh, yes,'' Tezza said, yawning hugely. ''There is that. If he had flagged, I could have made him come. You just put something, your finger, anything, into them, you know, the way they do to each other with their cocks. They lose control and shoot off. Jodd taught me that.'' She gazed off into the distance looking sleepy and perplexed.

Beyarra scrubbed hard, until Tezza said ''Ouch!'' and pulled her arm away. ''Don't hurt me, Beyarra. You know I love you. But I kind of like them too, I can't help it. Mating will be harder for you because you have no feeling for them. But I'll help you, you know I will.''

That evening after suppertea, Alldera came to Beyarra and took her aside to walk along the old riverfront below the City wall. Beyarra was utterly tongue-tied by guilt in the presence of her hero.

Could Alldera know? Was there a scent of sex about Beyarra, or maybe it was the lingering odor of the manna? *Please let her not know!*

Moonwoman was not in a lenient mood that night.

''I've heard,'' the runner said, ''about what happened in the Games Hall today, Beyarra. Are men so attractive that you and your friends can't wait a little while longer?''

Beyarra's heart hammered painfully. ''We were just scared that Bavell might die of the cough before anyone gets any use out of him. Tezza was ripe and wanted to try. Nothing bad happened.''

Alldera sighed. ''I've already spoken to Tezza. She cried the whole time. I told her not to make such a fuss.''

Beyarra stumbled because she couldn't see the riverbank path clearly through her own tears.

Alldera went on, ''You're right, there's no harm done; or anyway nothing to compare with all the harm of the old ways and the old days. I would have preferred not to have any of the Riding Women involved. . . . The point is, I don't want it to happen again until we're all ready. And I don't want you or the others talking about this time, either. Do you understand? We said we'd wait."

"You Free Fems decided to wait," Beyarra said, appalled but unable to stop herself before the challenge was out.

"Yes," Alldera said. "We did. When Newly Freed come and liberate Free Fems, then you can take over these decisions."

Cheeks burning, Beyarra asked lowly, "Don't you ever think of doing it yourself? That man Eykar made a daughter with you. Maybe he could make another now, even if you are old—I mean older—than before, I mean." *Oh, Lady, still my foolish tongue!*

Alldera looked up at the stars. "Beyarra, I just want your word not to try again, with anyone, until we've all agreed that it's time. All right?"

Beyarra promised.

Bargains and Dispositions

In the Great Hall of the Hemaway Company Alldera walked between heaped goods scavenged from the City. Sunlight swept down through high, empty windows which darkened and lightened swiftly as clouds flowed across the sky.

She drew from a stack one of the thick, straight wooden bows of the men. "So far, only Kobba can even string these things. Their cast could be farther than that of our bows, in skilled hands."

Gayala Rois took another and held it up, sighting along an imaginary arrow. "But you couldn't use this from the saddle. It's too long."

"Right, but you wouldn't want to ride against a dozen men armed with these in rough country, where a person can outscramble a horse. A horse is a large target, even for a bad archer."

The Rois threw the bow down. "A horse is never a target, to a human being."

Emla snorted mockingly down her long nose. No one

bothered to argue for the humanity of men. Alldera, who had her period and felt cramped and irritable, missed Nenisi Conor badly just then. Nenisi was nearly as dark-skinned as the Rois and not as pretty, but she was mature enough not to take an idea into her head as stubbornly as a root grown into a split stone.

She said, "No point wasting the wood—have these staves broken in half. Someone will have a use for the bits."

"As firewood," the Rois said, eyeing the bows malevolently.

They all understood that whatever could not be taken along to Lammintown was to be destroyed, to make sure that neither weapons nor provisions would fall into enemy hands.

"Wasn't there a longer knife with these others?" Alldera asked, stopping before an array of blades. "Very worn, with a notch near the tip?"

Emla lowered her gaze and said in a lavishly humble tone that Alldera hated, "I took it, Alldera. I'm regrinding the blade. It's good metal. Why should it lie here unused?"

"Why should these weapons disappear, one by one?" asked Ila-Illea of the Newly Freed, whose bright glance darted hungrily everywhere. A hero of the City's fall through her nimble climb up the causeway ruins, she had a round, swarthy, good-humored face and a lively fascination with weaponry and fighting skills. "They belong to all of us."

"Does it bother you both," Alldera inquired ironically, "that such man-made things are valued more highly than weapons we make ourselves? Emla, bring something of yours here to replace what you've taken."

She turned away from Emla's sullen face and made for the doorway to the courtyard beyond. Spread on a large, rough table was gear for making arrows—blanks of flint, bone, Ancient glaze-stone pieces and odd metal bits for striking into points, bundles of horse sinew, color pots for cresting so a person could know an arrow's owner at a glance. Two

Newly Freed were supposed to be sorting and packing up the best of these items for transport to Lammintown.

Juya-Veree lay on her back on the ground, staring at the sky.

"What's wrong?" Alldera said, alarmed. "Are you sick?"

Kastia-Kai, sitting with her back against the courtyard wall and sunning her crippled arm, said, "Nothing's wrong with her."

"Juya?" Alldera knelt beside the young fem.

"She's fine," the older unslave said, not moving from her place. She had changed her horsehair braid for a new one, not glossy black but a more natural-looking brindled gray.

"I'm looking at the clouds," Juya-Veree murmured. "I used to watch them fly over us, but I could never just stop work to look."

"You're not out here to look at clouds," Alldera said.

Kastia-Kai got up with a pouting expression and began poking through the things on the table. Just loudly enough to be heard, she said, "My bad arm hurts me."

Everyone was listening and trying to look as if they weren't.

Alldera took a lighter tone. "Come on, Kastia, you're tougher than I am, and this is work that needs doing, work we do for ourselves."

"But it's the Free Fems who do the deciding, and the Newly Freed who do the work," Juya said, climbing lethargically to her feet.

Emla answered heatedly, "That's not true, and it's not fair! Some people are just lazy. They wouldn't do anything if they weren't pushed. I didn't risk my neck taking the City so other people could lie around looking at the sky."

Alldera said, "Emla, do you have any liniment for Kastia-Kai's arm? If not, some of Sheel Torrinor's horse medicines work well on people too."

She turned to the tattooed youngster and took her lightly by the elbow. "I'm asking you to be patient." Juya stood with downcast eyes but did not pull away. She was an attractive girl and had bloomed noticeably in freedom. "Will you try, as a favor to me?"

Juya-Veree nodded slowly and Alldera let her go.

"Spoiled and lazy," Emla hissed under her breath. "Elnoa the Green-eyed had her faults, but in her camp we worked. These unslaves are no good for anything no matter who commands them."

Ila-Illea shot her a burning look but kept quiet. Alldera was relieved. She tried always to check this kind of talk, rejecting divisions the little army could not afford. Ila-Illea had, she thought, leadership potential.

"The Newly Freed aren't used to their freedom yet," Alldera said placatingly. "We've had years to get used to ours."

The Rois raised her eyebrows. "Why would freedom need getting used to?"

"Gayala," Alldera said. "Don't start."

Someone called, and she turned back toward the Hemaway Hall with a little warning shiver of the skin. Daya stood under the sagging porch roof with four armed sentries. She wore another of her signal-flag blouses, this one made of two green Chester Company pennants joined together front and back.

"A Muck wants to see you, Alldera," she announced. "A very particular piece of muck, or he'd be dead bones for having opened his mouth."

Eykar Bek, of course; there was no other "particular" Muck. Trust Daya to wait until she had an audience. *Did she ever love me?* Alldera thought. "Bring him along, here, out of the wind. And Daya; stay, will you? There may be a tale in it."

Doggedly she tried to find ways to include Daya and confer approval on her in public. True to form, on Reprisal Day Daya had struck no blow against any man herself. She had claimed to be instructed by Moonwoman to remain an observer, in order to get an overall view of the event for her stories.

Daya's current bedmate, pretty Beyarra-Bey, had also only watched; but she was Newly Freed. Her timidity and squeamishness were excused. And unfair though it seemed, she had begun to fall away from Daya after that day. She was not with the pet fem now.

Daya, beautiful in her finery, added, "I had him cleaned up for you, Alldera."

"Thank you." Alldera stepped up onto the porch and seated herself on the sill of a low window. People gathered, watching. Just as well; Alldera didn't want to have dealings with any man except before witnesses, especially not this man.

He came into her thoughts sometimes as she had known him in the past, proud and determined. She puzzled over the difference between the mingled hatred and respect she had felt for him as he was then, and her nagging interest and curiosity about him now.

There were to be no special relationships with slaves; she had stated this rule herself, for them all. If only someone had survived among the Newly Freed whom Alldera had known in the old days! That would have made a difference, surely? As it was, though, the only person she had found in her homeland whom she knew from those times was this man. It seemed that the bond that this created in itself, apart from the peculiar quality of their relationship in that period of their shared youth, could not be abolished by a rule.

At least, she noted with relief, today her heart did not speed with anticipation as she braced herself to face him. Too much had happened. She could not help but think of the three impaled fems, and the bloody rage of Reprisal Day; and she knew he must be thinking of these things too.

The phalanx of guards fell back. Eykar stood with his hand on Setteo's shoulder, holding himself upright and composed. He looked spectrally thin and white.

Alldera fleetingly wondered how it would feel to touch

that pale skin (as Tezza had touched Bavell), not as his slave anymore but as—as what? The roles would be reversed, that was all. She was only thinking of him this way because of what had happened with Bavell.

She briskly asked the escort to stay by the door and not let anyone else enter the courtyard. Beckoned, the Endtendant drew nearer and she unexpectedly caught his fresh-scrubbed scent. She quaked with a spasm of memory and of anger. *I asked not to see him, I didn't want to speak with him again ever—but here he is.*

He was silent, waiting, as she had once waited upon his will. She shouted, "What do you want, Muck?"

He hesitated, nervously wetting his lips. A disappointing figure in others' view, no doubt: not very tall, not very muscular, not even whole. It was embarrassing to have shared even distant events with him.

"I asked a question," she said, calm now. It was only a slave, after all, one of many.

Setteo whispered, loudly enough for everyone to hear, "Answer, answer, they want to hear your answer!"

"I come as a witness," Eykar said. His voice had a rusty edge. "As you appointed me."

"You see?" said Setteo admiringly. "You have nothing to worry about. Nobody answers as well as you do."

Juya-Veree giggled behind her hand and whispered to Ila, who said something that made her laugh again, more loudly.

"Setteo," Eykar said over their noise, "go sit over there, in the sun. He may do that? His clothes are still damp from this morning's rain."

Should she allow him to speak to her this way, or to speak at all? The shifting overlays of past and unfolding present disoriented her. At her nod, the mad boy slipped out from under Eykar's arm and went to lean against the wall, absently fingering the ends of the leather lace that he had bound around his temples.

Eykar stood favoring his bad leg like a lamed horse. He said, in a flat, carefully unchallenging tone, "We are dying.

All of us will die if we don't have someplace dry to shelter in and untainted water to drink. If you want any of us to survive for your own purposes, you must act to keep us alive.''

She had forgotten that he was a formidable person in his own right—exactly the kind of forgetting that had doomed the masters of bond fems to their present defeat and degradation. There, that was better—antagonism roused her.

''Men used to cut out the tongues of fems who spoke up too boldly,'' she reminded him, ''or, in some cases, who spoke at all. Try to keep that in mind. Sit on that block, there.''

Was he feigning some of this debilitation, limping so obviously? That would have been beneath him in former days, but this was now. *Pay attention,* she told herself sternly; *judge, evaluate. Use mind, not emotion, the present and not the past.*

She began pacing back and forth on the porch, in front of a wooden door propped across a couple of barrels. A dozen recurved femmish bows had been set out there to dry, the wet weather having weakened them. Alldera picked one up and turned it in her hands.

''Maybe something can be done about your living conditions,'' she said. ''But I don't give gifts to men. Will you barter?''

She watched him think it through: that he had nothing of value, except the knowledge in his head. She could all but hear the turning of his mind: Is it safe to speak? What does she want me to say? How far can I go, in truth or lies or a mixture of both? How far must I go to win something worth having?

The mobile intelligence of his face was frozen in masklike stillness while he thought. She knew just what it felt like to have thoughts racing behind such a mask. She had been there before him every step of the way. All fems had, in every passage of speech with their masters in the old days. This thought carried a mixture of vengeful pleasure and a curl of pain.

"Don't waste my time," she said. "Information for favors or nothing for nothing. Have we a bargain? Good. We know from the Newly Freed that at least thirty children were born alive in the Holdfast since the Fall. Only a few have been found in 'Troi, Oldtown, or the City. Are the rest in Lammintown? In Bayo? Or hidden somewhere else?"

He sat mute. An impulse to strike him rocketed through her. But this was no time for impulse. Nothing was more stupid in a master than thoughtless, emotional reaction.

"Don't test me," she said softly into his continuing silence. "I want to know this, and I will find it out."

"If I don't tell, if I can't tell, what then—torture?"

"Anyone will say anything to end torture. We learned that under your rule. Where are those youngsters?"

He straightened his scarred leg cautiously. "Let me think."

She felt a strange lightness behind her eyes. Knowingly, she was sure, he spoke into their singular connection, his voice and words pitched to it.

"No thinking," she snapped. "Answer!"

He looked away. "Some children were killed in the early years after the Fall. The young men had just murdered most Seniors to take control of the Holdfast, confirming belief in the innate enmity of sires and sons. I think they were in no hurry to raise up new sons to challenge their own power.

"And there were raids, battles, sporadic fighting for years after. Those least able to fend for themselves were the very old and the very young."

Not a new story, or an unlikely one. So it had been among femmish slaves when the harvests had been bad or when epidemics had scythed through the Holdfast population.

He went on, "As far as I know, most of the youthful survivors came into the hands of Erl the Scrapper. He collected them, having the sense to see the importance of the young to the future, if there was to be a future."

"You were with him at that time?"

"Part of that time, yes," he said with a flash of the nicety she remembered as characteristic of him. "I know of my own certain knowledge that two boys died of a fever that swept the City a few years ago. Another of the survivors is Setteo, though he was already a few years old at the Fall. You might ask him about the others."

Now he looked at her directly, and Alldera heard discontented murmuring among the watchers. To them he must sound insolent. He had only fallen into his old manner with her, as if they were still alone together in the camper, quarreling and sparring on their way upriver as captives of their enemies.

But that was long since over and done with. She said sharply, "We don't need impudent men or old men, only young and biddable ones."

"How can any man forget," he answered, "after what is called Murder Day in the pits?"

She turned her face from him, her heart beating hard. This was becoming dangerous. *Don't push me into a corner from which, in front of witnesses like this, I can only lash out and do you damage—you already damaged man. Don't you know anything?* But something in her was traitorously glad that he was not totally broken, not utterly changed.

" 'Murder Day,' " she said, with deep disdain. "Every day we lived as your slaves was our 'Murder Day.' The day you mean we call 'Reprisal Day,' and so do you, if you want to stay alive. Your kind don't choose the names for things anymore."

He seemed to shrink into himself, silenced, and she felt not triumphant but deflated. "Tell me more about Setteo," she prompted.

"He was already odd," Eykar said, glancing over at the boy, "given to visions and trances, when he first came to me. Bright, though. He loved the old books. He pored over the pictures and learned the names of all the animals. But he fell into other hands and came back as you see him."

"Liar!" Daya broke in. "He lies in what he doesn't say.

Ask him about the DarkDreamer, ask about Servan D Layo!"

Alldera, her body thrumming with adrenaline, turned back to Eykar. "If you survived, and Erl the Scrapper survived, surely your friend the DarkDreamer still makes his clever way in this world. Where do we find him?"

Silence stretched and stretched. Then he said in a colorless voice, "If he is still alive, he will find you."

Daya's arched nostrils flared. "That's a threat!"

Alldera commanded silence with a chop of her hand. She leaned forward. "Do you know for a certainty that the Dark-Dreamer is alive?"

"No," Eykar admitted. "Some rubbish came drifting down the coast last spring. It was thought to be a sign of the existence of people living farther north. No one else went to see, so after a while Servan did. I've heard nothing of him since."

"He could be dead." She longed to believe it. "He didn't take you with him?"

"We had parted company some time before. He knew where to reach me if he wanted to."

And always had, she thought, with the eerie sensation of thinking the exact thought at precisely the same time that he thought it, and with much the same tone. She pictured D Layo and tried again to overlay that handsome young face with lines, to fade the glowing hair and thicken the lithe, strong body.

But nothing would dim the DarkDreamer's remembered smile or the lazy, predatory gleam of his eyes. His reckless imagination made him more of a threat, old or young, than the whole crowd of prisoners from the City could ever be.

Eykar cleared his throat and said diffidently, "I've answered what you've asked. In return, can some care be given to the survival of the men in the pits?"

She would teach D Layo's lover to bargain with her. "You won't be in the pits much longer. We leave for Lammintown in two days' time."

She watched this news register. "Many men are too sick to survive a forced march!"

"Then they won't survive."

Ashen-faced, Eykar rose to his feet. "May I rejoin the others? There may be preparations we can make among ourselves to lessen the hardship of the journey."

Suddenly exhausted and sick of the sight of him, she signaled the escort with a quick nod. At once they closed in around him and Setteo and took them both away. Daya, following, looked back over her shoulder with hot, bruised-looking eyes.

Alldera wondered if there ever would come the moment to tell Eykar that he had a daughter living free in the Grasslands—she willed Sorrel to be his daughter, not D Layo's—and how she would feel if she never told him.

And how she would feel if she did.

IV

VI

Night Sea

T he Blessed Ones were gambling, throwing marked stones and shouting around a fire on the beach. One of the Angels was there too, on foot and boisterous with beer.

Setteo sat on the sand massaging his ankles and watching the water. Of course the Angels were fascinated by the sea: it reminded them of where they had come from, the Cold World of mysteries which he suspected even the Bears couldn't rule completely. It was well known that dead men lay by the thousands beneath the waves at the promontory of Endpath, up north. If that was the proper place for them, why not for all dead beings? Setteo was sure he had heard them sometimes: troops of dead stumbling seaward under cover of night; not the sort of thing most people would notice.

He remembered the Angels staring at the ocean on the day they had all arrived, dismounting to touch it and taste it, exclaiming to each other, gaping and blinking. One had climbed up to stand on her horse's rump, straining to see over the vast expanse to a farther shore. Since then, at any hour of the day or night you might find two or three of them riding slowly along the water's edge, their heads always turned so that their eyes looked toward the eastern horizon.

Just this past afternoon he had glanced up at the broken old watchtower on the clifftop and seen a mounted Angel gazing seaward. It was no surprise that a bonfire on the beach at night would have at least one of the Angels in hearty attendance.

Setteo had his own understanding with the sea, which would grow greater if tended. Already, if he synchronized his heartbeat exactly with the beat of the tides, he could leave his body and walk out on the water to the broken line of ferry pylons that paralleled the coast.

Not that he could do that now, of course, under the eyes of the Blessed and their mentors. Playing at being small instead of great, they might forget serious things; such as that you must not disturb the body of a spirit traveler or the journeying soul could lose its home for good.

There were times when he considered such a fate attractive, as when Daya-Blessed found his hoards of power things and scattered or destroyed them in her cruel, smiling way. However, the glazed bits he had taken from the City kiln yards, thrown for augury, had repeatedly fallen in patterns telling him that dying into the Cold Country for good was not for him; not yet anyway.

He could smell the wind of the spirit lands sometimes, as it sought him here in the Warm World to remind him of these things. The Blessed never seemed to notice it because it didn't come for them. The Angels noticed, though. Setteo was sure that they sometimes saw the Bears and became agitated because of it.

That Angel drinking with the Blessed now, the dark one with a coarse face almost like a man's, see how she started and shivered, and reached for the beer jar out of turn. Setteo observed shrewdly, but stayed away from the Angels. The Bears had made them from the souls of the dead, and the secrets of the dead were all secrets of pain.

In-rolling waves gnashed at the pebbles offshore. Some-day he might learn the sea's speech, though he was not eager to. He suspected that much of what the sea had to tell was like the river's murmuring (he could decipher that some-times), being richest in stories of storm and ruin.

But there might be traces of vanished sea creatures, even fragments of their fabled songs. The thought of finding such treasure made him shiver ecstatically.

There went Daya-Blessed, leaving the convivial bonfire to meet two others walking down from the streets of Lam-mintown. She trailed ribbons of fitful light that he knew from experience to be thoughts of hers toward him, which would shortly materialize in a shout for his presence. He got up and followed her.

"No fires at night, you know the rules," the taller new-comer said. This was one of the Meek, referred to among themselves as Newly Freed or unslave, named Leeja. She was excessively long, lean, and graceless, and her humor could be dangerous when its object was male. Setteo kept well to the other side of Daya-Blessed from her.

Daya said piously, "The moon protects us."

"She protects best those who protect themselves," said Leeja, who now called herself "Leeja-Beda." No matter how much they changed their names, of course, the Bears could tell who was who, and so could Setteo.

"Old Roona is our watch captain tonight," the other sen-try said. This was Kastia-Kai, with a patched old Senior mantle slung from her shoulders and over her head, one end trailing down her back. "She's not as strict as Kobba—"

"She's a lot smarter, though," Leeja remarked. "But of course that's not saying much."

"—but if any men come roaring out of the Wild drawn by our fires, I don't want it to be on my watch."

"Go tell them to put that fire out, then," said Daya-Blessed, "if any of them are sober enough to hear you."

Leeja-Beda stalked over to the edge of the firelight and

stirred up a swirl of halfhearted protest and laughter with her presentation of this command.

"Alldera should be holding her council here tonight," Daya said, "on the open beach where the wisdom of Moonwoman could be felt. But they are all such great warriors, she and her near-and-dear, that they don't need the help of anyone, not even the Lady."

Kastia-Kai glanced aside at her, eyes gleaming under their crepey hoods. She said dryly, "Free Fems like to take credit for everything themselves. Unslaves fought the battle of the City too, if people could be bothered to remember."

Daya-Blessed nodded. "I remember. But some Free Fems have no respect for anyone who isn't covered in battle scars."

"We are all the daughters of Moonwoman," Kastia-Kai replied. "Isn't that what Fedeka says?"

"You and I are not allies, Kastia." Daya-Blessed brushed a smooth arc onto the beach sand with her footsole. "But we agree in more than you may think. I have my talents, and I know some secrets."

"Ah," Kastia-Kai said. "Secrets."

They stood quietly, thinking shimmering thoughts visible but undecipherable to Setteo. Then Daya-Blessed added in a still quieter voice, "Perhaps someone from among the Newly Freed—you, Leeja-Beda, or Ila-Illea—could command as well as Alldera can, or better—with Moonwoman's guidance. Alldera is strong-willed, a daring conqueror, but when the fighting is over, will she be the best one to lead?"

Kastia-Kai glanced sharply at her. "Are you against Alldera, then?"

"I didn't say anything against Alldera. I only spoke *for* the greater interest of all of us. And I spoke to *you*, Kastia-Kai, not to, say, those fools at the fire over there. I know a thoughtful person, a person with some long-range vision, when I see one."

"It is true," Kastia replied cautiously, pleating the folds of her mantle where it draped over her bad arm, "that I find some people's appetite for violence very—foreign, even mannish; and I wonder how well that will serve when the time comes to stop fighting and start building new ways to live here. Did you see how Kobba's face fell when she heard that Lammintown was empty, so there would be no battle?''

Daya smiled condescendingly. ''People's prayers and offerings are what caused Moonwoman to empty this place for us. I value Kobba's strong arm as much as anyone does, but I think she should be grateful to the Lady for Her favors.''

''Have you spoken to Fedeka about—leadership?''

''No, only to you.''

Kastia said, ''Here comes Leeja-Beda. I'll think about what you've said. It's never too early to consider the future.''

Who would not think over the words of a Blessed straight from the Cold Country? Setteo sniggered and managed to make it sound like a sneeze when Daya-Blessed glared at him. He created a paroxysm of snufflings and blowings, shaking his head in frantic apology and moving away from them so as not to spatter them with his imaginary snot.

As Leeja-Beda rejoined them Daya said, ''I'm not ready to sleep yet tonight; I'll walk with you.''

''What about him?'' Leeja-Beda tilted her long head in Setteo's direction. ''I like my enemies in front of me, not behind my back.''

Setteo made a quick bow and trotted on ahead, a position he preferred anyway: he could hear more clearly what they said to each other. The three behind him spoke about the proposed expedition to Bayo, raising the same questions being debated in Alldera's council: Who was to go? What of those of the Newly Freed who wanted to go but could not ride horseback? Should the Angels stay in Lammintown, or ride down to Bayo too?

Setteo knew something about this last, but of course no one asked him. He had wandered on recent nights with the horses, understanding better and better their chewing, stamping speech. They said that the Angels argued among themselves.

The freckled one called Garriday, who was very unhappy out of the Cold Country and longed for her home, feared to see the numbers of captive men grow. She proposed a bloody course, for which support had increased among her fellows since the dawn of the three Christs: that the Angels should rise one night, kill all the captives, and ride for home with a detour through Bayo to kill any men there as well, leaving the Blessed to cope as best they could.

The horses, on the whole, thought this a good idea but favored leaving a few men alive to serve as studs, firmly broken and bridled to the will of the Blessed.

While the sea, Setteo suspected, thought in perspectives too long to be of any coherence to a mere person, the horses had trouble seeing ahead at all. Their uneasiness in this new place made them try hard, in hopes of conjuring their own return to the wide prairies of their home; but they had no real knack for it.

Kastia-Kai said no one should go to Bayo at all: ''There's nothing there,'' she insisted. ''Why don't the Free Fems believe us? We Newly Freed would have heard if anyone survived in Bayo.''

Which was nonsense, but Daya-Blessed didn't say so, and it wasn't Setteo's place to comment. He walked quietly on ahead, over the sloping surface where the receding tide had hardened the sand underfoot.

The men of the post-Fall settlements had passed around more outright lies than dependable gossip, and had rarely taken fems with them on trading missions for fear of losing them one way or another. Thus there had been little opportunity for exchanges of good information. There could be giants or dinosaurs at Bayo, and no one in other parts of the Holdfast need necessarily have heard of it.

Setteo rather hoped for dinosaurs, whose terrific images he had hardly dared to look at even in the safety of the Library. Remote and exalted ancestors of the Bears them-

selves, they were ultimate creators of the Cold Country and
the Warm World alike.

"Setteo!" Daya-Blessed's voice took that whiplash
sound that always made him flinch. "What do the men say
about Bayo?"

Setteo turned to walk backward, facing her. He knew an
acceptable answer. "What men always say about everything, Blessed—nonsense and cursing and lies."

"How would he know?" Leeja-Beda mocked, pointing
her beaky nose at Setteo. "He spends all his time around
you, Daya, not with the men. He's not crazy, just mad for
you."

"Only crazy, thank you, Blessed," Setteo said brightly.
He knew himself to be saner than any of them, but knew too
the sort of thing they liked to hear from him.

"He is and he isn't," Daya said. She looked small, silhouetted against the star-sparkling sea, but Setteo was not
fooled. In any light, she cast the long, ominous shadow of
her true and perilous self—if you had the eyes to see it. He
could feel her gaze burning his skin. "He wanders among
the Mucks when they're out in work gangs, and sometimes
he hangs around the edges of the quarry. Everyone takes him
for granted, but his ears work very well; his brain too, sometimes.

"Come on, Setteo, be specific: *what* nonsense, what cursing, what lies?"

Setteo glanced up at the cliffs. Few lamps shone in the
windows of the stone houses of Lammintown. A Bear was
plainly visible slinking along the edges of the stone quarry,
where the men were penned, beyond the northern margins of
the streets. The hunger of the Bears was insatiable, and a few
cases of fever had followed the captives to Lammintown.

"Men say that there are Ferrymen in Bayo," he began
cautiously, "preparing to strike northward and rescue their
captive brothers. Or they say the Ferrymen have run away
into the swamps and left Bayo as empty as Lammintown."

Most of this he had heard in conversation between

Beyarra-Bey and her friend Tezza-Bey, or among the Blessed themselves. This didn't make it safe to repeat, but it was better than nothing. For someone who saw the Bears, what was safe anyway? To remind them that he was harmless, he managed to tangle his feet together and sit down hard on the damp sand.

They laughed, except for Daya-Blessed. She stood silently regarding him. He wished he could see her expression, though with the scars on her cheeks, sometimes it was difficult to read her face at all.

"Where are the others, Setteo?" she said with velvet menace. "The other cubs, the ones much younger than you. Are they in Bayo? I am asking you, boy: where are the children?"

He dug his fingers into the sand and stayed where he was. "They died as the Librarian said, back in the City. The Bears like small, tender souls very much."

"He doesn't know any more about that than we do," Kastia-Kai said scornfully. "What are 'bears'?"

"Something in his mind," Daya said. She knew better, of course, coming straight from the Cold Country herself.

"What about Rozag?" Leeja-Beda said suddenly, in a bleak tone very unlike her and so doubly worrisome.

"Everyone knows about Rozag the prophet," Setteo said, his heartbeat speeding with alarm. This was a touchy topic. Bavell had gotten his nose smashed in a fight over the affair of Rozag the prophet, more than a year after Rozag's death. "That was not so long ago."

"Oh, it was all a lie," Kastia said, "spread by the men to frighten us."

"No, it's true," Leeja-Beda said. "I know of three little ones who were given to Rozag, and they never came back again. Make the cutboy tell you what happened to them."

Instantly the atmosphere darkened and Bears began to shout from the rooftops of Lammintown. Setteo crawled to Daya's feet and crouched there, hunching his limbs tightly to make himself small, very small.

"Rozag the prophet," he gabbled, "had a vision and went through the Holdfast seizing all the youngest ones that he could find. He said they were evil demons foisted on us by angry ghosts, and that they would grow up to turn against their fathers as the young have always turned.

"But if these young were burned on the bones of the dead, Rozag said, the spirits of the dead would feed on them and would relent and become friendly (which tells you how much the Bears told *him*—nothing)! Then each of the fems would grow pregnant and split open when her time came, and birth not a dangerous cub but a fertile adult, male or female. The old Holdfast would be restored as it used to be, but better.

"There was a good harvest that year. Men were afraid to lose the little gain they had made, afraid of each other, and, as the old songs taught them, afraid of their own young. Many little ones were given to Rozag and his followers, who made a huge fire and burned them all. Then they themselves leaped into the flames, chanting and praying.

"Everyone was mad that year," he added softly. "Madder than I am today. It was because the Bears spoke in dreams, calling for souls to eat. One way or another, sometime or other, everyone hears the Bears."

Daya-Blessed slapped him hard enough to make him dizzy. He cowered, his arms locked over his head, but he could tell by the fading of the Bears' voices that the worst danger was passed.

"No bears," Daya said. "We're talking about children, missing children. Did any survive?"

"Maybe in the caves," he gasped. "In the Lammintown caves or under the docks of the City or in the mines at 'Troi."

"We've been to the mines and we've searched the caves." Daya-Blessed grabbed his ear and twisted it painfully. "Are they in Bayo? What will we find in Bayo, Setteo?"

He tilted his head to ease the pain but managed to keep his

hands down and not to touch her. If you touched them, they
might really hurt you, even if you were only a mad cutboy.

"Ask me tomorrow, Blessed," he begged, "and I'll tell
you."

"All right," she said, releasing him. "Go think up a very
good answer."

She threw a handful of stones after him as he hurried
away. Hidden among the rocks, he saw how they returned to
the quenched bonfire to collect the heavy-faced Angel who
slept beside the ashes, abandoned by her drinking companions. The two Newly Freed dragged this Angel, who belched
and cursed, away between them.

Daya-Blessed stayed behind alone. She turned to face the
sea and the sliver of moon floating above it. Rattling the
white pebbles that she carried tied at her belt, she spoke
softly to the sky. Setteo crept nearer.

"—loves me, but she doesn't. How could she, why would
she, when there are warriors for her to love? And the signs
are clear: she leaves me out of her councils. Mother Moon,
what can I do? She has no regard for me anymore. She just
pretends to honor me and my stories. I never had a strong
arm, so I trusted in cleverness, skills, and tales. But what are
words in a time when deeds mean everything? War is all—
and look what that did for Tua! And Jebekka, Rozbajja, and
others now, our own dead that we could so ill afford to lose!

"Alldera has no thought for the spirits of these poor dead,
or for You, Lady, who receive and care for them. She's so
puffed up with her victories, she preens in the adoration of
silly children like Beyarra. Only some of these Newly Freed
understand that not all distinction comes from the point of a
lance or an arrow or a knife. They respect me as Your ser-
vant. But most are dazzled by the exotic Riding Women and
the crude aggression of savages like Kobba.

"So many different people, so many interests and
desires—I wish we had stayed in the Grasslands! We were
happy there. I still love her, but now everything is different.

"I beg You, Lady, accomplish what I am too small to do

alone. Check Alldera's course, bring her low, if only for a short time. Make her pay for Tua's death, that she invited because of her jealousy of Tua and me. Anyway, she needs failure. If there were a cabal against her, I could rescue her and then she would return to me. I would remind her to beg Your aid and forgiveness and recognize the true source of all power, even hers. Then she would remember who she is and what she is, the same as all of us—Your daughter, Your humble child!''

She turned sharply and scanned the beach. Setteo huddled deeper into shadow, terrified that she had sensed his presence. But his shielding spell, taught him by the Bears, fooled her eye, for she turned away again.

''She is proud, proud, proud,'' Daya-Blessed chanted passionately, stamping on the rumpled sand with each repetition. ''She always was, from the day she came to Elnoa's camp! She doesn't recognize the value of softness, flexibility, imagination—the talents of slaves. She scoffs at your aid and inspiration. Only heroes matter to her.

''I am not a hero!'' she wailed. ''Mother, speak to me! Tell me what to do! War has changed her from loving me to mocking my weakness with lying praise. She smiles on others, even enemies of mine like Emla and Kenoma, because they flourish in war, while I shrink.''

She lowered her head, digging her fingers into her hair. ''I grow older, Mother, and my stories are nothing. Even to these young unslaves I am only a curiosity—an aging pet who was never brave and is no longer beautiful. Beyarra tires of me already and makes fun of me, giggling in corners with Tezza and sighing after Alldera. Who will love me?''

She paced and wept beside the sea. Watching from hiding, Setteo tried to unravel the meaning of what he had heard. At last, near dawn, he climbed into a shallow cave and, in precious privacy, he rocked and sang himself into the spirit land.

The Bears accepted gifts from him: fragments of dried

meat that he had stolen from the stores of the Blessed at enormous risk.

In return, the Bears showed him Bayo.

When he woke, he went to find Daya-Blessed and soothe her spirit; for the Blessed in anguish were doubly dangerous. Besides, her pain had touched him. He had wondered at times, himself, who might love him.

He told her what he had seen: huge footprints leading south from the City—those were the old laver ponds—and a loose weaving of gray cloth laid over them, the strands of which were the stone causeways that had once stood like a maze above the ponds. Down at the end, on a crescent-shaped mound of earth representing mud-brick Bayo, lay a heap of salty, sodden ashes.

The bones of a skeleton, headless and disarticulate, had been scattered over this rank bier. The figure of a Bear was engraved in coarse black lines on each and every bone. Setteo brought one of these bones back with him.

Daya-Blessed said the bone was nothing but a bleached stick he had picked up on the beach. She threw it away. Which was how the Blessed acted when they forgot their deep knowledge. As if what he had seen could be disposed of so simply!

Sometimes she embarrassed him.

A Fine of Horses

Alldera, blessed with an unexpected hour of solitude on a cloudy afternoon, ran through the streets of Lammintown. She no longer had the wind for real speed and her once-broken rib ached, but her footsoles were still tough. Even after years on horseback, she rejoiced to find that she could cover distance quickly on her own two feet.

Speed-trained specially by her first master, she had run his messages in the City. She thought of herself as she had been then, a compact figure full of self-importance and the joy of her own speed, but maintaining that edge of alertness necessary simply to survive.

In those days, any man might have struck her dead on a bet; or interfered with her errand for his own reasons, incidentally getting her punished by her master for failing in her duties; or thrown her down for a few moments' pain and ignominy on her part, guilty pleasure on his.

Here in Lammintown on a crisp, bright afternoon of the Free Fems' rule, no men lurked and all the ways were open to her without risk or penalty. She ran reveling in this marvel, in which she could still scarcely believe.

Gangs of men, driven by the Whips who oversaw them, had been through this tier of the town pulling up the cobbles and dragging them away on wooden flats, so that horses could tread securely down the curving avenue. Between the stained and dilapidated faces of the old company buildings, the packed earth was still dented where the paving stones had been embedded. She was careful how she set her feet.

Winning, winning, winning, the rhythm of her footstrikes ran: we win, we win, we have come home to *win*.

The underlying purpose of their return had still to be addressed, of course: the creation of a generation of freeborn fems. Nothing so blatant as the mating of Tezza-Bey (so far, without physical consequences) had happened since that troublesome event, but there were other signs of increasing restiveness about procreative use of the men.

The latest was a rumor of two of the older Free Fems douching with concoctions of local plants to try to restart their menses. All the Free needed was to have good riders and archers self-poisoned by such foolishness, and then have to deal with a surprise counterattack, or a mass escape of prisoners!

She ran a zigzag course down a broad street toward the sea, thinking about her own bloodchild, grown freer than the wind among the Riding Women's tents. Sorrel's existence made it difficult for Alldera to admonish others on the subject of having children.

And she understood well the longing for something fresh, innocent, and hopeful to arise from the welter of bloody struggle in which they had all been living; something around which all of their own differences could be centered and resolved.

And differences there were, like the dissonance developing between unslave Ila-Illea and a Free Fem named Soa. These two had known each other as kits, before Soa's escape to the Tea Camp. At first, they had fallen into each other's arms with tears of delight, but now a chill deepened between them.

Ila, though no youngster, had proven herself bold in the taking of the City; Soa had come away from that fight with nothing special to add to her self-song except some rather unoriginal brags which had in time grown to include previously omitted details. Ila-Illea was openly skeptical, Soa was hurt and insulted.

Why couldn't they just build on the victory of each other's survival, like old Roona and funny, skinny Leeja-Beda? These two had worked once together as slaves when Leeja had been just a child fresh from the pits anxiously taking instruction from her elder in the old dye works. They were now affectionate companions. Maybe the gap in their ages made it easier. Roona seemed to have a steadying, mellowing effect on Leeja's easily flammable nature.

The downhill run was hard on Alldera's no-longer-young knees. She checked her pace, panting, sweat chilling on her skin. Mother, how she had missed the flavor of this damp coastal air!

On the beach ahead, people were lined up to shoot with the rough practice bows that the Newly Freed were learning to make. Spotting the gleam of Roona's leather cap, Alldera walked out toward them. Maybe Roona would have some ideas on how the breach between Ila-Illea and Soa might be mended.

Wrapped in her thoughts, she was quite close before she sensed something wrong: the archers' faces showed more than the tension of concentration. She paused, caught in a cowardly hope that nobody had noticed her yet, so she might sidestep some fresh tide of trouble. But stemming such tides was part of her job. Cursing under her breath, she went on across the sand.

Sheel sat bareback on a red mare and looked down the line of shooters. Anything she could do beside the sea rather than inland she did there. She said the sea called more to her than even to the other Women because she had been raised beside the Great Salty River on the western edge of the Grasslands. Wide waters that were merely strange to other Riding Women reminded her of her childhood days.

At the moment, however, all of her attention was clearly on her students. She did not look pleased.

"You want to draw as you bring your bow down. And don't stick your hand to your jaw and stand there wobbling around or you'll kill some innocent passerby when you finally do shoot. Concentrate as you draw and then let go. Unlike most of what goes on around here, this is not about *control;* you have no control, and if you're really good you never will. You're trying to develop your shooter's instinct, if you have one."

The archers shuffled their feet and fiddled with their weapons, facing a driftwood balk set upright in the sand twenty paces away.

Tamansa-Nan stood nearby but not in their rank, twisting her slim hands together. Her bruised-looking eyes were fixed on Ellexa, who had stepped out of line and stood glaring at Sheel like a statue of righteous wrath. The Chief Whip often spent spare time trying to improve her archery.

"You think you can just go on as if nothing has happened?" Ellexa demanded. Old Roona grabbed at her arm but Ellexa thrust her aside. "You damned Mares think you can do whatever you like around here. Well, not this time!"

Alldera suppressed an urge to wade in yelling, scolding, and cursing them for yelling, scolding, and cursing each other on such a fine day. What a nagging old Matri they brought out in her!

"What's all the shouting about?" she said equably.

"Alldera!" Ellexa strode to meet her. She still limped from an injury taken in Oldtown, but held her statuesque body proudly upright. "You haven't heard? Tamansa-Nan says that Juya the Newly Freed is gone to the Grasslands with two Riding Women. Juya calls herself 'Veree' now, on the say-so of Sheel Torrinor. And she's pregnant. She was pregnant when unslaved, but kept it secret. This Woman got the secret out of her, and now she has stolen both dam and cub out from under our noses!''

Alldera kept her face impassive while her thoughts whirled. *Oh, Sheel, what have you allowed to happen, with your Riding Camp ways and your Torrinor pride?*

''Sheel?''

The blonde rider swung one sinewy leg over and sat side-saddle to face her. ''Juya asked me for a new name. I gave her one, and suggested that she go birth her child in a camp of Riding Women. So what? I thought everybody was free now. Whose permission should she have asked?''

Tamansa-Nan said, ''Juya would never have agreed to leave! I knew her, she was my friend. Look, these are her love knots still in my hair.'' She spread the curtain of her hair with both hands so that the ribbons in it gleamed like jewels.

''Juya is a fem, not a Mare,'' Ellexa said. ''Her child should be the first one born free in the new Holdfast, in *our* Holdfast.''

''Well,'' Sheel said, turning to the Chief Whip with a look of frank antagonism, ''now she'll be the first child born of a Newly Freed in the Grasslands. She'll grow up knowing how to ride a horse and shoot an arrow and cast a lance. And she'll have a famous companion in the first child born to a Free Fem ever, my sharedaughter Sorrel, to whose tent Margora Garriday has agreed to escort Juya-Veree. What's wrong with that?''

'' 'Veree,' '' Roona said, shaking her leather-capped head. ''What kind of name is that, 'Veree'?'' She kicked at the sand with her knotty old foot, scowling.

Sheel said, ''A person came to me for a name, and I gave one from my own line's history. In my country that makes me her sharemother, with rights in her unborn child.''

''You have no rights,'' Ellexa shouted, her handsome features distorted with fury. ''You are not in your land now!''

''Any land under my horse's hooves is my land. Are we target shooting here, or getting ready for a brawl?''

They glared at each other. Ellexa, head truculently raised and silver locks fluttering from the bright headband round her temples, was not some nervous unslave to be easily faced down. She wore an embroidered belt she had taken as a trophy from a dead man in the City, and Daya's war songs told of her courage.

An attack on Sheel by any fem, Free or Newly Freed, would be disastrous, its consequences unthinkable. Alldera opened her mouth to intervene, but Tamansa-Nan erupted, screaming, "Wild Witch!" She raised clawed hands at Sheel. "Juya wore my love ribbons, not yours! Her cub is our cub, a child of our old lives in our own country, not of your foreign, evil ways!"

She snatched a bow from the hands of the unslave nearest her and aimed an arrow at the Riding Woman. Everyone froze.

Alldera said with clenched calm, "You'll miss, Tamansa, and Sheel will kill you before you can set another arrow."

Sheel nodded, looking annoyed rather than frightened. "For one thing, you should have three or four more arrows ready in your bow hand—not a problem, if you're holding the bow loosely as I've shown you all about twenty times. For another, I'd better tell you that playing shoot-the-sun at home I put seven arrows in the air before the first one hit ground, and that was not long ago."

Tamansa-Nan's hands were shaking so badly she might loose her arrow by accident. If she hit Sheel or Sheel's horse—

"Put that weapon up!" Alldera snapped. "Do as I say, *now*."

Tamansa-Nan lowered the bow. The arrow dropped on the sand.

Sheel said, "And you'll want to put that ornament you're wearing in your other ear, if you're going to draw the string out that far. Then you'll need longer arrows too, but you'll find they don't drive as deep."

"We want to know the truth about Juya," Ellexa declared. She flung down her bow and tucked her thumbs under her trophy belt, arms belligerently akimbo.

"I told you," Sheel said. "She went because she wanted to go."

Ellexa said fiercely, "We all know how those black Women with you tried to mate with one of our captives. You people have no morals. You seduced Juya and bribed her to go away—"

Alldera cut her off. "Tamansa-Nan, lend me that bow if you're not going to use it." Ellexa, offended into silence, stared down her sculptured nose as Tamansa-Nan let Alldera take the weapon from her hands.

"Now, will you all let me speak?" Alldera drew an arrow from a quiver set upright in the sand. "You've timed Juya's departure well, Sheel. With half our strength gone to Bayo we can't risk sending anyone after your friends. Any more than we can afford quarrels among ourselves when there are still men unaccounted for."

"You and I measure risks differently," Sheel said primly.

Alldera felt transported into some wide-winged, sun-shot tent full of Women. She smiled despite herself.

"Sheel Torrinor, don't try to insult me. We know each other too long and too well for that. I don't like what you've done. I don't like the loss of one fighter from our ranks, or any from yours, or the horses they've taken with them. We're not so rich or so secure here that we even know what we can spare."

Sheel scratched her eyebrow with her thumbnail. "I think you're worried about word of your doings getting back to the Grasslands, for fear of what the camps of Women might decide to do about it."

Alldera laughed. "Then I don't need to worry for a very long time. Juya's child will see puberty before the camps of the Women come to a conclusion about us here."

Sheel's eyes met hers for a moment of ironic understanding. The few Riding Women who were disposed to decide things quickly were already here, with Sheel.

Ellexa turned her lofty stare on Alldera. "So we do nothing?"

"What we all should be doing," Alldera said, "is learning to use these weapons better." She raised the bow and shot quickly, loosing the arrow from her chest. The wooden target emitted a loud *thock,* and the arrow stood quivering in the central diamond marked on the wood. She found herself giving silent, heartfelt thanks to Moonwoman.

Sheel said, "Hold the bow more aslant across your body, you'll shoot better."

"Does it rest there, Alldera-Chief?" Ellexa insisted. "Some people may wonder just who you are chief of—us, or these Wild people!"

"Ellexa, I am chief of this army and whoever is part of it, as long as they follow me."

Tamansa-Nan boldly held out her hand and Alldera gave her back the bow, adding in a conciliatory tone, "Quarreling over Juya's—departure"—she had almost said defection— "won't help us. We must trust each other, or fumble our victory away in plottings and arguments."

Roona nodded sagely. "No joy without trust; it's an old saying."

Tamansa-Nan dropped to her knees on the sand and said huskily, "No fem, Free or Newly Freed, trusts anyone more than she trusts Alldera Conqueror. But I loved Juya, and she has been robbed away like a slave taken by a high-handed master."

Ellexa said, "We ask for justice, Alldera. If we don't bring justice with us, why did we come home at all?"

Alldera looked her in the eyes. "Do you know what justice is in the Holdfast these days, Ellexa? I don't, and I don't think you do, either. We need time to learn it, make it, test it. We can't create it by decree."

She turned to the others, searching each face for a moment and thinking with surprise that she had become very good at this sort of thing. Out of the corner of her eye she saw Tamansa-Nan get up and brush sand from her knees.

"For now," Alldera said firmly, "making rough judgments seems to be part of my work, and I do it. My judgment made Ellexa Chief Whip over all the labor gangs; I don't hear anyone challenging that, do I? Friends, your work right now is learning what Sheel Torrinor has to teach about the use of the bow. Tamansa-Nan, you're on cooking crew today, aren't you?"

"I was, until I heard about Juya."

"Meals are important too," Alldera said gently, "to people whose masters used to starve them."

Tamansa-Nan flushed, a bright spot on each cheek. She turned and strode back up the beach, each step an angry stamp in the sand.

Roona cleared her throat. "I've seen pictures of men of Ancient times shooting longer arrows, tucking the hand against the ear the way Ellexa was doing."

"Then they were shooting on foot," Sheel said.

"We're on foot too."

"Only until I can get you all on horseback. When her arrows are all shot, a foot archer is helpless. An archer on horseback can get away and fight again. How is your aim, Roona?"

Roona showed her gappy, yellow teeth. "The eyes still work." She closed her big-knuckled fingers firmly on arrow and string, and aiming at the sky, began her draw as the bow came down. Everyone watched, except Ellexa, who kept her angry eyes on Alldera.

Alldera turned and followed Tamansa-Nan. She remembered being ordered by her elders at Bayo to travel to 'Troi with two strange young masters. How angry she had felt then, commanded by everyone, consulted by no one—young and powerless.

Tamansa-Nan seemed to be a person of fixed ideas. Although she carried a knife now, she still wore bond-fem dress—smock, sandals, a grass hat in sun or rain—without any concession to the greater comfort and utility of Grassland clothing.

"It was brave of you," Alldera said when she caught up, "to face Sheel Torrinor with this charge. I wish you'd come to me first, though."

"Nobody knew where you were," the unslave said. She kept walking and would not look at Alldera.

"I'll find you and tell you myself how all this comes out."

Alldera returned to the lower streets and ran for another twenty minutes, caught in a rush of poignant memories. How would Juya-Veree feel, housed with her pregnancy in a Grassland tent, as Alldera had been housed years ago? But Juya was there not as a runaway slave but as Newly Freed and chosen kin to Sheel Torrinor. What future would that bring her?

In some ways Juya was no loss to the fems. She was one of those who complained often of being weary of war and chafing under the necessity of being always prepared to fight or to work. A gentle soul in harsh times, and a lazy one.

Everyone dreamed of easier times. Alldera did herself, when she was overwhelmed by judgments, assessments, plans, and worries. She worked as hard now as she ever had under the whips and curses of her masters. There was an old saying about the dangers of achieving one's desires.

When she circled back to the beach, only Sheel was there, sitting on the wooden balk that had served as a target. She was looking at her reflection in a polished metal plate as she trimmed the hair back from her forehead in a wide strip from ear to ear.

"I thought you'd be back sooner." Sheel tucked the dish away in a drawstring bag. "Borrowed from one of your unslaves, in return for riding lessons. She's off on my horse now, practicing; poor Redshine! Do you like this effect? I'm tired of hair sticking to my face all the time, thanks to your awful weather."

"Where have your shooters gone?"

"I sent them away. They weren't concentrating, someone was bound to get hurt. Those toy bows they make are no good in damp weather anyway. Oh, you know that old one with the cap? She's a pretty good shot, a natural, I think.''

Alldera said, ''Come with me; I don't want us to be over-heard.''

They climbed to the top of the only work building still standing on the beach. Inside, the lammin harvest had once been cooked in vast kettles in ceaseless heat and stench, tended by young men condemned to the work as punishment.

Stray drops of rain pattered on the disordered roof slates. Sheel kept her face turned toward the sea as they walked together. It was full Rainy Season in her country now. Alldera remembered the first time she had seen the Women moving camp to find the new, fresh grass, and the astonished joy and trembling aliveness she had felt. It was that time at the tents again, and here was Sheel Torrinor stuck in Lammintown, watching storms tumble over the bay.

''I notice,'' the blonde Woman said dryly, ''that you don't leap to raise them up anymore when they slobber on the earth in front of you.''

''Some things aren't worth fighting about.''

Rising up the cliff face behind them like crooked stairs, Lammintown looked cold and dead. Its windows were dark blanks in the pale limestone walls. From the higher rooftops, sentries watched the coast and the dark margin of the northern forests.

If only the Bayo expedition would return! If only someone would signal now, today, that she saw them riding back from the south. Little Beyarra had gone with them. Alldera missed her shy, sprightly presence, and her absence had not improved Daya's mood.

Sheel said, ''If not for the ruined things still standing out there—'pylons,' right?—I would never believe that anybody actually traveled on that water.''

''Sailed right across it in the old days, according to some songs and stories,'' Alldera said. ''Or were wrecked and drowned trying to.''

"Sounds like something they would try," Sheel observed. They skirted a gap where the roof slates had fallen in to expose smoke-blackened beams and hollow darkness. "You know what?" Sheel said, hugging her cloak around her shoulders. "I think this 'leadership' is bad for you."

"Who says so?" Alldera said, stung; she thought she had been doing pretty well. But of course Sheel was talking about the effect of command on the commander, not on those led. "Oh, probably," she conceded. "But wouldn't it be bad for anyone? And I don't know how else to do the job."

"Well, with so many people who aren't even related to each other," Sheel allowed, "I suppose someone has to keep order; like a chief on a far-distant raid for horses."

"After all this time, you still surprise me, Sheel."

"Is that supposed to be flattery?"

In the Grasslands being "surprising" meant being mutated from the norm of one's Motherline. It meant people thought you were odd, unpredictable, and possibly sterile as well.

Alldera sighed. "I meant to compliment you, yes. They say that Ancient leaders ruled nations of millions. Here I am trying to keep about a hundred people from each other's throats and barely managing. Now and then, knowing what I know now, I think a person could do a lot worse than have a man like Jonkendy or Diragondi for a master."

"I didn't hear that," Sheel said.

Alldera sighed. "No. And I didn't say it. But I'm just a jumped-up message-carrier, Sheel, and sometimes it all gives me a headache, so sometimes I think it. Sometimes I honestly wish somebody else was in charge of me and everything else." She rubbed at tension in the back of her neck. "I think a lot about bringing up newer, younger people to share the work—and take it over, one day."

Sheel cleared her throat. "Not too soon, I hope. Don't misunderstand me. For what it's worth, I think you carry your authority well."

"But?"

They had come around to the south side, where the roof was dramatically fractured and blackened by some long-past explosion. Sheel kicked a fragment of slate out of her way. "They make an idol of you, Free Fems and unslaves alike. Their worship and obedience is a rein by which they hold you. Someday they'll turn and lash you with that rein."

Alldera shrugged uneasily. "You said yourself, without leadership they're just a mob; anyway, who else wants the job? Kobba has already refused it."

"Grass that bends under an east wind will bend under wind from the west," Sheel warned. "You should have gone home with my friends and Juya-Veree. I wish I had gone with them myself."

So they came roundabout to the point, Grassland-style. "What Women left with her?"

"Margora Garriday and Ayana Maclaster. They've been threatening to go for a long time now. At least this way their retreat is of some use."

Alldera thought about the six remaining Riding Women. She would have accepted the loss of the exceptional marksmanship shared by the Rois cousins in exchange for a fading of the gossip about their part in Tezza-Bey's illicit mating. Too bad it wasn't the Roises who had left.

Sheel added, "These people might have stayed, if you'd let them ride to Bayo with your scouts."

"Bayo is femmish business," Alldera retorted, "our childhood home and horror, not yours. As Juya and her child are ours, not yours."

Sheel sniffed. "Don't be ungrateful. By sending Juya away I have removed her and her child from the reach of vengeful men."

"Most fems, Free or unslave, would take that as an insult to their ability to defend themselves. Sending Juya home was a mad thing to do, and you know it!"

Sheel turned the corners of her mouth down. "If you

don't like my arguments, let's get right to your judgment.
You're going there anyway.''

The humid wind twitched at Alldera's sweaty hair and
clothes. She thought of the cases she had seen argued in the
Chief Tents of the dry, bright Grasslands. Pride was cru-
cial—pride in one's Motherline, one's camp. Here, in a quiet
moment without witnesses, Sheel might bend.

''I am going to fine you some horses,'' she said, ''for
making a secret family around Juya's child, that you did not
have first claim on. Will you pay your fine, Sheel Torrinor?''

Sheel's eyes narrowed. ''How many horses?''

''I'll have to think about it.''

The Riding Woman turned and stared seaward again,
holding her cloak close at her neck. *You are not my leader,*
her posture said, *though others may take you for theirs.* Alldera said nothing. A judgment was a judgment, not an argument.

Finally Sheel said, ''I will pay. Because you said *'they'*
would take it as an insult, and you called the Grasslands
'home.' You still are part of us, you won't demand something crazy. I'll pay, and I'll settle it somehow with the others.''

''Good,'' Alldera said, greatly relieved. ''I'll see that the
payment horses go to the people who are most upset about
Juya's leaving.''

She thought suddenly, with wistful pleasure, of her own
daughter having a younger companion, a second child of the
Holdfast. She owed Sheel something for that; but best not to
muddy matters in the eyes of others.

''Tell me, Alldera-Chief,'' Sheel said, ''how much longer
will you stay here? It's colder already than Cool Season in
my childhood, when weather was really weather on the
plains. Your people love you and follow you, but they are
restless and raw. There was another fight last night, two unslaves quarreling with a Free Fem. One tried to use her

hatchet. Tyn Chowmer took it away from her, or there'd have been blood spilled.''

They had squabbled over a bit of the rope with which Alldera had dragged Gunder to death at Oldtown. She hoped Sheel didn't know that repulsive detail. She thought with a brief stab of vivid pain of the feud-death of her own heartmother Barvaran in the Grasslands, not long ago. ''People quarrel. All people, any people, anywhere. Even Riding Women, Sheel.''

''With hatchets?'' Sheel said. ''On my side of the mountains you used them as tools to cut tea, but here—'' She shook her head. ''The Holdfast makes people crazy. You'll be crazy too, in the end.''

''There's a lot to do here still.''

''How long will you stay?''

Alldera turned toward the northern cliffs hulking under their coat of black trees. ''Ask me that when everything is secured.''

''And if it can never be secured?'' the Riding Woman persisted. ''Will you never come home?'' Alldera turned to her, eyes suddenly brimming. But Sheel's frowning gaze was bent on the sea. ''I ask on behalf of the people of the camps who care for you—Nenisi Conor, Patarish Rois who always tells the tale of how she was your first raid captive; and of course our daughter, Sorrel.''

Alldera said, ''Why do you hate this place so much? You never suffered here.''

''It is full of ghosts,'' Sheel said softly. ''The wind blows and blows but can't blow them away. The only clean, free thing here is the sea. Don't you feel it yourself?''

Alldera rubbed her hands together for warmth, at a loss for words. She had never thought of Sheel as a person of spiritual sensitivity. Finally she said, ''I have no time for ghosts. The living claim all my time and energy.''

Sheel said, ''And some who should not be living. A man, a 'special' man, has been pointed out to me. They say he is Sorrel's father, an assertion I find particularly offensive and absurd: that crippled scrap of manhood! If I kill him for you, will you leave these people to their own desires and come home?''

Alldera's body clenched with shock. "Don't you lay a hand on Eykar Bek!"

"Do you care more about that man than you do about Juya-Veree and her baby?" Sheel inquired. "More than about Daya, who is so unhappy here, or that infatuated child Beyarra? Be careful, Alldera. I want no tragedies to take back to our sharedaughter, Sorrel. I want no shame to carry home with me to the tents of my mothers.''

The Oracle

The quarries at Lammintown were better quarters than the clay pits had been, for which Eykar was immeasurably thankful (and wasn't it amazing what a man could come to be grateful for?). Rainwater drained out of the rough-cut chambers through cracks and grooves, keeping the floors fairly dry. Great shafts of stone had been split out along the base of the walls, leaving overhangs under which men could shelter.

But tunneling was impossible and the fems had ground the upper walls clean of climbable pathways. There was only one way out of the quarries, and the fems controlled it.

Though the weather was colder in Lammintown than in the City, the incidence and severity of the coughing sickness had lessened. Bavell still had a tenacious case of it. Eykar sat and listened, for the tenth time or so, to his endless worrying over the thing that had happened to him in the City.

Head hanging, the boy said in a tragic tone, "If anyone finds out, I'm done for. Arjvall suspects something, and he hasn't talked to me for days."

To the others the lad had told a story of being taken away to be examined for his cough by femmish healers. Some might guess what had really happened, but no one seemed anxious to pursue it. If it were openly acknowledged that Bavell had been mated to a fem, then something drastic would have to be done in response. Their numbers were too few for that now.

"I thought things were mending between you and Arjvall," Eykar said.

Bavell endured a spasm of coughing. "But what if he finds out?" His eyes glistened. "It was wonderful, sir. I thought I'd die of it, it felt so—because of the drug. I mean, I thought it was Arjvall with me; it was him I saw. But it felt different, it was different—I must have known, I remember knowing! But I loved it. I almost cried when it was over."

He cried now, and coughed some more.

Eykar patted the boy's shoulder. "It's all right. Sooner or later they'll get around to some kind of mating system with all of us; it's what they've come for. When they do, we'll turn to men like you, who've found pleasure in lying with fems, to help us do the same, for our sanity's sake."

"I can't talk about it," Bavell moaned, rolling his forehead against his folded forearms. "How could I, ever? The lads would think I'd been turned femmish. They would murder me, like they killed Doverdo. And they'd be right."

Eykar remembered, with intense discomfort, his own distraught and ignorant fears at the time of his first sexual experience with a fem, years ago. How did he dare to advise this bewildered young man?

He wondered if it had really been as he remembered with Alldera, and if it would be different now, and what was the significance of his heightened alertness whenever he saw her. Was there a kind of magic involved, a subtler form of enslavement than that of yokes and prisons? Who was he to say there was not?

Sometimes he thought that musings about sex with Alldera were a ruse of his own mind to keep him from thinking about Servan instead. If he thought about Servan, the great knotted tumble of love and hatred and lust and loathing that enmeshed him with that foul and glorious man would draw Servan here to him, and all hell would truly break loose for everyone.

So, better to think about Alldera, with whom he had lain and yet survived. Better to imagine doing what he had been too frightened and furious at the time to do—to try the weight of her breast in the palm of his hand, to test with his lips and tongue the soft skin behind her ear at the point of the jaw or in the hollow of the elbow where the blood beat palpably and fast.

Now there was a fullness in his groin which Bavell would be sure to misinterpret if he noticed it. What was a man to do with his recalcitrant, ungovernable body? Didn't it count for anything that he was no lad anymore but an adult, and that body worn nearly to death by hard usage that should have reduced it to lumpish apathy? At least his own reaction had become tamer. He was vexed and bemused, but no longer fell into the paroxysms of rage against himself that he recalled from his younger days.

His unwanted erection vanished moments later when he was summoned up into the full sunshine of a brilliant morning. Setteo was attending on Daya somewhere and Bavell was too shaky to be depended on, so Bek went alone. He limped up the stone ramp with his heart thudding hard.

Maybe it's my turn now, he thought.

Leeja-Beda, a fem in leather, waited at the rim, impatiently watching his painful progress.

Where was Alldera? A foolish, craven thought. For all he knew, she had ordered this—whatever it was to be. Not sex, judging by the way this fem's mouth curled in disgust. They wanted young men to bed with anyway, not an old wreck like him.

What then? It could be anything. It could be death. He wanted to weep with anger that for all he had learned in his life, he must still stand here at the top of the quarry ramp trembling in a sweat of dread.

Leeja-Beda's dark eyes had an unfocused look that Eykar knew well: manna-glaze. Fear churned his guts. The drug had unpredictable effects, especially on the inexperienced.

She strode off ahead of him without a word, leading him down the switchbacks of the path to the north end of Lammintown beach. He hurried after her as fast as he could. They entered the forecourt of a once-handsome house on the seafront. In the sand-drowned garden stood a fountain in the form of a man diving into water, undamaged and beautiful. Hands now dead had made that, Eykar thought, perhaps as a love gift to the Senior who had kept this private residence for his favorites. He looked back despairingly at it as he entered the building.

The dank front room was piled with wood cut from the Wild, the fuel stock with which the fems made fires to warm themselves, fires to cook their food in greater abundance than any but the richest Senior men had had in the old days—fires with which to burn enemies? Men had burned fems as witches, once. He had seen it, he had smelled the stinking smoke.

Leeja drove him on with a palm thrust against his back. He stumbled, his lame leg throbbing, into an adjoining chamber where a small fire licked at three logs steepled together on the tiled floor. The walls were painted with erotic pictures—men stroking and sucking and mounting each other—which startled hot blood into his cheeks.

A half dozen fems were gathered here, among them several he knew from the City. One of the Wild Women, black-haired and almond-eyed and exotic, sat on the sill of the empty window and swung her booted foot against the wall in a slow rhythm. They all looked at him expectantly.

His curiosity was, in its usual reckless fashion, busy framing questions he dared not ask. But his body was well schooled in submission. He kept his gaze lowered and sat where he was directed.

Then he smelled again the sweetish odor of manna, and Leeja said, "We have questions for the Oracle." Hands forced him down, his bad leg folded painfully beneath him. A cup was pressed to his lips. He twisted his face away.

A manna-scented hand clamped his nostrils shut. Flooded with mingled horror, relief, and greed, he drank the drugged beer down in a gulping rush. Inwardly, he laughed. They were wasting their resources on him. Without D Layo's guidance the "Oracle" was worthless. The drug was a poison to his system and might well kill him at last, quickly and without fire.

Don't think of fire or fire will come.

The wall paintings swelled and receded like a billowing curtain. A persistent horn note (real or hallucinated?) blared in and out of his hearing with this motion, almost drowning out the shouted questions of the real people in the room.

They hit him. He was consumed in the conflagration of pain that burst from the old scar on his thigh (*don't think of fire!*). His croaking cries caromed off the painted walls in colored flashes so bright they made him blink. They'd all go deaf and blind in here together, and serve them right.

"What's happening to the scouts who went to Bayo?" someone said in his ear. "What will they find there?"

He couldn't get breath to answer because of the smoke from his burning leg. Then his attention was caught by the floor under his hand, the colored tiles still bright beneath soot and grime. Servan would have liked those colors. Servan as a boy had aspired to be a potter in the kiln yards of the City.

Drops splashed on the floor and muddied it, drops from his eyes. Bony fingers prodded his ribs. "Where are the Ferrymen? Will they come back?"

On the wall nearby, a man hugging another's rear to his lap turned his flushed, wide face toward Eykar and winked a slow, humorous, lascivious wink.

A sending from Servan, of course. Servan was more beautiful than this painted image, but that was a fair rendering of his broad, smooth face, his burnished hair, the sweet and cryptic curve of his lips. The wink meant that he was not dead (*of course not!*), but busy scheming somewhere. Eykar squinted, trying to see more clearly past the film over his bad eye, at the blazing beauty of Servan's face, his muscular body, the robust grace of his hands.

He heard metal grate against the floor tiles, and noted with displeasure the dirt ground into his own knuckles. And redness. Someone had stuck a knife point through the webbing between his fingers. Pain-fire coiled up his arm.

He tried to rise and run, choking on his own smoke. His head exploded and he flew into the blackness of death.

Still his leg ached and his hand throbbed. His throat was so dry he was sure he couldn't swallow his own spit without pain. Someone was standing by the—was he on a bed? There were no real beds in the quarries. He tried to open his eyes, but they felt crusted shut (there must have been fire—).

"Lie still," came a familiar, peremptory voice. "You're all right. One drink of manna isn't going to kill you now if it hasn't yet."

"Don't think they meant to kill," he whispered (feeling nothing in his throat, it was completely numb after all). "Wanted answers, prophecy—I used to do that. Didn't say anything, though."

"You are amazing," Alldera said after a moment. She sounded angry as well as incredulous. "How do you dare address me at all? Each time you do it I'm astonished all over again. Maybe next time I'll smash your teeth in for you, you arrogant Muck."

"*You* dared," he said, and a giggle escaped him, shocking, foolish, demeaning. "You spoke to me, positions reversed."

"Our positions are not reversed," she hissed. "I was your slave because I was weaker than you, that's all. You are my slave because your kind beat us and starved us and fucked us and worked us to death for generations. You're just paying what you owe."

He didn't have it in him to be frightened again so soon. "No argument," he muttered. "But I have paid."

Silence. Then she crouched beside the bed, warm and looming, and said very softly—he felt her breath heat his cheek—"Whoever you paid and however you paid, you didn't pay me, Eykar. I don't know that you ever can."

At once she was up and pacing again. "You're lucky to be alive right now, do you understand that?" His attention slid away from the razor edge of her words (*can't hold an edge,* he thought, and nearly giggled again). Her clothing rustled as she moved nearby, patterns of sound and motion uncannily familiar. He felt her looking at him. His hands remembered her hands, warm and blunt and strong, taking hold of his, pulling him up off the ground and onto his feet. He clenched his fists.

"Far from being heroically silent under the influence of manna," she said, "you complained mightily about life in the quarries. You don't like the food, the cold, the heavy work with inadequate tools, and the general squalor that surrounds you. Did you expect a sympathetic hearing from *us*?"

"It was manna talking through my mouth."

"Well, your mouth said things Leeja-Beda might have cut your throat for, if not for your connection with me. I warned you not to trade on that. Use your head, and stop making trouble for us both."

He licked his lips, dry tongue on dry surface. "Nothing to do with you. An Oracle can't speak if you've killed it."

The air was full of the quiet sound of her breathing, and someone else's low, untuneful humming. He didn't have to look to recognize a signature of Setteo's presence. Taken together, the sounds were soothing. He hoped Alldera wouldn't talk again and disturb the blessed quiet.

"They say that after the Fall, you traveled with the Dark-Dreamer," she said. "According to Leeja herself, men actually donated manna for D Layo to dose you with so he could interpret your ravings as prophecies. I've never heard anything so crazy or so stupid. You were always oversensitive to the drug, and still are, obviously. Were you so desperate after the Fall that you had to take such idiotic risks?''

He tried to look at her, couldn't, and started up, terrified, in the bed. ''I can't see!''

''Open the other eye.''

She was seated on a bank of rugs and cushions, her back against the wall of a plain, cold room; her room, he was sure, an upper chamber of Lammintown called ''Cliff's Eye.'' Her hands were busy at something—mending?

He remembered her sitting like that, near enough for him to feel warmth radiating from her smooth, tan skin, in the camper years ago. The two of them had been caged together, young, scared, snarling at each other as they were lugged the breadth of the Holdfast, almost, to meet his dreadful father.

She was better-looking now. Free life had made her flourish at an age which in the old days she would probably never have reached. The childish roundness of her face had gone, leaving her features sculpted into strong shapes. Her eyes were thoughtful under hooded lids and edged by sprays of fine lines.

Even threaded with gray, her hair looked much thicker and darker than he remembered. The length of it had been gathered into a single broad braid worn forward, over one shoulder, like a fat, glossy ribbon.

He had not touched her hair that other time, in the camper. He had been too terrified and furious to play games of sensuality then. Now it all was small and far away, that old, shameful moment; as if someone else had done it, and someone else had suffered it. So why did he feel water leaking from the corners of his eyes?

If she noticed his tears, she gave no sign. Her expression was sternly expectant. Casting hastily about, he recalled her query about the drug. He concentrated on speaking clearly.

''I didn't decide to be a prophet. Servan bought me from the Trukkers after the Fall of 'Troi. They knew I had sabotaged Maggomas' defenses, meant to kill me for it. Servan saved my life." He smiled. "My price was two fems and a 'boy,' in reality a grown man, skin scoured and greased to make it soft and young-looking. Typical of Servan, to cheat.

"By the time I knew what he had planned for me, I was drowned in the drug. Years recovering, after. If I ever did." He paused, seized by panicky disgust: *shouldn't have told, shouldn't have spoken to her.* In Setteo's hearing too.

"You don't look much like a man who's been spoiled and petted for his prophetic gifts," Alldera remarked. She frowned at the length of thread she was carefully drawing through cloth stretched on a wooden frame. The moving yarn made a small, arid sound.

"Oh, that's because I wasn't," he said with absurd casualness; but how else could this be spoken of? "Contrary. Sometimes, if the 'prophecy' was unwelcome or if something extra had been paid, Servan allowed a little rough handling of the famous Oracle. They did some damage, but I'm still here."

She froze for an instant (or was it his mind that froze?), the thread pulled taut, her eyes fixed on him. Then she took another stitch and said dryly, "Sounds like the masters I remember. Did you learn to enjoy their attentions?"

He couldn't answer, could only watch the movements of her busy hands.

Glaring suddenly at him, she blurted in a tone of revulsion, "I thought he was your lover!"

There; he was released. She had given vent to his feelings, so he need not. He answered lightly, "He was angry that I had refused Raff Maggomas' empire. He paid me back many times over for that. Many, many times. I let him. Didn't care."

One good thing about speaking of slavery to one who had been a slave: she didn't reproach him for the lack of brave gestures in his story. And she didn't press him for tasty details. *That's two good things,* he thought.

"How long did this go on?"

"Oh, years," he said with a loose wave of one hand. He

didn't want to calculate exactly. "Some of our divinations actually came about. Great reputation for a while. We were rich. In our heyday, I grew rather plump." He squinted along his stripped and scrawny length, draped in a faded quilt. "But Servan got bored and decided to go do something else."

She made a satirical sound, then swore and scowled at the thread, held taut from the canvas. "Where did this knot come from? All I did was pull it through." She fiddled with it, lips compressed. "More likely he was afraid the failed prophecies would catch up with you and he didn't want to be there for the reckoning. He had a strong streak of practicality, as I recall."

"He traded me to Erl's men for some old maps they'd found, and went off to look for—something or other. Without Servan my 'visions' were a mishmash. Erl let me alone after a while."

She licked the end of a new thread, flattened it, and worried it through the needle's eye. "So now Leeja-Beda and her friends decided to try. Maybe she hoped to use your 'gifts' to challenge Fedeka's moon worship, because Soa, who she used to love but now hates, has become one of Fedeka's fanatics. What is it with people anyway? Why must they complicate things?"

He didn't want to hear complaints about her own people that she would later regret having made in front of him. "What are you making?"

She held it up. Inside the circular frame she had stitched a whorl of black, gray, and earth-toned undulations and arrow shapes. "Beyarra-Bey showed me how to do this. She *says* it's relaxing. This will be a shield cover when it's done, for one of the Riding Women."

Witches from the Wild, he translated automatically. He wished he could take hold of her muscular hand and draw off some of her hardihood for himself.

She said, "That was prime manna from the Scrapper's

own stores that they dosed you with. What did it show you?''

As if in a dream he heard his own voice say calmly, ''I saw fems become monsters, as men were when we were your masters.''

''No,'' she said. ''We'll do it much better.''

Suddenly he was painfully, nervously alert. ''How?'' he said, hitching himself up on one elbow. ''You'll have the same blindnesses we did, you'll commit the same excesses. It's already happening. They took Bavell—''

''You're not going to tell me,'' she said coldly, ''that a fem riding a man to orgasm in a sweet drug dream is the same as a man raping a femmish slave at his whim?''

Dangerous ground; he tried to shift it. ''Do you know what lies are told in the daily tallies of men's deaths?''

She rose, set the sewing aside, and began to pace the room again. ''Early this morning Kobba took a man out of the quarries. He was given weapons to defend himself and died fighting, cut to pieces on the beach by four Newly Freed. It's not the first time something like this has happened, and it won't be the last. Is that what you're referring to?''

Who had it been this time? he wondered hopelessly.

She came closer, her lips set and bloodless. ''It's not murder on impulse, man-style. Fems who never dared speak up to a master must find the courage to strike a man, to wound him, to kill him in battle. People need to do it first in a situation that's safe for them, to know that they can do it.''

''But what about the younger men, the ones who could learn better than they've been taught—the ones there's some hope for—I try to change their thinking, but with this—this slaughter going on—''

''Don't whine,'' she snapped. ''The Endtendant of Endpath never whined.''

He cackled, half weeping at the same time. ''The Endtendant of Endpath was a brash boy, obsessed with his own 'high destiny.' How you must have laughed at me. You must still be laughing.''

She seated herself again, studying him. "Not at all. Your 'destiny' was high enough to save my people from Maggomas' disgusting plans."

"An accident. That was not my goal."

She sat forward, elbows on knees, pensive. "You know, early on, when I saw there was no risk you wouldn't take, I thought you might be a god." Her brows drew together. "Nonsense, of course. I wasn't a witch or a demon, and you weren't a deity. Eykar, don't expect me to be a god now. We're not about to shrug off ages of suffering, smile, forgive, and start fresh as if nothing had happened. Fems are human beings."

"You *were* human beings." He blinked up at her. "You're becoming vengeful criminals."

"If we are," she said, "then that's what you made us."

He winced, and kept trying: "Haven't you come back to be something else than our creation? Something new, something of your own not crippled by those old times?"

For a moment she looked away, her eyes wide and unfocused. "Yes," she said at last, a gusty exhalation, a sound that filled him with dread because it was a sound of defeat. "But that was before the dawn of the Impaled Ones by the river."

She blinked and shook her head impatiently. "No, even before that—I still think about Gunder sometimes, and that was at Oldtown. I remember how the rope juddered and yawed, yanking that *man* over the ground at my horse's heels, and how my muscles sang when I slammed my lance into the other one, his friend. I thought my heart would burst with joy. And you know exactly what I'm talking about."

"Yes." His forearms seemed to ring again with the blow, powered by rightful fury, that had killed Raff Maggomas on the terrace in 'Troi. They were both silent for a little, she leaning close enough to touch but not touching, he gripping the edge of his blanket with trembling fingers.

"I did want something else," she said, returning to this again because, he could see, it pained her, "something much cleaner and brighter. But Eykar, who can make a new, whole self without spending the ocean of old poisons first?'' She looked at him with bitter tenderness. ''It's only because of you that I ever hoped we could all do better together. But you're a sport, a freak among your own sex, or maybe just a man so far out ahead of his fellows that your existence is as good as meaningless.''

''You can't know that,'' he began, but she cut him off.

''I know what I learned from three dead fems spitted like chunks of meat at the City that morning.'' She sat back, her face set and impassive. ''And you're not going to tell me that the men in the quarry would behave with anything less than their old savagery toward us if they were free to. You're not going to offer me such a huge, glaring lie, are you?''

He bit his lip and was silent.

''Good. So you do understand that we will do whatever it takes to break you all, and we'll keep you broken for our freedom's sake and the freedom of our daughters after us.''

''But it's endless, then, with no forgiveness, ever!''

Her hand darted out too fast and too close to follow. He thought, *Now I'm dead.* Fingers pressed hard on his mouth. She spoke so softly that he had to strain to hear. ''I could kill you as you lie here, like this.''

Her hand closed in the warmth of his own breath against his face.

''No one would stop me, and no one would blame me,'' she murmured. She withdrew her hand, brushing his lips with tremulous fingers. ''We shouldn't talk about these things. When I think of the past I feel so much rage—you're lucky today. Other deaths have bled off a little of the impulse—Gunder's death, his friend's, all the deaths you charge me with. So I can put my hand on you and not draw your blood, every drop of which you owe to me and mine a thousand, thousand times over. Every drop, every single drop, Eykar.''

He closed his eyes and lay there shaking, listening to the small sounds as she resumed her needlework. When he could bear the quiet no longer, he broke it himself. "Why did you bring me here? What are you doing to me?"

"Whatever I please," she said. "It's my turn."

His limbs jerked convulsively beneath the quilt, moved by agony that had no physical cause. "Send me back," he begged. "Send me back to the quarries."

"You're not thinking," she said. "Even without knowing of our past connection the men won't trust you now. You've been too long here with me. I'll have to keep you close until we return to the City." A slight pause. "Then you can go back to living in the Library."

His eyes flew wide. "It's not—you didn't—"

"I had it sealed. Things there should be as you left them."

He threw his forearm over his face to cover his eyes. When he looked around himself again, only Setteo remained, still singing tunelessly to himself. The unfinished shield cover lay in a small heap on the couch, but Alldera had gone.

Bayo

Beyarra-Bey clung miserably to her saddle. She would never get used to this awful jouncing, legs spread apart as if for a monstrous man in the old breeding rooms, for hours on end. She envied those of the Newly Freed who took to this hideous mode of transport (so high off the ground, so far to fall). She envied the Free Fems who rode like Riding Women, and she wished there were Riding Women with them now.

How she had begged Kobba to be allowed to come! She had needed to get away from Daya's cruel moods and heartless mockery, increasingly bitter since that awful day when Daya had hit Tezza-Bey with her whip.

Of course there had been attractions too, in the idea of the ride to Bayo. Beyarra had wanted to see the infamous kit pits which she, born shortly before the Fall, had never known. Also, she had lost a game of pitch-pebble to Kenoma, who in matters of debt was not a very nice person and who had demanded her one precious belonging, her silver earring, in payment. All in all, a temporary absence from Lammintown had seemed like a very good idea.

And besides, at home Tezza had been pestering her. She wanted Beyarra to help her steal one of the younger men from the quarries, hide out up at the old shelter on the way to Endpath until they both were pregnant by him, and then return to Lammintown in triumph as mothers-to-be of the first freeborn children of the new Holdfast.

A mad plan, and directly counter to the promise Beyarra had made to Alldera. But everyone made mad plans in the face of wild conjectures; no one was immune. The unslaves said among themselves that the Free Fems were afraid to lie with males under any conditions and so kept putting off the moment for everyone.

"They don't really want us to have cubs," Tezza had complained (and she had not been the only one to do so), "because they're too old to do it."

Tides of rumor surged ceaselessly through the ranks of the unslaves. Some suspected a conspiracy between Alldera and the Riding Women to steal any new children for themselves. Hadn't Juya-Veree been sent off, pregnant, to the Mares' country?

Some whispered that Alldera and the Free Fems would ride away with the Wild Women if a force of men attacked, leaving the Newly Freed to face their vengeful masters alone. Even if they stayed to fight, wouldn't the Free Fems kill pregnant unslaves rather than risk them falling alive into men's hands?

Beyarra knew she would never make a name for herself as a fighter of men, like Ila-Illea, for example. What could a not-very-beautiful, not-very-talented, not-very-brave unslave do to be valued for more than her youth? So many others had greater claims to recognition.

She could present her child to Alldera as a proof of her faith in the Free Fems' goodwill, as a personal achievement, and as a gift of love and gratitude. So Beyarra was tempted by Tezza's plan; but reflection made her cautious. Some

Newly Freed looked forward to abandoning training they hoped never to use against men, and instead prove their worth in a more natural way. Beyarra shared this feeling, but something about becoming somehow a *dependent* again, even on account of pregnancy, repelled her.

Since Juya-Veree's departure Kastia-Kai and others talked about all but locking up pregnant fems to make sure that nothing happened to them or their cubs—their *children*.

And she had promised Alldera, after the mating of Bavell, not to get involved in anything secret like that again.

Nobody riding with Kobba talked about anything but reaching Bayo. Kobba didn't look at people with a glance that tried to measure how fertile they might be. She cared about toughness and nerve, purpose and resolve, now, in the present.

Beyarra shook her head, astonished at her own thoughts. It was amazing how many and complex reasons a person could have for doing or not doing a thing, once the slave's primary reason—because a master said so—was gone.

It hadn't been easy to arrange. Kobba hadn't wanted Beyarra-Bey to come on this hard, long ride down the coast.

"But I'll never get to see anything," Beyarra had complained, stroking Kobba's coarse, yellow hair. "We'll start mating, and I'll get pregnant and be kept close to make sure nothing bad happens to me. It will be like being penned up again by my masters."

And Kobba had shifted hard against her and muttered, "No fem will ever be penned again by anyone, not while I live."

"No, I know it," Beyarra had answered, abashed, and inflamed too by the surge of strength and heat in Kobba's long, supple torso and the startling softness of her breasts. If you had to sleep with someone to get something you wanted, it was much nicer if that person had an attractive body.

Since the occupation of Lammintown, Kobba's famous celibacy—based on her fabled loyalty to Great Elnoa of the Tea Camp—had crumbled. Now she changed her bed companions with brutal casualness. But she needed to be held, by someone, more than most people realized.

So she had let Beyarra-Bey come with her in the place of that fool Shanuay, who was flaunting her chestnut hair among the Riding Women these days. If anyone remembered how Kobba had claimed that gutless person as her own daughter, they kept quiet about it now. Kobba, having no better idea of how to be a ''mother'' than anybody else did, seemed willing to forget that moment and let Shanuay fend for herself.

Now, jouncing along hanging on with both hands and gritting her teeth, Beyarra-Bey wished she had let Shanuay—or anyone else—come instead.

An autumn storm hovered off the coast. Thick black clouds boiled slowly over the water and the wind gusted with a promise of violence. They had already ridden through one cloudburst that had horses and riders slipping about on wet earth and slimy leather respectively. Blinded by the downpour and in the rush to cover the arrow quivers she carried, Beyarra had dreaded being left behind. Who would notice the loss of one rider, and a terrible rider at that?

The only good thing about horses was that they stayed together, and so she was not lost. Her white mare plodded along, head bobbing like a ridiculous toy and sharp back shifting in an agonizing rhythm, between a brown horse in front and a black one behind. Ila-Illea's blotchy-colored mount, on Beyarra's right, looked as if it had a skin disease.

No horse could travel on the white horse's left because she defended that flank with flashing teeth even if not attacked, a quirk for which the creature had been named Fang. That was what passed for personality in a horse.

On the left now was the long pale beach, littered with rubbish cast up by the tide. Out at sea you could still distinguish several of the ferry pylons that paralleled the coast, though many had been washed away.

''How much farther, do you think?'' Beyarra-Bey asked, trying to sound hearty and eager.

Ila-Illea, a natural and enthusiastic rider as well as an intrepid warrior, laughed and flicked her lightly on the thigh with her rein ends (the things some people thought of as flirting!). "That's the sixth time you've asked in an hour. The answer is still, *soon*. The pylons are curving inland, which means Bayo Inlet is close by."

"Could—people at Bayo see us now, from there?" Beyarra said with a renewed gripping in her guts. For her, fear tended to mean loose bowels, and there was nothing more embarrassing than having to halt the entire group while you got off your horse to squat behind the marsh grass.

"Oh, there's nothing to fear," Ila-Illea said confidently. Her ragged black hair grew low on her forehead and close around her cheeks, framing the flash of her wide, white smile and the sparkle of her eyes. She had adopted the loose headwrap of the Riding Women and wore it with more dash than Beyarra-Bey would ever have suspected in her, when they were both slaves in the City.

No one believed that Bayo was still functioning after all these years: Rovers marching on watch in twos, men with whips driving fems to the milkery or the rendery or out to gather salt, or reeds and grass for weaving.

Such stories! But Roona had sworn to the truth of it all. She had never been allowed to eat waterweed, and had never even seen grain, in her bond-life. After the Fall, these foods had become staples for everyone.

Beyarra was born at a time when surviving fems were a rarity, to be worked and disciplined by their masters but not neglected or casually destroyed. She had thought of men as corrupt, selfish, and foolish rather than as monsters of cruelty.

Now men scrambled each day for the rations lowered on platforms into the quarries as soon as everyone was in his place to be counted—he or his corpse. Then up they came, a few at a time, to be driven to their tasks under the direction of the gang Whips, until it was time to go back down again.

They would have a bad time when this storm reached

Lammintown. Beyarra did not admit it even to Tezza, but sometimes she was sorry for them. She even missed beery Rab, with whom she had spent some pleasant evenings when he was relaxed by drink. He had never hit her, though he had occasionally threatened to.

"There," said Ila-Ilea, pointing. "That's the mouth of Bayo Inlet."

They all set their mounts to the tooth-jarring trot that Beyarra-Bey hated. Every time Fang swung slightly to one side or another to avoid the roughness of the marshy ground, Beyarra juddered along all atilt and desperately clinging to her saddle until the great, smelly, grunting beast swerved in the opposite direction and carried her jouncing at that angle instead.

Preoccupied with anxiety and discomfort, she wouldn't have seen even a ferryboat licking along toward them over the land. And there was a ferryboat.

What else could that dark, sloping hulk be, half in the water and half on land, its curved flank lifted to the sky? A horse might look like that, a gigantic horse dead and rotted with its ribs exposed.

Kobba declared a rest (praise Moonwoman!). She set two Free Fems to keep watch, lying on their bellies along the tops of the low dunes farther to landward. The others dismounted and walked up to the wreckage.

Beyarra-Bey just managed to slide down from the saddle without her numbed legs collapsing under. She hobbled along beside Kobba, clutching her rein ends and hoping Fang would follow but not so fast as to run her over.

"Looted," Kobba said. "See where the winch was, on the deck there? Nothing's left but the bolt holes." She stuck her head inside a huge gap in the hull and pointed where light filtered down through the broken decking. "Nothing left in here, either."

The smell inside reminded Beyarra-Bey of picking mushrooms under the City docks. She had found a bloated corpse there once, a suicide.

"Maybe fems from Bayo took all the metal?" she ventured.

Kobba grunted. "Men, more likely, but whoever did it, it was a long time ago. We'll camp here on the way back. Let's chop up some of this planking now and stack it. Maybe we'll risk a fire tonight."

Kobba wore the ears of men strung from her belt, shriveled dark things that were horrid to the touch. Some people preferred other trophies (some took none at all and frowned on the practice). Kobba said now that she would not give the men the satisfaction of thinking their miserable sexual equipment worthy of notice, although it was well known that she had in fact taken such prizes at first and boasted of it.

Her collarbones stood like knife hafts at the opening of her rain-darkened leather shirt. Her necklace of flattened iron nails—which in quiet times she worked on, pounding and grinding them into arrow points—gleamed. Anyone Kobba protected was as safe as could be.

They continued inland. Mounting Fang again was agony. The rule had been that no one could ride to Bayo who was not able to spend a day in the saddle and then do it again the next day, at any speed. So far, luckily, no speed had been required.

Ila-Illea began to sing an old song about Bayo. She had a strong, flat voice that made Beyarra wince.

"Flutes of the falling sun,
Voices of the dead and gone,
Sighing with the sea,
Promise of rest and ending,
Sing over my cublings.
Which of them comes from me,
Which sturdy kit,
Ears pricked to flute-voices?
Ask for no sending,
Best not to know.
Flute songs of Bayo

Men's songs, fly over us.
Voices of small ones
Murmur soft and low.''

Someone began another song about a slave who deliberately courted death at the hands of the Rovers after they had
murdered her lover.

Kobba raised her hand and the singing stopped. ''We're
here.''

No flutes piped in Bayo now. The silence carried only the
tide-wash in the narrow bay they had followed, and that just
when the freshets of wind veered off and left the air still.

''But where?'' Ila-Illea said, turning in her saddle, her
eyes squinted small beneath her dark brows. ''The waterway
is too narrow for a boat here. We must have passed Bayo.
It's gone!''

''No, there,'' Kobba said, pointing.

They approached a long, eroded mound. Beyarra dismounted to look at it more closely (and to get off the cursed
horse again). The surface was rough with fragments of masonry half-sunk back into the earth of which they had been
made.

''There's nothing,'' Emla cried bitterly. ''Thank the
Lady, Ellexa didn't come—she had hopes—but it's all broken down and destroyed, there's nothing left!''

''Better so,'' Kobba said.

They spread out, examining the ground. Now and then
someone would bend to pick up something, or just squat and
stare without touching. Ila-Illea took up a mashed straw san-
dal, flung it down again, and scrubbed her palm on the skirts
of her tunic. The wind carried snatches of low conversation
from fems conferring, kicking the grass aside, nodding,
pointing: that was the milkery, look, a fragment of glazed
pitcher; and that was the rendery, nothing left now.

Emla walked wildly about pulling at her dark hair with its
white streaks (left by some terrible Grassland suffering, people said). Ila trotted awkwardly after her, touching her gin-

gerly and pleading with her to be comforted. Discomfited by
such sorrow in someone she didn't much like, Beyarra-Bey
kept away from them both.

This was where the men slept, Kobba said, forbidden territory that no Bayo fem had ever seen. And that was the salt
warehouse, and this is where they stored our food, and
wasn't it here that marsh grass was woven?

Beyarra, finding the interest of such a barren place
quickly exhausted, watched the sky anxiously. The storm
must soon break. There was no shelter. The miles of causeways that had once joined Bayo and the City had been pulled
or had fallen down. At this end of that old system only stone
blocks remained, tumbled here and there amid the tall grass
that grew over everything.

"What's that?" Beyarra said suddenly, pointing at a
glimmer of white in a thicket at the west margin of the
mound.

"That's where the kit pits were." Kobba set off at a rapid
pace. Beyarra-Bey tried to follow, but Fang suddenly
balked, refusing to be led a step forward.

Beyarra pulled on the reins, breathless and frustrated,
until Ila-Illea, her round face lit with suppressed laughter,
came up and whacked Fang on the rump. The white mare
started forward with an indignant snort. Hot-faced, Beyarra
hurried ahead, ignoring the menacing thumping of Fang's
hooves on the earth just behind her.

Kobba stood by a pile of white sticks.

Beyarra bent closer. A pattern of dark cavities and ir-
regularities resolved into a skull's face, gaping from its
cushioning on a casual nest of—bones. She was looking at a
midden of bones.

"Well," Kobba said in an odd, hoarse voice, "the kit pits
used to be here. It seems they've been filled up."

Beyarra-Bey shivered so violently that her teeth clicked
together. "But who were all these people? So many! Were
the pits very deep?"

"Not so deep as the quarries of Lammintown," Kobba

said, her bitter smile quirked to one side by the newly healed scar down her cheek. "Who do you *think* they were? The sisters and daughters and mothers we hoped to find alive here."

The others looked and exclaimed, stooping to examine the grisly heap. Kobba set her jaw and was silent. In their deep, shadowed sockets her eyes gleamed.

Rain began to patter down on the bones and the grass. The horses pulled at their bits and flicked their ears nervously at the low growl of thunder over the sea. Everyone remounted and rode back to the beached ferry hulk and sheltered there. They had little to say to each other. Ila did the cooking, driving out the smells of damp and mold with good rich odors of stewed meat, pine nuts, and noodles.

Used to working in the kitchens of the City, Ila-Illea had lately shifted from refusing to do her old slave tasks to taking them up again with evident pleasure. She commandeered Emla's help, distracting her from the steady sobbing she had kept up all the way back from Bayo. Emla's black-lashed eyes, that normally darted and studied and missed nothing that her clever mind could turn to good use for herself, were reddened and blurred with tears. Beyarra-Bey was glad of Ila's presence.

They ate quietly, sitting close together and picking bits from the stew to feed to lovers and friends. It was a custom of the Free which Beyarra-Bey thought too tender and beautiful to indulge in lightly. Though she watched longingly as one would touch the lips of the other and then suck the shiny juices from her own fingers, she renewed her vow not to exchange nourishment with anyone until she found her own true love (who, she had reluctantly concluded, was not Daya, nor Kobba either).

After the meal, she sat with Kobba by the gap in the ferry's flank. There would be no hugging together tonight, and not much comfort; and moon's horns, how Beyarra's body ached from riding all this way!

"Might there be others, live fems," she said tentatively, "hiding in the marshes? Daya has a story about that."

Kobba snarled, "If she were here I would thrash her for her lies." Beyarra-Bey considered, with mixed feelings, the idea of Daya trying to argue a way past Kobba's anger. "No one," Kobba added, digging into the soft, rotten wood beside her with the point of her knife, "can live in the marshes, or Bayo would have emptied long ago. But you can go and look if you like, when we come back in drier weather and bury those poor bones. Or maybe we'll burn them, with men bound and burning in their midst. Or grind the bones to powder and stuff the men's mouths with it until they suffocate."

Beyarra said quickly, "I think the bones have been there a long time, maybe since before the Fall, even. Other people might have escaped since."

Kobba studied her for a silent moment, looking her up and down. Then she said, conversationally, "You'll be mating with men soon, a youngling like you. Mating, conceiving, and producing, if you have it in you to do that. Pray to Moonwoman that your children are all daughters. If you mean to be around me, better pray hard for that."

She turned again to look out at the slashing rain, and Beyarra-Bey looked too, and gaped, too breathless with shock to make a sound.

Two slight figures bent to the gap in the ferry wall, looking in: pale faces, eager and young. One of them said, "Strangers? Who are you?"

"Who are *you*?" Kobba cried, leaping to her feet.

Quickly the newcomers conferred. Then, "We are Bayo-born," one said. "And we want to know: will you take smoked meat and leather in trade for one of those big creatures that you ride?"

Strong Drink

T hey are the same."

"They are not." Sheel sat hunched in her saddle, her back to the wind. "Their hooves soften from moisture and spongy ground, and they're fat from this rich grass."

"Well, fewer horses colic now," the Rois said. She spat. The weather was colder and she had developed, like others among both Women and fems, a phlegmy cough. "Anyway, those are the same changes you'd see in a herd at home after a very long wet season."

"It's different. The sky is different, the earth is different, the water—" Sheel shook her head, thinking of how the sea stretched forever toward the east. Who could have imagined the sea! "The pregnant mares are too fat, too soon. Their foals will be hard birthing and become big horses. Big, fat, clumsy horses that need a lot to eat."

"Stronger and faster horses than the ones at home, maybe," Ray Rois said approvingly.

"Do you want to leave stronger and faster horses than

ours in the possession of these people?'' Sheel said. ''Some of these fems were the slaves of men less than a full season ago!''

''Oh, the Free Fems will keep the unslaves in line,'' Ray Rois said with a wet chuckle. ''They are getting good at bossing other people around, starting with those 'Dirts' of theirs.''

''And the missing men of this place? Who will keep them 'in line' when they come back?''

''I thought we were talking about horses,'' said the Rois, affectionately slapping the neck of her mount. ''And not everybody believes there are any men out there, certainly not men who can outride these fems.''

''Men are forked like us, even if they carry different equipment between their legs,'' Sheel said. ''A man could sit that horse of yours, if he was let.''

The Rois laughed. ''I don't believe they could ride at all, with that tender sex-flesh of theirs stuffed between them and a horse's backbone.''

''They'd manage, if it meant the difference between freedom and slavery,'' Sheel said. ''You could design a saddle with some kind of special pocket—''

The Rois scowled and stuck her lips out, looking seriously offended. ''No horse of mine would accept such a rider!''

''Oh, is that so? So what was it that carried away to exile the Ohayar Woman who treacherously murdered your ancestress Annaminay Rois? The Ohayar was an enemy of the Rois line, but a Rois horse, Downy, carried her out of your foremothers' reach.''

''Why are you yelling at me? I'm your friend.'' Ray began to cough in earnest, covering her mouth with her hand.

I yell because I dreamed of what the men stole from me. I dreamed of Paysha, freed to die, run onto a pole like a foal set to roast while she was still alive, Sheel thought. *I liked her, and she might have come to like me. I liked it that she led the fems up the south side of the City. I think about her,*

but she's dead, killed in horror by filthy, semihuman crea-
tures. Milk and welcome, how I hate this place and every-
thing in it, and sometimes my friends and relations too.

At least Ray Rois didn't swill hot beer every chance she
got like Tyn Chowmer. Tyn was so changed—in former
days, it would be Tyn Chowmer riding here with Sheel.
Today it was Ray, coughing almost as alarmingly as some of
the men did.

"You need some thorn-broth for your throat," Sheel said
roughly, ashamed of having snapped so. "But I have none
that I brought with me left, and I haven't seen any growing
in this mad place."

Ray wheezed, "I'm fine. Listen, there's a lot that makes
no sense to me, either. Here they are dropping the final 'a'
off their names because that 'a' was part of their slavery—"

"Except for Leeja-Beda," Sheel interjected, "who insists
on 'honoring' her slave years in her new name. Don't forget
her."

"Maybe, since it's her, it's all a joke, you think? Hey, I've
had some good laughs here, with everything else. I'll never
forget the sight of that little Tezza-Bey, bouncing on top of
that terrified man with her breasts flopping. I wish you'd see
how funny these people are!"

She laughed now, marveling. "Whatever the fems do,
there's always one that wants to do differently. Did you hear,
Fedeka wants the men to call them not 'master' but 'Hero'?
Only the word has to be different because 'Hero' is what the
men used to call their Rovers. So what do they do? Change
the last sound to 'a'! Now a man must call a fem 'Hera' if he
speaks to her! Does that make sense?"

"No," Sheel said glumly, "but Fedeka said Moonwoman
wants them to do it, so it doesn't have to make sense. What
makes least sense of all is having live men around to talk to
them at all."

"That's all about breeding," Ray said in that madden-
ingly knowing tone she had adopted about such matters
since the mating of Tezza-Bey. "Why are we heading

uphill? We're not going to find what we need on the headland. Anything that grows up there is all wind-twisted.''

"It would be the wrong wood anyway," Sheel said, "and any shoots we cut will rot instead of seasoning, in this damp. How could a person expect to find good arrow shafts in a country that's barely seen a bow until we came along?''

Ray Rois whistled. "Sheel, Sheel! You ride extra watches, you startle as if enemies lurk behind grass blades, you pick arguments with everybody—what's wrong with you?''

"This country is bad for me, that's all. I would give a lot for a piece of sweet, fresh cream cake from home. The milk the mares give here doesn't taste right, have you noticed?''

Ray looked down, fiddling as she rode with bright bits of plastic. She was knotting them into a woven strip of fabric she had looped around her knee.

"Let me say something you won't like to hear, Sheel Torrinor, as your relation and journey-mate. Some people feel that the badness you feel here, you brought with you in your own heart. Maybe you'll feel better when we leave the coast and go west again. Maybe not everybody should come to this 'sea.' ''

" 'Some people,' '' Sheel said savagely, "are stupider than rocks. It isn't the sea, it's the whole place. It's poisoned with suffering.''

"A place can't be bad, it's only a place," the Rois objected reasonably. "This isn't home, but it isn't bad.''

"You Roises are the most complacent—'' Sheel began hotly. "The land isn't even shaped right here. Men made it flat as water to grow more of their damned drug on it. Did you ever see such unnatural flatness in your life?''

"The salt flats on the lands of Steep Cloud Camp?''

"That's not like this, you know it's not! And here there's this great water at the land's edge, running under the land, maybe.''

"Does it?'' Ray looked startled. "I never heard that.''

"The Grasslands have curves and hollows like a woman's

body, one of your mothers', or your tent-sister's or your first
lover's smooth back. This—'' Sheel waved angrily at the
horizon. ''They smashed the life out of it and rolled it flat
like a sheet of stretched leather. Like something dead.''

''You worry too much,'' the Rois said soothingly. ''As
soon as Alldera's scouts return from that south-town, Bayo,
things will change. Nobody wants to winter here. And once
we get back to the City, we're halfway home. We won't stay
in the Holdfast forever.''

Maybe we should be, Sheel thought.

She drew rein near the ruined watch tower on the cliff
above Lammintown. All that was left was one roofless
room, its grassy floor littered with tumbled building stones.
There were no bones, for a wonder, but the place felt tingly
with ghosts. She watched her companion narrowly for a reaction, but the Rois, coughing again into her cupped hand,
apparently sensed nothing.

Sheel could not explain to this easy-minded youngster
what she had come to fear most: that they must somehow be
contaminated by the generations of bloody savagery soaked
into Holdfast soil. If a person could be infected by the angry
spirits of anyplace in the world, that place would be the
Holdfast. You wouldn't want to carry that back with you to
the Grasslands.

Better to die here, she thought, staring broodingly westward where the sun lowered. Although with no sharu to scatter your bones, your soul could never leap free into the night
sky, to camp forever with your ancestor mothers and the
spirit horses of the sun and moon. You would be cut off forever in an alien place, blown here and there on raw, rainy
winds.

I'm a fool, she thought, *to have come up here to this
ghost-infested place with such dark things on my mind. Bad
dreams and bad moods come to me with the ebb of my
menses. Old age beckons and laughs at me. I should be
home, among friends and family at such a time. I should be*

teaching my sharechildren how to be good Women, not riding blind and foolish in an alien place that hates me.

No, it's not me, it's this place! This bad land makes me a fool all the time.

"You look sad, Sheel Torrinor," Ray Rois said, peering at her with concern. "Maybe you and I should head west early."

"You're eager to go back there," Sheel said dourly. "You liked that 'City'?"

"There are a lot of things to find there if you're lucky." The Rois held up what she was making of the cloth strip, a bright glitter in her dusky fingers. "I gathered these colored pieces there, fragments of old things from before the Fall, maybe before that even. Say what you like about the Ancients, they made things to last! I'll sew this to my bridle, or make an armband of it and give it to my line sister when I see her."

More likely she was making the ornament as a love gift to that shameless Shanuay, who had managed to insinuate herself into the bedding of each of the Riding Women in turn, excepting only Sheel herself. This was not a subject that Sheel could bring up without losing her temper; better to keep silent.

Someone hailed them: "Sheel Torrinor! Rois cousin! Have you seen that Chowmer Woman?"

Three figures approached, two Women on horseback—Suasayan Tulun and the Salmowon, whose pale, too-delicate skin was wind-chapped and whose reddened nose dripped in damp weather, which here meant most of the time—and Tamansa-Nan, the dark-haired unslave who was Juya's friend, on foot. She always seemed to turn up when there was some trouble for the Riding Women, peering out accusingly from under her wild cloud of curls.

"Why would Tyn be out here?" Sheel said, directing her question to the Women as if the fem were not there.

Ayalees Salmowon said, "She had a headache and went wandering out of our tent last night. She hasn't come back."

Tamansa-Nan said guardedly, "I saw her drinking man-nabeer with some Newly Freed up here on the cliffs around moonrise."

Sheel swore. "Sharu bite my bones! This isn't the first I've heard of Riding Women poisoning their brains with that damned brew! What's the matter with everyone?"

But she knew. Mannabeer gave strange, rich dreams.

Echoing her thought, Ray Rois murmured, "They told me I might meet their Moonwoman in the fog of this man-nabeer, but all I saw were three sharu gambling with a Woman's knucklebones."

Sheel said, "Who of us saw Tyn Chowmer last?"

"Gayala Rois saw her," the Tulun said. "She's gone looking for her."

Sheel said, "We'll look too."

Why did her heart knock so hard with alarm? Tyn Chowmer was a tough and seasoned raider who might spend time alone if she felt like it. Grumbling bitterly over the ner-vous chatter of her own fearful thoughts, Sheel rode with Ray Rois west down the cliffs' backslope toward the drifting horse herds.

"I've said a hundred times, I don't sleep soundly knowing that living men are guarded by fems who drink that stuff. But I never thought I'd be traveling with Women, true Women of the Grassland camps, who would rot their minds with it!"

"Tyn said you had some yourself, Sheel Torriner. What did you see when you drank it?"

"The Grasslands, whole and entire from end to end," Sheel said after a moment. "I felt I was floating in the sky, like a dead person's spirit. I haven't drunk any since. Tyn!" she shouted. "Answer me!"

They found the Chowmer near noon. She lay by a stream beyond the grazing herd.

"Drowned," said Tamansa-Nan, kneeling lithely beside the dead Woman. "It looks like she tried to drink and passed out with her face in the water."

Sheel dismounted. No one spoke as she swiftly stripped the corpse and ran her hands over its cold and doughy skin, that she had known warm and comforting, and every scar and mole of which she recognized. She searched for wounds and for bruises other than the discolored patches where the blood had settled under the skin of the Chowmer's face and front.

But there was nothing. The unslave was right: Tyn Chowmer had gotten drunk and disoriented with mannabeer and had drowned in a brook.

They brought the body down a narrow cliff path to Lammintown, riding close together and ignoring the fems who turned from their own business to watch with wondering eyes. Gayala Rois rode to meet them, and all proceeded together toward the tents of the Lammintown camp, which were pitched in a grassy swale south of the town near the lower stretch of beach.

Tamansa-Nan walked behind them. Her face was unreadable. She was probably glad of the death of a Riding Woman in payment for the loss of Juya-Veree.

At their own tent the pale Salmowon, who was the dead Woman's closest kin here, embraced Sheel. This showed she thought no blame attached to Sheel for the Chowmer's death, although Sheel was the leader of their "raid."

They took the corpse inside. With effort they disposed Tyn Chowmer's heavy body decently on a horsehair blanket and sat discussing what to do. Curses and cries were all that rose to Sheel's lips. It seemed likely to her that this thing had happened because she had sent Juya-Veree away, pregnant, into the Grasslands. Some horrible balance that she did not understand was being demonstrated: two femmish lives required one dead Woman in exchange. The ratio seemed just to her.

If she spoke of this, they would think she was crazy. Probably she was. She kept silent and gnawed on her grief and her guilt and her loss.

Near dusk a fem came walking from Lammintown and sat down in the lightless tent across from Sheel.

"We feel your loss, as cousins of your lines," she said formally. It was Alldera. "People have asked me to come tell you that. Will you leave it to me to attend to the unslaves who were drinking with our cousin Tyn Chowmer, and who perhaps might have prevented this from happening?"

"Do as you like," Sheel said. A gulf had opened around her where the Motherline of the dead Woman had previously traveled with them, and a raw, hurtful space where Tyn herself should be.

"Don't strangle your grief, Sheel. Tears heal, if anything can, and we all need to see them. My people are grown harder than stone as it is."

"Are they?" Sheel jerked her chin in the direction of the shrouded body. "Tyn was sleeping with that unslave Shanuay. She said the fem cried in her sleep every night."

"We all cry secretly in our sleep," Alldera said. "No one wants to think of herself as a merciless killer. We didn't come here to swarm over everything in our path like hungry sharu."

"Don't talk about things you don't understand," Sheel grated. "The things of my country are not the things of yours."

Alldera said, "I'm sorry, Sheel. I wouldn't have any Woman of the camps swallowed up by this angry old homeland of mine, least of all a lover and comrade of yours—"

"And companion of your bloodchild on her maiden raid."

"That too." Alldera sighed. "Now do you understand? We slipped out of the Grasslands as secretly as we could because we hoped no Women would follow."

"You knew *I* would follow."

"I knew you would want to," Alldera said. "I hoped others would stop you. I wish they had." She touched Sheel's knee very lightly and added, "I don't drink beer myself. Not since a time in the Tea Camp when I was feeling sorry for myself and began to drink in earnest. If I hadn't gone to Fedeka, I might well have died of drink. I might have died as Tyn Chowmer has died.''

"What can I say to you?" Sheel ached for one of her own blood, another Torrinor, to speak with.

"Say what's in your heart.''

Sheel could not deny Alldera's right to ask this. Alldera had spoken her own feelings when Sheel's heartmother, Jesselee Morrowtrow, had died, and before that their sharemother in Sorrel's family, Barvaran.

"It is in my heart,'' Sheel answered hoarsely, "that while I loafed in my saddle thinking about how I might die in this country, another Woman did die here. Maybe she died my death.''

After a shocked silence, Alldera expostulated, "This is sick and foolish talk, Sheel, not the talk of a Torrinor Woman! Don't let the sea air turn your mind soft and make you unfit to go home.''

"Alldera Holdfaster,'' Sheel said, "don't you say 'home' to me, as if we shared one. I thought we did, but I was wrong. Holdfaster you were and Holdfaster you are, you and all your tribe. You know nothing of any consequence to me or mine. Go back among your own kind.''

"I will,'' Alldera said. She sounded not angry but very tired. "And you may do the same, soon, I hope. When our patrol to Bayo gets back—''

"What if they don't return? It could happen.'' Sheel jabbed her forefinger at the shrouded corpse. "There are Women in the Grasslands who have been expecting Tyn Chowmer's return any day now, but they will never see her again.''

Alldera said steadily, "Here's a lesson you can learn from me if you care to, Sheel: no matter how much pain you feel, the truth is that Tyn Chowmer came here with you because she chose to, just as the Free Fems chose to follow me. And then she chose to drink beer with manna in it until she couldn't walk straight. The fault, if there was one, isn't yours. Leave your friend the dignity of her own choices, such as it is.''

Alldera got up and left.

That night Sheel and the others watched by the body, singing what they knew of the Chowmer's self-song and telling tales of her life and doings as they had known her. In the morning Sheel went out to collect fuel for a pyre. They had determined to burn the corpse and carry home as much ash and bone as could be recovered, to be scattered on the plains.

As Sheel saddled her bay mare, Ayalees Salmowon rode up with a man trailing her on foot, his neck in a noose. He plodded along with downcast eyes. His skin was grimy with quarry dust and he coughed explosive, rattling coughs that almost shook him off his feet. He was young, and someone had once broken his nose for him.

Sheel caught the Salmowon's rein. "I thought we were all bringing fuel for a funeral fire today. Why have you brought this instead? We agreed, no men at our tent, ever."

The Salmowon tugged the rope. The young man stumbled, and the watching Women laughed. "I won him playing flipstones with some Newly Freed two nights ago. He's sick. They say he would have been given to Fedeka for Moon-woman anyway."

Sheel looked at the young man's matted hair and stubbled cheeks with distaste. "What good is the creature to you?"

The Salmowon nodded toward the femmish tents. "They sacrifice to a Woman in the moon, and they have had victory against their old enemies. Here in the moon's own country, I will sacrifice in the name of my dead kinswoman."

The man, hearing this, grasped the rope in both hands and cried, "No, Hera, please—"

Sheel strode over to him, drawing her knife, and slashed his knuckles across. When his hands flew away from the knife, she sliced his exposed throat, stepping aside to escape the sheeting blood. He dropped to his knees, clawing the air that he could no longer draw. The Women gathered, murmuring. The man twitched and spasmed, his rag-bound feet kicking weakly on the ground and then sagging loosely apart. Dark stains of blood and urine spread under him.

The Salmowon swung down from her saddle. "Sheel Torrinor, this thing was mine that you've killed!"

Sheel bent and wiped her blade on the dead man's rags. "This thing," she said through gritted teeth, "was such filth as we agreed to leave to the fems, since they must have them. And let me remind you, daughter of the Salmowon line, that the fems hold these creatures in common. No one should have handed one of them over to you in settlement of private debt."

"That gives you no right to do this!"

"Until now," Sheel said coldly, "you've made nothing of your kinship to Tyn Chowmer, who was my friend and my lover."

Ayalees, red-cheeked under stress in that hectic Salmowon way, said furiously, "All the same, all the same, Sheel Torrinor. You are wrong."

"I say I'm right." Sheel looked at the others. "At home, Women do not make sacrifices of others' lives except in feud, and no man could ever be involved in a matter of honor. If we are to do a new thing in a new place, the raid chief who led you here is the one to do it, and to face whatever praise or blame comes from it when it is told in our home tents."

"Fine words," the Salmowon retorted. "I spit them back at you, Sheel Torrinor."

"Then speak against me in our Grassland camps," Sheel said, "unless you insist on starting a feud with me here and now, where neither of us has kindred of our own blood to advise us or negotiate between our Motherlines."

For a moment Ayalees looked as if she might accept the challenge. Both Roises were listening intently and could be dragged into a fight, especially if the Tulun aggressively took her lover's side. Even if the Tulun held back with the caution of her line, other Grassland lives than Tyn

Chowmer's could easily be bled away on Lammintown beach this morning.

Ayalees Salmowon turned to twitching her lead rope free from the corpse. "I raise no feuds while raiding. But we have a blade between us now, Sheel Torrinor. I hope neither of us is cut by it in the end."

A mature, Womanly decision, and what a person would expect from the Salmowons. Some things at least stayed firm, even in this land of upset and unrule. Sheel could have kissed the Salmowon, whom she strongly disliked.

One of the Roises said, "That's surely the young fellow Tezza-Bey mated. Those fems were right to try to breed him while they could."

Sheel mounted her horse. "I won't stay here and listen to a lot of trivial talk about some dead man."

She rode away without another word, heading out toward the horse herds. For the moment the dull, grinding sense of loss and failure was lifted from her.

Be first and last, Tyn Chowmer, she said strongly inside herself as she rode. *I beg it of your spirit, and the spirits of your line: be our only death in this alien land.*

The Crest of the Tide

T he Market Arc of Lammintown was flooded with a
joyous riot of noise that beat from wall to wall like
waves crisscrossing on the beach. The mob parted,
whooping, and a band of screaming riders galloped down the
curving avenue waving javelins and hatchets overhead.

"Here they come again!" Daya said.

"Good, let them," Alldera answered. "Let them gallop
and shriek till they drop!"

They sat together on a hastily thrown-together platform
draped in blankets, horsehides, and carpet. With them were
the seven stranger-fems from Bayo. These were viewed as
loot and prizes as much as rescued kindred; and that, she
thought recklessly, was fine with her.

To hell with always being *sensible,* reminding people of
what was right, what was necessary, what was possible.
They were conquering warriors, magnificent in victory even
in the sight of those harsh judges, the Riding Women of the
Grasslands. Damned if she wouldn't be part of the feasting

instead of soberly planning and calculating while others
bawled their joy at the sky.

The riders reined to a jostling halt before the dais and
screamed unintelligible salutes. Two of the Bayo-born
clutched nervously at each other, smiling inanely and clearly
in terror for their lives.

Beyarra-Bey nearly fell off her plunging white mare, but
her face, shining with perspiration, was radiant. Her friend
Tezza-Bey clung on behind her, shrieking with laughter.

Then they all peeled aside into the ruins of the old Blue
Company Hall. Another squad of riders was already milling
in confusion at the lower end of the Arc, preparing to charge
in turn. At the front, Leeja-Beda pretended to lose her balance and fell backward onto her horse's rump, skinny legs
flailing in the air.

"Look at that fool clowning around," Daya said scornfully. "These show-offs who think they can ride after sitting
a few times in the saddle! She'll get herself trampled to
death."

Poor Daya, so sour; probably because she had not been
with the scouting party and could not claim any of the glory
of having found the Bayo-born. Though from what the
scouts had said, these hardy refugees from the old kit pits
had actually found them. One way or another, they were
found: survivors of the slave town who had found refuge in
the swamps. Their arrival in Lammintown had set off this
explosion of jubilation like lightning igniting dry grass.

They were like living fragments of a dream all the Free
had shared, a dream Daya had given shape to in her stories.
She had earned her place on the dais, her brilliant clothes
that everyone admired, everything good that came to her.

Alldera reached impulsively to hug the pet fem, but Daya
evaded her: "Give your accolade to the Bayo-born, or the
scouts. That's what people want to see."

Some of the returned scouts were being carried, lurching
above the mob, on the shoulders of friends and lovers. Others gathered alongside the dais, hemmed in by admirers

pressing gifts on them. Only the Riding Women had stayed apart, insisting on keeping watch on the herds, and on the men in the quarries, while the fems feasted.

It was intolerable to see Daya sitting dark amid the revelry. Impulsively, Alldera grabbed Daya's hand and pulled her to her feet (*Am I chief here, as Daya and others keep saying I am, or not?* she asked herself) and down off the dais after her.

"Come on, this is yours too!"

Two of the seven strangers, flushed and exhausted-looking and still alien in their clothing of woven grasses and swamp leather, made as if to follow. Alldera waved them back. "Stay and enjoy your fame!"

She plunged into the crowd, clasping the hands held out to her, returning hug for hug, breathing the mixed reek of leather, smoke, beer, and food. Two groups of labor fems spun in swift circle dances, flinging their heads back and ululating at the sky. Alldera felt ebullient enough to join them, but shy of intruding on their pleasures.

Looking back, she saw the Bayo-born youngsters sitting as she had left them, waving anxiously over the heads of the surging crowd to those known to them from the scouting party.

"A victory!" Roona cawed from horseback, her wrinkled old face split by a huge grin. "Seven children of Bayo, living and free—who would have thought?"

She leaned down to press Alldera's fingers between her own crooked hands. People surged around Alldera, patting her, plucking at her clothing so that she would turn and see the bright tears in their eyes, their mouths wide with shouts of triumph and words of praise lost in the surrounding din.

"Talk to Kobba!" she yelled. "Give your praise to Ila-Illea, and little Beyarra-Bey too! To Emla! They are the ones who went to Bayo and brought the seven home!"

"Alldera Messenger, you sent them there!" Kastia-Kai cried, and others echoed her words.

Even Daya's brittle manner seemed to soften in the glow

of celebration. She said into Alldera's ear, "Don't worry, none of the scouts are being neglected. But no one will forget who our real leader is this day. You can't ask them to do that."

Alldera grabbed her around the shoulders. "I don't, I'm not. I'm not asking people to do anything, for once!"

She staggered through the reeling crush, half leaning on Daya. Her blood pulsed to the beat of the drum Leeja-Beda had hung from her saddle and was whacking with a water bottle, sharp elbows flying. Ila-Illea, aproned and grimed with cooking stains and smoke, squirmed through the crowd and thrust a spitted chunk of hot meat into Alldera's hands. Two early foals had been killed, and the luscious scent of their roasting flesh floated out from behind the wall of what had once been a private garden.

"Eat," Ila said with a broad smile that showed the gap where she was missing two teeth on one side. "You brought us to this feast day. Taste the best of its meats, Alldera-Chief!"

Alldera felt that she could fall forward into their adulation and be supported, floating as if carried by a hundred hands. She tore at the meat and chewed with a great show of zest and pleasure, to the loud appreciation of the audience.

A tongueless one stepped forward and put a necklace of rounded, sand-worn glass pieces around Alldera's neck. Alldera pressed the half-stripped spit into her hand in return, and the yells and blessings and laughter grew louder, until the group fell back to make way for yet another charge of riders. These, led by Kenoma in her red shirt, carried a ragged banner over their heads and threw fragments of tea brick to those on foot.

Alldera scuffled in the dust for a prize with everyone else, laughing and shoving and sticking her leg out to trip a rival scavenger. She was challenged for it, but Emla the masseur, of all people, stepped in as her champion.

The two wrestlers surged and swore in the cleared space the spectators had made. Wily Emla won two falls of three, and Alldera took off the necklace of glass and put it over Emla's dusty head.

"That may have been a mistake," Daya remarked later, when they climbed together toward the rainwater tanks in the cliffs above the town. "Giving away a gift just given to you."

Daya and Emla were old enemies. Alldera, winded but happy, paused on a paved landing where labor fems with water buckets used to be allowed a brief rest. "Not today," she protested, laughing. "No grudges, no rivalries today!"

Daya looked pale. "I'm sorry if I spoke out of turn."

"No, no, I didn't mean that," Alldera assured her. She started up the wide, shallow stairs again, her eyes on the sky above the beetling cliff's rim. "You can always tell me serious things, you know that."

"There will be a gathering for Moonwoman tonight, the last before we leave for the City. Will you attend?"

"Ask me again later," Alldera said automatically. She did not want to argue about Fedeka's ceremony now. Warm and half-giddy with the pleasures of the day, she reached her arm through Daya's and climbed in step with her.

Down below, the revelers sang self-songs and parodies of self-songs, joke songs, and boasting songs. A shifting skirl of voices drifted up from the humming streets.

"—down with a stroke of my blade," came words yelled ecstatically over the rest.

"And the flying drops of Muck-blood
Were not so many as the lives of friends and lovers
I saw soak into the sands of Lammintown beach
In the days of our bondage, the years of our Hell—"

Then an outburst of argument, followed by gales of laughter.

Daya said, "There are questions about these seven from Bayo."

"Their story will come out in time, when they learn to trust us more."

"What if there are hundreds of them in hiding down there in the swamplands? What if they're in league with men?"

"Men? What men?" Was this what people were saying?

"The missing Ferrymen, or Bayo men who followed these kits into the swamps—I don't know. They're so *young*. Who sired them? Who are they, appearing out of nowhere?"

"That's how we've appeared, from the unslaves' point of view," Alldera pointed out. "Anyway, you should be pleased. These Bayo-born are right out of your tale of the Found Ferry, but happier."

"That was fable, not history. And I don't like the greedy way they look at the horses. They're not nearly impressed enough by the Riding Women, either. I don't trust them."

You didn't find them, Alldera thought. *My poor friend, this isn't turning out to be a heroic adventure for you. Only your stories are heroic; but that should be enough.*

They passed two people who had come up this way ahead of them. Views from the water-tank stair were famously grand, but these figures stood oblivious, intertwined where two joined walls trapped sunlight.

Alldera glimpsed the face of Tamansa-Nan, slack and droop-lidded with passion, over the lifted, enclosing shoulder of someone in the stained leather shirt of a Free Fem. Tamansa-Nan's earring, a colored stone wound in a thin wire, graced the other's ear now.

Embarrassed, Alldera climbed past without speaking, two steps at a time. She did not wish to overhear the words that Tamansa-Nan's lover was whispering.

At her side, Daya murmured, "Who gets your love tokens now, Alldera? Into whose mouth do you press the choicest morsels with your own fingers?"

Flushing, Alldera glanced at her. Sunlight gleamed on the curve of the pet fem's throat. "Are you asking for yourself, or for someone else?"

"I'm asking for you. If you are lonely, you shouldn't be."

"The penalty of greatness," Alldera said facetiously. She paused on the next landing and stretched her back. "Who can I invite to my bed—"

"Anyone you like," Daya said.

"Who could I invite without starting a flood of rumors that could water a whole field of grudges and complaints? If I favor a Free Fem, that means to some people that I despise the unslaves. If I sleep with one of the Newly Freed, they'll say I'm an overbearing would-be master, taking advantage. Shanuay flirts with me—as she does with everyone, sooner or later—but if I incline toward her, does that mean I approve of her fickle ways?"

Daya gave a dainty sniff. "Shanuay would sleep with sharu if there were any here."

"Shanuay flies from comfort to comfort through chaos that terrifies her," Alldera said. "I chose a poor example. But can you imagine the jealousies and resentments if I were to turn to one of these Bayo youngsters now, for instance, rejecting—apparently—all the rest? And as for making my bed in the tent of the Riding Women, those unnatural aliens from a foreign land that wasn't even supposed to exist—" She shook her head and sighed gustily. "It's a lucky thing I'm not still in the hungry heat of my youth, I guess."

The pet fem said nothing. Alldera wondered if she was offended by some unintended slight; she was so easy to upset these days.

"Sorry if I sound irritable," the runner said. "Come on, here's the last flight of steps. I'm not angry at you for sniping at Shanuay. I'm not even angry at her. I just—I want—" She stared at the worn stone steps as she climbed them, searching for words. "You know, sometimes I think I have the makings of a terrible tyrant. I hope you never have cause to make a story about that."

"It would never occur to me."

"I mean, if I found a magical root, say, that would make anyone brave and strong who ate it, don't you think I'd force it down the throats of people like Shanuay?"

"You wouldn't have to," Daya murmured. "Many people would rush to eat that root."

"I know, I know, I'm talking nonsense—I can't express things with a storyteller's gift. The thing is, it maddens me sometimes, to think that you can't *give* people freedom. We come home and knock the yoke of slavery off the bond fems' shoulders once and for all, but someone like Shanuay still won't hold up her head like a free person."

"I thought that was the lesson of Elnoa's Tea Camp."

Alldera laughed and nudged Daya's elbow with her own. "It's a good thing nobody but you, Daya, knows what an idiot I am. You're right. I wonder how often I have to learn that lesson before I really know it. You have no idea how often I wish I were as clever and preceptive as you, or as strong and sure as Kobba."

Daya looked at her sideways, a quick, unfathomable glance. "You need someone to soften your impatience and sharpen your sight, someone to talk things over with so you catch all the nuances. That's why I asked who's sleeping with you."

Nettled that the pet fem was clearly not offering herself, Alldera said, "Look, when you aren't still hand-feeding Beyarra-Bey, then you can ask me about love."

On the ledge with the deep pools of storm runoff they stopped, panting and shaking the tightness out of their legs.

The rock was warm under Alldera's bootsoles. She flopped down gratefully with her back against a bucket stoop. After a moment's hesitation, Daya settled beside her. Far below, two Riding Women relieved of sentry duty cantered their mounts back and forth on the beach.

"All this excitement has made me more foolish than usual," Alldera confessed. "I spoke out of turn. I know I don't own you and never did."

Daya did not reply. Alldera thought of Tua, and before that Grays Omelly in Stone Dancing Camp; and who knew how many others? Kenoma, she had heard, had been Daya's lover years ago while traveling with the tea wagons. A glaze of sweat made Daya's face gleam, and Alldera breathed in her warm, perfumed odor. *You should have let me keep you.*

"I have no right to complain if other lovers make you happier than I could," she said.

"Oh, happy—" Daya said with delicate disdain. "Beyarra-Bey is easily dazzled, she scarcely knows who it is that kisses her. She bores me, a little; she's so young." She paused. "Anyway, since she went adventuring to Bayo she has no use for me. I've seen her making sweet-eyes at you, though."

Alldera reached back and began to undo her braid, which felt damp and messy. "I heard that she and Kobba were a couple, riding down to Bayo."

"Kobba has let her go again since. Beyarra would be a good bedmate for you. She's timid, but she worships you, and she'll always be the first bond fem who joined us."

Alldera's heart beat harder. How many more times was Daya going to make her beg? "I would rather have you back yourself than playing matchmaker between me and Beyarra."

The pet fem's lips tightened. Her fingers nervously toyed with the strap of bells she wore tied around her other wrist. "You shouldn't say things you don't mean."

Alldera groaned. "Sometimes I wonder whether you and I understand each other at all anymore. At least let's enjoy this feast together, without any claims or arguments or bad memories."

"We should have brought something to eat," Daya said. "More food stuffed into our bellies, less to pack and carry back to the City with us. That's what the unslaves say, the lazy bitches."

Alldera frowned. "I think some of them are still opposed to going back—mostly the ones who wanted to stay there in the first place! But it's foolish to sit here in Lammintown through the winter storm season. Can't they see that?"

"They see it. They just don't like it. They say that doing what you're told is for slaves. Like work."

Alldera started her braid again. "Well, I've spoken to Kastia-Kai about heading inland in no more than a week's time. I meet tomorrow with Tamansa-Nan as well, to do more prodding and persuading. Anyone else, you think? What about Leeja-Beda? I think a lot more goes on behind that satirical mask of hers than people think."

"She's killed a man with her own knife, so she's a hero of the new Holdfast," Daya said. "That's all anybody needs to know, isn't it? Of course you should consult her."

"There are all kinds of heroes. You know how I feel about that."

"I think I know how you wish you felt."

Oh, it was useless. Alldera tied off her braid, shut her eyes, and leaned back against the bucket stoop. Drumming throbbed down below, crossing a chanted dance-song with a faster rhythm. She bade to the forefront of her thinking the things that kept her awake at night; the things she needed to talk over with the cleverest and most farsighted of her advisors.

All the Holdfast's centers had now yielded up their living occupants. The irresistible expansion that had carried the Free Fems victoriously from the Wild eastward had reached its limit at the coast. Something else must happen now: discipline, and the will to consolidate their grip on the Holdfast, and then the creation of the truly "free" fems: the children of the conquerors.

It was one thing to launch the arrows of femmish fury at their justified targets. That had been her dream, and, against all probability, it was accomplished. But the prospect of trying to organize a workable life here daunted her. She knew she was expected to do this, but had not the faintest idea of how. Discussions in the Grasslands had never gone, realistically, beyond simple victory. Neither had her own thinking, she admitted ruefully to herself.

She turned to Daya. "Emla was mashing the kinks out of my back yesterday, and do you know what she said? She said sometimes she dreams of the Grasslands, and thinks of going back there. And I think Kenoma says the same every day, to somebody.''

"Kenoma has been sick with one thing or another since the day we came down from the mountains. Have you seen that rash she's got on her elbows now?'' Daya sounded more disgusted than sympathetic.

"I know you don't like Kenoma, but people do respect her with or without a rash.''

The pet fem went on with light malice. "Still, it seems Kenoma's homeland doesn't agree with her no matter how respected she is. The only thing she likes about being home is that red shirt she found. She sold off the scrap from it very dear, because nobody knows how to get that color anymore. People joke about wearing the 'red rag' ''—as all fems had once had to do when menstruating, to warn men of their unclean state—''but they treasure the stuff all the same. Kenoma likes that, even as she sneezes and scratches and wishes she were back on the other side of the mountains.''

Squinting, Alldera thought she could see flashes of Kenoma's red among the revelers even from this distance. It cheered her to think so, and she smiled.

"As for Emla,'' Daya added, openly acerbic as she turned her attention to her old Tea Camp rival, ''she misses the old days of her influence with Elnoa the Green-eyed, which despite her best manipulative efforts she hasn't been able to duplicate with you.''

"Oh, she's more straightforward than she was. A lot of us have changed, though sometimes I'm afraid it's all come too late. I worry that we'll get restless for nomadic life, now that we face the slog of planting and mending and building. The Newly Freed aren't the only ones who shy away from real work.''

Almost too softly to be heard, Daya asked, ''Are you sleeping with Eykar Bek?''

"What?'' The horizon of the sea seemed to jolt in front of Alldera's eyes. ''Of course not!''

But she had thought of it. Seeing him daily in her quarters, helpless and naked under his thin gray quilt . . . Astounded by the arrival of the Seven of Bayo, so young and evocative of Sorrel, of the possibility of new, freeborn daughters . . . Hearing people comment on the musculature of this Dirt or that, or speculate about whether Setteo could still raise his rod, as some cutboys could . . .

Did Eykar have sex with Setteo? she wondered when she saw them together; did the cutboy tend to all the needs of the Endtendant's body, in D Layo's absence? Or did Eykar still rule those impulses—surely he still had them—with the same cold loathing that she remembered? And if he did or he didn't, what should that matter to her?

Sometimes she had to leave her quarters in Cliff's Eye because she was disturbed by Eykar's nearness, the warmth beating steadily from him out into the room. Femmish lovers had melted her body's core and torn her heart (Daya foremost among them). Yet that pale-eyed man with all his scars and weaknesses was sealed to her in some way that overbore all others, and that neither of them seemed able to understand or to remedy.

The pet fem rattled her Ladystones nervously in her hand. "You say no, but you keep him by you. We said we would hold all our prizes in common."

"I don't recall you insisting on common ownership of Setteo," Alldera snapped.

"That was different—our first prisoner, a symbol, a—a special trophy! Are you jealous that I was the one to take him captive and not you?"

Bewildered by the intensity and lightning shift of this attack, Alldera stammered, "Daya, I never—"

"Because I can't stand against you," Daya rushed on, "you know that! A mere storytelling pet fem against the great runner, Alldera Messenger! So you've taken over Setteo too, by attaching him to Eykar Bek. Now you have them both. Do you think people don't notice? We always said there would be no special men, none favored, none lifted by so much as a hair above the others so that they could look up to him as a leader.''

"Eykar is already special to them, he always was—"

"And to you. 'Eykar'—you call him 'Eykar' as if he were a friend.''

"Should I call him 'Bek,' as if he were a master?''

The pet fem swallowed hard. "I was there when you met him, between Oldtown and the City. I saw you take his hands.''

"I was surprised, that's all," Alldera said. "I've told you, I never expected to find him still alive.''

Daya said bitterly, "He fell and you raised him up the way a fem would raise up her fallen lover.''

Alldera's heart pounded. It hadn't been that obvious, it couldn't have been that obvious. *What hadn't? What, exactly?* "I was moved, Daya, that he and I had both survived, after all we'd gone through together in those days, and separately since. I couldn't pretend not to be glad—''

"You *are* glad. That Muck is more special to you than any of your own, with all the blood that stains his hands. People see how you mock me, Alldera, and make a fool of poor, love-struck Beyarra. People say that the only one you have any real feeling for is this man.''

Alldera saw who it was who said such things: the storyteller herself, to whom everyone else listened.

"Did you think of him every time you lay down with me?'' Daya said. "Even in the old days in the Grasslands, was it really him you hugged to you and whispered to and stroked with hungry hands?''

At last, a rock of clear denial on which to steady herself. "No, Daya, never; not with you, not with anyone, Free Fem or bond fem or Woman of the camps. How can you think such a thing? It's long since you and I were lovers, but it hurts me to think that we're no longer even friends.''

"You don't need a friend," Daya shrilled. "You have your pet, your lover, your master back again!''

Alldera stood up. "Why did you come up here with me? You want something. What is it?"

Daya was silent, savagely twisting and retwisting a lock of hair beside her ear. She raised her head and met Alldera's gaze. "Turn Eykar Bek over to Fedeka for tonight's ceremony. I'll give up the cutboy too; my prisoner, my one claim to fame. We'll do it together."

"*No.*"

"Don't you see anything?" Daya's eyes were huge, pleading. "It isn't just the men who revere Eykar Bek. Leeja fed him manna because she thought he might be still an Oracle, a source of mystical truth. Other unslaves feel this too, though they'd deny it if you asked. They grew up seeing their masters hanging on the Oracle's manna-mad ramblings. We can't have challenges to Moonwoman's authority, certainly not using the drugged babblings of a Dirtmuck from the quarries!" She brought her fists down on her knees. "The Lady must consume him in front of everyone."

Alldera burst out, "I've never heard such—"

"There is only one Divinity!" Daya cried. "You can't deny Her, you are the champion She favors. You may not feel the need for help from beyond this world, but your followers do. They can scarcely believe in their freedom sometimes, let alone their own power. In your heart, even you sometimes look to the Lady, I know you do! Give Eykar Bek to Her tonight."

"For pity's sake, he's half-blind and lame besides!"

"Pity?" Daya snarled. "You dare to speak of that creature and pity in one breath?"

Alldera stepped back from the lip of the ledge, clenching her clammy hands. It was a killing fall from here to the landing below, and she was suddenly afraid. "Daya, listen. A master of the old days might slaughter a burned-out, crippled slave for the sake of a superstition. I won't. And I won't let you or Fedeka soil yourselves so, either."

"Superstition?" Daya raised hands cramped by rage into claws. "You still think the power of Moonwoman is a lie?

Who do you think has inspired you to lead us this far? Do you think you've done it all yourself?''

"Of course not! How can you say that to me? No one knows better than I do—I've had *your* help, Ellexa's, Fedeka's—''

"Other *selves*," Daya said witheringly. "Each little self brandishing its tiny talents and shrieking for its share of fame. Who appointed you over the others, if not Moonwoman? Who do you pray to for wisdom and strength? To Moonwoman, or to your man-Muck? You look to him to give you another child because you're the great Alldera, and one free cub isn't enough for you!''

Alldera flinched. "I'm no mother for any child. If not for the Riding Women, Sorrel would never have lived to be born. I'll leave all that to younger people, the ones still soft enough to find new ways. I don't sleep with Eykar, Daya.''

"So plausible," Daya hissed. "Such a good speaker! You always were, and you learned that in the old Holdfast, from your masters and at your masters' will.''

Alldera's lips felt stiff and clumsy. "If you ever loved me, stop talking before you say something neither of us can forgive.''

"No, you stop trying to shut me up! Listen, listen to me for a change, you never listen to me anymore! I'm begging you: let Fedeka offer Eykar Bek's blood to the protector of all fems, our Mother the moon.''

"No, I told you.''

"Traitor!'' With a convulsive gesture Daya tore free her Ladystones and flung them out into the air. They clicked and bounced against the cliff as they fell.

Alldera's fear vanished. Daya was no physical threat to her, she could do no more than hurl away a few pebbles. Even the blood sacrifice the pet fem demanded must be accomplished by Fedeka's hand, not her own. Daya couldn't strike Alldera any more than she could strike even a disgraced and degraded master. She simply did not have the courage.

Alldera bent forward—sure enough, Daya recoiled from her—and brushed dust from her pants. She felt suffocated in sadness.

"You do what you like with Setteo," she said heavily. "He is yours by the rein regardless of any duties he's been given since. But if Fedeka wants Eykar Bek, she can come try to take him herself. Now, get out of my way. I have the trek back to the City to organize."

She descended alone toward the raucous festival, stepping carefully because her sight was blurred with tears.

V

The Cold Country

Setteo stood by the stone wall and made the slow steps, each foot up and down in place, that he knew would bring him to the fugitives. Wherever Givard had fled with Tezza-Bey, he could be found by a detour through the Cold Country.

It was dangerous. If here in the Warm World the Blessed and their Angels were angry, the Bears would be in a more dangerous mood still, perhaps enraged enough to overwhelm Setteo's skills.

He did have skills, after all. While the Blessed searched the caves above Lammintown, Setteo had made an ameliorating spell with the horses' help. He had woven a small net of tough cliff weed that he hoped might contain the fury of the pursuit until he could bring help from the Cold Country.

Not that he owed anything to Tezza-Bey, let alone to Givard. But the tide of violence seeking after the two of them was hideously destructive. If you refused to range your powers against destruction, you did not deserve to have them; and Setteo had bought his abilities at too high a price for that.

So he worked furtively in his own way, while here sat Alldera-Blessed in the Cliff's Eye and directed her search for the runaways. The central chamber, leached from the stone by seeping water, was furnished with a chest, a wooden seat, and a couch of leather cushions. A section of roofing on rough-hewn blocks made a table on which maps of the cliff's passages were spread.

Alldera pored over them, frowning and biting her lips, while Daya-Blessed rummaged among the maps that had been packed up for the return to the City (delayed now, of course).

The Librarian stood at the window-opening staring out over night-shrouded Lammintown. He radiated waves of black despair shot with flashes of fear. And no wonder: Alldera-Blessed was speaking to him in the deadly tone in which demons are summoned.

"We'll find them," she said, smoothing out a creased chart with fire-bitten edges. "Old Roona hid in those caves years ago. She and Kastia-Kai between them know the passages inch by inch even without maps."

The Librarian said hollowly, "New caves and passages may have been discovered since, Hera."

"It doesn't matter. We'll find them." She brushed dust from her hands with unnecessary force. "Horns of the moon, I'm tired! We should all be on our way back to the City now. How did this happen?"

"It wouldn't have," Daya-Blessed said, with a glance of hatred at the Librarian, "if you'd listened to me."

Daya's fingers twitched with nervous irritability. She missed her whip. Setteo had felt the keen kiss of that little whip more than once. She did not carry it anymore when she was around Alldera-Blessed.

Setteo, biting his fingertips, tasted blood at last. He drew lines on the stone beside him, vectors that would lead him into the Cold Country. With his other hand he held the grass net to his mouth and breathed on it as he shuffled in place, unnoticed, he hoped, by anyone.

"I did listen to you," Alldera said. "I didn't happen to like what I heard."

Daya's voice rose. "It was only a matter of time before someone else took a male pet for herself, once you'd set the example. I thought it would be Shanuay; I know her kind. Only with a man will that one ever feel 'safe.' Instead it's Beyarra-Bey's best friend! It's a joke, Alldera, and maybe not the only one, either. Where is little Beyarra tonight? Gone to pick out a Dirtmuck for herself?"

Alldera straightened up, working her shoulders in circles. "She's off searching for Tezza, like everyone else. More maps, please."

Setteo shut himself away from them and sank into stillness. With a convulsive effort he stepped out of Cliff's Eye and into the Cold Country.

There, there was the chill of ice under his feet. He squinted against the pallid glare, tucked the grass net into the waistband of his ragged pants, and began to walk slowly straight ahead. It was not a good idea to hurry in this place, or you could be transformed into one of the Flying Souls whose pictures he had seen in old books in the Library. Your feet elongated into thin blades and your arms into long, trailing sticks, and you fled forever, flashing over the surface of the white spirit world in terror of the Bears.

He walked over ice dotted with what looked like small ponds of black water. Behind him lay a vast white plain. Ahead, the ground reared itself into a range of white ridges crossing his path from as far as he could see on either hand, under a silver sky. Though no breeze stirred against his skin, he heard a faint, rhythmic sound like the soughing of wind.

He was not surprised when one of the low white hillocks toward which he advanced shook itself and stood, yawning so that he could see past its yellow fangs into its pink, steaming gullet. The susurration in the air was the concerted breathing of the Bears.

This one had the human-shaped, amber eyes of one he had already met and dealt with, for when they accepted him not as prey but as a strong spirit traveler, their eyes changed toward him. Emboldened, he approached.

"Elder Brother, I see that you are warm and fed and rested. May we speak together a little?"

"Well, I see that you are thin, fearful and driven, and too small to make a mouthful let alone be my brother," said the Bear, emitting breath stinking of carrion. "Why have you come?"

"For my pleasure and to see my friends and relations." Setteo had found that it was helpful not to be too precise with the Bears at first. "But also I am puzzled, and there is always wisdom to be found here."

The Bear grunted and fell to biting at something stuck between the pads of one massive forepaw.

Moving his feet subtly (if you forgot and stood still, you could be frozen to the ground and never return to the Warm World again), Setteo said politely, "How can the Meek, whom the Blessed call 'Newly Freed,' inherit the earth if they rush to serve their old masters again? I am thinking of Tezza, called Tezza-Bey, who has set Givard free and run away with him."

The Bear lifted its pointed nose and sniffed thoughtfully. "Put your hand into my mouth, and an answer will come."

Setteo swallowed the bile of fear, walked closer, and extended his right hand. If the Bear knew that he was lefthanded, it did not care. It brought its jaws together, just touching his skin with its fangs.

As the heat of the Bear's maw closed around his arm up to the elbow, from deep down its throat came a threadlike voice: "The Meek already own the earth and always have. No one can give them what has always belonged to them; they must claim it for themselves. But fear still holds them in its jaws. They must first find their courage."

"Thank you, Elder Brother," Setteo said, carefully withdrawing his hand.

The Bear licked its glistening lips. "A hand is all bones,"

it remarked comfortably. "The part that I would choose has already been taken, so I consider your fee paid."

It nosed him with rough playfulness in the crotch, then curled up and closed its eyes and became a hill again. The hill just behind it at once rose up.

He skirted a string of round black ponds and stood before the second Bear, stepping in place on the ice. Before he could frame a question the second Bear said, "If you want to find these runaways, anoint your feet with a salve made of the fat of horses and scrapings of their hooves. Horses' spirits can go where they themselves cannot, even into the caves and passages of the Lammintown cliffs."

"I have no time to make such a salve," Setteo said. "Would you have any of it with you, that I can purchase?"

"Reach into that pond," the Bear said, nodding at the nearest circle of black water.

Squatting down and setting his teeth, Setteo thrust his left arm up to the elbow in the frigid water. Something brushed against his fingers, and he caught it and drew out—a miniature horse, curled up in his palm, heavy as a stone and covered in silvery slime. The water held, he realized, the souls of the waiting-to-be-born, including the young of the horses.

"I have caught a prize," he announced, getting carefully to his feet with the cold, throbbing creature in his hand. "May I present it to you?"

"Give it here," said the Bear. It seized the fetal horse and gulped it down. Setteo, fearing he would be next, almost forgot to keep moving. He was very cold now, and his thoughts and capacities of motion were slowing.

"Get ready, here it comes," said the Bear with a huge burp. Setteo was just in time to cup his hands under the Bear's muzzle: out of its mouth dropped a gob of silvery paste with a stench so rank that it nearly made him faint.

Trying not to breathe, he sat down and daubed the stuff onto the bottoms of his feet. It burned and tingled but otherwise had no observable effect.

"Something for you, something for me," said the Bear, and it ambled away.

Behind it lay a smaller Bear with a yellowish pelt and its front paws curled under the fur of its chest. It barely raised its head as Setteo approached. "What is your question?"

"I don't have a question," Setteo said, for he felt great fear of this Bear. What he had meant to ask was forgotten.

"But I have an answer," said the Bear. "Will you come to me, or shall I come to you?" Setteo saw, with a great dull beat of horror, that the Bear had the tiny, black, empty eyes of one that he had never met before. It did not see him at all but looked directly, with a mindless hunger, at his soul.

"I'll come to you," he stammered, after a paralyzed moment. His desperate brain flared into thought. "I have some fine craftwork to give in exchange for your answer."

The yellow Bear growled; it clearly had fresh human soul in mind for payment. But it made no further objection, and when Setteo came and stood by its head, it coughed once and announced, "The Country of Anger has no boundaries once you stand upon its burning land. The only way out of it is by flying up into the quiet sky above. But to fly high enough to see beyond its borders takes the power of more than one wing."

"What does that mean?" Setteo said, dry-mouthed.

The Bear raised its head skyward. Setteo, following its gaze, saw a thing that had not been seen in the Warm World for generations, though he recognized it from pictures of Ancient times. Creatures glided through space, the ones called "birds," soaring on slow beats of their great white wings.

Words came into his mind direct from the Bear's: "There is your Second Coming indeed." The deep eye pits of the yellow Bear smoked with greed. "Now step nearer."

"Of course," quavered Setteo, drawing the grass net from his waistband. "Here is the gift I spoke of. I want to arrange it properly, to bring out its finest qualities for you. Will you be so kind as to close your great jaws for a moment?"

The Bear rumbled softly to itself and reared its head back

to examine what Setteo held. "What is it? That looks to me like a little mat of grass, a wad of rubbish, a piece of trash."

"That's the magic of it, Great Brother, that has let me bring it safely so far among people who would take from me anything that appeared precious. I am only a slave in the Warm World, after all. In my hands this seems nothing; but fitted to your exalted person it will assume its true and wondrous form."

The bear's head lowered grudgingly within his reach, the pitiless eyes still fixed on him. Setteo blew warm breath on his fingers. "It will become a mesh of fine golden thread and sparkling gems," he said with enthusiasm.

Gently he draped the net over the Bear's muzzle, looking at it from one angle and then another and making little adjustments. Then quick as thought he knotted the opposite corners beneath the Bear's jaw and sprang backward.

"Mmmf!" cried the Bear, rearing up and pawing wildly at its own face; for here in the Cold Country the grass net was as strong as the magic of the place itself, and could not be broken.

As Setteo stumbled out of reach, the Bear lunged after him. He threw himself aside. The bear crashed past him and fell headlong into a black hole in the ice, sending up a great fan of black spray. And from that jagged hole nothing else emerged.

The plain trembled underfoot, the sky echoed with sounds of ice splitting and grinding. Other hills, low and white, began stirring and rumbling, and a high, keening note rang through the Cold Country.

Setteo turned and ran back the way he had come. The ointment on his burning feet lifted him into the air. Darkness closed around him like a fist, and cold stone jarred his staggering steps. He sagged against a chilly wall, breathing with gratitude the smell of good, earthly stone-dust.

Though no Bears had followed him, still he was not alone. Two people hurried along the narrow passage ahead of him. They were very frightened. Setteo listened with their ears, felt the biting currents of air with their skins, and breathed with them the smoke of the small stone lamps that each one carried.

His true, inward self that traveled without flesh hurried after the fugitives. His spirit eyes, freshly sharpened by visiting the Cold Country, saw them clearly and read the auras that their own spirit bodies emitted.

Tezza-Bey was afraid the men were planning some outburst over Bavell. The Angels had first won him while gaming with the fems and then murdered him, and the men were eager to strike back. But in the crushing response of the fems to any such demonstration, Givard might die. This seemed to Tezza-Blessed an unendurable waste, as everyone would come to realize, too late. So they would thank her in the end for preserving the lad, and welcome her back with feasts and dancing, if she could preserve Givard and his seed.

Givard, who thought himself capable of grand, even gallant action (at least when he wasn't frightened out of his wits), meant to dash into the Wild in search of the vanished Ferrymen, taking Tezza with him and protecting her, for which she would of course be lastingly grateful. If she wasn't—that part was a haze of anger, longing, and desperation, in colors too bright to look at for long.

Foolish children, so intent on ascending through the caves to the watchtower, where Tezza-Blessed had hidden supplies for their flight. With shocking suddenness hands reached down and drew them, struggling but not daring to scream, up. Setteo followed, soundless and effortless on his anointed feet.

Blesseds held the runaways inside the torchlit walls of the broken tower room. They stared at their captives with slitted eyes worse, much worse, than even the eyes of the third, yellow Bear.

He was grateful to be only present in his spirit self. He reached for the grass net that he had woven to try to give the two fugitives some protection—and remembered where he had left it. Unarmed, he could only watch.

If the captors would give their fury the outlet of speech, it might be softened. But they said nothing, and Tezza-Bey clung to Givard's arm in an agony of silent terror. Only Givard uttered a sound, gasping out part of the Chant Protective. He had the words wrong.

Power stirred in Setteo, power from the Cold Country. He felt it rise up his legs and his trunk, and he opened his mouth to release it.

Nearby something huge and heavy growled. One of the captors lifted a heavy stick in her hands. Setteo saw the gesture clearly with his spirit eyes, by the light that shone from the silver coat of the Bear that stood beside him.

"Oh rose thou thy stick," Setteo sang, releasing the spell that had come home with him from the Cold Country. "The invisible bird that flies in the night—"

Inexplicably, the first blows fell as he finished the verse: "—he doth thy life destroy!"

And hearing the words he was speaking, he realized that it was not a spell of protection but a spell of death. So staves and fists and stones rose and fell without mercy, to a rough rhythm of grunts and exclamations.

He fell with the victims and kept falling, down, back toward his fleshly body where it stumped along stupidly beside the wall of Cliff's Eye. Blesseds argued here in Alldera-Blessed's rooms, making a discordant noise that he thrust away.

Level with his face he saw the blood lines he had made. He smeared his palm over the marks and, released from their power, began to inch along the wall toward a gap leading out of the chamber.

He needed solitude to recover himself, and to think out the meaning of the answers he had been given. His tingling legs would barely move, but he was still protected by the aura of his travels. He slipped away unnoticed, sucking tearfully at his bitten, smarting fingers.

He had brought magic for Tezza-Bey and Givard from the

Cold Country and it was the wrong magic. The Bears had tricked him, for their own impenetrable reasons.

But was that his fault? Maybe Givard should have been less rough with Setteo back when men were masters in the City; maybe that would have made a difference. He padded silently along a lightless passage in the rock, grieving that he had not been able to focus enough to ask other questions, about how the men might survive, and what leverage they might find to shift the brunt of destruction away from themselves. Questions about the future.

It was something he would do well to remember: sometimes he bested the Bears and won from them what he needed; but sometimes the Bears won.

Necessity

❧❧

A sliver of moon had risen over the sea. Eykar's heart beat thick with dread. Inevitable retaliation must be triggered by Givard's escape. Volatile Givard, blowing hot and cold, veering from loudmouthed bravo to lofty idealist to whining coward: how many would die for his folly?

Someone had come a moment ago, and Daya had gone out with them, leaving Alldera marking off on one of the maps another section of the caves that had already been searched.

"People will say you knew about this beforehand," Alldera said. "Did you?"

"Didn't you always know everything that was happening before your masters did? We're as good at slavery as you were, Hera."

Her hand holding the marker stopped moving over the map. She gave him a long and steady stare. "Eykar, were they going to meet anybody? Were they running away to join someone else in the Wild? You know who I mean."

He moistened his dry lips. "You must ask them, Hera. I don't know."

"You should have stopped Givard."

"I wasn't there to stop him," he said, "because you've kept me here with you."

Her nostrils flared angrily. "I don't think you knew anything about it."

"As you say, Hera."

She did not answer but sat at the improvised desk gazing at nothing. The sag of her shoulders and the slack curl of her fingers where they rested on the map betrayed enormous weariness. A brave, determined man could attack her now while she was alone and strengthless in her stone room, and break her neck with one twist of his hate-filled hands.

Eykar had been subject to nearly delirious passages of exhaustion himself in recent weeks. Looking at her bowed head—gray streaks in the hair, the scalp showing pale at the part—what he felt was sympathy. Perhaps that meant he was not a man at all, certainly not a brave one. He didn't care.

The scar on his thigh itched. If he scratched it, it would stop itching and start to ache. If he didn't scratch, after a while it would begin aching anyway. His eyelids felt sandy with sleepiness. No one would sleep until the runaways were caught; and they would be caught, because the fems would not stop searching until they were.

Leaning in the window opening, he dreamed that he rode on horseback, a thing he had never done and had no wish to do. In the dream he sat close against Alldera's back, his hands clasped together under the moving warmth of her breasts. She turned to shout something, and he kissed the corner of her mouth, and then they were facing one another on the horse's back, locked body-to-body and wound about in the rich braid of her hair. Beneath the hooves of the horse the earthen tones of Alldera's needlework flowed away—

"—found," Daya said triumphantly.

While he dozed, his dream stirring and swelling his genitals, the pet fem had returned. "They're heading for the old watchtower. It won't be long now. We can take the gallery passage to the clifftop.''

"Eykar!" How quickly he had grown used to that tone; it barely stung any more. Fortunately his body had settled down again, and he could stand to answer a command without embarrassment or worse.

Another fem had come with Daya—Ellexa of the Silver Hair, who wore slung slantwise from her shoulder a fine embroidered belt she'd taken from Erl the Scrapper's corpse. She glanced at Eykar with contempt. "We don't need this Muck with us."

Daya said slyly, "Alldera doesn't trust other fems to let her pet alone, since Leeja tried to poison him with manna."

"No man has seen the gallery passage, ever," Ellexa said. "No man should."

"He stays with me," Alldera said, shrugging on a horsehide vest over her shirt.

There was a beat of peculiar silence shared exclusively by Ellexa and Daya; Alldera did not notice. Then the pet fem tugged down her sleeves in a businesslike gesture and said, "Well, get him his crutch, then—where's that worthless cutboy of mine?"

"Not far off, Hera," Eykar said, automatically protecting Setteo. "He never is."

"It's my place to dismiss him or not," Daya said, examining her nails. She never looked at him anymore. The day she looked at him might well be the day she killed him. "Not yours."

"As Setteo very well knows," Alldera remarked tartly. "So he ignores what Eykar tells him and does as he likes. No wonder we can never find him when we want him." She caught up a headless spear shaft from a heap of damaged weapons in the corner and tossed it to Eykar underhand. "Lean on that. Make sure you keep up."

The pet fem, blanching, cried, "What are you doing?"

Alldera gave her an exasperated look. "Should he lean on you instead?"

"We don't arm men!" Ellexa protested.

"Oh, don't be ridiculous," Alldera said. "Are men so mighty that you're afraid of one cripple with a stick against three armed fems?"

She took a small clay lamp from the table and shouldered her way past them (he remembered the ghostly glow of rows and rows of those same lamps on Lammintown beach, lighting night work by a gang of labor fems—in another life, of his many lives). The other fems fell in behind her in chastened but resentful silence.

Eykar trailed them into passages he had never seen. Fearful of a fall in the lurching shadows thrown by their lamps, he cursed Setteo for his absence.

The fems did not look back. He was left to hustle after them as best he could, past the wavering, water-carved walls, past the flickering images carved and painted above sooty smears where the fires of runaway fems had burned in former days. He saw spirals, carefully traced shapes of spread-fingered hands, counting-series of lines in groups of fives—counting days in hiding?

Then came crude stick figures shown running, or walking bent under heavy loads, or wrapped in each other's arms, or transfixed by barbed slashes, or straining upward to escape the stylized flames that surrounded them. Other figures pursued them, entrapped them, tormented them—squat monsters with rough-drawn, pendulous male genitals, wide mouths full of pointed teeth, and whips in their fists.

As the ceiling angled upward the trickle of these figures became a flood, drawn by different hands in greasy soot and colored clays. Tumbling over and under and around each other, pursued and pursuers flowed densely along the billowed stone.

This too was a map, of sorts: a map of the fems' rage and pain, generations in the making; just as Alldera had said. He read his own kind's future there, and his heart quailed.

The three fems stopped. The way divided into several smaller passages. Daya studied a diagram, holding the edges

of the map against a bare place on the wall with her elbows
and forearms.

"We should have taken the longer way." Ellexa glared
back at Eykar, who lowered his gaze and pretended not to
look at the drawings. "When Tezza-Bey and her Dirtmuck
are caught, what will you have done with them?"

Alldera was adjusting the strap across the instep of her
boot. She said something Eykar did not hear. He edged
closer. One of a slave's few resources was knowledge.

"They have to be punished," Ellexa said. "People expect
it."

"Damn, these straps have stretched." Alldera looked up,
her face deeply scored and shaped by shadow. "Are you
putting in your bid to personally cut the throats of Tezza and
this boy?"

"You shouldn't scoff," Daya remonstrated softly. The
whites of her eyes gleamed. "The unslaves in particular
need an example of what happens to a fem, any fem, who
conspires with a man, any man, for any purpose."

Eykar leaned against a boss of stone. On a smooth hollow
beside it someone had drawn three figures impaled on poles
beside wavy lines for water; a new picture, in fresh pig-
ments.

"Tezza-Bey is little more than a child," Alldera said.
"She grew up in a different Holdfast than the one we knew.
Bearing and raising free children is the example I hope she'll
set."

Daya's lip lifted in a delicate sneer. "Should weaklings
and traitors be allowed to breed? Or to live, even?"

Alldera looked from one of them to the other. "All right,
Tezza has behaved like an idiot. You want to kill a fem for
making mistakes, like a master culling his femhold of those
not deft enough to serve soup without spilling it?"

Daya's scarred cheeks paled. She rolled up the map with
trembling hands.

Ellexa said, "We want to make sure nobody else lets
some Muck seduce her into turning traitor."

" 'Traitor' isn't a word I like to use about my own people," Alldera said. "And I don't like to hear you use it, either."

"Someone will punish Tezza and her Dirtmuck," Daya said, "with or without approval. No one will blame that person for what she does."

Again Eykar sensed that tension between her and Ellexa, and this time he saw by Alldera's frown that it disturbed her too. There was something here against which her words broke and subsided leaving no impression, like water over rock.

In a different tone, soft and sorrowful, Daya went on, "Kastia-Kai came here last week to mourn a friend who died years ago in Lammintown, someone she had thought then might have been her own dam. She'd meant to come alone, the way most people visit the gallery, but I tagged along. She reminded me of how runaways who hid in these tunnels were hunted out and killed as sport for Lammintown men. Someday these passages and chambers could echo with fems' screams again, if Tezza-Bey's stupidity is imitated by others."

The unspoken accusation hung in the air: like your own stupidity, Alldera, in keeping Eykar Bek by you, which has encouraged Tezza-Bey in her folly.

Alldera indicated the wall of images with an emphatic wave of her hand. "No matter how stupid any of us may be about any particular man, none of us could ever forget all this."

In the flickering lamplight the eyes of the others looked flat and cold. Alldera waited, clearly unwilling to resort to the style of authority fems identified with men's mastery. But Eykar feared that here, with these people, only iron hardness would do. Perhaps guilt—because she had truly favored him—tainted and undercut her faith in her own strength. She could not effectively counter that charge.

She didn't try. "Are we here to argue about me and that man over there? Let's stick to our problem with Tezza-Bey.

Remember how Matri Mayala said that we Free Fems would act like masters to the bond fems? To kill Tezza-Bey out of hand is to do exactly that. No, the unslave must be allowed to speak for herself, as we were never allowed to do. Then we'll decide how to respond.''

"But how?" Daya said intently. "*How* will you respond?"

"We'll decide then," Alldera said. "All of us together, like sensible people who respect and care about each other."

"Even 'sensible' people will say," Ellexa said, "that you're being lenient in this case because Tezza-Bey is free-name-friend to your favorite, Beyarra-Bey, among other reasons."

Alldera answered levelly. "People can say what they like, so long as they come say it to my face—as you're doing now, Ellexa. But we'll argue that, publicly, when we come to it. Which way, Daya?"

Daya pointed with the rolled map. She and Ellexa avoided each other's eyes.

They left the gallery passage and ascended a much steeper, narrower one. Dropping the spear shaft, Eykar hauled himself up with both hands, concentrating on his progress and trying to outdistance his fear. But all the way a voice in his mind told him, *Poor, foolish Givard isn't the only one who's a dead man tonight. You have heard too much to live.*

The passage led them out behind the ruined watchtower overlooking Lammintown harbor. The night breezes seemed almost warm by comparison with the chilly currents in the caves. Torchlight blinded Eykar. Alldera strode out ahead, hailing the torch-carriers.

As he stood catching his breath and blinking, Eykar was seized roughly from behind. A knife point stung his neck, commanding silence. He was shoved through a gap in the walls and slammed against cold stone inside, all so quickly that he barely had time for panic.

A few paces away on the fractured paving of the watch-

tower floor lay a tangle of what his light-shocked eyes took
at first for discarded clothing or horse gear. Then the shapes
resolved into two bodies, laced and smeared with black
blood. Givard he knew by a Blue Company pennant tattooed
on one outflung arm. The head was a shapeless ruin. Poor,
foolish boy.

The other was Tezza-Bey, by whom in former days Eykar
had been served more than one cup of Erl the Scrapper's
sour, cloudy beer. She had been plain "Tezza" then,
homely, timid, and eager to please. Now her limbs were bent
at sickening angles and her face was a welter of blood. Firelight gleamed dully on the white of one half-open eye.

He thought numbly of the body of Doverdo, savaged in
secret for a similar transgression. His throat constricted,
holding back a cry, a curse, a protest: no use.

A fem stood by the corpses, turned away from Eykar, her
attention fixed on the doorway. She wore a striped mantle
around her head and shoulders and she carried one arm
tucked to her side. He recognized Kastia-Kai's stance.

The breath of his guard smelled beery.

"—what you mean," came Alldera's voice, ringing with
impatience. She marched in buoyant with energy and authority, throwing back her hair.

Daya and Ellexa crowded behind her, blocking the entry.
Alldera advanced alone. For all her quick step and alert carriage she was a fool of Fate; she still did not know why she
had been brought here.

Ellexa's hand dropped stealthily toward her boot top.
Many of the Free carried knives sheathed that way.

"Who did this?" Alldera's shocked stare rebounded from
the dead to the faces of the others. "Why haven't you raised
the alarm?"

No reply; they waited for some signal. He could summon
nothing in himself—no warning shout, no rush of heroic
strength. He was paralyzed by foreknowledge as bitter as
bile.

"Couldn't you cover them, at least?" Alldera reached for

the mantle that Kastia-Kai wore. The garment was given without a word. Alldera knelt with it by the bodies. "We sent out search parties, not executioners!"

"*You* sent," Ellexa said caustically. "*We* did what needed to be done. Someone has to."

Broken stone dug into Eykar's shoulder blades. His guard's knife shivered faintly against his throat. This was the knife of Tamansa-Nan, who had disemboweled a man chosen apparently at random on Murder Day.

Eykar hungrily sipped air, tasting its sea tang. They would kill Alldera in front of his eyes. If he was lucky they would kill him right after, quickly, still in the heat of action.

"Ellexa—" Alldera began sternly, and stopped. She looked back at the doorway, began to rise. "Daya? What is this?"

"Necessity," Daya hissed, and everyone burst into motion.

Kastia-Kai and Ellexa rushed Alldera, raised blades catching firelight. With a snarled curse Tamansa-Nan abandoned Eykar, lunging in after them.

Alldera sprang to her feet, flinging up the striped cloak as a shield. Retreating, she snatched at her own knife, sheathed at the back of her belt, rider-style. Daya stepped in behind her and pinned her reaching hand. Then there was a flurry of struggles, blows, and effortful sounds that filled time and space to the exclusion of all else.

"Stop, that's enough!" one cried: Ellexa, stepping back. A single blade, dulled with red, swung down again. Ellexa pulled and slapped the others away from their quarry. "That's enough, I said! It's supposed to look like the work of one man and a half-witted boy, not a pack of starved sharu!"

They stood away. Someone panted, "But she's still alive, Ellexa!"

In a moment they would turn to him. He had nowhere to go. Since he must die, let it be there with the only one of these people he had ever really known.

He limped hurriedly past the fixed, flushed faces of the assassins. Through his mind ran a gabble of prayer addressed indiscriminately to the fems' moon-goddess and to Setteo's Bears, not to let him stumble or collapse. The attackers made no move to stop him.

He lowered himself clumsily to the ground and lifted Alldera, working himself between her and the walls so that he could support her, his legs stretched outside of hers. Wetness spreading from her ribs warmed his right arm; yet she was breathing. She must have fended some blows off with Kastia's mantle, now a stained and sodden tangle around her.

Settled at last with nothing more to be done, he let his breath flood loose out of him. Their two heartbeats thumped like the footsteps of people running together.

She nudged his hand with blood-sticky fingers. "Sheel?"

"No."

She struggled. Absurdly embarrassed by her rejection in front of the assassins, he pinned her weakly threshing arms inside his encircling grip. "There's just me. Sshh."

Tamansa-Nan advanced, lean and menacing in the firelight. She turned her knife and held out the leather-wrapped pommel to Eykar. "You're taking the blame anyway, Muck. You might as well do the deed."

A scalding rage burst through his terror: "Butcher! Do it yourself!"

Then he buried his face against Alldera's hair. If he saw the killing blade descend he would have to scream. Alldera had not screamed. He did not want to disgrace himself, or her.

The Watchtower

For a moment, Alldera thought she had come imperceptibly awake to find herself lying with Beyarra again, that Beyarra's soft mouth and tongue languorously explored the lines at the corner of her eye and Beyarra's arms pressed in warmly on the sides of her breasts. Moved on upwelling pleasure and heat, she tried to turn her own face upward to catch the girl's lips with her own parted ones.

Pain savaged her body. Cut surfaces slid searingly one on the other so that she gasped and whimpered. *Oh, it hurts,* she thought, stunned. And this was Eykar's bony body supporting her, not Beyarra's rounded, resilient flesh.

Someone cried, "Tamansa, no! We can't let a Muck kill her—it's only supposed to *look* as if they did it."

Tamansa-Nan thrust one arm out, holding Daya back. "I don't care. Because of her I've lost my friend Juya and Juya's child to Witches who fuck with horses. I want to watch Alldera while her own special man-Muck cuts her throat."

Over Tamansa-Nan's arm Alldera saw the scarred face of the pet fem, the eyes like lightless holes. A knife sleeved with blood was clenched in Daya's wiry hand. How pitiable, that the only blood Daya was able to shed in the Holdfast was Alldera's. You could barely see the stains on her blouse—a useful thing, after all, that bright patchwork of men's flags.

Eykar whispered in her ear: "Don't move, don't say anything."

She wished she had managed to mark at least one of them. She wished they had killed her clean.

"Shh," he said, although she had made no sound other than the distressed drawing of another breath. "Let them talk. They'll quarrel."

He was right, of course. Doesn't the slave come to know the masters better than they know themselves?

Daya turned furiously on Ellexa. "It's all wrong, you've made a mess of it!"

"You thought it wouldn't be a mess?"

"Why did you stop us?" said Kastia-Kai. Alldera knew that querulous voice well. "I'd have finished her!"

Everyone began talking at once.

"It has to look right, it has to look—"

"That *Muck* is supposed to have—"

"—have gotten his hands on a weapon? Didn't anybody think?"

"—off the cliff, not cut her to pieces!"

"He wouldn't, nobody would believe—"

"—a Muck! Of course he would!"

"—all decided, what's wrong with everybody now?"

"I only wanted—"

"—be like this. You said—"

Their voices crackled with rage and fear. They paced the small stone room, gesticulating, all dramatic flash and shadow in the light of the sputtering fire. Alldera concentrated on the pain chewing her body, but their voices kept intruding.

"What are you afraid—"

"—never thought you meant—"

"We should have done what *I*—"

"Well, let's do it, then, let's—"

"—your fault, don't pretend—"

"The watch will hear! Do you want—"

"—distracted them, we arranged all that—"

"Coward! Why don't you—"

"Someone will come. We can't just—"

"—use your *brains,* will you!"

"You should have let us—"

Every time they looked over at their handiwork, she saw desperation gleaming in their eyes. Good. Let them shake over what they'd done, let them curse and revile each other.

Eykar kept repeating some inane query in a whisper: "How bad is it? What can I do?"

She lifted one hand away from her side and held it up, trembling with strain. Her knuckles were sheathed in blood and more leaked between her clenched fingers.

"Grabbed a knife, hung on." She had meant to wrest the weapon away and turn it on her attackers. She remembered everything as if it had happened to someone else, but the pain was hers. "Hurts like Hell."

He undid her belt and drew it free. He fastened the clasp and worked the loop of leather over her head and down so that her wounded hand was supported by a rough sling.

Lucky, she thought, resentful of the pain all this cramped, subtle jostling cost her, *to have something to do,* something that was within his capacity even in his fear. You could have danced to the beat of his hammering heart. Odd, to be so close again, and to sink into him so deeply for comfort, and not to mind now where his bony hip pressed her so uncomfortably. It was all right, as long as she could borrow his warmth.

Nothing he could do would help in the long run. They meant to kill her, the four of them (and apparently others not present now). They probably already had, if she could just stop fighting, let go, and die.

But her resistance was fueled by fitfully flaring rage at how Ellexa and Daya had set a trap for her, urging a death sentence against Tezza-Bey and Givard in order to sanction the already accomplished murders of the fugitives. If she had said, "Yes, we must execute them both immediately," would they have called off the attack on her? If so, for how long?

She grunted angrily. It hurt; everything hurt. Eykar continued making useless gestures of repair while the fems' voices swarmed and snapped. With a rag worried from somewhere, he wrapped her bloodied palm and then her closed fist. The bleeding lessened.

She rolled her heavy head back against him. A gash on the side of her neck leaked a slow, hot trickle down her skin. She thought she remembered the blade that had struck that blow glinting in Kastia's fist, and she struggled to hold on to that thought, as if there would be a reckoning.

Well, why not? A greedy, angry, madly hopeful appetite for survival continued its clamor. Her senses busily collected information, insisting that she was still alive. Eykar's cheek pressed, bristle-rough, against her temple. His skin was tacky with sweat, and he sighed each breath with effort. Dead weight she must be, almost as heavy as a corpse.

"—quiet, I said!" Daya cried across the babble of charge and countercharge.

In the brief silence that followed, Kastia-Kai protested, "This isn't what I agreed to!"

Alldera thought vengefully, *Too late for tears now.*

"Outside, everyone," Daya ordered. "We need to talk calmly. They aren't going anywhere."

Tamansa-Nan swung her booted foot into Eykar's bad leg—he flinched hard and gasped—and turned away.

"Somebody should stay here and keep watch," Ellexa said. "You all know how I feel about this. Daya can speak for me."

The others filed out through the crooked doorway, whispering and looking back over their shoulders.

"Finish me yourself, Ellexa?" Alldera whispered. "Should have done it years ago when your patrol caught me leaving Elnoa's camp against orders."

The weakness of her own voice frightened her. *What are they fussing about? Just wait a little and it will all be over.*

Ellexa sank down, her knee joints cracking, and fed sticks to the fire. "If Kastia and I had done this alone," she said morosely, "the way we first planned, it would have been finished ten minutes ago."

She tugged her embroidered knife belt straight, rubbing at a blood spot on it (*Some dead man's blood, or mine?* Alldera wondered). "But no, Kastia must have others in on it, to spread the 'support,' meaning the guilt, around. It could have been so simple!"

"But why?" Alldera groaned. "Why?"

Ellexa flicked a pebble onto the motionless chest of Givard. "We caught these two and killed them, against your *orders*," she sneered. "No one was willing to be shamed and punished for doing what had to be done. But we knew you wouldn't admit that we were right, and you confirmed that out of your own mouth."

"Excuse," Alldera said. "It's about the men. All, not just Givard. Everything, for you, about the men."

"Of course," Ellexa rejoined, scowling. "Your Muck, there, is still their leader and Setteo is their spy, but you protect them both. We could lose everything because you don't see how dangerous these two are, like all their kind. And how easily these unslaves can still be influenced by them. You wouldn't listen, not even to me; and I'm no careless killer of men.

"I spoke up in favor of fining Leeja-Beda, remember, after she hacked down that Dirtmuck in one of my work gangs. Do you think you're the only one among us who's sick of bloodletting and brutality? I am a civilized person, even though I was a slave. But these two runaways—it couldn't be allowed. You're corrupted, you don't see it. And that's why.''

"Treachery," Alldera spat weakly. "The vice of slaves."

Ellexa rubbed her palms on the thin, tough grass. "Well, your solicitude for the men is more than a vice. It's a deadly threat to everyone's freedom, though some people are still too blinded by hero worship to notice. You made me Chief Whip over these Mucks. I notice." She looked with thoughtful hatred at Eykar. Alldera felt his arms tighten shakily.

"But," Alldera said with energy, and fainted. When she came to again she heard the blurred rise and fall of voices outside the shattered chamber as the others argued, she remembered only intermittently about what.

Ellexa had turned, hiding her face from the firelight.

"—that man's head," she said venomously. "The first trophy of a master's death at our own hands. And you, who had stayed in camp, who had not yet struck one blow against a living man, you scolded me for it. You shamed me in front of everyone, for the death of a man."

"I said I was sorry." Alldera reached toward her and relapsed against Eykar again, her head whirling. "Later, at Oldtown. Apologized, Ellexa."

Ellexa rose to her feet and stood over them. "This isn't personal anymore. I've been watching you. You care more about the unslaves than you do about us because you share their softness about men. You conspire with these Newly Freed youngsters to parcel out the captive Mucks among them. You even sleep with one of these spineless unslaves. Her kind will become the mothers of the children of the new Holdfast, never mind how they've been collaborating with their masters for years!"

She looked over at the two dead runaways. "I'm years past my last bleeding, but I'm still a living person, and I think. Just because I don't talk all the time, that doesn't mean my head is empty.

"What will we be, we Free Fems who came and fought and won? Old, barren, useless, figures of fun when our faces flame and sweat and we have to go to Fedeka for medicine just to keep our bodies balanced. We'll be unrespected and cast aside.

"So despite our wishes and our warnings, other unslaves will do as Tezza-Bey did, emulating you, Alldera. They'll throw our victory away and end up slaves again, them and us and all their daughters in turn. You expect me to stand by and watch you make way for that to happen?"

She glared down at Alldera with a terrible, drawn face. "Have you forgotten poor Tua, our first death here? I taught her how to choose the right tea leaves to pick, on the other side of the mountains. You didn't know that, did you? And now she's dead. She didn't die for nothing. I won't let it be for *nothing,* in the end!"

Alldera thought of Tua's dripping body drawn from the well in the Oldtown yard. "Sorry," she whispered. "Mistakes. You win anyway. Kobba should have been leader; I always said so."

Ellexa began to speak but left off, shaking her head. She squatted down again and held her hands out over the licking flames.

In minuscule increments of motion Eykar shifted his position and stretched his bad leg. Alldera jabbed at him weakly with her elbow. "Don't—hurts!"

But she held onto his forearm with her hand that was undamaged. She clung to the warm, shivering life in Eykar's angular body, fearful of what he could not shelter her from no matter how long or how determinedly he held her.

Like pain. When the muffling effect of shock receded, the pain would be left exposed, full strength. She could barely cope with what was getting through now. *Think of something else.*

Think of the conspirators displaying her dead body and telling lies about what had happened. They would assign to themselves heroic roles and actions that had come too late or been foiled by the clever brutality of Eykar Bek, the Dirt-muck Alldera had recklessly kept near her. Some would be-

lieve them, some not; Daya was a persuasive narrator. Ellexa, Chief Whip, had authority.

True, Alldera had staunch adherents (like little Beyarra-
Bey, for whom she felt now a throb of helpless loss). But to
many of them Alldera was a legend, a deity in spite of herself. People can believe anything of a legend. Their feelings
about such a person are large and malleable, not intimate and
truly knowing.

Daya, whose scent and taste and mercurial nature Alldera
had known better than she had known herself, who had been
closest to her and a part of her own story, had misunderstood
everything; everything.

Daya would explain, and they would believe her. Well,
maybe Fedeka wouldn't—assuming the dyer wasn't part of
the plot herself, on Moonwoman's behalf.

What would Sheel say? In the Grasslands, as sharemother
in Alldera's child she would have called a feud on the killers. Here in the Holdfast she might judge the cost of vengeance too high. But Sheel would feel something, maybe
more than Sorrel would when she heard. (Lucky Sorrel, who
was not part of this bloody land with its old hatreds. That
was real freedom; surely to have given her that was a success
no later failure could erase!)

If some fems didn't believe the lies—if people took sides,
breaking the difficult unity of the Free, they could still lose
all. Their triumph could slip away while they fought for
power over each other instead of over their enemies.

She twisted in Eykar's arms. "We learned it from you!"

"What?" Damn him, was he deaf?

"It was you, you," she gasped, hitting her head against
him in her need to pass on her pain. "We learned it from our
masters—treachery!"

"Yes, Hera." He tightened his hold and crowded his head
against hers, muffling her strengthless violence.

Why wasn't it Nenisi Conor of the Riding Women, or
sweet Beyarra-Bey, holding her here at the end of her life?
Why wasn't it Daya the pet fem, whom she had loved long

and who had once loved her, triumphantly beautiful with her scars or without them? Where was Nenisi, black as deep water, mother and mentor and joy of those years in the Grasslands?

Alldera pressed her blood-smeared cheek against her man-slave's neck and wept.

Unslave

B eyarra hated the caves at night. She hated Lammintown, with its cold winds and its nearness to the
gloomy northern Wild, at all times. But Tezza-Bey
was hiding somewhere in these dark passages, and Tezza-
Bey was her freename friend. Now Tezza-Bey had done
something so foolish and dangerous that she would need all
that well-placed friends could do for her.

She had always had a daring imagination, behind that soft,
foolish face of hers. Since Beyarra would not break her
promise to Alldera—since Beyarra-Bey slept now in Alldera's bed, and might even tell her of the plan to run away
with a young man—Tezza had done it on her own.

And with Givard, of all people! A blowhard and a coward,
a dangerous sort even for a master—

Muck, Beyarra corrected herself as she hurried along following the mental picture of one of the maps she had tried to
memorize in Cliff's Eye. Dangerous even for a Dirtmuck.

*I never thought she would do it alone; but she has, and I
didn't warn Alldera beforehand. I could have said some-*

thing, but I never thought she would try it alone. Round and round her guilty thoughts chased each other in useless circles that could change nothing.

Only action could do that.

Beyarra stopped, feeling a current of cold air on her cheek. A side passage here led out at a deep crack in the cliff's lip. This was not the way that Tezza had planned to go; it was too exposed. But there was no telling what Tezza-Bey had let Givard persuade her into attempting.

Now it seemed obvious that Tezza had nursed a special liking for Givard all along. Maybe she had never meant to share him at all. The silly fool, to pick a time when the watch, changing after suppertea, could scarcely avoid spotting the two runaways entering the caves!

Now Tezza had people like Kobba and Ellexa after her, and Beyarra-Bey rushing around trying to save her. There was no rest, it seemed, for the free.

What Beyarra feared more than losing her way forever or falling into some unmapped chasm was running into the searchers herself. She did not think they would believe that she was only trying to help them find the fugitives.

What, exactly, to say to Tezza when she found her Beyarra had carefully thought out: she must persuade her friend to throw herself on Alldera's mercy and take her punishment. Alldera was a great and thoughtful soul; she would understand, she would be merciful. She would take pity on her new lover and her lover's foolish friend.

Wouldn't she? Beyarra swallowed a sob of desolation and stopped to blot her eyes.

"So slow!" hissed someone very close on her left. "Too late!"

Beyarra froze, her thoughts flying in terror. The searchers would have challenged her, and they had torches. So who was this?

"Tezza?" she squeaked.

"Lost in the Country of Anger!" came the agitated response. "Like your Chief-Blessed herself, though she at least is still alive, I think. The yellow Bear said nothing can help her escape but 'birds.' You aren't a bird.''

Setteo.

''What are *you* doing here?'' Beyarra was petrified that he would touch her in the darkness.

''I am waiting, Blessed; for you?'' He sounded doubtful. It was rather insulting.

''But where are they—Alldera, and Tezza?'' Beyarra was petrified now that she had had a moment to consider the meaning, such as there was, of his words. Tezza dead, Alldera in danger—she hoped it was only the cutboy's madness speaking.

''The Country of Anger has no boundaries,'' Setteo said eagerly. ''The only way out is by flying up into the sky. But to fly high enough takes the power of more than one wing. Birds have two. How many have you, Blessed?''

If he was here, the searchers probably were not. She straightened her shoulders and tried to produce a convincing tone of command. ''Take me to Alldera and Tezza-Bey.''

''But then they will kill us too, Blessed,'' he whined. ''Death is the only harvest in the Country of Anger.''

''I order you, Muck!'' she cried. ''Do as I say!''

Silence. Where was he, exactly? Beyarra, her voice choked with fear and frustration, thought suddenly of Erl the Scrapper's home hall in the City: two ''wings'' joined at the kitchen.

''Setteo, if a building has two wings, is it a bird?''

After a moment he said, ''Will you trick me, Blessed? Of course. Two wings make a bird.''

''Good, that's the right answer.'' Swallowing her dread and reaching into the darkness, she caught his hand in a spasmodic grip. ''Now, I am the east wing and you are the west wing. When we join hands, like this, we can fly away out of the Country of Anger and bring Alldera and Tezza-Bey with us.''

''Of course, Blessed,'' he answered with alacrity, giving

her fingers a shy squeeze. "Quick, though. The Bears are roused tonight."

She had no more idea what Setteo's eternal "bears" were than the nature of a "bird." Imagining something slimy sniffing along her path through the caves, Beyarra trotted after Setteo. She was so upset, and so astounded by her own daring, that she completely lost track of where they were among the cliff passages.

Suddenly he let go of her hand and with a muttered incantation began to climb. She struggled after him, concentrating on groping from hold to hold. Before she knew where she was, cold wind whipped her hair and she stumbled out onto grassy turf under a cloud-blurred scrap of moon.

Breakers pounded the rocks far below. She hastily backed away from the cliff's edge, sucking at a stinging graze on her knuckle.

Setteo tugged her sleeve, drawing her toward a rough mass that stood black against the stars. There, a glow of light moved as they moved, and vanished—inside the old watchtower? But why would Alldera be here? Had Tezza-Bey and Givard tried to hide inside those broken walls? And lit a *fire*?

Hearing femmish voices from somewhere around the side of the ruins, she backed a step. If other people had found the runaways, wasn't she too late? Wouldn't she just put herself in danger too if she tried to help now?

But she already was in trouble. A person who would deliberately sneak away with Givard all by herself wouldn't shrink from trying to throw blame on an absent and innocent (well, comparatively innocent) friend. Full of sick anxiety, Beyarra crept up on the voices, trying to think out what she could say in her own defense.

Three people—Daya and a couple of unslaves by the sound of them—were quarreling. Beyarra-Bey listened, pressed to the stone wall out of the wind.

They said terrible things, so terrible that at first she could not believe what she was hearing. Tears of shock and horror chilled on her cheeks. Tears for Tezza, whom they said they had killed. A grievous blow; but life as a bond fem had taught Beyarra that fools often died of their folly.

They also said that Alldera was stabbed and dying.

Beyarra remembered not last night's kisses but her own arrival at the Free Fem's camp outside Oldtown, and Alldera joking about not being tall. Anyone might find her way to the bed of a great person, but that moment of first meeting was Beyarra's own. Her heart swelled with anguish.

What they said could not be true.

She crept away along the watchtower wall and climbed carefully up on some heaped rubble to peer inside. A fire burned on the ground, and by its light she could make out a person squatting nearby. Someone else, a dark, shapeless, bulky form, lay propped against the wall.

Two others were sprawled with the peculiar stillness of the dead in the middle of the shadowy enclosure: poor Tezza, and Givard. She had seen many dead people in her life, and was steadied rather than shaken by the sight. The Country of Anger, indeed. All slaves knew that land, dark with blood and strewn with corpses.

Beyarra backed away and whispered into the darkness, "Setteo! Setteo! Where are you?"

Her groping hand closed on the cutboy's short, greasy hair. She bent close—he smelled sharp and rimy, like sea wrack from the beach—and said into his ear, "Setteo, no birds are strong enough to fly Alldera out of here. Go get help from your Angels."

"Oh, yes," he whispered quickly. "Angels too have wings, although these are not visible in the Warm World."

Oh, Mother Moon, if only he wasn't too mad to do what was needed! "Run and find Sheel Torrinor or one of the others—you know who they are. Bring them here, as fast as you can!"

"I have no tokens to take me safely among the Angels," he whispered back. "Give me something for them, Blessed."

He was right; without some sign, why should they follow

him? But Beyarra had only a small knife she used for sewing, and no one put weapons in the hands of Dirts.

She took hold of the silver ring her first master had had fixed to her right ear, set her blade against the narrowest part of the lobe, and with a stifled gasp cut the bauble free. Warm drops spattered her neck. She tucked the earring into Setteo's hand and curled his fingers shut on it.

"Here's your token." She only hoped it would mean something to the Wild Women.

He was gone with scarcely a sound. She was straining for the faintest trace of his departing footsteps when harsh hands seized and lifted her bodily off her feet.

"Got him!" someone shouted. "Another runaway!"

"No, it's a fem—a spy!"

Hot urine burned down her legs as they dragged her into the tower and turned her face to the glare of the fire.

"Beyarra-Bey," Tamansa said. "What are you doing here? Who cut you? Ugh, you stink!"

"I was looking for Tezza," Beyarra gulped. "She's my friend, I wanted to help—"

Kastia-Kai prodded Beyarra with her crooked finger. "Tezza's past help. What are we going to do with you now?"

Beyarra stammered, "Kill me too, I think." She could not stop the spate of words and didn't care, since she had so completely and publicly shamed herself in her terror. "Why not? You have no decency in you. You're no better than masters yourselves, to kill Tezza-Bey, a bond fem all her life just like you and me. And to attack Alldera Messenger— shame on you, traitors!"

Daya looked distantly down at her. "I am no traitor. I serve the interests of Moonwoman before anyone else's. And I protect those I love, Beyarra-Bey. I have loved you, but you never loved me."

Beyarra locked her gaze on Daya's pale, scarred face. "You are a killer, and your friends here are killers, like you, and cowards, like you! We told the Bayo-born that we were bringing them home to live with heroes!''

"What a creature!'' Tamansa-Nan said scornfully. "All loyalty but no sense, and no guts; as you can smell right now, if you try.''

Beyarra blubbered, ''You've always hated me, Tamansa, but my weakness is nothing to yours. Cowards! Criminals! You do the men's work for them and then boast of your courage and your virtue!''

All wrong—she should dominate them with her cool composure, cleverly stalling, giving Setteo time to fetch help. Instead she rushed on, fighting the completion of murder with a torrent of tears and condemnation.

"I know the brave stories you tell, Daya, about how the Free Fems turned warrior and won the Holdfast with Moonwoman's help. I could tell those stories as well as you tell them, but even if I walk away alive tonight, I never will. I'll cut my own throat before I tell any tales that I've learned from a scheming pet fem who's struck down her own friend and leader!''

Daya said impassively, ''Alldera and Tezza-Bey have both spat on the wisdom of Moonwoman and the safety of their own people. Both are traitors with men.''

"Kill me too, I don't care!'' Beyarra stormed. "I'm ashamed to be Newly Freed, and ashamed to be the first to have joined the Free Fems. I don't want to listen to your sly, cruel voice anymore, and I don't want to live to see what the Army of the Free becomes without Alldera Messenger to lead it.''

Kastia-Kai said, ''I don't have to listen to this.'' She held her bloodied knife rather unsteadily to Beyarra's chest. "You're so young and so stupid, you don't know anything!''

Daya seemed to erupt, her face dark and distorted with rage. "Be quiet, Kastia! You're a bully and a fool.''

"What? What names are you calling me?''

"The names,'' Daya said scathingly, ''that belong to you,

Matri-mate. You helped kill poor Tua, maybe you twisted the cord yourself. How could I think I could work with you? You should have died with your friend Mayala.''

"Stop it, both of you, and listen to me!" Tamansa-Nan said. She hovered over the victims, the dead and the still living. "This can still work. We'll say that Eykar Bek and Givard killed Alldera and Tezza-Bey, and Beyarra-Bey tried to save her friend and was killed by the Mucks too."

They were quiet, thinking.

The energy drained out of Beyarra, leaving her feeling faint and very cold. Her clammy pants—castoffs of Alldera's tailored by Beyarra to her own use—clung icily to her seat and legs. These people would shove her off the cliff's edge, and all she could do was stand there weeping.

"It's too much," Ellexa said somberly. She shook her gleaming silver hair back from her face, now stark and tragic-looking in the fitful firelight. "How many bodies do you count, Tamansa-Nan? These two on the ground, and those two over there, and now this little unslave as well?"

"Not Beyarra," Daya said. "She's not at fault."

Ellexa ignored her. "I said I would help kill Alldera and see the Man Who Killed His Father die for it. Well, Alldera is still alive, the man is still alive, and Tamansa says we have three deaths to go."

"Only three?" Tamansa-Nan demanded. "How many fems, bond and Free, have died for lesser reasons in your lifetime, Ellexa?"

Ellexa shook her head. "Beyarra-Bey made herself unslave when she saw the chance. We Free Fems didn't have to do it for her. Her death would be one too many and one too heavy for me."

She lifted her regal chin and walked over to put her arm around Beyarra's shoulders. Beyarra-Bey trembled, trying not to collapse against Ellexa like a strengthless cub.

Kastia-Kai threw her knife down. "I'm not part of this. I only pretended to strike. I changed my mind, but I thought you all would kill me too if I said so. I'm only an old bond fem—"

"That won't save you if Alldera dies," Tamansa-Nan said nastily. "Or if she lives, either. You think we can switch sides and still survive this mess? You think Alldera will ever forgive any of us? Who's for going with me, into the Wild? Who's got that much courage, at least?"

Kastia-Kai shook her good fist in the air. "Daya, why did I listen to you?"

Daya said, "Listen to me now, you fraud—all of you, you cowards! No, be quiet, *listen*. I am the greatest coward of you all, and the greatest coward thinks best for a gang of cowards."

They seemed mesmerized by her voice, which dripped self-loathing and despair. "Listen," she continued, "and you'll see I'm right: if you're not going to finish it, then you must try to mend it. Go and fetch Emla. She's a healer these days, second only to Fedeka. She'll help if she can, because it will lift her up at the same time that her enemies are cast down."

Beyarra-Bey gulped. "I've already sent for help."

"Of course you have," Daya said. "There is one hero with us, and she has already acted the hero's part. Look at her, my company of cowards: look at my little former bed-mate, and learn how someone looks who acts from nerve instead of fear."

Beyarra could think of nothing to say to this except to ask if it really was all over. But if she questioned, someone else might also question; and then indeed the answer might be no, despite what the pet fem said.

So Beyarra stood still in her reeking clothes and stared silently back at the circle of murderers.

One by one they looked away.

Maps of Heaven Cut in Stone

Eykar Bek, plucking weeds from the damp earth of the terrace garden, straightened his back and looked inland. The visitors were still there, camped on the loading dock built into the rocky spit that led out to Endpath.

One of the visitors stood outside their tent talking with a mounted Woman black as storm clouds, though which of the Rois cousins it was he could not have told at any distance.

The spring morning was fresh and cool. He had salvaged a patched, musty cloak from his old quarters in the south tower room. Wrapped in faded black, he would be nearly invisible to the visitor against the jet wall of upper Endpath rising behind him.

The others of this latest embassy from the Army of the Free had ridden off somewhere, leaving horses—two, he thought, but his sight was unreliable—tethered by the dock. In all likelihood it was about the horses that these two were speaking.

Eykar had expected the visitors to be gone this morning, their errand as vain as that of the earlier groups—at least one delegation per month right through the cold heart of the winter. Even Sheel Torrinor had declared herself, guardedly, impressed by the persistence of Alldera's people.

Perhaps Fedeka, leader of this latest crew, would not be put off as easily as the others. His narrow garden, built up of windblown dust and compost tended by each Endtendant in turn, might not be harvested this summer, after all. A pity. His reward here had always been the pleasures of solitude and simple labor within earshot of the breakers. The last thing he had ever expected was to return to his old post with all its horrors scoured away but its meager joys still open to him. He was not in charge here now; no decisions fell to him beyond those concerning the tangle of uprooted stems and roots in his hands.

It came to him as he stood there, in a fortress now held by fems against fems, visited by fems on pressing femmish business, that he had been mistaken all along about his situation.

Alldera's personal attention to him, based on the unique history the two of them shared, had misled him into thinking that the core of the Free Fems' return to the Holdfast was the forging of a new relationship with their former masters. In that relationship he had seen a necessary, though risky, place for himself as an intermediary.

What nonsense! The central matter of the femmish conquest was, of course, the relations of the fems to one another, among themselves, and to the Wild Women who had returned with them. His masculine arrogance had told him otherwise, an error he had been blind to because he had believed all the arrogance beaten out of himself. What a fool! Even Setteo the cutboy, that unlikely minor hero of Alldera's rescue, had clearer self-knowledge.

He turned away from the low shoreline cliffs and limped seaward along the terrace to toss the weeds into the sea.

Beyarra-Bey stood at the south tower, watching him. She had wrapped a blanket around herself. With her pointed face and upswept hair, she made an elegant silhouette.

"You're sure none of those things are edible?" she said.

"As sure as any Endtendant ever was, yes, Hera, I am," he said. "And necessity made some great gardeners here."

He waited, dusting his palms one on the other. She was the easiest of all to talk to, when no one else was near. He owed her his life and Alldera's and had gladly ceded her a corner of his garden. She had planted a flowering vine in memory of her friend Tezza-Bey, and he had twice seen her weeping there.

They had an unspoken understanding: although Beyarra was Alldera's lover, Eykar was entitled to his own special relationship with the runner, because of the events of that night in the watchtower. He and Beyarra were not rivals but allies, though cautious ones.

She stared at him, perplexed. "You look so—contented here. Some people would go mad from being locked up in this awful place."

"Many Endtendants did," he said, "over the years."

"*I* will, if we don't leave soon! Each time people come begging Alldera to go back, I'm afraid it will be the last time they ask. I think there are ghosts here."

He said gravely, "Yesterday before suppertea I thought I heard men singing an old chant of lovers' death together, up on the east terrace. There was no one, of course."

She tightened her blanket about herself.

Eykar leaned against the terrace wall, his grimy fingers absently exploring the facing of pitted stone. "Maybe Hera Fedeka can persuade everyone that it's safe for Alldera to return."

Beyarra-Bey looked close to tears; a strange hero. "Everyone wants to go. If only Alldera—"

"Ah," he said, and waited for her to lead the way across this dangerous ground.

She hesitated. "Maybe if you speak to her?"

"Too risky. Emla wants to kill me as it is."

"Oh, Emla," Beyarra said. "It's not personal. She just needs to put plenty of distance between herself and that murderer Ellexa because they were lovers once. So she tries to make herself indispensable, and she hates it when her patient wants your company more than hers.'' She giggled, her eyes sparkling.

''That's only sometimes,'' Eykar said, thinking of fevers from which Alldera had wakened in a screaming panic at the sight of him.

''All memories are mixed,'' the little unslave said kindly. ''When she's herself Alldera knows what you did for her.''

''I did far less than you did yourself,'' he said, ''Hera.''

Her color deepened and she gnawed anxiously at her thumbnail. ''Oh, that was just—it doesn't make my advice any good. But Alldera knows *you* wouldn't tell her it was safe to leave if it wasn't really safe.''

''Pardon, Hera, but what would a slave, marooned here for months, know about femmish politics in the City?''

She drew herself up, small but determined. ''Do you refuse to help persuade her?''

He bowed. ''I'll try. Where is she?''

''On the east upper walk, for the morning sun. Emla and I helped her out there an hour ago.''

From the east walk one could look out to sea and not notice the visitors camped on the spit. The landward view of the dock was blocked by the shallow dome of the central chamber's roof.

''I'll go,'' he said, ''but can you secure us a little privacy? Some people would as soon tip me over the edge as have me talk alone with Alldera.''

Beyarra-Bey nodded, brightening. She enjoyed a touch of intrigue. He would not be surprised to learn that she had slipped out of Endpath on her own to meet with the visitors.

''Shall I call Setteo to help you?'' she said. ''I think he's fishing off the lower terrace again.''

''I can manage.'' He limped past her to the south tower room.

''There are no fish anymore,'' she called after him, ''are there?''

"I never saw any, Hera. I think he's trying to magic them back from even before the Ancients' times." And enjoying the effort. How odd that of them all, only the cutboy might be said to be happier than Eykar was himself, here in this black house of sorrows.

The south chamber was built around a scorch-marked hearth where generations of Endtendants had burned dried sea wrack against the winter damp. Beside the hearth a narrow stair mounted past bright slits in the outer wall. The wind whined through the openings, turning the stairwell into a tunnel of icy drafts.

There was no railing, some freezing soul having long ago burned it for fuel. The hollows where brackets had held it had become handholds, polished smooth by the use of many Endtendants since. Eykar used them to offset the weakness of his lame leg.

For years of his young life, he had inhabited this place with four drug-numbed servants who were also his keepers. For years no one came but sick, wretched men looking for ritual death at his hands. Now everything was so changed that he never knew whether to laugh or cry.

How many times had he stepped through this upper doorway—not panting and sweating and in pain, not in those days? He looked out across the broad pavement that ended in an open drop, fifty feet to the foam-bitten rocks below.

Alldera, her back to him, occupied the single seat—a massive stone block—that gave on that prospect. Each Endtendant had found ways to cushion the bench, using grass or fabric or even turf cut from the shore. Alldera, huddling in a thick cloak, sat on a pad of folded blankets.

"They're still here," Bek announced. "From the City. You can't put off seeing them forever."

He avoided the honorific "Hera" deliberately, to provoke something besides the brooding grief in which she had been sunk all winter. He could not bear signs of weakness in her after all she had surmounted. Besides, very inconveniently, her pain hurt him, and he had more than enough of his own.

She glanced back at him, her face set, and did not reply.

"This is not a solution," he said. "You know it as well as I do."

No answer.

When they had first brought her to Endpath, which a handful of people could hold against a host if need be, he had helped Emla and Beyarra-Bey to tend Alldera. Now that she was better, he was careful not to touch her, although the impulse to do so was often strong. Sometimes he remembered that night in the watchtower, feeling the deep tension of shock slowly loosening in her body within the fragile shielding of his arms. Today he just wanted to rub the stiffened fingers of her wounded hand and feel the suppleness begin to return.

And there were moments when he thought he saw the signs of response in her, in a glance, a look lingering unaccountably on his face when he was turned partway from her and might not notice. But the attack had left her as sensitive as if she had been flayed, and he was a slave here, not a free person who might risk an unbidden touch. He must depend entirely on words.

He said, "Do you realize that this group has waited six days?"

"How long did you live here as Endtendant?"

"Years. But that was different. I was an official murderer, with nowhere else to go."

Whitecaps trimmed the incoming waves like foamy scarves. Under the waves lay the ashes of generations of men who had come up the pilgrim path. He thought of them with a tenderness which he had not felt for the doomed but living men at the time. He wondered if she thought of them at all.

"These visitors come as suppliants," he said. "Even at this distance, they reek of contrition."

"Stop telling me what I know, Eykar."

A footing firm enough to support honesty existed between them. Still, that footing might be snatched out from under

him at her will. So it had been between them when he
had been the master and she the slave. She had taken heart-
stopping risks then. He took one now.

"All right, let me tell you what *I* know. If your enemies
held power in the City, they could have starved us all out
months ago. Instead, supplies have been sent regularly since
we came here. These visitors have something to offer you,
surely. Isn't it time to find out what? You can't be afraid of
your own kind for the rest of your life."

"What do you know about it? You weren't attacked by
your friends." The querulous voice, the fearful voice that it
was agony to hear.

"I was Endtendant. I didn't have friends."

"I'm not going to give them anything they want, that's
all," she muttered vengefully. But he saw by the trembling
of her lips that she was deeply afraid, in her flesh and her
bones. He knew how crises of pain and shock could do that
to a person long after the wounds themselves had healed.

"What about what *you* want?" he said. "Is it this, to live
in this castle of death for the rest of your life?"

"Who sent you up here?" she said suspiciously, and
looked away again. "Better you than Kenoma anyway; she
talks about nothing but her own health and how much better
she feels here at Endpath than down in Lammintown. And
she's always making sucking noises that I can't stand, with
those pits or stones or whatever she keeps in her mouth. At
least Sheel will tell a joke now and then."

Now that Kenoma felt better, she seemed filled with a
restless energy that made Eykar very wary. He suspected her
of filching from the food supply to assuage her ravenous appetite, but he didn't dare say anything; Alldera trusted her.
The blonde Riding Woman Sheel and her black-skinned co-
horts, who had never spoken a word to him, he both feared
very much and thought magnificent.

"Endpath is hard on them all," he said. "They don't have
manna to make them dream sweet dreams, as my Rovers
did."

"Don't rub your leg like that. Sit down, if it's bothering you."

She drew her robe aside to make room on the bench. He lowered himself with a grateful groan and stretched out both legs, spreading his cloak over them like some arthritic old Senior with bad knees.

"I used to come up here in all weathers," he said, "watching for demons in the ocean, or for a ferry tying up with supplies for my Rovers and me. Sometimes I slept out here."

"You did?" she said skeptically. He could see why. A bleaker, more barren spot could scarcely be imagined.

"Summer nights, I used to sleep on this bench. I saw comets; or visions, when rations ran short."

"Visions." Alldera laughed abruptly and pulled her robe closer about her. "I've seen some myself. I've seen the ghosts of all the Holdfast fems who ever prayed for help and begged for mercy and died anyway, the ones who didn't live to see us win. Maybe what was done to me was a kind of blood price, exacted as a penalty for my failure."

"Failure?" he said blankly. "What failure?"

"Failure to save them, of course! Dams and kits, generation after generation—apart from a pathetic handful of fugitives—every one of them died a slave. I came in time for nothing but a scraggly, leftover remnant, probably both the first and the last Holdfast fems who get to die free."

He was silent, thinking of his own ghosts, the ash-men under the tide.

She rocked, huddling in her wrappings and murmuring, "So many. More than all the waves in the sea."

Pulling himself together with an effort, he said firmly, "These are unhealthy thoughts, Alldera. Maybe not untrue ones, but certainly unhealthy and dangerous."

She stopped rocking and shot him a mordant look. "Well, you would know, wouldn't you, Endtendant?"

With relief he took up the opportunity to shift their discourse out of these dismal waters. He pointed.

"Over there on that parapet is my picture panel. Each of us in turn chose a spot to make his mark, to fill the time between death dreams. Some of the work is very fine."

He wanted to get her up on her feet so that he could induce her to turn and look to landward, where the embassy waited.

She slumped against the seat. "So you're an artist too? Beyarra should have taught her needle skills to you, not me. What did you write on your piece of the wall?"

"Come and look." He gathered himself to rise.

"Just tell me, Eykar. I'm not stirring from here."

He sighed. "Stars. I made maps of the heavens as they look from here. It wasn't an original idea; Endtendants before me did the same. You could study the history of the stars, if they have a history, on that wall. I spent whole days puzzling out the traces left by my predecessors."

"And what did you learn?"

"I don't remember. Sometimes it's as if I never left, and sometimes this place hardly seems connected to me anymore. Alldera. Do you want Endpath connected to you, in the tales of your own people?

"Do you want to sit here and watch the sky and the sea until you begin seeing phantoms with your open, waking eyes? Do you want to condemn your friends to become nothing but your Rovers, attached to you and existing only to attend you? You can grow old here cutting your own star map into black stone, and die surrounded by the ashes of a hundred thousand dead men. Listen to me. I know what I'm talking about."

"It's not just me," she said, staring straight ahead with fierce concentration. "It's them too. They put their lives on the line for me, bringing me up here, guarding me, keeping me alive. Some people must hold that against them. Given the opportunity, those people will punish them."

"That's not what you're afraid of."

"I mean you too, Bek." She shot him a look of naked emotion forged that night in the watchtower. "For your own safety, I should send you off into the Wild with Setteo. You did that for me, remember.''

"A cripple and a madman, starving together in a forest! I'm better off with you, despite the risks." And he took another one, deliberately. "You promised me the Library. Was that a lie?"

"What if it was?"

His heart twisted. "If I thought that were true, I would drag you to the edge now and throw you down to the rocks!"

"Watch out," she said, her lips white. "Watch out, Eykar."

"What for?" He pushed up off the bench and took a limping step away from her, flooded with violent despair. "You're no danger to anyone. You've let them change you. You let them bleed all your courage out of you with their knives that night."

"Who," she said, "do you think you're talking to?"

"Alldera Chief, Alldera Conqueror. I'm talking to her, or to no one." He was begging and didn't care. "I have legions of dead behind me. Don't make me mourn for a person still living now too. I can't stand it."

She offered a faint, satirical smile. "What you can't stand is having wasted your gorgeous rescue on a boring, cowardly, ordinary person instead of a hero out of men's chants and femmish stories."

"As you say, *Hera.*"

She ignored the sneer. " 'Hera' is meant to stand for 'hero.' You tell me, from all your knowledge of history you've gleaned from your precious library: what kind of hero is attacked by her own people?"

"*No,*" he said. "You don't understand, you have it all wrong. A handful of former slaves, frightened and confused by war and reversals of everything they thought they knew, lost their nerve and turned on their leader. That's all."

"No it's not." She squinted up at him. "And you should know better. Look: in the old days when you gave me orders, that made me know I was a slave. When a Matri acting for you told me what to do, that made me know I was a cub as well as a slave—altogether, a person completely without significance.

"Don't you see? I made too many decisions, gave too many orders. I made my own people feel small and childish. No wonder they attacked me, as if I were a master, or a Matri."

"Well, maybe they *are* small and childish. Maybe it's their fault, not yours."

"Then I don't want them!" she shouted. "I don't care if they say they want me back. I don't want them!"

He saw her lower lip tremble again. It maddened him. "I don't understand you! Didn't you tell me not to expect fems to be gods? They were slaves! What do you want from them? Isn't it enough that you've all come home, you've fought us and beaten us? Isn't victory with a little blood on it, a little shame on it, good enough for you?"

"Don't talk to me like that." She fixed him with a murderous glare. "You have no right. You've spent your life infatuated with a murderous criminal who did nothing but crap on you for his own profit and pleasure, and invite other men to do the same. You settled for that—scorn, betrayal, abuse—you lapped up what your *lover* D Layo dished out, and then you crawled back for more! You don't ask anything of people. I do."

He clasped his hands behind his back to keep from striking her. "But you ask nothing of yourself. When you were a slave you were afraid all the time, but you had courage. You showed it to me. What you're showing me now I can't stand to look at."

She turned away with a sharp intake of breath.

Spent and panting, horrified at his own outburst, he considered what he would give to take back everything he had just said. Maybe she would have him killed now, and regret it later; or not. Maybe they could never ever find a way to soothe and heal each other, only to rip and tear.

She sniffed, scrubbed at her nose with the edge of the

blanket, and muttered, "So don't look. You make a really rotten slave, I hope you know that. The Lady must favor you or you'd never have survived this long. Fedeka would probably cut my throat if she heard me say that. She'd certainly cut yours.

"Well, I'm fed up with being lectured and yelled at by a damned slave." Alldera thrust the blanket aside and began to lever herself up onto her feet. "Go tell Kenoma to invite our visitors in. Let's get this over with."

Angry Hearts

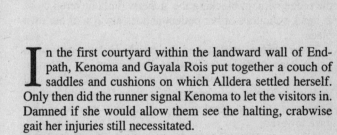

I n the first courtyard within the landward wall of Endpath, Kenoma and Gayala Rois put together a couch of
saddles and cushions on which Alldera settled herself.
Only then did the runner signal Kenoma to let the visitors in.
Damned if she would allow them see the halting, crabwise
gait her injuries still necessitated.

Sheel stayed outside with the Endpath horses: no matter
what happened, no horses were going to end up as strays,
vulnerable to capture by strangers.

Beyarra-Bey, bluish with cold in a pretty two-cloth smock
which left arms and neck bare, fussed and dithered until
Alldera asked her to go prepare refreshments for the visitors.
Setteo had hidden himself somewhere, asking his Bears for a
happy outcome, no doubt.

Alldera stationed Eykar well back behind the couch, sitting on an upturned cauldron from the brew room. She didn't
want to see his face registering reactions to whatever was
said here today.

Her left hand she placed in plain sight on her knee, the

fingers spread on a frame devised by Emla to straighten and
stretch the scarred tendons. Emla said the full range of motion would eventually return. Alldera doubted it.

She squirmed uncomfortably. Her shirttail was bunched
under the skirt of her leather jacket, and she could not reach
with her good hand to fix it. She should have kicked Bek into
the sea before letting him talk her into this meeting!

Horses whickered outside the wall. People appeared at the
gateway where Kenoma, barbarically regal in her faded
scarlet tunic, searched them carefully for weapons. For once
she was not chewing anything, in honor of the occasion.

The Rois cousins stood like dark statues on the walls of
the enclosure, arrows nocked to their bowstrings. Kenoma,
with a clutch of javelins on hand, took a place along the wall
behind Alldera and to one side, where she could command
the scene without blocking the archers. Emla hovered close
at hand, solicitous of her patient and, as always, of her own
place.

Three visitors approached the couch: Fedeka, decked in
pale tokens of her Deity; Ila-Illea, flamboyant in a patterned
shirt and hung about with the empty scabbards of several
knives; and Daya, dressed simply in worn Grassland leather.
She came last and stood quietly, apparently composed, her
gaze lowered.

Alldera swallowed a lurch of panic—still, after all this
time! Daya, she noted, had grown her hair out into a wavy
mass bound up on her nape. There was a shocking amount of
gray.

*Here we are grown old in our efforts, and enemies at the
end. How did this happen to us?* If only Daya would come
and embrace her; if only Alldera could bring herself to go
take the pet fem by the hand and kiss each scarred cheek—

If only Daya had not been the one to prevent her from
drawing her knife in the watchtower.

"What do you want?" Alldera blurted; a starker beginning than she had intended.

Fedeka's seamed lips tightened with anger at the sight of

Eykar Bek. The several necklaces of pale pendants that she wore clicked softly as she made the circle with her fist that called down Moonwoman's blessing on their gathering. "We are glad to see you well," she said.

"I am not 'well,' " Alldera said, "but I'm not dead, either."

Ila-Illea grinned and tried to hide it. Alldera remembered her from those first heady days of conquest as a spirited person with a lively sense of humor. She remembered liking Ila.

"I asked to come to you before," Fedeka said with a chill glance at Emla, "but I was turned away."

Alldera shrugged. It hurt. "Emla volunteered her abilities, and Sheel Torrinor knows a few things about healing. My friends didn't trust you, Fedeka. They still don't, and I still don't. For all I know you were in on the murder plot, you and Daya together; its leaders, even."

The dyer blinked and looked away, and Alldera thought, *I've hurt her feelings. Well, good.* Fedeka's big fingers rubbed at a polished white disc of shell suspended on a thong on her chest. Daya carried a long string of white glass fragments knotted at her belt; a replacement for the Ladystones she had thrown from the well-ledge above Lammintown.

Fedeka said, "If we had caused that terrible event, the Army of the Free would have killed us both by now. People were frantic with rage and grief, Alldera. There were trials. I'll answer you as I answered then: some fems were eager, even fanatical, in their need for you to publicly accept Moonwoman. It was in the hope of forcing you to it that Daya rashly joined the conspirators. But neither she nor I ever intended your death."

"You don't sound particularly sorry about it, one way or the other," Alldera observed.

"I am sorry," Fedeka said soberly, "but there are tides in events as well as in oceans. I don't quarrel with the Lady's choices."

Ila-Illea diffidently lifted her hand for attention. She wore no visible moon tokens.

"We want you to come back," she said earnestly. "I speak for the unslaves. We all agree that no one had a right to just murder Tezza-Bey and her Muck-Boy, let alone attack you. People are still horrified by what happened. Everyone is sorry."

"Everyone," Alldera said. She looked hard at Daya, who did not meet her eyes. " 'Everyone' can't be running things in the Army of the Free. Who's taken charge?"

"A council," Fedeka said, "was chosen. Two members were named by the Free Fems, two by unslaves. The fifth place is reserved for you."

So they did all right for themselves in her absence. She felt a sense of betrayal and letdown, at war with grudging pride in them, that they did not need her. "They govern well, your council?"

"They manage." Fedeka's shoulders relaxed and she went on confidently, "We got back to the City later in the year than we had planned, but with Moonwoman's help we're coping. The Bayo-born are elusive and baffling to deal with sometimes, but we've begun trading with them for some of what we need. Meanwhile, we're planting gardens and digging good wild roots in quantity. Our storage rooms are filling up. We have our disagreements, but everyone works and no one starves. Eleven good, sound foals have been born already in our herds."

"Then what do you need me for?"

"You led us here," Fedeka said simply. "We took back our homeland with you as our Chief, and the Lady's help."

"Keep going, you're just getting to the good part."

"Only the hands of a few enemies struck you, and they failed," the dyer said. "Moonwoman watches over her own. The rest of us want to welcome you home and show our sorrow for what happened without our knowledge or consent."

Alldera stared at her. Fedeka looked steadily back at her. "I suppose Kobba is on your council?" Alldera probed. "How did she feel about the attack in the watchtower?"

Fedeka blinked, taken off guard. It was Ila who responded. "Kobba would have come here with us, but she's our Chief of the Watch now, she had too much to do. She didn't ask to be on the council. With you—gone, people clamored for her. She'll step down to make a place for you if you ask her to, or you can name someone else of your own choosing instead."

Like maybe yourself, young Ila? Alldera thought. "How do you know she would agree to that?"

"Well, I asked her," Ila said. "How else?"

Her brash forwardness made Alldera laugh. She had to turn away to hide the spasm of pain that this cost her. Emla started forward with an exclamation of concern. Alldera waved her away. They all waited in silence for the runner to recover.

Deep in her gut there began the dull ache that sometimes woke her at night, pain left over from a blade stroke that should have killed her. Perhaps Daya had held that knife.

"What about you, Daya? Tell me your *story*."

Daya said in a subdued tone, "There are many stories more important than mine. Ellexa, known to us both as far back as the Tea Camp days in the Grasslands, hanged herself at midwinter in the old potteries of the City. She used that bright-sewn belt she took from Erl Scrapper when she killed him."

There was a small sound. Emla stood swaying, her knuckles pressed to her mouth. She had been quick to distance herself from Ellexa, once her lover, but plainly this news hurt. Alldera too felt the loss, as of anyone from Elnoa's camp. They were fewer than when they had crossed the border last summer.

Daya continued softly, "Tamansa-Nan ran away, on foot, with Leeja-Beda."

Fedeka nodded. "Leeja-Beda was one of the plotters. Poor old Roona has been heartbroken about it."

Leeja the clown, making comical use of her gawky frame and long-nosed face with its bright, malicious eyes. Alldera remembered her entertaining others at the river, after the taking of the City, and dancing by firelight with exaggerated awkwardness an old story-dance with Roona.

"She decoyed the cliff watch away inland that night," Daya continued, "so that no one was near the watchtower. They say that she and Tamansa-Nan have gone together to find Juya-Veree and her child and bring them back to the Holdfast. Maybe they hope to win enough favor by this to overcome the burden of their crime against you."

I let it go with just a word or two when Leeja-Beda took Eykar to be an Oracle because I had fined her once already and I wanted her support. I wanted her not to be angry at me.

"Kastia-Kai—"

Alldera cut off the recital with a gesture. "Don't tell me, I don't care. They all let me know in no uncertain terms that they were done with me, so I am done with them. I asked about you, Daya. I see that you haven't run away or killed yourself."

"No one dared to touch me," Daya said faintly, "because I had been close to you, and because Fedeka spoke for me. Under her instruction I have dedicated the remainder of my life to the service of Moonwoman."

"Your instruction, Fedeka?"

"Yes." The dyer nodded. "Too many of our lives have been wasted by our masters"—another glare in Eykar's direction—"and by time, for us to throw away even the least of our own."

"Well, I hope Daya is more faithful to you than she was to me. Where is your little whip, Daya? Don't you carry it anymore? I'm not there to forbid you."

Daya whispered, "I burned it and offered the smoke to Moonwoman."

"And your pretty shirt of company pennants too, no doubt, that had my blood all over it."

Fedeka said gently, "There has been a lot of blood, Alldera, a lot of hurt, for everyone. Why do you begrudge your people the comforts of ritual that Moonwoman's worship can provide? Not everyone believes as I believe, I know that.'' The dyer smiled. ''But everyone can find some rest and refreshment of spirit in the Lady's rites; even someone as guilty as Daya, here. Isn't that worth something?''

Alldera looked impatiently from one to another of them. ''Is that all? If there's more, say it now. I don't want to have to go through this again.''

Daya said haltingly, ''Can you and I speak privately?''

Alldera clapped her good hand down on her knee. ''No. Talk now, in front of these people, or never. Daya, whatever else you did or didn't do that night, whatever you meant to do, you prevented me from fighting back. I haven't forgotten, and I never will. I don't want to be alone with you again, for any reason. That man there by the wall can be alone with me and armed to the teeth, sooner than I would let you near me with empty hands.''

Daya made a terrible keening sound.

Leaning painfully forward in her seat, Alldera added, ''Once I loved you, and maybe you loved me. Now, by your own doing, I'm afraid of you.'' She lifted her hand, lashed clawlike to its frame. ''And if I ever recover my full strength, you had better be afraid of me.''

The pet fem raised her eyes, luminous with pleading. ''I am not afraid now, but I was then. I thought Eykar Bek had seduced you and turned you against Moonwoman, the source of all our strength—even your own, Alldera, if you would only admit it!

''Eykar Bek is a man with the blood of thousands on his hands from his days here in Endpath, a man whose sire once planned to raise fems like livestock for men's food, and a man other men might follow. But you saved his life and kept him by you. He is still by you now—'' She stabbed her finger at Eykar. ''A man who was once master of your body, and who violated you. Do you forgive him but refuse to forgive me?''

Alldera shook her head sadly. ''I've forgiven you so many times for so many things, Daya, and it never seems to do any good. As for him, what do you expect from a man when he's master? At least he's never tried to cut me to pieces! From my own I expected better.''

"Then you expected too much!" Daya cried.

Alldera studied her, marveling. "So I am to blame? You dare say that to my face?"

"Your actions made some of us afraid," Fedeka interposed quickly. "Who was close to you in Lammintown? Not your old friends, not Daya or me or Kobba. Not Moonwoman, whose name you jeered. A man was close to you—an enemy, taken to yourself at a whim, it seemed, and against your own rules."

"Fine words," Alldera said bitterly, "well practiced, no doubt, in arguing your innocence. But I remember how often I sought you out, you and others, to talk with you and ask your opinions and explain my actions. And I am not convinced."

Reddening, Fedeka kept quiet.

Daya said, "Don't you see that you seemed already an outlaw against your own? You were bent on leniency toward Tezza-Bey even though she helped a man escape, and that set the seal on my fears. I am not brave, Alldera, as everyone knows. I'm only a storyteller. My fear made me misjudge you and mistrust the Lady Herself."

"I'll tell you how I see it, Daya. You exaggerated the dangers of Eykar Bek's presence because you knew people were uneasy about it. You raised assassins against me like some jealous pet fem in a Senior's hold. I think you have never forgiven me for Tua's death. I don't forgive myself, as well you know. But you still had to have your revenge."

Daya dropped to her knees on the stones of the courtyard. The air whispered with the tension of bows drawn full, and Alldera heard Kenoma's quick movement at the wall. Daya was lucky. If Sheel had been there, an arrow would already stand in the pet fem's throat.

Ignoring the weapons, Daya spread her arms wide and

lifted her tear-stained face. "I never meant for them to kill you! That was Tamansa's idea, and Ellexa agreed—"

"Oh, get up and stop squealing!" Alldera barked. "No one's on trial here. The verdict is already known."

Daya rushed on: "I got in too deep, and when I tried to withdraw they threatened me. I had to agree to everything. But in the end I saved you, I stopped them, remember? I was horrified, I couldn't believe how far it had gone! I only wanted you to need me again—to respect me—" Her voice broke. "You weren't to *die*! I was wrong, but I saved you. I saved you despite everything!"

Useless to object that it was Ellexa who had interrupted the attack, Eykar who had come to Alldera's aid, and Beyarra-Bey who had shamed the assassins into retreat. Daya would remember only how when the tide had turned against her, she had turned with it. She would tell it and tell it and tell it her way until people thought that was how it had happened, because she was a gifted storyteller and because she needed them to believe.

Already, no doubt, she believed her own lies: that on that night she had been if not a hero, at least no villain. I only meant good. . . . Stronger people forced me. . . .

"Get up, Daya," Alldera said wearily. "Go sit over there and let others speak. I don't want to hear anything more from you."

Beyarra, bringing a tray, passed Daya with a grimace of distaste as the pet fem silently obeyed. Alldera felt a spasm of anger against not Daya but Beyarra-Bey; anger and sadness. It pained her that Beyarra's naivete, her youthful good looks and energy, had taken the place of Daya's complex luster.

She remembered Daya smiling in delight, forgetting her scars as she found for the first time the joys of riding over the plains at the gallop. Daya joking weakly and rudely from her own sickbed in Fedeka's camp—

Daya, leading Alldera to the tower room and the assassins' knives. That was what Daya had become.

"This is wearing me out," Alldera muttered. "I'm not used to visitors here."

Emla's hand pressed Alldera's shoulder protectively. Mouth quivering, Daya looked away from her longtime rival, and Alldera felt deep pity for the pet fem. She would have shrugged off the masseur's triumphant touch but had not the energy.

Fedeka said, "Alldera, come back to the City. Not now—later, when you're stronger. Come at the solstice. I'm crafting a ceremony of victory and reconciliation for that night. It won't mean as much without you. People want your leadership again. Most never even thought of doing without it. We are all racked and weakened by the outrage done to you, all the blaming and the grudges and the claims and counterclaims. Come help make us whole again."

Alldera rubbed her eyes with her good hand. All she wanted at this point was to get rid of them and sink back into the dark peace of Endpath.

"You heard," Emla said. "She's tired."

"A drink of heartsteep will help, as you know very well, Emla," Fedeka said severely, "if you remember what you learned from me."

"Everyone wants you to come home, Alldera," Ila begged. "Many people have come all the way up here from the City to see you, but the Riding Women turned them away. We've built cairns all along the route, monuments to Moonwoman in your name."

"With sacrifices, no doubt. How much thinner are the ranks of the captives now than when I left?"

Fedeka shook her heavy head. "We had no second Day of Reprisal, Alldera, although I won't pretend we didn't argue about it. People accepted that the Muck Givard paid for his arrogance as Tezza-Bey paid for her weakness, and there it should rest."

Alldera saw Beyarra-Bey wince, her smooth, rounded forehead creasing painfully at the mention of her dead free-name-partner. She felt both sympathetic and impatient:

Beyarra-Bey still had nightmares about that night. She retained a childish softness that was attractive one moment, trying the next.

Fedeka continued, "Our war is won. When less blood seeps into battlefields, less blood needs to be offered to the Lady. Things don't stand still and refuse to change just because you're not with us, Alldera." She rubbed her broad hand over her face. "May I sit a moment before we go? My legs are older than yours."

Old debts were owed to the dyer. Alldera nodded at the refreshments Beyarra had brought. "You may as well enjoy our hospitality, having come all this long way."

Under watchful eyes the emissaries fetched cushions for themselves and sat. Fedeka chewed seedcake slowly with her few teeth and handed the tray on to Ila-Illea, who picked over the selection with interest.

"Do you mean to stay here for good, then?" Fedeka asked mildly. "It's a heavy responsibility for our outpost at Lammintown, keeping watch over you and your friends all this way up here."

Emla looked severely at the dyer. "Does this council of yours want to abandon Lammintown completely?"

"It's been discussed," Fedeka said coolly, and turned back to Alldera. "What would you advise?"

"I would advise you not to ask me for advice, Fedeka. Nothing will divide people more than creating your own council and then undermining it with 'advice' from your former chief."

"But you're our wisest person." Ila looked near tears. Perhaps she had just begun to realize that their embassy would not be successful. "Alldera Chief, when we left the City six unslaves and two Free Fems were pregnant. There will be children soon. They should grow up knowing our greatest hero, the mother of our new life! We have a right—"

"Hush." Fedeka nudged her warningly. Her eyes

gleamed between their wrinkled lids. "*We* have no right to speak of rights here."

"They were smart to send you, Fedeka," Alldera said. "Pour some tea, someone. My throat is dry with talking."

Beyarra barred Ila-Illea from rising in response and served Alldera herself. Wary, no doubt, of poison. Some might consider that the better of two evils—a dead hero, safely enshrined in Daya's stories, rather than the live, unforgiving survivor of an assassination attempt.

Alldera was sure that nothing so base as poison would come from the hand of Ila, who had climbed the causeway ruins to lead the Free Fems into the City. But Beyarra's care touched her, and made her ashamed of her impatience with the youngster.

Fedeka glanced around the courtyard. "Perhaps we could deal better together out of the sight and hearing of that Muck," she said.

Alldera didn't bother to answer.

Fedeka lowered her voice. "The Mucks believe he's here with you for some purpose of his own, and that he's protected by powers inherited from his father. They say among themselves that he'll join somehow with the DarkDreamer D Layo, and together they'll make changes of the kind you can imagine."

"They don't tell you such stories, surely?"

"We have informers among them now. Only a few, but they work hard." Fedeka smiled. "Men are no more proof against threats and bribes than we were when we were slaves."

"Tell your informers to spread word of what Eykar did that night at the tower. That should topple him from his pedestal."

Fedeka made a negative grimace. "They've heard that, and other tales about him too. They say it's all lies, and continue to pin great hopes on him. He's as much of a problem as ever, Alldera."

Well, so am I, Alldera thought; *are we joined at the soul,*

Eykar and I? So what's it to be, the two of us limping off into the Wild to die, or creeping back to civilization to live, if we're let? She glanced at Eykar—what a prim, poised bit of wreckage he was, how sure of his place, and of her. Did he think she owed him something, because of that night?

He's only a slave. Use him. Her cheek twitched with tension, but she smiled. "You won't go back empty-handed. Take Eykar Bek with you, and Setteo too."

"We didn't come for them!" Ila burst out, drawing back.

Alldera silenced her with a look. "If neither of them is dead by the time of your ceremony, Fedeka, I'll come to the City. You understand? If you can keep those men alive I guess I can trust you to keep me alive too, whatever grudges and wild ideas some people still may hold. So I'll come; but not as anybody's chief. It must be a clean slate for everyone—no revenge, no assumptions, no demands."

Fedeka at once held out her broad hand. "Agreed. We'll do our best, and Moonwoman will decide."

Elated as if by a victory (though she was not sure what she had won), Alldera clasped the dyer's thick, beringed fingers. Over her shoulder she called to Eykar, "Go find Setteo. Tell him to prepare for the journey."

Her unspoken thoughts seemed to ring in the air between herself and him: *I decide when you are forgiven. And you are not forgiven yet.*

He got up and bowed, wordless. She had to smile, seeing their essential likeness to each other again confirmed: both too broken-down for pride, too obdurate to die, never prepared but always journeying at the bidding of a perverse, insatiable Fate.

Epilog

A Traveler

Sheel found Alldera walking slowly along the curved,
windowless wall of the Deathdream chamber. Early
summer sunlight glowed down through the glass-block
apex of the domed ceiling. The gloomy space beneath
seemed to revolve silently around this central column of
misty silver.

What a relief to see Alldera moving easily, no longer
cramped and canted by injury. Even the short time Sheel
had been away to the City had made a difference. Alldera's
torso once again rose straight, if not springily, from her
solid hips. The plant of her slightly toed-in footfalls was
firm.

Imagine anyone healing well at Endpath!

"Haven't you had enough of this murder room?" Sheel
called from the entryway. She hated being back here. She
hated to walk on the black floor, still crusted with salt from
its last flush of seawater a decade and a half ago, when Eykar
Bek had fled his work here.

"I want a last look around," Alldera answered. "It's

wonderfully satisfying. It feeds the soul the masters said I didn't have.''

''On what? There's nothing to see, even,'' Sheel grumbled. She wished this were true. After the Fall the Seniors once in control of the Holdfast had made a stand here. Young men had starved them out and then tried to destroy the place.

Pale stars of impact scarred the polished walls where stones had struck, spraying glassy splinters on the floor. Here and there were sooty traces of fires the Juniors had lit in a vain effort to heat the walls enough to crack them when the cold tide rose outside. Undamaged stretches were chalked over with curses, plaints, and the names of men long dead. Even the metal doors to the sea chutes were dented and scratched.

Sheel had not paused to wash and rest after the long ride up, but she realized that she might as well have. Alldera was in no hurry to depart. Let the eager escort Sheel had brought her wait in the sun, let the songs of praise skirl up outside of Endpath. She lingered, here of all places!

''Pilgrims used to come in at that doorway you're standing in,'' Alldera said, pointing. ''It's built to admit only one at a time, protecting the Endtendant and his Rovers from attack; symbolic too, of course. The men who made the Holdfast loved abstractions.''

''I know that. I heard what you used to talk about down here with that man Eykar.''

''So that was you, prowling above us with your bow in your hand.''

Sheel followed her glance to the skeletal iron walkway that circled the domed ceiling. She shuddered involuntarily. What was it with these people and high places, and how had she ever had the nerve to climb up there herself, not once but many times?

''Even in this light,'' she said, ''I could have put an arrow in his heart before he did you any harm.''

Alldera laughed, not her old free laughter but the husky,

covered sound that her recovery had left her. "He was probably in more danger from you here than he's been in since, at
the City."

"He asked me to bring you a message, something about a
garden. I guess he meant that piss-poor little strip of dirt he
planted, on the terrace."

"What about it?"

"I don't remember." She almost added, "I don't carry
messages for men," but remembered in time that as a slave,
Alldera had done just that.

"But he seems well; you remember that."

"You asked me to go to the City and make sure he was
really all right, and I did. I said so already. No wonder people think you really care about the creature!"

"I do," Alldera said with composure. "Apart from anything else, he saved my life at the watchtower, Sheel."

"He saved his own life." They needed to be closer together to talk like this. Sheel stepped through the doorway,
kicking rubbish aside. "If they'd killed you, he'd have been
next."

Here came that look that Sheel hated, smoothing Alldera's expression into a mask. It meant *you don't understand,* and always made Sheel feel as if she had walked into
a wall.

"So?" she demanded, taking a solid stance with her arms
folded. "What is it that I'm too stupid to comprehend? I'd
like to hear it, even if my Grassland brain can't possibly take
it in."

Alldera shook her head and did not reply. She stepped up
onto the round central plinth. The chamber was bare now of
the legendary implements of death—the deep brass bowl,
the chalice, the shallow dipper Sheel had heard described.
Light pearled eerily over the runner's head and shoulders.
She might have been a vision of the celestial Divinity that
Fedeka worshipped.

Deciding firmly for the practical, Sheel said, "Are you
going to keep him by you back there in the City?"

"Probably."

"You *are* crazy! People will see that your problem with him is still there, despite what happened."

"The *problem* was there before I took Eykar out of the quarries. It would still be there if he and I were both dead now, along with poor Tezza-Bey and that boy. The problem is men and fems, masters and slaves. Of course it's still there."

This is the part I really don't understand, Sheel thought, and kept her mouth shut.

"Remember the bond fems who tried to shield their masters from us when we invaded the City? A complex link has bound men and fems for generations. You can't dissolve it just like that."

This was too much for Sheel's restraint. "Slavery," she spat. "*Slavery* is a link?"

The runner hesitated only a moment. "We don't like to admit it, any more than the men do, but yes, I think it is. And around it and despite it, there have always been men and fems who were drawn to each other rather than to their own kind, in body and spirit. You wouldn't see that—"

"I don't want to see it, it's disgusting." Sheel stamped her feet irritably, anxious to get into the saddle again. "You're not saying, I hope, that you actually slept with this Eykar creature, willingly, while you kept him in Cliff's Eye. When people say so, I call them liars to their faces. I'll be very embarrassed if they've been right all along."

"They aren't." Alldera looked away briefly, and Sheel wondered if her answer was a lie. "But such joinings of—of affinity have happened in the past. I think they'll go on happening whether people approve or not."

Sheel exploded air angrily from her mouth. "Then nothing you've done here will ever be secure!"

"Well," Alldera said thoughtfully, "no, I guess not."

Sheel felt naive, if not actively foolish. She didn't like the feeling. "You should have let me kill him. I should have killed him despite you.'' She smacked the wall with the flat of her hand.

"I wouldn't have forgiven you for it, Sheel," Alldera said. "With or without actual sexual coupling, Eykar and I do matter to each other. Even though we've used each other shamefully, I can't pretend we don't—'' She hesitated. "Care.''

"Was Nenisi's love worth nothing to you, then?'' A low blow, but Sheel felt desperately out of her depth.

"All love is worth something, isn't it?''

Sheel stared hard for a moment at this person who stood poised like a spirit of glowing mist, speaking of men, fems, Women, and love all together and looking at her with an open, quizzical gaze that made Seldera seem about fourteen years old.

"Don't ask me," Sheel said finally. "None of this will ever make sense to me.''

The runner tipped her head back and gazed up into the ghostly light as if a better answer might be discernible there, if she only searched hard enough.

Sheel was seized with intolerable restlessness. "Look, are we leaving today, or not? I can tell you, Beyarra-Bey will pitch a fit if we ride into the City without you. She couldn't bring herself to come back here with me—I think she hates Endpath more than I do. But she talks of you all the time and meddles in every part of Fedeka's feast, trying to justify being there making ready instead of coming back up here to fetch you.''

"I miss her too," Alldera murmured.

"Let's go, then." Sheel forced herself to reach into the ghostly light and take Alldera by the arm. "Let's get out of this death pit.''

"Don't rush me." Alldera trapped her hand and drew her in a slow stroll around the vaulted chamber, their footsteps sighing from wall to wall. "Walk with me a minute.''

"Don't you trust your own people yet?" Sheel said. "I was careful about who came back with me. Daya, now—I have to tell you, I thought about a quiet little knife between her ribs before I left.''

She paused, interested that Alldera didn't jump in at once with a protest. After a moment the runner said calmly, ''If I didn't trust Fedeka to keep her under control, I wouldn't be going back, Sheel. Or maybe it's Moonwoman I'm trusting, I'm not sure. Anyway, I don't think what happened was all Daya's fault.''

''No? So whose fault was it, then?''

''It's too complicated for blame. Sometimes I feel as if I went to the Grasslands and caught wild lightning, saddled it, bridled it, and rode it home to strike fire where fire needed to burn. I shouldn't be surprised that I got scorched!''

A note of bitterness sounded under the surface humor in her tone. Sheel glanced sharply at her. ''The men are in your power, and no fems are slaves in your country. Isn't that worth it?''

Alldera looked down at her scarred hand, slowly flexing the fingers. ''Tua would say yes.'' She swallowed audibly. ''I don't know what the three impaled ones would say.''

''The dead don't talk. What do *you* say?''

''I say, it's not a bad bargain.'' The runner's head came up. ''I've thought a lot about this; more than was good for me, maybe. I'd take the same path again.''

''Luckily for you, you won't have to.'' Sheel slapped her palms together briskly. ''Your path leads now to a feast in the City, *if* we're not too late arriving to get any food. You owe a good meal to everybody who's been shut up here on camp rations all winter.''

An unreadable glance, which made Sheel's skin prickle. ''I heard you practicing for Fedeka's celebration, singing your self-song, before you went down to the City.''

''Not much else to do, here on this rock.''

''Singing to the sea, Sheel, which we'll turn our backs to today. Is that why your song ends now with a farewell?''

They came around, for the third time, level with a flight of shallow steps that led down into the brew room, a chilly nook in which the Endtendant had once cooked up his murderous draught. Sheel stopped, turned, and leaned her back against the wall beside the steps.

Alldera had made room for a reassuring answer, which was probably what she was hoping for. But this was not a place for evasions. Sheel swallowed hard and told the plain truth.

"My song ends that way because I'm only stopping in the City for Fedeka's feast. After that, I'm going home. All of us Riding Women would have left months ago, if not for wanting to make sure you were safe. We miss the Grasslands and our families, not to mention the fact that nobody has anything left of the tea we brought with us. I myself have a sharedaughter I haven't seen for ages. I want to bring her news of her bloodmother."

"Kiss Sorrel for me when you see her." Alldera's eyes glittered. "I haven't been a true mother to her. It's lucky she has other mothers to do it right. I really did want to be like you, you know—a Riding Woman instead of a fem, mother and daughter of an honorable line—no wonder you used to look at me with such contempt!" Sheel could not deny this, and kept silent. "That's changed now, isn't it? It means something to you, that we've won here. So why will you go away and leave us?"

"I'm telling you. You're not listening. It's *because* you've won. You don't need us. And we ought to leave." Sheel crossed her arms and rubbed her biceps roughly. She'd been a fool—no, a coward—to imagine that these things could be said in some light, painless way during the ride back to the City.

"I dream bad dreams here," she said. "We all do. We don't belong. We look funny, walking your paved streets and your planted fields with our saddle-bowed legs. We're clumsy and nervous in your stone rooms. We're stupid because there's so much that makes no sense to us no matter how often it's explained."

"You can learn," Alldera said. "I came to your country and learned what I had to."

"I've learned more than I wanted to already."

Alldera paced, her hands twisting together. "I know you're homesick. Now you know how we felt on your side of the mountains! We stood it; why can't you?"

"We stand it," Sheel said, "about the same as you did in our country: badly. We eat too much, we drink too much, we gamble away our property, we quarrel among ourselves, and some of us—we grow too casual of our ancient enemies, the men; too curious, too disdainful. We rot here, cut off from our own."

"Ah, Sheel," the runner coaxed. "Don't go."

"Be happy," Sheel said with a painful grin. "You've won." She reached out and halted the Free Fem's agitated pacing. Turning Alldera's hand in her own, she felt along the heavy-boned wrist and strong, stubby fingers. The palm was deeply scarred, but the hand could still grip.

"You've beaten me, Alldera Holdfaster. You're the stronger of us two." She let the square, callused hand go. "And I'll say that in my self-song. There's no shame in being bested by someone more powerful than oneself."

"*What?* What are you talking about?" Alldera cried on a gust of incredulous laughter. "You can't compare a seasoned warrior of the plains with a broken-down Holdfast runner!"

Sheel eyed her critically up and down. "You'll harden up again. Mothers mine, you are tougher than dry-season grass and meaner than swarming sharu, you fems! I've seen you fight, remember. Bitterness strengthens your arms, the marrow of your bones is vengeance, and your memories have no end. What have we Riding Women to match all that?"

"Freedom," Alldera said. "Freedom you were born to, Sheel, that you didn't have to win from anybody."

Sheel grunted. "Maybe that's why it's a little delicate, our freedom; a little fragile, next to yours. We're not immune to corruption."

"Corruption!" Alldera's eyes narrowed with alarm. "What corruption?"

"I don't want us to learn to keep slaves."

"But you don't—oh. Ayalees Salmowon's winnings. Of course, I see. That was my fault, Sheel. I wasn't paying attention, to let that happen. And if Bavell's death causes trouble between you and the Salmowons, I'll make reparation myself in your place."

Sheel put a finger to her own lips and then reached out to touch Alldera over the heart, an old Grassland gesture of gratitude. Then she pushed away from the wall. "Anyhow, we're not going right away. The others want to stay for the ceremony, out of courtesy. Well—Ayalees Salmowon insists. Since Tyn Chowmer's death, she's taken to Fedeka's stories of some great Woman in the moon. She needs to live with her own people again so she won't get crazy. We all need to."

Outside a muffled drumbeat began, doubling the throb of the sea. "They're calling you," Sheel said.

Alldera struck her hands together, creating a clatter of echoes. "And I'm calling you! Don't you hear me? Stay, Sheel. Are you afraid of becoming like us? Look around: this death room is part of each Holdfaster's heritage, but it's no part of you or yours and never will be. You're only a traveler visiting an exotic land, there's nothing of ours that you need. But we need you. We need a person without the taint of this place's history to help us choose new pathways."

Sheel said angrily, "I don't know how, that's what I'm saying! Outside my own country and away from my own people, how could I make such judgments? Don't ask me for help, it's foolishness."

"But I do ask it." Alldera caught her by the arm and looked urgently into her face. "Look, you know as well as I do that whatever I mean to do, one way or another I'll keep pushing these fems. Look how I'm pushing you!"

She gave Sheel an exasperated little shove and swung away from her again, restless with energy. "My life gives me glimpses of how people can be better than they are, and then I want them to do that, be that, whether they want to or not, and right now too. Damn Eykar, he can go drown in his damn books now and leave the other men to manage as best they can. He's just a slave. But I'm Alldera Conqueror, and there's no humble, selfish obscurity to keep me safely out of other people's business. Help me, Sheel."

Sheel covered her eyes with one hand. "Please, put your modesty away, it's blinding me. A great Motherline should spring from your body's child, if there's any justice."

"Fems aren't Riding Women." Alldera paced away from her, hands behind her back. "Though I'm not sure we're fems anymore, either. We were slaves, isn't that why you despised us? But we're not slaves now. Are we Women, if we're free? Can we be Women of the Holdfast, as you and the Nenisi and the rest are Women of the Grasslands? Help me to make it so."

Sheel's throat felt tight. "You ask too much, and of the wrong person. You should come home with me and ask Nenisi."

"It's your objective advice I want, not the blind encouragement of someone who loves me."

"Who says I don't love you?" Sheel pressed her lips together, too late to hold back the forceful, traitor words. Alldera turned on her an eager, dazzled look and Sheel's heart gave a panicky thump. Hastily she added, "The others are set on going back. I'd be left alone here, the only Riding Woman in a foreign land."

Alldera grinned. "Oh, more will come riding over the mountains, if only to shake their heads at us—us Holdfast Women, and our shocking ways. Besides, your Salmowon friend may be too caught up in Moonwoman worship to leave at all. Salmowons have a mystical streak, don't they? You have to stay and keep her out of Fedeka's clutches."

"Blood of my mothers," Sheel said fervently. "I knew we should have left you in that damn desert where we found you!"

"You did try, remember."

Sheel flung her head back, baring her throat. "All right, all right, you win again! Just sling your rein around my neck and count me captured, why don't you! I can see I'll never be able to buy back my freedom!"

But her spirit bounded as if released from a heavy weight.

At the sight of them the escort from the City raised a roar. The first rank of riders flipped lances trimmed with colored pennants into the air and caught them again, all in unison, while reining their mounts in sinuous patterns at a tight canter.

"Oh, damn, how beautiful—they'll make me cry," Alldera muttered happily, halting in the outer gateway.

In fact her cheeks shone with tears and her nostrils had reddened unbecomingly. Sheel wanted to straighten Alldera's hair and wipe her eyes for her, and send her out to them haughty and composed to accept what was, after all, no more than her due from her own fractious people. But Alldera was no daughter of hers, to pet and handle with such familiarity.

Sheel's own eyes stung. She was thinking of the old Grassland tale of Leotana Sharavess who, deeply wronged by close kindred, was found in exile in the southern wastes by her devoted cousin and brought home for vengeance, which she turned instead into a legendary occasion of generosity and forgiveness.

This was completely different (though who could be sure, exactly, of what anything meant among fems?). Still, the self-song of Leotana beat through Sheel's thoughts in a swinging dance rhythm that evoked joy won from tears and honor from rage.

Striding at the head of the cavalcade, on foot as always, Fedeka led the ride south from Endpath. She bristled with brightly dyed reeds that were fastened to the back of her shirt and rippling from her sleeve. She sang Alldera's self-song in a distanced, narrative form encompassing recent events that Alldera had not yet sung herself.

> "Wounded to near death by filthy betrayers,
> She came to her refuge long years after seeking.
> Black rock of old murders opened to take her.
> Endpath, midnight castle of the tears of men.
> Ocean-cold spirits were called up and sung up
> From under the waves of the all-cleansing waters
> By the lame wizard Eykar
> Now tamed and commanded.
> They paid their tribute
> Their deep debt of healing
> In aid to the watchers
> The loyal, the faithful ones,
> Kenoma, Beyarra-Bey, Emla the healer,
> And warriors, grim-faced and blacker than Endpath
> Riders from over the long western desert—"

"She's got some of it right," Sheel said doubtfully.

"Not enough," Alldera said. "Hey, I have a present for you, but I don't know whether it's good enough for a grim-faced warrior from across the desert and all that."

Sheel said gruffly, "What present?"

"You'll see. I'll give it to you at Fedeka's ceremony."

They descended the Endpath road, past the tumble-down shelter halfway along, and turned west below Lammintown where the cliffs flattened to the shoreline. All the way Fedeka's powerful arm wove in a sinuous pattern as she sang.

The others sipped from their water bottles and joined in here and there at will. Now and then someone would ride up and fix a token—a colored braid or metallic pendant—to Alldera's saddle or her horse's reins.

Sheel watched the runner warm and loosen in this flood of adulation and passionate pledges. Soon she rode joking and singing among them as if there had been no attack, no estrangement. She looked almost as young as when she had first come to the Grasslands, carrying her child and childish herself, years ago, escorted by a much younger, more arrogant, and disdainful Sheel Torrinor.

Sheel wondered if Alldera's ''present'' was going to be that lumpy piece of sewing work she'd been swearing over for months, using it as exercise for her stiff hand. What in the world was a Woman of the Riding People to do with something like that?

I'll give it to Sorrel when I go home, she thought, *and say that her bloodmother wants her to have it.*

Femmish conversation and laughter rang all around her. She thought of how she had ridden into this country, full of foreboding that she would be swallowed up forever in Alldera's land of bones. Maybe that was what was happening, in a way, but she found she couldn't summon up much apprehension.

She dropped back among the other Women and lagged on purpose a little behind them all. She wanted to look back as long as she could at the slanted coast. Her heart felt too large for her chest.

It was no small thing, to have ridden with the Free Fems to their country and fought their enemies with them, and to have helped preserve the life of their leader and return her to her people. And it was no small thing, either, to have seen the wide blue sea.

BEST OF SF FROM TOR

THE BEST OF SF FROM TOR